HER NEW YEAR
B

GILMORE

MILLS & BOON

First Published in Great Britain 2017
By Mills & Boon, an imprint of HarperCollins*Publishers*
1 London Bridge Street, London, SE1 9GF

© 2016 Harlequin Books S.A.

Special thanks and acknowledgement are given to Jessica Gilmore for her contribution to the Maids Under the Mistletoe series.

ISBN: 978-0-263-92264-6

23-0117

Printed and bound in Spain
by CPI, Barcelona

A former au pair, bookseller, marketing manager and seafront trader, **Jessica Gilmore** now works for an environmental charity in York, England. Married with one daughter, one fluffy dog and two dog-loathing cats, she spends her time avoiding housework and can usually be found with her nose in a book. Jessica writes emotional romance with a hint of humour, a splash of sunshine and a great deal of delicious food—and equally delicious heroes!

For all the amazing Mills & Boon Romance writers—
past and present.

Thank you for being so welcoming to new writers and
so generous with your time, experience and wisdom,
and thank you for writing such amazing books.

It's an honour to work with you all. x

CHAPTER ONE

Early December, Chelsea, London

'WAIT! STOP! OH, NO…' Sophie Bradshaw skidded to a halt and watched the bus sail past her, the driver utterly oblivious to her outstretched hand. 'Just great,' she muttered, pulling her cardigan more closely around her and turning, careful not to slip on the icy pavement, to scan the arrivals board in the bus stop, hoping against hope the next bus wasn't too far behind.

She huffed out a sigh of disappointment. Tonight London buses were definitely not running in pairs—she would have to wait twenty minutes until the next one. And, to add insult to injury, the light snowflakes that had been falling in a picturesque fashion over Chelsea's well-heeled streets all evening had decided to pick up both speed and strength and were now dancing dizzily through the air, blown here and there by some decidedly icy gusts of wind. Sophie eyed a taxi longingly. Would it hurt? Just this once? Only, last time she'd checked, she had only forty pounds left in her bank account, there was still a week to go until payday and, crucially, she still hadn't bought any Christmas presents.

She'd just have to wait and hope her best friend, and fellow waitress, Ashleigh, joined her soon so that she could forget her freezing hands and sore feet in a good gossip about the evening's event. Sophie hadn't received one thank you in the three hours she had toted a laden tray around the expensively dressed party-goers, but she had experienced several jostlings, three toe-tramplings and one pat on her bottom. It was a good thing her hands had been occupied in balancing the tray or the bottom patter might have found himself wearing the stuffed prawns, which would have been momentarily satisfying but probably not the best career move.

Sophie shivered as another icy gust blew through the bus shelter and straight through her inadequate if seasonally appropriate sparkly cardigan. Why hadn't she brought a coat, a proper grown-up coat with a hood and a warm lining and a waterproof outer layer? 'Vanity, thy name is Sophie,' she muttered. Well, she was getting her just reward now; nothing shrieked high-end fashion like the 'frozen drowned rat' look.

Huddling down into the cardigan, she turned, hoping once more to see her friend, but there was still no sign of Ashleigh and Sophie's phone was out of battery—again. The snow-covered street was eerily deserted, as if she were alone in the world. She blinked, hot unwanted tears filling her eyes. It wasn't just that she was cold, or that she was tired. It was that feeling of being invisible, no more human or worthy of attention than the platters she held, less interesting than the cocktails she had been handing out.

She swallowed, resolutely blinking back the tears. *Don't be a baby*, she scolded herself. So her job was hard work? At least she had a job and she was lucky enough to work with some lovely people. So her flat was so small she couldn't offer Ashleigh even a temporary home? At least she had a flat—and, even better, an almost affordable flat right here in Chelsea. Well, 'right here' being a twenty-minute bus ride away to the unfashionable edges of Chelsea, but it was all hers.

So she was a little lonely? Far, far better to be lonely alone than lonely with someone else. She knew that all too well.

She straightened her shoulders and lifted her chin as if she could physically banish her dark thoughts, but her chest still ached with a yearning for something more than the narrow existence she had lived since moving to London just over a year and a half ago. The narrow existence she'd trapped herself in long before that. What must it be like to be a guest at one of the many glittering parties and events she worked at? To wear colour and shine, not stay demure and unnoticed in black and white?

With a sigh she looked around once more, hoping that the bright smile and can-do attitude of her old friend might help her shake this sudden and unwanted melancholy, but although the snow fell thicker and faster than ever there was still no sign of Ashleigh. Nor was there any sign of the bus. The board in the shelter was resolutely sticking to an arrival in twenty minutes' time, even though at least five long minutes had already passed...

Sophie blew on her hands and thought of the warm, inviting glow of the hotel lobby just a few metres behind her. She was staff—and temporary staff at that—but surely, after a night run off her feet catering to some of the most arrogant ignoramuses she had ever had the misfortune to waitress for, they wouldn't mind her sheltering inside for just a few minutes? Besides, a snowstorm changed the rules, everyone knew that. Even a posh hotel turned into Scrooge after the three ghosts had visited, welcoming to one and all. And it would be easier to keep a lookout for Ashleigh if she wasn't constantly blinking snow out of her eyes...

Mind made up, Sophie stepped cautiously away from the limited shelter of the bus stop and onto the increasingly snowy pavement, her feet sinking with a definite crunch in the snow as she began to walk back towards the lobby. She kept her head down against the chill, picking up speed as she neared the door, and warmth was in sight when she collided with a tall figure, her heel slipping as she did so. With a surprised yelp Sophie teetered, arms windmilling as she fought to remain upright, refusing to surrender to the inevitable crash but knowing that any millisecond now she would fall...

Just as she started to lose the battle a strong hand grasped her elbow and pulled her upright. Sophie looked up, startled, and found herself staring into a pair of the darkest brown eyes she had ever seen, framed with long thick lashes. 'Careful! It's snowing. You could hurt someone—or yourself if you don't look where you're going.'

Italian, she thought dreamily. She had been saved by an Italian man with beautiful eyes. Then his sharp tone permeated the fog in her brain and she stepped back, sharply moving away from his steadying grasp.

'Snowing? So that's what this white cold stuff is. Thank you for clearing that up.' She stopped, the anger disappearing as quickly as it came as shock flared up on his face—followed by the ghost of a smile. It was a very attractive ghost; he was probably rather gorgeous when he relaxed. *Not relevant, Sophie.* More to the point, she *had* bumped into him. 'I'm sorry, you're right, I wasn't looking where I was going. I just wanted to get inside before I turned into the little match girl. I've had to admit defeat on finding transport. It's looking like I'm going to have to walk home...' She looked ruefully down at her black heels. They were surprisingly comfortable—comfortable enough for her to wear them to work—but patent court shoes probably weren't high on most Arctic explorers' kit lists.

'Typical London, just a few flakes of snow and the taxis disappear.'

Sophie didn't want to contradict him and point out that there was a little more than a drop of snow—several inches more in fact—or that she wasn't actually looking for a taxi but for a far more prosaic bus. 'It's always the same when it snows,' she said airily, as if she were a real Londoner, blasé about everything, even the fairy-tale scene unfolding before her, but instantly ruined the effect by shivering.

'And you've come out inappropriately dressed.' The disapproval was back in his voice, but before Sophie could react, he shrugged off his expensive-looking coat and wrapped it around her. 'You'll catch pneumonia if you're not careful.'

Pride warred with her frozen limbs and lost. 'I... Thank you... Although,' she couldn't help adding, 'it wasn't actually snowing when I left home.' She snuggled into the coat. The lining felt like silk and there was a distinct scent on the collar, a fresh citrus scent, sharp and very male, rather like the smartly tailored man standing in front of her. She held out her hand, just the tips of her fingers visible, peeking out of the long coat sleeves. 'Sophie Bradshaw.'

'Marco Santoro.' He took her outstretched hand and, at his touch, a fizz of attraction shivered up Sophie's spine.

She swallowed, shocked by the sudden sensation.

It had been far too long since she'd had that kind of reaction and it unnerved her.

Unnerved her—but she couldn't deny a certain thrill of exhilaration too, and almost without meaning to she smiled up at him, holding his gaze boldly even as his eyes darkened with interest.

'I must be holding you up,' she said, searching for something interesting to say but settling on the banal, unsettled by the speculative look in his eyes. 'I should give you your coat back, thank you for coming to my rescue and let you get on your way.' But she couldn't quite bring herself to return the coat, not when she was so blissfully warm. Not when she was so very aware of every shifting expression on his rather-nice-to-look-at face with cheekbones cut like glaciers, the dark stubble a little too neat to be five o'clock shadow. She also rather approved of the suit, which enhanced, rather than hung off or strained over, his tall lean body. She did like a man who knew how to dress…

She'd given him the perfect getaway clause. One moment of chivalry could have marooned him here with this sharp-tongued girl for the rest of the evening. All he had to do was say thank you, retrieve his coat and be on his way. The words hovered on his tongue, but Marco paused. There was something he rather liked about her defiantly pointed, uptilted chin, the combative spark in her blue eyes. It was a nice contrast to the tedium that had made up his evening so far.

'Take your time and warm up. I'm in no hurry. The fresh air is just what I needed after being in there.' He gestured behind him to The Chelsea Grand. 'I was at the most overcrowded, overheated party imaginable.'

'Me too! Wasn't it awful?'

'Unbearable. What a shame I didn't see you in there. It would have brightened up a dull evening. No one ever enjoys these Export Alliance affairs, but it's necessary to show willing, don't you think?'

Her eyes flickered. 'Oh, yes, I hope the evening wasn't too much of a bore.'

Marco deliberately didn't answer straight away, running his gaze over Sophie assessingly. She was a little under average height, with silky blonde hair caught up in a neat twist. Her eyes were a clear blue, her mouth full. She wasn't as poised as his usual type, but then again he was bored of his usual type, hence the last six months' dating detox. And fate did seem to have brought them together; who was he to argue with fate? He smiled straight into her eyes. 'For a while there I thought it was. But now, maybe, it has…possibilities.'

With interest he watched her absorb his words, his meaning, colour flushing high and quick on her pale cheeks. She stepped back. 'Well, it was lovely meeting you, Mr Santoro, but I really should try to get back before I need a team of huskies to whisk me home. Thank you so much for lending me your coat. I think I'm warm enough to risk another five minutes looking for transport.'

'Or,' he suggested, 'we could wait out the storm in the comfort of a bar.' There, the gauntlet was thrown; it was up to her to take it or not.

He rather hoped she would.

Sophie opened her mouth, then closed it again. Marco could practically see the arguments running through her mind. She didn't know him. It was snowing and impossible to get home. What harm could one drink do? Was she acknowledging the sizzle of chemistry in the air? That indefinable quality that stopped him from taking his coat and walking away, that stopped her from saying a flat no. He could almost smell it, rich and ripe.

Sophie sighed, a tiny sound, a sound of capitulation. 'Thank you, a drink would be lovely.'

'*Bene*, do you know somewhere you would like to go? No? Then if I may make a suggestion, I know just the place.' He took her arm and she allowed him, as if the process of saying yes had freed her from making any more decisions. She was light under his hand, fragile as he steered her away from the hotel and down to the lights and bustle of the King's Road. Neither of them spoke, words suddenly superfluous in this winter wonderland of shadow and snow.

The bar he'd selected was just a short walk away, newly refurbished in a dazzling display of copper and light woods with long sleek tables for larger groups and hidden nooks with smaller, more intimate tables for couples. Marco steered Sophie towards the most hidden of these small areas, gesturing to the barman to bring them a bottle of Prosecco as he did so. Her eyes flickered towards his and then across their small hideaway with its low table for two, its intimate two-seater sofa, the almost hidden entrance.

'Excuse me for just a minute, I'm going to freshen up.'

'Of course, take your time.' He sat down and picked up his glass and smiled. The dull evening was suddenly alive with possibilities. Just the way he liked it.

What am I doing? What am I doing?

Sophie didn't need to look at a price list to know the bar was way out of her league—each light fitting probably cost more than every piece of furniture she owned. And she didn't need to be a mind reader to know why

Marco Santoro had selected such a small, hidden table. The whole scenario had seduction written all over it.

She'd never been the kind of girl handsome men in tailored suits wanted to seduce before. What would it be like to try that girl on for size? Just for once?

The loos were as bright and trendy as the bar, with huge mirrors running all along one wall and a counter at waist height. Sophie dumped her bag onto the counter, shrugged off the coat, hanging it onto the hat stand with care, and quickly tallied up her outfit. One dress, black. One pair of tights, nude. One pair of shoes, black. One silver shrug, wet. Hair up. Make-up minimal. She could do this.

It didn't take long; it never did. Hair taken down, shaken and brushed. That was one thing about her fine, straight blonde hair: it might be boring, but it fell into place without too much effort. A colour stick added a rich berry glow to her lips and colour to her cheeks and a sweep of mascara gave her eyes some much-needed definition. A quick sweep of powder to her nose, an unflattering scarlet after ten minutes in the snow, finished her face.

She looked at herself critically. Her face was fine, her hair would do, but even though she'd added a few stitches to the Maids in Chelsea standard black dress to improve the fit, her dress was still more suitable for church than an exclusive bar. She rummaged in her bag and pulled out a white ribbon. Two seconds later she had tied it around her waist, finishing it with a chic bow. She added oversize silver hooped earrings, looped a long, twisted silver chain around her neck and held the shrug under the dryer for a minute until it was just faintly damp. Not bad. Not bad at all. She closed her bag, slung the coat nonchalantly around her shoulders and took a deep breath. It was a drink. That was all.

An hour, maybe two, with someone who looked at her with interest. Someone who didn't know her, didn't feel sorry for her.

An hour, maybe two, of being someone different. A Chelsea girl, the kind of girl who went to glamorous parties and flirted with handsome men, not the kind of girl who stood on the sidelines with a tray of drinks.

Sophie wasn't remotely ashamed of what she did for a living. She worked hard and paid her own way—which was a lot more than many of the society women she cleaned for and waited on could say—and Clio, the owner of Maids in Chelsea, the agency Sophie worked for, had built up her successful business from scratch. Maids in Chelsea was known for supplying the best help in west London and Sophie and her colleagues were proud of their reputation. But it wasn't glamorous. And right now, she wanted just a few moments of glamour. To belong in the world she served and cleaned up after until the clock struck twelve and she turned back into a pumpkin.

Didn't she deserve this? It was nearly Christmas after all…

CHAPTER TWO

New Year's Eve

'THAT'S FANTASTIC, GRACE. No, of course I'm not mad, I'm really happy for you. So when do I get to meet him? Tonight? He's taking you to the Snowflake Ball. That's…that's really, really great. I can't wait. I'll see you there. Okay. Bye. Love you.'

Sophie put her phone down and stared across the room. If there had been room on the floor, she would have slumped in a dramatic fashion, but as every inch of the tiny sitting room/dining room/kitchenette was covered in bolts and scraps of fabric, she could only lean against the wall and swallow hard.

Did Cinderella feel resentment when she was left alone and everyone else went to the ball? No, she was quite happy to sit by the fire with the mice and Buttons and weave straw into gold before letting down her hair and eating an apple.

Okay. Maybe Sophie was muddling up her fairy tales a little.

But, crucially, Cinderella was excluded from the ball completely. How would she have felt if she had been made to attend the ball as a waitress and had to watch her stepsisters waltzing by in the arms of their handsome tycoons and earls? There would have been less singing, more teeth-gnashing then.

Not that Sophie had any inclination to gnash her teeth. She was happy for her friends, of *course* she was. It was amazing that they had all found such wonderful men and goodness knew they deserved their happiness—but did they all have to find true love at the same time? And did they have to find it just before the Snowflake Ball?

She sighed. Last year had been such fun, waitressing at the prestigious event with Emma and Grace, and she'd been looking forward to introducing Ashleigh to the glitter and sparkle that were the hallmarks of the charity gala. The ballroom always looked amazing, the organisers ensured there were plenty of breaks, tips were generous and there was a short staff event afterwards with champagne and a delicious buffet. In fact last year had been the best New Year's Eve Sophie could remember. But this year everything was different. First Emma had bumped into her estranged—and secret—husband, Jack Westwood, aka the Earl of Redminster, and after a few difficult weeks the pair had blissfully reconciled. Then Ashleigh had fallen for gorgeous Greek tycoon Lukas while house-sitting for him. Sophie had been over the moon when her old friend had phoned her on Christmas Eve to announce her whirlwind engagement—she'd never heard Ashleigh sound so happy.

But she had to admit that she had been a little relieved that Grace, like Sophie, was still single, still employed at Maids in Chelsea and would still be waitressing at the ball. There was only so much loved-upness a girl could take.

Only while Sophie had endured overcrowded trains back to Manchester on Christmas Eve to spend an uncomfortable two days back tiptoeing around her family's habitual disapproval and enduring the same old lectures on how she had messed up her life, Grace had spent *her* Christmas being swept off her feet by hotelier Finlay Armstrong. Swept off her feet and out of her waitress clothes and into a ballgown. She *would* be at the Snowflake Ball tonight, but, like Emma and Ashleigh, she'd be there as a guest, not hired help.

'You are officially a horrible person, Sophie Bradshaw,' Sophie said aloud. 'Grace of all people deserves all the happiness in the world.' She'd been alone in the world, even more alone than Sophie, so alone she'd chosen to work over Christmas rather than spend the holidays on her own. The rift in Sophie's family might seem irreparable, but at least she had them. Yes, Grace deserved every bit of luck and happiness the last week had brought her.

But didn't Sophie deserve some too?

She pushed herself off the wall and picked her way over to the sofa, resolving once again to do something about the material strewn all over every surface as well as the floor. She did deserve happiness; she knew that even if she didn't always feel it. Her ex, Harry, had done far too good a job of eroding every last bit of confidence from her for that. But happiness for her didn't lie in the arms of a man, no matter how titled or rich or handsome he was. It lay in her dreams. In her designs. In her... And if waitressing at this ball would help her achieve those dreams, then waitress she would—and she would smile and be happy for her friends even if they were divided from her by an invisible baize door.

Only...was Harry right? Was something wrong with her? Because she had had her own little romantic adventure this Christmas, but, unlike her friends, hers had ended when the clocks struck—well, not twelve but five a.m. It had been her choice to creep out of the hotel room without leaving as much as a note, let alone a glass slipper, but she couldn't imagine Jack or Lukas or Finlay leaving a stone unturned if their women simply disappeared without a trace. But although her heart gave the odd unwanted leap whenever she saw dark hair above an expensive suit—which in Chelsea was about thirty times a day on average—the last she had seen of Marco Santoro had been his naked, slumbering torso, dimly lit by the light of the bathroom as she had gathered her belongings together.

And okay, she hadn't looked for him either, not even when she'd confessed her one-night stand to her friends just a few days ago. Not only was Marco Santoro out of her league in every way, but Sophie had allowed infatuation to cloud her judgement before. She wasn't foolish enough to mistake lust for anything deeper, not again.

Although it had been an incredible night…

The sound of the buzzer interrupted her slide into reminiscences just as she was picturing the curve of Marco's mouth. Sophie shivered as she pushed the all too real picture away and picked up the answerphone. 'Yes?'

'Sophie, it's me, Ashleigh.' Her old friend's unmistakably Australian tones sang out of the intercom and Sophie's spirits immediately lifted. So all her friends would be married to insanely wealthy, influential and hot men? It wouldn't really make a difference, not where it counted most.

'Come on up.' She pressed the buzzer and looked around wildly. Was it possible to clear a space in just twenty seconds? There was a knock on the door before she had managed to do more than pick up several scraps of material and, with them still clasped in her hand, Sophie opened the door to discover not just Ashleigh but Grace and Emma as well, brandishing champagne and a thick white envelope.

'Surprise!' they sang out in chorus, surging into the room in a wave of perfume, silk and teetering heels. The dress code for the Snowflake Ball was white or silver, but blonde, tall Emma had added red shoes and accessories to her long white silk shift, Grace, glowing with happiness, was sultry in silver lace and Ashleigh had opted for a backless ivory dress, which set off the copper in her hair and the green in her eyes. They all looked gorgeous. Sophie tried not to look over at her black waitress's dress, ironed and hung on the back of the door.

'How lovely to see you all.' She narrowed her eyes at Grace. 'You must have called me from just around the corner.'

'From the taxi,' Grace confirmed, her eyes laughing.

'Congratulations again. Finlay's a lucky man and I'll tell him so when I finally meet him. I'd hug you, but I don't want to crease your dress.'

'Where are the glasses?' Emma, of course, was already at the counter optimistically known as a kitchenette looking in one of the three narrow cupboards allotted for crockery and food. 'Aha!' She brandished them triumphantly, setting them down before twisting the foil off the bottle. It was real champagne, Sophie noted, a brand well out of her price bracket. Funny to think just a few weeks ago they would have happily been drinking cheap cava from the off-licence at the end of her street. So the divide between her lifestyle and her friends' had begun. Just as it had ten years ago when she had opted for paid work and domesticity while her few friends went to university.

She pushed the thought away as the champagne cork was expertly popped. 'Not for me, Em. I can't. You know what Clio says about drinking on the job and I need to be at the hotel for staff briefing in an hour.'

'Now, that,' Ashleigh said triumphantly, 'is where you are wrong. We've asked Keisha to cover your shift and you, Miss Sophie Bradshaw, will be going to the ball! Here you are, a formal invitation.' She thrust the envelope towards Sophie, who took it mechanically.

'I've always wanted to be a fairy godmother,' Grace said, holding out her hand to accept one of the full glasses Emma was handing out.

Sophie stared at the three beaming faces, completely flabbergasted as she took in their words, the envelope still clutched unopened in her hand. 'I'm what?'

'Going to the Snowflake Ball!'

'We're taking you as our guest!'

'You didn't think we'd leave you out, did you?' Ashleigh finished, taking a glass from Emma and pressing it into Sophie's unresisting hand. 'Cheers!'

'But…but…my hair. And what will I wear?'

'Oh, I don't know,' Emma said. 'If only one of us was an aspiring fashion designer with a wardrobe crammed full of original designs. Hang on a minute…' She strode into the minuscule bedroom—so tiny Sophie could only fit in a single cabin bed—and pulled back the curtain that divided the crammed clothes rails from the rest of the room. 'Ta-dah!'

'I couldn't wear one of my designs to an event like this! Everyone else will be in dresses like, well, like yours. Expensive, designer…'

'And you will outshine us all in an original Sophie

Bradshaw.' Grace beamed at her. 'Oh, Sophie, it's going to be a magical night. I am so very happy you are coming with is. Let's get you ready…'

Why on earth did I agree to attend this ball?

More to the point, why did he agree to attend the Snowflake Ball every New Year's Eve? It was always the same, filled with the same people, the same talk, the same tedium. Marco cast a scowling look at the crowded ballroom. Oh, it was tastefully done out with abstract snowflakes suspended from the ceiling and the glitter kept to a minimum, but it was still not a patch on Venice on New Year's Eve. His was a city that knew how to celebrate and New Year was a night when the stately old city came alive.

He hadn't spent a New Year in Venice for over a decade, although there were times when the pull of the city of his birth ran through his veins like the water in the canals and he missed the alleyways and bridges, the grand old *palazzos* and the markets with an almost physical ache that no amount of excellent champagne and food could make up for. His hands folded into fists. Tomorrow he would return home, not just for a fleeting visit, some business and a duty dinner with his mother and sister. Tomorrow he would return for a fortnight, to host the Santoros' annual Epiphany Ball and then stay to walk his sister down the aisle.

Tomorrow he would step into his father's shoes, no matter that he wasn't ready. No matter that he didn't deserve to.

Marco took a deep sip of wine, barely tasting the richness. He wouldn't think about it tonight, his last night of freedom. He needed a distraction.

His eyes skimmed the room, widening with appreciation as four women stopped at a table opposite. They were talking over each other, faces lit with enthusiasm as they took their seats. His gaze lingered on a laughing blonde. Her silver minidress was an interesting choice in what was a mainly conservatively dressed ballroom, but Marco wasn't complaining, not when the wearer possessed such excellent legs. Excellent legs, a really nice, lithe figure and, as she turned to face him as if she were aware of his scrutiny, a pair of familiar blue eyes. Eyes staring straight back at him with such undisguised horror Marco almost turned and checked, just to make sure there wasn't an axe murderer creeping up behind him.

The girl from the snow. The one who had disappeared...

Marco muttered a curse, unsure whether to coolly acknowledge her or ignore her presence; it had been a novel experience to wake up and find himself alone without as much as a note. Novel and not exactly pleasant; in Marco's experience women clung on long after the relationship was over, they didn't disappear before it had even begun.

And they certainly didn't run away before dawn.

His eyes narrowed. She owed him an explanation at the least, apology at best. There were rules for these kinds of encounters and Sophie Bradshaw had broken every one. Besides, he was damned if he was going to spend the evening marked as the big bad wolf with Little Silver Dress going all wide-eyed at the very sight of him. He had a fortnight of difficult encounters ahead of him; tonight was supposed to be about having fun.

Mind made up, Marco took a step in Sophie's direction, but she was already on her feet and shouldering her way through the ballroom. Away from him. So she liked to play, did she? He set off at an unhurried pace, following the silver dress as it darted across the crowded room and through a discreet door set in the wooden panelling. The door began to close behind her, but his long stride shortened the distance enough for him to catch it before it could close fully and he slipped inside…

To find himself inside a closet. A large closet, but a closet nonetheless, one filled with towering stacks of spare chairs, folded tables and several cleaning trolleys. Sophie was pressed against one of the tables, her hands gripping the sides, her heart-shaped face pale.

He allowed the door to close behind him, leaning against it, his arms folded, staring her down. '*Buongiorno*, Sophie.'

'Marco? Wh-what are you doing here?'

'Catching up with old friends. That's what I like about these occasions, you never know who you might bump into. Nice corner you've found here. A little crowded, lacking in decoration, but I like it.'

'I…' Her eyes were wide. Scared.

Incredulity thundered through him. He'd assumed she had hidden because she was embarrassed to see him, that maybe she hadn't told her friends—or boyfriend—about him. Or because she was playing some game and trying to lure him in. It hadn't occurred to him that she would be actually terrified at the very thought of seeing him.

Although she had fled from his bed, run away from her friends the moment she had recognised him. How many clues did he need? His mouth compressed into a thin line. 'Apologies, Sophie,' he said stiffly. 'I didn't mean to scare you. Please rest assured that I will leave you alone for the rest of the evening.' He bowed formally and turned, hand on the door handle, only to be arrested by the sound of her low voice.

'No, Marco. I should apologise. I didn't expect to see you here, I didn't expect to see you ever again actually and I overreacted. I'm not… I don't really do… You know. What we did. I have no idea how these things work.'

What we did. Marco had spent the last three weeks trying to put what they'd done out of his mind. Tried not to dwell on the satin of her skin, the taste of her, the way she laughed. The way she moaned.

Ironically he usually did know how these things worked. Temporary and discreet were the hallmarks of the perfect relationship as far as Marco was concerned. Not falling into bed with strangers he'd met on street corners. He was far too cautious. He needed to be certain that any and every prospective partner knew the rules: mutually satisfying and absolutely no strings.

But somehow that evening all his self-imposed rules had gone flying out of the window. It had been like stepping into another world; the snow deep outside, the city oddly muted, the world contracting until it was only the two of them. It seemed as if there had been no other route open to him, booking the hotel room an unsaid inevitability as they'd moved on to their second drink, walking hand in hand through the falling snow but not really touching, not yet, waiting until the room door had swung closed behind them.

And then…

Marco inhaled, the heat of that night burning through his body. He didn't know what he'd have done if she'd been there when he woke up, pulled her to him or distanced himself in the cold light of day. But he hadn't had to make that decision; like the melted snow outside, she was gone. He'd told himself it was for the best. But now that she was here, it was hard to remember why.

He turned. Sophie was still staring at him, her blue eyes huge in her pale face. 'How these things work?' he repeated, unable to stop the smile curving his mouth. 'Does there have to be a set path?'

Colour flared high on her cheekbones. 'No, I'm not looking for Mr Right, but neither am I the kind of girl who spends the night with a stranger. Usually. So I don't know what the etiquette is here.'

'Nor do I, but I'm pretty sure it doesn't require us to spend half the evening in a cleaning closet.'

'No,' she said doubtfully as if the cleaning closet were actually the perfect place to spend New Year's Eve. 'But what happens when we get out there? Do we acknowledge that we know each other or pretend that none of it ever happened?'

The latter was certainly the most sensible idea— but hadn't he decided he needed a distraction? Sophie Bradshaw in a silver minidress was the epitome of distraction. Marco stepped away from the door, leaving it a little ajar, and smiled as ruefully as he could. 'Are those my choices? They seem a little limited. How about I throw a third option in there—I ask you to dance?'

'Ask me to dance?' Her eyes were even wider than before if that was possible and she pressed even further into the table. 'But I walked out on you. Without a note! And I ran away as soon as I saw you.'

'*Sì*, both of these things are true, but if you dance with me, then I am willing to overlook both transgressions.'

'I did mention that I don't want a relationship, didn't I?'

'You did. Sophie, I am also not looking for anything serious and, like you, I'm not in the habit of picking up strangers in the snow. So if neither of us is interested in a relationship and neither of us indulges in one-night stands, then why not get to know each other better? Retrospectively. Unless you're here with someone else?' His hands curled into loose fists at the thought, the thrill of possession taking him by surprise. It was only because they had barely scratched the surface of their attraction, he reminded himself. Only because spending the evening with Sophie would be safe and yet satisfying. No expectations beyond fun and flirtation, although if the evening did end the same way as their past encounter, he wouldn't complain. His gaze travelled down the sixties-inspired minidress to the acres of shapely leg, lingering on the slight swell of her hips. No, he wouldn't be complaining at all.

'No. I'm here with my friends and their husbands and fiancés. They are all lovely and doing their best to include me, but they're all so madly, sickeningly in love that I can't help feeling like a spare part.'

She was wavering. Time to press his advantage. 'Then this is fate,' he said promptly. 'Every time you feel like a spare part, dance with me. We can have a code.'

Her eyebrows raised. 'A code?'

'*Sì*, you rub your nose or tug your ear and I will know you need rescuing from the tedium of romance.'

'They don't mean to be tedious.' But the wariness had disappeared from her face and she was smiling. 'What if you're not watching, when I signal?'

'Oh, I'll be watching,' he assured her. 'But just in case you forget to signal, let's make an appointment now to see the new year in together. I'll meet you…' He paused, trying to think of a landmark in the ballroom.

'Outside this closet?'

'Perfect. Yes, I'll meet you outside here at eleven.'

'But that's a whole hour before midnight.'

'You owe me half an hour of dancing for running out on me and half an hour for escaping into a closet.

I'm Italian, the hurt to my *machismo* could have been catastrophic.'

A dimple flashed in her cheek. 'Okay, eleven it is. Unless I need rescuing, in which case I'll...I'll twizzle my hair. Deal?'

'Deal.' Marco opened the door and held it, standing to one side while Sophie passed through it, brushing past him as she did so, his body exploding into awareness at each point she touched. He took her hand as he stepped out of the small room and raised it to his lips. 'Until eleven, *signorina*. I look forward to further making your acquaintance.'

Marco leaned against the door as he watched Sophie disappear back into the ballroom. Yes, she would do very nicely as a distraction, very nicely indeed. Suddenly he was looking forward to the rest of the Snowflake Ball after all.

CHAPTER THREE

'Who is that hottie? What?' Emma looked round at her friends, indignation flashing in her eyes at their splutters. 'I'm married, blissfully and happily married, but I still have eyes—and, Sophie…that man is sizzling. Tell us all.'

Sophie slid into her seat uncomfortably aware that her cheeks were probably bright red under her friends' scrutiny. 'There's nothing to tell,' she said, picking up her white linen napkin, dislodging a drift of small glittery paper snowflakes as she did so. 'I didn't miss the starter, did I? I'm starving.'

'Tell me my eyes are deceiving me and I didn't just see you emerge from a closet with him.' Ashleigh leaned in to stare intently at her and Sophie's cheeks got even hotter if that was possible—she was almost combusting as it was. 'Ha! You did. Nice work, Soph. Quick work though. We've only been here for twenty minutes.'

'I didn't go *into* the closet with him.' Sophie reached for her glass of champagne and took a much-needed sip, wincing at the unexpectedly dry taste. She pushed it aside and grabbed some water instead. 'He followed me in there.'

'He did what? I take it back. He's not hot. He's

creepy. Well, kind of both. Do you want me to set Jack on him?'

'I'm sure Lukas would be only too glad to have a word,' Ashleigh chimed in with a dark look over at the corner Marco had disappeared into.

'Finlay can be very intimidating,' Grace said, smiling dreamily at her very new and very large pink diamond ring on the third finger of her left hand.

'No, thanks for the offer, but I don't need defending.' Sophie lowered her voice. 'I know him. He's the guy...'

Three faces stared at her blankly.

She sighed. It wasn't as if there had been many—or indeed any—guys since she'd moved to London. 'The guy. From a few weeks ago. The export party guy. You know, in the snow... Italian, we went to a bar...'

'Oh, the one-night-stand guy?' Ashleigh exclaimed.

'Just a little louder, Ash, I don't think he heard you over on the other side of the room, but just one more decibel should do it.'

'What's he doing here? It must be fate.'

'No, Grace, it's not fate. It's embarrassing, that's what it is. I didn't expect to see him again, that's the whole *point* of a one-night stand.'

'Ah, but the real question is are you going to see him again? Now that he's the one-night stand and the quickie-in-the-closet guy?' Emma's eyes were twinkling.

'We did not have a quickie in the closet. Your mind! Call yourself a Countess?'

'It's My Lady to you.' But Emma's smile was rueful. Her friends hadn't got tired of teasing her about her newly acquired title. Sophie wasn't sure they ever would.

'You didn't answer the question, Sophie. Are you going to see him again?'

'Look, just because the three of you are all besotted doesn't mean that I'm looking to settle down. I've been there and done that and it very much didn't agree with me. I have agreed to dance with him later. But that's all I want. Honestly.'

But the scepticism on all three faces showed that none of them believed her. And she didn't blame them because she wasn't entirely sure she believed herself. Oh, she didn't want or need what her friends had, she wasn't hankering after a diamond ring the size of Ashleigh's or Emma's, nor, beautiful as it was, did she want to wear Grace's huge pink diamond. She was quite happy with a ring-free third finger, thank you very much. In fact Sophie's ambitions were as far from domestic bliss as it was possible to get. She wanted to make something of herself. Prove to her family—prove to herself—that she hadn't thrown her life, her chances away when she'd moved in with Harry. She didn't have the time or the inclination for romance.

But shocking as it had been to see Marco, it hadn't been unpleasant. After all, Emma was right: he was smoking hot. Smoking hot and charming. Smoking hot, charming and very, very good in bed. Not that she was planning to sleep with him again. Once was an excusable lapse, twice would be something far too much like a relationship.

But a dance wouldn't hurt—would it?

Sophie had had no intention of using any of the secret signs Marco had suggested. She kept her hands firmly on her lap, on her knife and fork, or wrapped around her water glass to ensure that she didn't inadvertently summon him over. But, as the night wore on, her resolve wavered. It wasn't that her friends and their partners intentionally excluded her, but they just couldn't help themselves. They kept separating off into cosy little pairs to sway intimately on the dance floor, no matter what the music, or to indulge in some very public displays of affection over the smoked salmon starter. In some ways it was worse when they emerged from their love-struck idyll and remembered Sophie's presence, tumbling over themselves to apologise and making Sophie feel even more like a third—or seventh—wheel than ever.

Then when the men sauntered off to the bar between courses, leaving the four friends alone, the conversation turned, inevitably Sophie supposed, to Grace's and Ashleigh's forthcoming weddings.

'Definitely a church wedding,' Grace said. 'Probably in Scotland, although it would be a shame not to hold the reception at The Armstrong. After all, that's where we met. The only thing is a church can be a little limiting. Do you think it would be okay for the bridesmaids to wear short dresses in a church?'

'The bridesmaids were in minidresses at the last church wedding I attended. They were certainly effective.' So effective that Harry, Sophie's ex, hadn't been able to take his eyes off the head bridesmaid as she had paraded down the aisle all tumbled hair and bronzed, lithe legs. Nor, it had transpired just a few hours later, had he been able to keep his hands off her either. Sophie swallowed, reaching for her water blindly to try to mask the metallic taste she always noticed when she thought about that night. The taste of humiliation. Not just because Harry had treated her like that; if she was honest with herself, he'd behaved like that for far too many years. Nor was it because he had chosen to do so in front of all of their friends; after all, Sophie had spent many occasions making excuses for him or turning a well-practised blind eye. No, the scalding shame she still experienced every day was because it had taken such a blatant humiliation to force her to act, to realise that this bad boy couldn't be redeemed and he wasn't worth one more of her tears.

How had it taken seven years? Her parents had known it almost instantly, as had her few friends. And yet she'd chosen Harry over every single one of them, sure that she saw something special in him nobody else could see. Maybe if she'd been more confident, maybe if she hadn't felt so alone when she met him...

No, there were no maybes. She had only herself to blame. What a fool, young and blinded by lust and romance. Never again.

She looked over at her friends, forcing a smile. 'I have a request, no, a demand. You must promise to seat me at a table full of fabulous, fun single ladies. No set-ups with your cousin's best friend's brother's boss just because he visited Manchester once and so we'll have lots in common and no nudging me towards the best man because that's what happens at weddings. I want a party table.'

'It's a promise,' Ashleigh agreed, turning to greet Lukas with a brilliant smile as he put another champagne-filled ice bucket down on the table along with another bottle of mineral water. Maybe she was too used to cheap cava, but Sophie just couldn't drink the champagne; every sip tasted sour. Not only was she a third wheel, but she was a sober third wheel...

What was wrong with her? She *should* be having a good time; she looked okay, her dress had got several appreciative comments, which was always warming to a designer's ears, the food was really tasty, the band talented and the ballroom looked like a very tasteful winter wonderland. It was New Year's Eve and she was out with her best friends being wined and dined. Sophie straightened. She was being selfish. She shouldn't need anything more.

Except...

Sophie's gaze slid, not for the first time, over to the large round table at the other side of the room. Marco was leaning back in his chair, a glass clasped elegantly in his fingertips, apparently deeply involved in a conversation with the couple sat next to him. Only a slight inclination of the head and a tilt of the glass towards her in a light toast betrayed his awareness of her scrutiny. But he knew, she had no doubt. He'd known every time.

It was only nine o'clock. Two hours until their promised dance.

The third of the six courses had been cleared away and Emma and Jack had taken advantage of the hiatus in the meal to dance—if you called moving very slowly staring intensely at each other dancing. Grace and Finlay were sitting opposite Sophie, but there was no point trying to chat to either of them; they were looking into each other's eyes, emitting so much heat Sophie had moved the water jug closer in case they suddenly combusted. As for Ashleigh, Sophie hadn't seen her friend for several minutes, but at last sight she had been towing Lukas determinedly towards the closet Sophie had discovered earlier.

She had a choice. She could spend the next two hours sitting here feeling sorry for herself or she could allow herself some real fun. The kind of fun she'd been too busy accommodating Harry to enjoy before. The kind of fun she hadn't allowed herself since the breakup. Just looking at Marco made her stomach fall away and her breath hitch, but she was no longer a naïve teenager who couldn't tell the difference between lust and love. And that was what this was: pure and simple delicious lust. If she knew that, remembered that, then what harm could a few more hours in Marco's company do?

And as the thought crossed her mind her hand rose, almost by its own volition, and, with her eyes fixed on Marco, Sophie slowly and deliberately wound a lock of hair around her finger and smiled.

He'd been aware of her every second of the evening, from the moment she'd walked away from him to rejoin her friends. The swish of her hair, the sway of her hips, the curve of her mouth. It was as if an invisible thread stretched across the vast room connecting them; every time she moved he felt it, a deep visceral pull.

It was unlike any reaction he'd ever had towards a woman and it wasn't hard to work out why; he didn't need a degree in psychology to realise that she was probably the first woman to walk away from him and he was completely unaccustomed to not calling the shots in all his relationships, personal and professional. No wonder his interest was piqued.

Not that he wanted her to know it. Knowledge was power in every relationship, no matter how temporary.

But Marco knew every time Sophie slid a look in his direction, he felt the tension in her as if it were his, he knew she would cave in eventually and so, with a surge of triumph, he watched her as she reached up and wound a lock of silky blonde hair around her finger, a provocative smile on her full mouth—and a challenge in her eyes.

Marco's expectations of the evening had risen the second he'd caught sight of the elusive Signorina Bradshaw; at that look in her eyes they took flight. 'Excuse me,' he said, pushing his chair back and languidly getting to his feet. No need to rush. She wasn't going anywhere. 'I have some personal business to attend to.'

He held Sophie's gaze as he moved with predatory grace across the dance floor, his steps slow and easy until he came to a halt in front of her. Sophie sat alone on one side of the table, the only other occupants breaking off from an intense conversation to watch, open-mouthed, as he extended a hand. *'Signorina?'*

Sophie arched an elegant bow. 'Sir?'

He smiled at that, slow and purposeful. 'Would you do me the honour?'

'How very unexpected.' Her eyes laughed up at him. 'I don't know what to say.'

'I believe the words you are looking for are "Thank you. I would love to."'

'Are they? In that case thank you, I would love to.' And she slipped her hand into his and allowed him to lead her from her chair and onto the dance floor.

She slipped into his arms as if she had never left, every curve fitting perfectly against him, her arms resting naturally around his waist. 'Are you having a nice evening?' It was a strangely formal question considering the way her body was pressed to his.

'I am now,' Marco answered gravely and, with some satisfaction, watched the colour rise in her cheeks. 'Have you attended this ball before?'

'I was here last year.'

'No, I was here also. How on earth did I miss you? Impossible.'

She smiled, a dimple peeping out. He remembered that dimple; it had enchanted him the first time she had smiled, snowflakes tangled in her hair, slipping on the snowy ground. 'Maybe you weren't looking hard enough. So this is a regular event for you?'

He shrugged. 'Usually. One of my clients always has a table and so here I am.'

'How very convenient. Don't you want to…' But she trailed off, shaking her head. 'Never mind.'

'Don't I want to what?'

'I'm just being nosy. It's just, isn't spending New Year with clients a little, well, impersonal? What about your friends and family?'

His stomach clenched. Tomorrow would be all about family—with one glaring omission. 'My clients are my friends as well, of course. Most of the people I know in the UK I met through work. What about you? Who are the people you are here with?'

The dimple peeked out again. 'Work friends,' she admitted. 'London can be a lonely place when you first move here.'

'You're not from London?'

'Manchester, and no, I'm not spending New Year with my family either. I did Christmas and that was more than enough.' A shadow crossed her face so fleetingly he wondered if he'd imagined it. 'How about you? Whereabouts in Italy are you from?'

'Venice.'

Her eyes lit up. 'Oh, how utterly gorgeous. What an amazing place to live.'

Amazing, thrilling, beautiful, hidebound, full of rules and expectations no man could be expected to keep. 'You've been?'

'Well, no. But I've read about it, watched films, seen pictures. It's at the top of my bucket list—lying back in a gondola and watching the canals go by. Masked balls, *palazzos*, bridges…' She laughed. 'Listen to me, I sound like such a tourist.'

'No, no. It is a beautiful city. You should go.'

'One day.' She sounded wistful. 'How can you bear to live here when you could live there? London is cool and all, but Venice? There's a story, a view around every corner.'

'And a member of my family, or an old family friend, or their relative. *Sì…*' as her eyes widened in under-standing '…Venice is beautiful, captivating, unique, all these things and I miss it every day, but it is also an island. A very small island.'

'Gets a little claustrophobic?'

'A little. But London? Here a man can be who he wants to be, see who he wants to see, do the work he feels fitting. Be his own man.'

'London's not that big,' she pointed out. 'After all, I've bumped into you twice—literally the first time!'

'Ah, but, *signorina…*' he leaned forward so his breath touched her ear and felt her shiver at the slight contact '…that was fate and we don't question the work-ings of fate.'

They were so close he could feel her heart racing against him before she pulled back. 'Still, small or not, it must be a wonderful place to live. Are your parents still there?'

'My mother,' he corrected her. 'My father died ten months ago.' He steeled himself for the usual hit of guilt, regret and anger. Guilt his father's heart had been weak-ened in the first place, regret they had never patched up their relationship—and anger his father would never now admit that Marco had a right to a life of his own.

'Ten months ago? That's so recent, I'm sorry.'

'Thank you.'

'She must miss you, your mother.'

He allowed a smile but knew it was wintry at best. 'Miss me? I'm not sure. Miss telling me how to live my life? Every day.'

'I know a little about that. What does your mother want that's so terrible?'

Marco shrugged. 'What every Italian mother wants for her children, especially her only son. A place in the family business under her eyes, a wife, children, the usual.'

'And you aren't hankering for *bambinos* clustered around your knee?' She didn't sound disappointed or disapproving, which made a refreshing change. So many women seemed to see Marco's lack of interest in a family as a personal affront—or, worse, a challenge. 'Sunday morning football, wet wipes in every pocket? I have two brothers and they both have kids. I know the drill.'

'I like my life the way it is. Why complicate it?'

'And I take it no interest in a wife either.' She smiled, a small dimple charming him as she did so. 'Your poor mother.'

'She only has herself to blame,' he said lightly. 'My marriage is an obsession with her. I remember going to my mother's friend's house and while the mothers talked I played with the daughter. She was a nice girl, sporty. We got on really well. When we left my *mamma* asked me if I liked her and when I said I did she said *bene* she would make a good wife for me. I was five!'

'All mothers do that. My mother was convinced I'd marry Tom next door. He played the violin and sang in the church choir, always said hello and helped shovel snow or rake leaves. Perfect husband material.'

'And yet he isn't here with you tonight?'

'Well, it turns out that Tom prefers boys to girls, so even if I had been tempted, it was never going to happen.'

'Lucky for me.' He pulled Sophie in close and swung her around. 'Tell me, *signorina*, why are we here in this beautiful room dancing to this beautiful music and discussing my mother? I can think of many more interesting topics.'

Her eyes laughed up at him. 'Such as?'

'Such as how very sexy you look in that dress. Such as how very well you dance. Such as what shall we do with all this time until midnight?'

Sophie swallowed, her eyes luminous in the bright, pulsing disco lights. His eyes were drawn to the graceful column of her neck, the lines of her throat, and he ran his thumb down her skin, feeling her pulse speed up. 'Do?' she echoed a little hoarsely. 'Why, *signor*, you asked me to dance and so far we've just swayed to the music. Less talk, more dancing. It's New Year's Eve after all.'

There was no conversation after that, just dancing, movement, an intimacy that could only be conjured by two bodies caught up in the same beat. Sophie could *move*, hair flying, eyes shining and silver minidress glittering in the disco lights as she swayed and turned. 'A childhood full of dance lessons,' she told him during a breathless break. 'I did it all, ballet, jazz, tap. I have medals and everything.'

But as the night neared midnight the music slowed and she was back in his arms. The ballroom was filled with anticipation as the seconds began to tick away, people gathering in groups ready to welcome in the new year. Marco steered Sophie to a secluded corner of the dance floor, not wanting the shared jollity, the drunken group embraces that so often marked the new year's first seconds. *'Felice anno nuovo.'*

'Happy New Year, Marco.' Her eyes were half shuttered, her lips full and inviting. He knew the taste of them, the sweet plumpness of her bottom lip, knew the way her hands wound into his hair as a kiss deepened, how her skin slid like silk under his fingertips. Just a dance, he'd said. Surely they'd both known that after the night they had shared they couldn't possibly stop at dancing. Besides, it was New Year's Eve; it was customary to kiss.

And how he hated to be rude. Just one kiss, to round off the evening, to round off their brief but, oh, so pleasing acquaintanceship.

Sophie purred her approval as he lowered his mouth to hers, her hands tightening on his shoulders, her body swaying closer until he felt every curve pressed tight against him. Marco was dimly aware that the room was erupting with cheers as the new year dawned, could hear bangs and pops as the balloons and streamers were released and the first chords of 'Auld Lang Syne' began to echo around the room, but it was as if he and Sophie were separated from the cheerful celebration, hidden in some alternate dimension where all he knew was her mouth under his, her body quivering under his caress, her touch on his neck, light enough to drive a man mad.

And then it was over as she stepped back, trembling and wide-eyed. 'Thank you for a lovely night. I don't think… I mean, my friends will be looking for me.'

It took a few moments for her words to penetrate his fogged-up brain. All he wanted was to pull her back in, take her mouth again, hold her still. Marco inhaled, long and deep, pushing the dangerous desire deep down where it belonged.

'It was my pleasure. I am glad I got to meet you again, *signorina*.' He took her hand, bowing formally over it, then stepped back, a final farewell. She hesitated for the briefest of seconds and then, with a quick smile, turned away.

A pleasant interlude and now it was over as all these interludes eventually were. Unless...

Tomorrow he returned home. Returned to a wedding, to play a part, to the weight of parental expectations, no less heavy with the loss of his father. Returned to guilt.

He could do with a distraction.

Sophie obviously wasn't looking for any kind of relationship; in fact this was the third time she'd walked away from him without a backwards glance. A wry smile curved his mouth; thank goodness her response to his kiss had been so all encompassing or he'd be wondering if the attraction was one-sided. And she had never seen Venice...

She would make the perfect distraction, for himself and for his family.

Marco didn't want to take any more time to think his idea through, not when Sophie was disappearing into the revelling crowd. 'Sophie?' She stopped and turned, a confused expression on her face.

He crossed the distance between them with a few long strides. 'My mother will be holding her annual party on the sixth of January, for Epiphany. I have to be there, to co-host, in place of my father. Would you like to be my guest?'

The confusion deepened. 'Me? Come to Venice? But...'

'You said yourself how much you want to go.'

'Yes.' She looked tempted for a moment, then frowned again. 'But, Marco, I hardly know you. You don't know me and I'm not really looking for anything, for anyone. I like you, I like spending time with you...'

'And I like spending time with you and I really would like to get to know you better. And that's all this is, Sophie. A couple of days in Venice, a party and then we go our separate ways. What do you say?'

'Of course you should say yes.' The ball might officially be over for another year, but the evening was far from finished yet—after all, as Emma pointed out, they hadn't properly celebrated Grace's engagement yet—and so they had all piled into taxis and gone back to The Armstrong, the hotel Finlay owned and where the newly engaged couple had met, to finish welcoming the new year in in style. It was a novel experience for Sophie to be escorted up to the exclusive suite as a guest, not a maid, and to sink onto one of the comfortable sofas, the room-service menu at her disposal and the promise of a car to take her home.

A novel experience for Sophie, but all her friends seemed to take this level of luxury almost for granted; even Grace stepped into the private lift as if it were an everyday occurrence for her. And now it was. Grace, just like Ashleigh and Emma, was marrying into some serious wealth.

This evening, lovely as it was, was exposing the very clear differences in Sophie's future and the paths her friends were headed down—and made her even more determined to shape hers the way she had always intended it to be. This year she'd put some serious effort into the website she'd recently set up and start trying to sell her designs. She clenched her hands at the familiar twist of excitement and fear. What if Harry was right? What if she was wasting her time?

Grace plumped down onto the sofa opposite, heaving her bare feet onto the glass coffee table with a sigh of relief. 'I agree. Go, have fun. It's always quiet at work at this time of year—and we've been run off our feet for months. Take some time off. You deserve it.'

'I'll lend you the fare if you need it. Consider it an early birthday present.' Ashleigh seated herself next to Sophie and nudged her. 'Venice, Soph. You've always wanted to go.'

'Marco offered to pay for my ticket. No, don't look so excited. He has loads of air miles from his work. It's not a big deal.' Actually it was. Sophie didn't want to admit how much his casual 'I'll cover all expenses, it's the least I can do, you'll be far more of a help than you realise' had touched her. Harry had not only always expected Sophie to pay her way but frequently his as well. He was a musician after all, above mundane worldly tasks like making a living. 'It's just, I hardly know him.'

Grace raised her eyebrows knowingly. 'Didn't look that way from where I was sitting tonight. The chemistry between you two...*oof*!' She fanned herself dramatically, ducking with a squeal as Sophie threw a cushion at her.

'What do you need to know?' Ashleigh asked, squeezing Sophie's hand. 'What would make you feel better about going?'

Sophie shrugged, unable to articulate the prickle of unease that ran over her when she thought about accepting Marco's casual invitation—or, more worryingly, the ripple of excitement overshadowing the unease. 'I don't know where he lives. I don't exactly know what he does for a living. I don't know if he likes music or books or walks in the country.'

'What *do* you know?' Emma curled up next to Grace. 'Tell us about him.'

'He's Italian, does something to do with art and antiques. Erm…he's lived in London for ages but really loves Venice, you can hear it in his voice. He has a gorgeous accent, dresses really well, his suits look handmade to me, beautifully designed, great fabric.'

'Focus, Sophie. We want to know about the man, not his clothes. How does he make you feel?'

How did he make her *what*? When Sophie had packed her bags, the shattered remaining pieces of her pride and her bruised heart and moved over a hundred miles away to start again, the one thing she had guarded herself against was feeling too much. It was thanks to her emotions she had fallen into such a sorry state in the first place. She picked up a cushion and cradled it close, as if it were a shield between her and the rest of the world while she thought. 'He makes me feel sexy. Wanted. Powerful.' Where had those words come from? But even as she spoke them Sophie knew that they were the truth—and that not once, in seven years, had Harry made her feel any of those things. Desperate, insecure, weak, needy, pathetic? All the above. Never powerful. Never wanted.

She straightened, turning to stare at Ashleigh half excited, half terrified. 'I should go, shouldn't I?'

'You should totally go. Who cares about his address and what exactly something in art and antiques means? As long as he isn't a drug smuggler and doesn't live with his wife and six kids, it's irrelevant. Sexy and powerful? Now, *they're* relevant.'

'Who knows where it might lead? Look at me. I went to Scotland for a bit of adventure and came back head over heels. Go for it!' Grace practically clapped in excitement, but Sophie shook her head emphatically.

'I am so happy for you, Grace, for all of you. But believe me, I'm not going to come back engaged. Marco made it very clear he's not interested in anything long-term and that suits me perfectly. There's a lot I want to achieve, that I need to achieve, and wedded bliss is very far down that list. But this will be good for me. I've been so scared of being sucked back into a relationship I've gone too far the other way. This is a big city. I should date and see people occasionally, live a little.'

'Live a lot,' Emma corrected her. 'You should, Sophie, you deserve to. And we'll be cheering you on every step of the way.'

CHAPTER FOUR

'LIVE A LOT,' Sophie reminded herself as she passed through the customs gate and into the arrivals hall. Her new mantra. She'd been repeating it throughout the flight, torn between excitement at seeing Venice—and Marco—at last and apprehension about the next few days. What if she and Marco had nothing to say to each other now she was here, or what if his mother didn't like her?

No, those negative thoughts were old Sophie, not new, improved, positive, life-grabbing Sophie. Pushing them aside, she scanned the arrivals hall, impatient to see Marco. She hadn't spoken to him since New Year's Eve as he had flown out the very next day, but he had sent an itinerary with her ticket and promised that she would be met at the airport.

Maybe he was running late…

As she scanned the waiting crowd again a sign bearing a familiar name caught her eye and, as she paused to read it again, the bearer, a slight man in his forties, formally dressed in a chauffeur's uniform and cap, caught her eye and smiled. 'Signorina Bradshaw?' he asked in heavily accented but perfect English. 'Signor Santoro asked me to meet you. He has been called away.' He handed Sophie an envelope as he deftly relieved her of her suitcase and bag.

Disappointment warred with a cowardly relief. Work had predictably been quiet over the last few days, leaving Sophie far too much time to second-guess her decision and, even though she'd tried to bury herself in her designs or wrestle with the unnecessarily complicated content management system on her still-not-live website, she often found herself sitting still staring into space, her heart thumping with panic at the prospect of stepping outside the narrow life she'd built herself.

The envelope was thick, more like an invitation than a piece of office stationery, and it took Sophie a couple of moments to open it and pull out a piece of crisp white paper. She unfolded it and scanned the brief lines.

Sophie,
Please accept my most sincere apologies but I am
unavoidably detained. Gianni will escort you to
my mother's house and I will see you at the party
this evening.
A dopo,
Marco

No kiss, she noted. What did that mean in a time when even her dentist included an X on her check-up reminder? Pocketing the note, she smiled at Gianni. 'Thank you for coming to meet me. I'm ready whenever you are.'

She'd spoken too soon. As she got her first glimpse of Venice Sophie realised that nothing could have prepared her for her first glimpse of the magnificent island city. Gianni led her out of the airport and, instead of heading to a car park, Sophie found herself at a dock.

'This way, please,' Gianni said, briskly walking her past the ferry port and the queues for the water taxis. Sophie wanted to stop and take in the strange sight of passengers embarking onto a row of boats, swaying on the gangplanks as they tried to balance their suitcases. All around her, voices exclaimed, yelled and barked in a mixture of languages, the fresh salt smell of the sea mixing with the less romantic scent of diesel.

They walked on for another few minutes until Gianni gestured her forward onto a gangplank that led onto a gleaming wooden boat. Two seats at the front were shielded from the elements by a simple screen and a further three comfortable-looking leather benches were arranged around the walls of the small glassed-in cabin. Gianni heaved her suitcase and bag onto the cabin floor, but when he gestured for Sophie to step inside she shook her head. 'Oh, please, can I sit up front, next to you? I've never been to Venice before.'

Gianni cast an assessing look at her quilted coat and the black velvet jeans she'd chosen to travel in. '*Sì,* but it gets cold on the sea. Do you have a hat?'

'And a scarf and gloves,' Sophie assured him as she took her place beside the driver's seat—or pilot's seat. She wasn't entirely sure of the correct term for a boat driver.

It took just a few moments for Gianni to cast off the ropes and expertly manoeuvre the boat out of the dock and around the fleet of ferries, water taxis and hotel boats out into the lagoon. Sophie sucked in a breath of sheer exhilaration as the boat accelerated through the clear blue water and headed towards the most beautiful place she'd ever seen. The island city rose out of the water like a stately dame.

'"Age cannot wither her, nor custom stale her infinite

variety",' Sophie quoted as the bell tower in St Mark's Square came into view. It seemed so familiar and yet so new—a picture she'd seen a thousand times and yet never really got until now. Sophie's heart squeezed and she knew she would always love this ancient city. It was in her blood already, taking further root with every breath.

She couldn't speak as Gianni steered the boat into the Grand Canal, just stared, almost overcome by the beauty all around her. Boats passed them, turning down narrow canals, bridges arched overhead and, glancing down a canal on her right, Sophie thrilled as she saw a boat piled high with a colourful variety of fruit and vegetables moored to the side, the owner twisting up produce in paper bags as he sold to eager customers.

It wasn't just the beauty of the city, it was the life thrumming through it. This was no museum, a place existing merely for the multitudes of tourists. It was a living, breathing place—and for the next two days she would be part of it. Would belong.

At that moment the boat began to turn and headed towards a small gangplank and a set of stairs leading directly to a door to an imposing cream-coloured building right on the Grand Canal. What was going on? She'd done a little research and knew that the hotels overlooking the famous canal were exorbitant. Sophie had expected a little B & B somewhere further out of the city. 'Wait, where are you going?'

Gianni looked puzzled. 'To Palazzo Santoro, of course. Signor Santoro asked me to convey you directly.'

'The *palazzo*?' Sophie's hands tightened on the side of the boat. Marco hadn't mentioned a *palazzo*—especially not one right on the Grand Canal. Her stomach twisted. Girls from the Manchester suburbs didn't belong in places like this—not unless they were serving drinks. She took a deep breath. *Palazzo* probably didn't mean anything grand. Maybe Marco's mother had a flat in this building. No one actually *owned* a building this big, no one Sophie was ever going to meet.

Before she could completely gather her thoughts the boat had stilled and Gianni was lifting her bags out of the back of the boat and extending a hand to help her disembark. Sophie climbed gingerly over the side of the boat and followed Gianni, treading carefully up the stone steps. He rapped smartly on the door and, as it opened, set Sophie's bags inside, gave her a friendly nod and ran lightly back down the steps and into the boat. She looked around wildly, hoping for a clue as to where exactly she was going, but all she could see was the open door. And her suitcase and travel bag were inside.

It fleetingly crossed Sophie's mind that no one knew exactly where she was—or who Marco was—and she could enter this house and never be seen again. But if it was a kidnap plot, it was far too elaborate a set-up for a waitress living on the outer edges of Chelsea. She took another step up the last step and entered through the ornately carved wooden door and came to an abrupt standstill.

Had she fallen down a rabbit hole? Sophie had cleaned and waitressed in some seriously swanky homes over the last year or so, but she had never seen anything quite on this scale or of this antiquity. The door led into an immense tiled hallway with a wooden-beamed ceiling and aged-looking frescos on the wall and ceiling, the only furnishings a few very old and very delicate-looking chairs. The hall ran the entire length of the building; she could see double doors at the other end, windows on either side, the sun streaming through the stained glass at the top. A gallery with intricate wrought-iron railings ran all the way around the hallway, accessed by two wide staircases, one at either end of the hall. Sophie could see several closed doors running the length of the room, discreetly hidden in the faded frescos.

What she couldn't see was any sign of life. She stepped further in, swivelling slowly as she took in every detail, jumping at the sight of the elderly woman, clad in sombre black from throat to calf, standing statue-like almost behind the open door. 'Oh, hello. I mean *buongiorno*.' All her hastily learned Italian phrases seemed to have disappeared from her head. '*Je m'appelle…* No, sorry, that's not right. Erm…*mi chiamo* Sophie. Marco is expecting me, isn't he? The driver, boatman, he seemed to think he was at the right place.'

That's right, Sophie, just keep babbling.

She was struck by a sudden thought: maybe this was a hotel and the Santoro was just a coincidence—it could be a totally common name like Smith or Brown. 'Should I check in?' she enquired hopefully. A check-in desk she could cope with. House rules, room-service menu, hopefully a fluffy white robe.

The woman didn't respond. Instead she bent slowly, so slowly Sophie could almost hear the creak of her waist, before picking up Sophie's suitcase as if it weighed less than an empty pillowcase. Sophie, who had stepped forward to stop her, froze in place as the woman stepped forward, the suitcase almost swinging from her hand. It had taken all Sophie's efforts just to heave that suitcase onto the Tube. She eyed the woman with respect and stood back out of her way as the woman strode past her with a grunted 'This way' as she did so. Sophie followed meekly behind, along the hallway, up three flights of the sweeping staircase and onto a long landing peopled with portraits of men in tights and women with fans. Sophie was panting by this point, but the woman seemed completely at ease and Sophie yet again promised herself a regular routine of Pilates, Zumba and body pump.

They came to an abrupt halt outside a wood-panelled door. The woman pushed it open and gestured for Sophie to step inside. With a wondering glance she did so, her aching legs and heaving chest instantly forgotten as she turned around in wonder.

The room was huge, easily twice the size of Sophie's entire apartment with three huge floor-to-ceiling windows overlooking the canal, shutters swung open to reveal the Juliet balconies outside each one, Venice framed like a living breathing picture within. Although the walls were painted a simple pale blue the ceiling was alive with a fresco of cherubs and angels, partying riotously across the room, edged in gilt matching the elaborate gilt headboard on the huge bed and the elegant chaise positioned before one of the windows. A huge mirror hung opposite the windows reflecting the watery light. The woman—a maid? Marco's grandmother? A complete stranger? Sophie had absolutely no idea—opened one of two matching doors on either side of the bed to reveal a dressing room, complete with dressing table and two wardrobes. The other door led into a bathroom so luxurious Sophie thought she might never be able to leave it.

'The family will gather in the reception room at six,' the lady intoned and left, shutting the door firmly behind her, leaving Sophie standing in the middle of the room torn between giddiness at the gorgeousness of her surroundings and fear at trying to find her way through this huge house to meet a set of people she didn't even have names for.

'Breathe,' she told herself. 'Live a lot, remember?' But as she sank onto the bed she was painfully conscious that all she wanted to do was hide away in this room.

Okay, here was what she knew: this was not an apartment; Marco's family appeared to own the entire, immense and very old building. Therefore the family party was unlikely to be just a few close friends, a glass of sherry and some pineapple and cheese sticks in the kitchen. The only person she knew was Marco and he wasn't even here and didn't expect to be until the party. She lay down and stared up at the cherubs, hoping they might be able to help her.

On the other hand she *was* in Venice. Sophie sat up and rolled off the bed, almost running to the window before the thought had fully formed, staring out with rapt eyes at the *palazzos* opposite, at the boats sailing below. She was in *Venice* and about to go to a party with a gorgeous man before returning to the most beautiful room she had ever set eyes on. So she was a little daunted? Time to pull on her big-girl pants—well, the nicest underwear she owned *just in case*—and try to enjoy every moment because she knew all too well that moments like this didn't come her way all too often.

'Come on, Sophie. Enjoy it. It's just a couple of days...' Two days of being someone new. Nobody here knew her, nobody here knew that she was twenty-six, had wasted the last eight years of her life, that she worked sixteen hours a day trying to pay her bills and get her own business off the ground. She wasn't Sophie Bradshaw, reliable employee of Maids in Chelsea, waitress, chambermaid and cleaner. She was Signorina

Bradshaw, the kind of woman who went to glamorous balls and got invited to stay in *palazzos*. Why not be that woman for two days? After all, she wasn't expecting to see Marco again after she went back to London. What harm could it do to live the fantasy, just for a little while?

But as she turned to look back at the ornate room fear struck her once again. How would a girl like her ever fit in a place like this? Even if it was for just a couple of days?

Marco adjusted his bow tie, painfully aware that he was running almost inexcusably late. It had been a long six days. Since his move to London Marco had kept his visits back to Venice as brief as possible—he'd been confident in his contacts in Italy; it had been the rest of the world he'd needed to concentrate on. But a decade was a long time and it was becoming painfully clear a couple of days twice a year was no longer enough. He needed to start spending some significant amounts of time here if he wanted to continue to grow his business.

His mother was also making it very clear that it was time he stepped up and assumed his role as head of the family. Only, guided by her, of course… His mouth thinned. He'd already fought that battle with one parent and he wasn't sure either of them could count a decade-long standoff as a victory. And now his father was gone it all seemed pointlessly self-destructive anyway.

But how could he complain about the burden of his name when every now and then it opened doors to homes and estates that were kept firmly shut to less exalted sons of the city? Today he had spent the day with an impoverished old Venetian family who were reluctantly selling off some of their family treasures and trusted Marco to do the job for them both lucratively and discreetly. Neither would prove to be difficult; he had a long list of potential buyers who would pay more than market value for first refusal on the beautifully carved furniture, Renaissance paintings and elaborate silverware.

A negotiation like this took time and he had been all too aware that while he was sitting drinking coffee with the Grigionis and dancing ever so politely around his commission, Sophie had arrived to an empty house with nobody to welcome her but Marta, who was a most excellent woman but not the most gregarious of people—and the chances were very high that she would run into his mother before he could warn Sophie just what he was bringing her into.

Several times over the last few days he had been on the verge of cancelling Sophie's visit. His mother had been so focussed on finding him a suitable Venetian bride he'd hoped Sophie's presence would throw her long enough to give him some space—but he'd underestimated her desire to see him wed. His father's death seemed to have intensified her hopes, and nationality no longer seemed to matter. His mother's eyes had lit up at the news he had invited a date to the party and she hadn't stopped asking him questions about his English 'friend'.

At least with Sophie by his side she wouldn't be able to introduce him to any eligible female guests with that specifically intense focus she usually employed. No, it was probably a good thing he hadn't cancelled. Sophie was here for just a couple of nights, not long enough for his mother to get too attached to her but long enough to throw her off the scent for the rest of his visit. Bringing a diversion was an excellent idea; he didn't know why he hadn't considered it earlier.

The clock had finished striking six when Marco strolled into the salon, adjusting his cuffs as he did so. Sophie was already there talking to his mother and his sister, Bianca, looking a little paler than he remembered but stunning in a pale pink beaded dress, which hung straight down to mid-thigh from two simple knotted straps. Her long blonde hair was knotted up with tendrils curling around her face, her only jewellery a pair of striking gold hoop earrings, which trembled as she moved. His blood began to pulse hot at the sight of her exposed neck. Inviting her had been an excellent idea for several reasons.

'Sophie,' he said, striding over to her and kissing her on both cheeks in welcome. 'Welcome. Did you have any trouble finding us?'

'No, no, even I would find it hard to get lost when a boat delivers me straight to the door.' Bianca and his mother laughed, but Marco's eyes narrowed. There was a tartness in her voice he hadn't heard before, the blue eyes icy and cold. Was she cross because he hadn't met her at the airport? He hoped not. Maybe a decoy was going to be as much trouble as a real girlfriend.

'Mamma, Bianca, please excuse us, I would like to make my apologies to Sophie properly for not being here when she arrived,' he said, smoothly drawing Sophie's arm through his. The pre-party drinks were being held in the reception salon, the largest sitting room on the first floor. Like most of the public rooms it overlooked the Grand Canal. Marco walked Sophie over to the furthest window, away from prying ears. 'I hope Gianni found you all right. I'm sorry I was detained.'

'No, that's fine.' But she was still staring out at the canal, her face set. 'I just wish you'd warned me, that's all.'

'I didn't realise until yesterday…'

'No! Not about being met, for goodness' sake! About this…' She looked around and he realised with a stab of compunction that her lips were quivering. 'Marco, every woman here is in a full-on ballgown. They look like they are going to a coronation, not a family party. And me? I'm wearing a little party dress I made myself. I look so underdressed.'

'You look beautiful.' And she did. Although she was right, all the other women were in floor-length, brightly coloured silk and chiffon gowns.

'And this house! Family party, you said. You forgot to mention that the family is the Borgias! I've never been anywhere like this. My bedroom is like a five-star hotel.'

'You don't like it?' Marco was struggling to understand the point she was making. So the family home was big and the party formal? Women usually loved the *palazzo*, and they loved knowing he was the future owner—owner, he supposed, not that he had any intention of setting up home here even more.

'Like it?' She made a queer noise, part gasp, part sob, part laughter. 'It's not the kind of place you like, is it? It's magnificent, beautiful, incredible, but it's not the kind of place I know as home. I don't fit in here, Marco. Not in this house, not with this kind of wealth. Your mother is wearing a diamond tiara that's probably worth more than my parents' house.' She shook her head. 'Oh, God, listen to me. I sound like the worst kind of inverted snob. I just didn't expect any of this. I'm more than a little thrown.'

Marco had never heard this kind of reaction before. True, most women who walked into the *palazzo* knew exactly who he was, briefed by their *mammas* just as he was by his. But even the wealthiest and most well-bred visitor got a covetous look in their eye when they realised the whole of the building still belonged to the family and therefore, by extension, to Marco. This kind of appalled shock was new, but it was also a relief, like a long sip of cold water after a lifetime of rich, creamy milk.

And she did have a point. He'd brought her here for his own selfish reasons; it hadn't occurred to him to warn her just what a Santoro party entailed.

'Just be yourself, Sophie. I promise you, everyone will love you—and they will adore your dress. I'm sorry, it didn't occur to me that this would all be a little overwhelming, but I promise to make it up to you. Tomorrow I'll show you Venice, not a tiara in sight. What do you say?'

She didn't answer for a long moment, indecision clear on her face. Then she turned to him, eyes big with a vulnerable expression in them that struck him hard. 'Are you sure I look all right? I'm not letting you down?'

'Not at all,' he assured her. 'In fact I predict next year most of the younger women will be glad to break with tradition and wear shorter dresses. Come, let's go and mingle and I will tell you three scandalous secrets about every person we meet. I promise you won't be intimidated by a single one by the end of the evening.'

CHAPTER FIVE

ALTHOUGH MARCO WAS true to his word and did indeed tell Sophie such scandalous secrets about every person she met—she refused to believe they could be true; *surely* that regal lady over there wasn't an international jewel thief?—she was still a little intimidated. Intimidated by the glitter and the air of self-possession displayed by every well-dressed guest, by the rapid flow of Italian all around and the familiarity with which each guest greeted each other. She felt too English, too parochial, too poor, too self-conscious, and although Marco was a charming and attentive host Sophie couldn't help thinking longingly of the city outside the old *palazzo*, ready to be explored and discovered.

But when Marco took her arm in his, when he leaned in close to whisper yet another outrageous lie, when he caught her eyes, laughter lurking in his, as his mother not so discreetly quizzed Sophie on her future plans and whether those plans involved marriage and babies, then she was pulled away from the room, away from her insecurities and into a world where all she saw was the tilt of his mouth, the warmth of his smile and the promise in his dark eyes. Anticipation flooded through her at the knowledge that when the clock struck twelve her night would only just be beginning… At least she hoped it would; she hadn't splashed out on a gorgeous new nightie in the New Year sales for nothing. The bits of silk held together with lace would hardly keep her warm after all.

She was aware of Marco's eyes on her and heat flooded through her as their gazes snagged and held, the rest of the room falling away. No, the other women in the room could do their best to attract his attention—and many of them were—but Sophie knew she wouldn't be sleeping alone that night.

After drinks and appetisers and a formal, beautifully presented meal for fifty, the party moved into an even grander and bigger room. Here yet more guests joined them, the numbers swelling into the hundreds as a band played at one end and immaculately dressed waiters circled with trays of drinks. Marco's mother had 'borrowed' him to greet an elderly relative and Sophie hovered by the window, unsure where to go or who to speak to—if she could make herself understood, that was. It was all too reminiscent of standing at the back of one of Harry's gigs, not quite knowing what to say or whether she was welcome in any of the close-knit, self-possessed groups.

'I'm sorry, it must all be a little too much for you. We are bad enough when it's just the family, but when all of Venice is here? I wish I could run and hide, so I have no idea how horrifying you must find tonight.'

Sophie turned to see Marco's sister, Bianca, standing beside her, a sympathetic smile on her heart-shaped face. She was very beautiful in a classically Italian way with masses of dark wavy hair and huge brown eyes fringed with lashes so long they made Sophie gasp with envy, tall and shapely with a generous bosom spilling out of the top of her low-cut strapless dress.

'It's a little more than I was expecting. Marco didn't quite communicate the full scale of the evening. I didn't expect to meet so many people. As you can see I'm not really dressed appropriately...' She gestured towards her dress self-consciously, aware that the hand-sewn beads and cheap fabric paled beside Bianca's ravishing emerald silk gown.

'Your dress is *bellissima*,' Bianca reassured her. 'I have heard many envious comments. Of course, you have such lovely ivory skin. That pale pink would make me far too sallow. I predict next year half the younger women will break with convention and wear something a little more fun and fashionable.' Bianca echoed her brother's prediction.

'Thank you.' Sophie didn't think her skin looked lovely or ivory, more the pale blue an English winter turned her naturally pale complexion. She'd much rather be blessed with Bianca's gorgeous olive skin and generous curves.

'And the cut, I love how it is so modern and yet looks so vintage. Who's the designer?'

'Oh, well, I am.' Sophie always felt absurdly diffident when admitting to designing or making her clothes. Her friends were supportive, asking for commissions and nagging her into starting a website to sell to a wider audience, but they were her friends—it was their job to tell her to follow her heart and aim high. Showing her work to other people was exposing. Harry had always told her that she was wasting her time and the problem was she didn't only believe him then, she still half believed him now.

'You made this? But, Sophie, it is incredible. No wonder it fits you so well. You are so talented.'

'Thank you, but it's not that hard...'

'Of course it is! I can barely thread a needle. Do you make all your clothes?'

'Most of them,' Sophie admitted. 'Some from scratch, with new material, but many of my clothes are do-overs. I buy them from charity shops or in sales, tear them apart and put them back together again.'

'How creative.' Bianca sighed. 'I tried for years to find my talent, but no matter how many private lessons I had I remained tone deaf, turned into a plank of wood on stage, and I'm still incapable of drawing better than a five-year-old. Antonio tells me not to worry, that handling spreadsheets is a talent in itself, but I'd much rather be a dancer than an accountant.'

'You're an accountant?' Sophie always thought of accountants as faded and grey—not vibrant and full of life like the woman in front of her.

'Head of Finance at Antonio's company. It's how we met. He says marrying me will stop me being head-hunted—I let him think that. I don't want to shatter his illusions! But I'd like to work for an international company if I get the opportunity. All those complicated tax laws would be really interesting.'

'Quite.' Sophie had no idea what to say, all her preconceptions tumbling down. It had been too easy to look at Bianca and see nothing but the beautifully dressed daughter of an obviously wealthy family—but there was clearly a lot more to her than that. 'As someone who can dance and sew but gets a cold sweat at the thought of a budget I have to say I think you got the better end of the deal.'

'Maybe. So where did you and Marco meet?'

Here it was. The interrogation. Sophie had already been through something similar from Marco's mother, an aunt and his godmother. 'At a party. Actually after the party, it was snowing and we sort of…collided.'

'How romantic.' The dark eyes were keen and focussed very intently on Sophie. 'Snow and an unexpected encounter. And you've seen much of each other since?'

'I wouldn't say much.' She forced a laugh. 'How friendly everyone is and they all want to know about me.'

'You must think we're all very nosy. But this is the first time in a long time that Marco has ever willingly brought a date to any occasion—and definitely the first time he brought someone Mamma hasn't set him up with. So you see, we are all consumed with curiosity to find out more about the mysterious English girl who has captured my brother's heart.'

Who had *what*? What exactly had Marco intimated? 'I wouldn't go that far. We are still getting to know each other. It's very early days…'

The two women had drifted over to one of the uncomfortable formal-looking sofas and Bianca sat down with a relieved 'Oomph, my feet are so swollen. How I am going to manage a whole wedding in heels, I don't know. I usually wear flats, I'm so tall. But Mamma insisted I wear heels on my wedding day. Luckily Antonio is tall too, so I won't tower over him!'

'You're getting married soon?' Really, it was absurd how ill prepared she was to meet this family. Next time a gorgeous stranger suggested a spontaneous trip to a family party she would insist on crib sheets and a written exam first.

'Next week.' Bianca sighed. 'Only, I think I ate too much over Christmas and I'm really scared my dress won't do up. The shame! But look at the size of my breasts! I'm going to be falling out of it, I know it.'

'But you must have a final fitting booked, surely? There will be something they can do. Let out a seam or fit a false back. I wouldn't worry, a good designer is always prepared for some fluctuation in weight.'

'But she's not here. She's gone to New Zealand for the whole month and won't be back until after the wedding. I didn't think it would be a problem. My weight doesn't usually change…' Bianca's voice trailed off and she looked so woebegone Sophie couldn't help sympathising.

'I could take a look,' she suggested. 'Make a few suggestions. Obviously it depends on the fabric and cut, but I might be able to help.' As soon as she said the words she wanted to snatch them back. What was she thinking? A wedding dress? A designer wedding dress no doubt, costing thousands and made of the best silks and laces. As if she were qualified to do as much as tack a hem on that kind of gown, let alone attempt some kind of alteration, but, Sophie realised with a sinking heart, it was too late to backtrack. Bianca was clutching at her arm, gratitude beaming out of her eyes.

'Really? You'd do that?'

'Well… I…'

'Oh, Sophie, that's so wonderful. *Grazie*. It's such a relief to know that you're right here. Wait, when are you going back to London?'

'The day after tomorrow, but I'm sure I can find time to look at it before I go, make some suggestions.'

'The day after tomorrow? But the wedding isn't for another week! What if something else changes?'

Sophie's smile froze. She'd heard tales of bridezillas but had never had to deal with one before, not even at work. In fact Emma's vow renewal was the first time she'd been directly involved with the bridal party, not a duty invite or a plus-one on the guest list—somehow she'd let her few school friends slip away through the Harry years and had never really connected with his friends' ever-changing parade of girlfriends.

'I'm sure it will be fine...'

But Bianca was shaking her head. 'So much could go wrong—a button could loosen or a hem fray or my veil need adjusting. What was I thinking to choose a designer who isn't here for the wedding? It has to be perfect. But if you were here, I wouldn't have to worry.'

'Bianca, no one would notice if a button was loose, I promise.'

'And what if I get bigger? Or smaller? With all the stress, I don't know if I'll lose my appetite or eat chocolate for the next seven days. Everything is very unpredictable at the moment.' To Sophie's horror Bianca's voice began to waver. She wasn't going to cry on her, was she?

'It's only a week. I'm sure it won't make any difference if you eat nothing but chocolate, not at this stage.'

'And this is your first time in Venice, no? You can't possibly see the city in just one day. Marco should have known better. You must stay, see the city properly and then come to the wedding. I would love to have you.' She turned to Sophie, her smile wide again, all traces of tears miraculously disappeared. 'There, now we are all happy, me, you and Marco. Perfect.'

'What will make me happy?'

Sophie's stomach turned as Marco strode up beside them. He'd think she'd been plotting with his sister, think the *palazzo* had turned her head and she wanted to stay, to inveigle her way into his family.

'Nothing. Bianca is panicking a little about her wedding, but I'm telling her not to worry,' she said quickly.

He raised an eyebrow. 'Don't tell me, the flowers are out of season and so you need to call the whole wedding off? She used to be quite sensible,' he added to Sophie, 'until this wedding nonsense.'

'It's not nonsense. Wait until it's your turn,' Bianca said indignantly. 'But, Marco, wait. I have a wonderful idea. Sophie should stay here with us until the wedding and come as your date. What do you think?'

Sophie should *what*? Marco froze to the spot, eyes narrowed at his beaming sister. Had she been consulting with their mother? Was this some elaborate plot? Was Sophie in on it? He cast her a quick glance. No, her cheeks were red and eyes lowered in mortification.

'What do I think?' he repeated.

'He thinks it's impossible.' Sophie reached up and took his hand, giving it a reassuring squeeze. 'I have to get back and he doesn't need a date anyway. I don't want to cramp his style.'

'Nonsense,' Bianca said. 'He would love to have you there.'

Amusing as it was to hear the two women politely disagree about what he did or didn't want, it was time to take control. 'Of course I would love to have you attend the wedding with me, Sophie, but if you have to get back, then there is no more to say. Besides, I have a lot to do over the next few days and I would hate you to be bored here alone.'

Bianca shot to her feet and glared at him. 'It's my wedding and I want her there. I need her, Marco.'

'But…' He wasn't often at a loss for words, but seeing his usually sensible, logical sister so het up robbed him of all coherent speech. 'Bianca, Sophie's said she needs to get back. You can't force her to stay.'

But as he said the words he began to consider just what would happen if Sophie *did* stay. He'd warned her he had to work so there would be no expectation for him to be responsible for her—and then when they returned to England he'd give it a few weeks before casually telling his mother they had parted company. In the meantime… He laced his fingers through hers, enjoying the smoothness of her skin against his. In the meantime it had been too long since he had enjoyed one of his discreet affairs. Two nights and a day wasn't long enough, not when every time she moved the beads on her dress shimmered, showcasing the outline of her breasts, the shapeliness of her calves.

And she'd made it very clear to him she wasn't interested in anything long-term…

'Of course, if there was some way you could arrange things so that you could spend a few more days with us, then you would be very welcome, Sophie.' He smiled at her. 'Besides, bitter experience has taught me that Bianca usually gets her way, so it saves time if you just agree with her at the start.'

'But…you don't want, I mean, this is a family occasion.'

'Three hundred guests, at least a hundred of whom are my parents' business associates and another hundred Bianca and Antonio's clients. I wouldn't worry about gatecrashing.'

Her mouth opened and she stared at Bianca incredulously. 'Three hundred guests?'

'You see why it has to be perfect? Please, Sophie, say yes. I'll be in your debt for ever.'

Marco knew not many people were able to resist

Bianca when she turned the full force of her charm on them and Sophie was no different. 'I suppose I could take a few more days off work. I have a lot of holidays saved up. I'm not a miracle worker,' she warned his sister, 'but I'll do my best. Okay, if you really want me to, I'll stay, but, honestly, you might be better off consulting a professional.'

'I am so happy.' Bianca clapped her hands. 'When can you take a look? Tomorrow?'

It was time to intervene. 'Tomorrow, Bianca, Sophie belongs to me. You can have her the rest of the week. No…' as she tried to interrupt '…you need to practice patience, my child. Sophie, there's someone over here I would like to introduce you to. Bianca has been monopolising you long enough.' He pulled Sophie to her feet, giving his pouting sister a mock bow. '*Arrivederci*, Bianca.'

'Who are you introducing me to?' Sophie asked as he walked her away from the party, opening a door hidden in the ballroom panelling and ushering her into the small adjoining salon, lit only by a few low lamps. 'I hate to break it to you, but the party is that way and there's no one here. Unless it's some ancestor of yours,' she added, looking up at the huge portraits hanging over the mantelpiece. 'He doesn't look overly impressed with your choice of date.'

'That's my great, great, many more greats grandfather Lorenzo Santoro. He didn't approve of anyone or anything by all accounts, a problem in pleasure-loving Venice.'

'I won't take it personally, then.' She turned and faced him, her hair gleaming gold in the low lights, the dress swaying seductively around her thighs. 'So if you don't want to introduce me to Lorenzo, then who am I here to meet?'

'Me. I haven't seen you since New Year's Eve, almost a week ago, and I've neglected you shamefully since you got here. I think it's time I made amends.' He noted with some satisfaction how her colour rose at his words, tinging her cheeks, throat and décolletage a delicate rose pink.

'Oh...' She looked up at him then, the blue eyes earnest. 'Marco, it was really nice of you to ask me here in the first place. I'd really hate for you to think I was trying to force you into extending my invitation. Your sister seems so worried about her dress, I offered to help and the next thing I knew...'

'Sophie, I know exactly what my sister is like, please don't worry. If you wish to stay for the wedding, then I would love for you to do so, but if she railroaded you...'

'She did, but it's not exactly a hardship to stay here and explore Venice a bit more.'

'Then it's settled, you stay. And, Sophie?'

'Yes?'

He took a step closer. 'Let's get one thing straight. I wasn't being nice when I asked you here.'

'You weren't?'

'Not at all. I wanted to see you again.' His gaze dropped to her full mouth. 'I wanted to renew our acquaintance.'

'To renew our acquaintance?' she echoed. 'So that's what they call it nowadays.'

Another step. 'Do you know what this room is?'

That elusive, kissable dimple peeked out at the corner of her mouth. 'Another room for unsuspecting guests to get lost in?'

'Did you see how the door was almost hidden in the panelling? It's an assignation room. Ancestors would slip away in the middle of a ball to meet their lovers here discreetly.'

'Not Grandfather Lorenzo surely?'

'Probably not him. But the rest of the Santoros. We're a degenerate lot.'

'Consider me warned. So, Signor Santoro, did you bring me here for nefarious purposes?'

His voice was soft but full of intent and satisfaction ran through him as he saw her shiver, her eyes dilating at his words. 'I wanted to say hello to you properly.'

'And how were you planning to do that?'

She was teasing him, leading him exactly where she wanted him to go, exactly where he wanted to be. Here, now, no need to plan or think ahead. Just two people enjoying all the benefits of mutual attraction. He took another step and then another, backing her up until she hit the wall, her breath coming in short pants. Slowly but with absolute intent Marco put one arm on the wall and leaned in so she had to look up at him, her body guarded by his, surrounded by his. It took all his strength not to pull her in close, crush her against him, not to lose himself in that mouth, that small perfect body, her sweet-smelling hair. 'Hello.'

'Hi yourself.'

Her mouth curved, the dimple provoking him, daring him, tempting him and, with a groan, he succumbed, dipping his tongue into the small hollow, her answering shiver pushing the last restraints away. With a smothered growl he swung her up in his arms, capturing her mouth with his, inhaling, demanding, needing, taking as he carried her over to the chaise, discreet in the corner of the room. Her kiss was equally fierce, her hands twisted in his hair as he lowered her onto the green brocade. Sophie lay, hair fanned out around her, eyes half closed, chest heaving. Marco stared down at her, trying to regain some vestiges of control. She extended a hand, her eyes wicked in the lamplight. 'Come on, then, *signor*, show me just how a Santoro conducts an illicit liaison.'

CHAPTER SIX

'GOOD MORNING, SLEEPYHEAD.' Marco looked up as Sophie entered the ridiculously huge breakfast room. He looked completely at home—not surprising, she reminded herself. This *was* his home. He sat back in a comfortable-looking chair, newspaper spread open before him on the polished table, coffee in one hand. It was all quite normal—or at least it would be if the table weren't large enough to seat thirty, every chair an antique and the view out of the line of shuttered windows not one she had seen in a hundred iconic photos.

'It's only eight a.m.—and considering I'm still on London time and got lost three times finding the breakfast room…' Was this whole room seriously just to eat breakfast in? It was plausible. The *palazzo* was big enough to have a brunch room, afternoon-tea room, supper room and midnight-snack room if the owners wished. 'I think I'm pretty bright and early.'

Especially as the man lounging opposite with a wicked grin in his eyes had kept her up half the night, leaving her room sometime in the early hours. It was better to be discreet, he'd said; his mother would be calling the banns if she found him in there—but Sophie hadn't minded. Sex was one thing, it was just intense chemistry, but sleeping together? That was real intimacy.

Marco smiled, the slow, sexy grin that made the breath leave her lungs and her knees weaken. 'I thought we'd get breakfast out, the Venetian way. Are you ready to go or do you need more time?'

'Ready? I've been ready since you mentioned this trip, ready since I got a passport, since I first saw Indiana Jones. I mean, we have canals in Manchester, but it's not quite the same. And the sun's shining. In January! What else could I possibly need?' Sophie had dressed with care for a day's sightseeing in a grey wool dress she had bought from a Chelsea charity shop and then redesigned, taking it in, shortening it and adding pink and purple flower buttons in two vertical rows to the flared skirt. A pair of black-and-grey-striped tights, her comfiest black patent brogues, her thick black jacket and a bright pink hat and gloves completed her outfit. She bounced on her toes. 'Let's go.'

Marco took a last, deliberate swig of his coffee before pushing his chair back and languidly getting to his feet. 'In that case, *signorina*, I'm at your service. I thought we'd start the day on foot and head onto the water later. Does that sound agreeable?'

'On foot. By boat, or even on a donkey. I'm happy any way you choose.'

Sophie had been too anxious the day before to really take Venice in. She had clear flashes of the city like snapshots of memory: the first glimpse of the Grand Canal, the flaking pastel paint on the canal-side *palazzos*, a gondola, boats crammed with people pulling in at a stop as nonchalantly as a red London bus stopping outside her flat. The greengrocer boat bartering and trading just like a market stall at the Portobello Market and yet strange and exotic. But the whole had escaped her and she was at fever pitch as Marco guided her along the gallery and down the stately staircase back into the vast hallway. It was almost an anticlimax when Marco ushered her out of the *palazzo's* grand double doors, at the other end of the hallway from the water door she had entered by, to find herself on a street, no water to be seen.

Okay, it was as far from her busy, traffic-filled, bustling London home as a street could be. Narrow and flagstoned, almost an alley, with aged buildings rising on either side. Doors lined up on both sides, some preceded by a step, others opening directly onto the street, and shuttered windows punctuated the plaster and stone of the graceful buildings. Voices floated from open windows, the Italian fast and incomprehensible. The air throbbed with vibrancy and life.

She hadn't expected this somehow. Venice was a fairy-tale setting, a film backdrop, a picture; she had forgotten it was a home too. How could Marco bear to live away from this unique beauty?

'This way,' he said, slipping on a pair of sunglasses against the sun's glare. He was more casually dressed than she had seen him so far in a pair of faded jeans, which clung perfectly in all the right places, a thin grey woollen jumper and a double-breasted black jacket. Somehow he managed to look both relaxed and elegant, a combination few British men could pull off. 'Hungry?'

'A little,' she admitted. 'Actually a lot. I could barely eat anything last night.' Nor had she managed much in the day, her stomach twisting with nerves.

'We don't usually have much for breakfast in Venice,' he said to her dismay. 'A coffee, maybe a brioche or small pastry standing up at the bar. But on a special occasion we visit a *pasticceria* for something a little more substantial. You do have a sweet tooth, don't you?'

Obviously it was far more sophisticated to say no, actually she only liked to nibble on raw cacao and a few olives were more than enough to satisfy her snack cravings, but honesty won out. 'Like a child in a sweet shop.'

'*Bene*, then I think you'll be more than happy.'

The next few hours slipped by like a dream. First Marco took her to a little neighbourhood *pasticceria*, which showcased a breathtaking array of little pastries and cakes in the display cabinets under the glass and wood counters. People dressed for work queued at the long polished wooden bar, where they quickly tossed back a small, bitter-looking coffee and maybe ate a pastry before ducking back out into the street, another caffeine seeker seamlessly moving into their place. Breakfast almost on the go. Marco and Sophie elected to take a little more time and sat at one of the elegant round tables, where Marco introduced Sophie to *frittelle*, round, doughnut-style pastries stuffed with pine nuts and raisins. 'They are usually eaten during *carnivale*,' he explained as Sophie uttered a moan of sheer delight at the taste. 'But some places make them all year round.'

'I'd love to see *carnivale*,' she said, licking her fingers, not wanting to waste even the tiniest crumb. 'It sounds so exotic.'

'It's crowded, noisy—and utterly magical. I have missed the last few, thanks to work, and every year I wish I'd been able to make the time to be here. There's nothing like it.'

Her curiosity was piqued by the longing in his voice. 'But you could live here if you wanted, couldn't you? You were working yesterday. Couldn't your business be based here?'

'Like I said in London, Venice is a village on an

island. There's no escape. Besides, it's good to try somewhere new, you know that. Where are you from? Manchester, didn't you say? You moved cities too.'

He was eyeing her keenly and Sophie shifted, not comfortable with the conversation turning to her and her decision to move to London. 'I think every home town can feel like a village at times. So, what else are we going to do today and will it involve more cake?'

After their brief but sugar-filled breakfast Marco led her along some more twisty streets. At the end of every junction she could see water, her throat swelling with excitement every time she heard the swish of waves lapping against stone, until finally she was walking along a pavement bordering not a road, but a broad canal complete with boats; private boats, taxis, even a police boat serenely cruising along. Sophie had to stop and photograph everything, much to Marco's amusement—especially the fat ginger cat sunning himself on one of the wooden jetties.

She was especially charmed when their route brought them out at a *traghetto* pier and Marco, after a quick conversation and handshake, gestured for her to get in and stand in the long, narrow boat. Two more passengers joined them before the two oarsmen—one at the front and one at the rear—pushed off and began to steer the boat across the Grand Canal.

'These are the traditional way to cross the Grand Canal.' Marco was standing just behind her, one hand on her shoulder, steadying her as the boat rocked in the slight swell of the water. 'There are seven crossings, although there were many more when my parents were small. The businesses have often been in families for generations, passed on from father to son.'

'Why are there two prices? Is one a return?'

'One for tourists and one for residents, but Angelo here considered you a resident this time.'

'Because I'm with you?'

'And because he said you have beautiful eyes.'

Sophie could feel her cheeks heat up and she was glad Angelo was too busy rowing to notice her reaction—and that Marco couldn't see her face at all.

After disembarking from the *traghetto* they headed to the tourist mecca of St Mark's square. It was still too early for many visitors to be out and about—and now that the Christmas holidays were finished Venice was entering its quiet season—but they were far from alone in the vast space. People were taking photos of the ubiquitous pigeons and the imposing tower or were sitting outside one of the many cafés that lined the famous *piazza*. Sophie's camera was in her hand instantly, every view, every angle needing capturing whether it was the blue of the canal and the lagoon beyond or the old palace, dominating the other end of the square.

Three hours later Sophie was light-headed and slightly nauseous. They had toured the Doge's Palace, crossed the infamous Bridge of Sighs and, thanks to an old school friend of Marco's, got a chance to see some of the hidden parts of the palace including the *pozzi*, tiny, dank, dark cells where Casanova had once been imprisoned. When Marco suggested a walk down to the Rialto Bridge she gave him a pleading smile. 'Can I have some lunch first? I know it's early, but I'm hungry and my legs don't seem to want to walk anywhere without sustenance and a sit down.'

'*Sì*, of course.' He didn't seem at all put out that she hadn't fallen in with his suggestion. It was so refreshing; she'd never been able to make off-the-cuff suggestions to Harry. At the merest hint that his itinerary didn't suit her he would fall into a monumental sulk, which would need all her best cajoling and coaxing to pull him out of. Her heart clenched at the thought. What had she been thinking of? To allow such a spoilt brat to dictate her life for so long? Of all the ways to choose to assert her independence. If she could only go back in time and talk sense into her eighteen-year-old self, then…eighteen-year-old Sophie would probably have ignored her as she'd ignored everyone else. Too giddy with lust, with independence, too convinced it was love. Too foolish.

But no, she wasn't going to sully one moment of this perfect day thinking about her past, indulging in regrets. She was in Venice with a gorgeous, attentive man and he was about to provide lunch. Life really didn't get much better than that.

Marco knew the perfect place for lunch. Close enough to St Mark's for his hungry companion, far enough away to avoid tourist prices and menus. A locals' café, with fresh food, a menu that changed daily depending on what was in at the markets and a bustling, friendly atmosphere. He used to eat there with his father, but when long, conversational lunches had turned into lectures with food he had stopped coming. He couldn't wipe out the last ten years of cold civility, couldn't repair his father's heart—but maybe he could reclaim some of the spaces they used to inhabit.

They had barely set foot over the threshold when he saw her, straight-backed, elegant and as lethal as a tiger eyeing her prey. His chest tightened. She hadn't come in here to wait for them, had she? Surely even his mother wasn't that conniving. But it was barely noon and she usually ate a little later than this. And that was an unusually triumphant look in her eyes.

'Marco, *vita mia*, how lovely to see you and your *bella* friend.' She leant in and embraced Sophie, who returned the traditional two kisses with a dumbstruck look Marco was sure must be mirrored on his own face.

'Mamma,' he said drily. 'What a coincidence.'

'*Sì,*' she agreed, but even though her eyes were wide and candid, Marco knew better. 'But a lovely one, no? I barely got to talk to Sophie yesterday. I hear you are staying for Bianca's wedding? We are delighted to have you with us for longer and, Sophie, *cara*, please consider the *palazzo* your home the whole time you are in Venice.'

There was no way out. Half amused, half annoyed, Marco accepted his mother's invitation to join her and they were soon seated at an intimate table for three so his mother could begin her interrogation. At least the food would be good, he thought as he ordered a *vermicelli al nero di seppia* for himself, a dish he refused to eat anywhere other than Venice, and advised Sophie, who still looked a little pale, to try the risotto. He then poured them all a glass of the local Soave and sat back to watch the show.

'So, Sophie, what is it you do in London?' And she was off... If Sophie had any secrets, they would be expertly extracted before the bread and oil reached the table.

Or not. By the end of the meal Marco knew very little more than he had at the start. Maybe she was secret-service trained because Sophie Bradshaw had avoided every one of his mother's expertly laid traps like a professional—and what was more, she had done it in such a way Marco doubted his mother had noticed. She had mentioned two brothers and nieces and nephews—and then, while his mother had gone misty-eyed at the very thought of babies and grandchildren, had turned the tables and asked his mother so many questions about Bianca's forthcoming wedding his mother had been quite disarmed. Very clever.

Marco leaned back in his chair and eyed Sophie thoughtfully. It hadn't mattered that he knew little more than her name when she had been due to spend less than forty-eight hours with him, but now she was staying with his dangerously excitable family for over a week he found himself a little more curious. Who was Sophie Bradshaw and what did she really want? Was she really as happy with a casual relationship as she'd made out? She liked fashion and designing—although she had told his mother that she took other jobs while she worked to get her business off the ground. What other jobs? She came from Manchester but at some unspecified point had moved to London. She had two brothers and five nieces and nephews. That was it. All he knew.

He didn't need to know more. Why would he? After next week he would probably never see her again. But he'd never met a woman less willing to share—and there was a shadow behind those blue eyes that made him suspect there was a reason she was so reticent.

Whatever the reason, it was her business; he didn't need to get involved. Once you got involved, then expectations got raised, then things got messy. He knew that all too well.

It was with some amusement that Marco watched his mother kiss Sophie on both cheeks and embrace her warmly as they left the restaurant—and even more amusement that he heard Sophie suck in a huge sigh of relief. 'Well done, you held her off beautifully.'

'I thought I was going to crack any minute.'

'It was a good move to bring up Bianca's wedding. That's been her sole focus for the last year and the only thing guaranteed to distract her.'

'It nearly backfired though.' Sophie pulled on her gloves as they emerged into the bright, sunny but cold street. 'She managed to bring every question back to me. Would I prefer an A-line or a fitted dress, didn't I agree that an heirloom tiara was classier than a newly bought one, what colour scheme did I like, would I prefer a princess cut or a pear shape or maybe I wanted sapphires to match my eyes? I got the impression if I gave a straight answer to any question I'd have a ring on my finger and find myself frogmarched down an aisle whether I wanted to be or not.'

Her tone was light, but her words still struck him. He'd expected his mother to take an overactive interest in Sophie, but it was frustrating to have it confirmed that nothing had really changed, that ten years of exile, all the drama and anger had been for nothing. His mother had no intention of respecting his decisions. He tried to keep his own voice equally light, not to let his anger show. 'You can see why I asked you here. Mamma is obsessed with weddings. While she thinks there's a chance we might end up together she won't be busy matchmaking. It's perfect. I owe you, Sophie. Thank you.'

There was just the most infinitesimal pause before Sophie echoed, 'Yes, perfect. As long as I don't crack. Don't leave me alone with her, that's all I'm saying. I'm not sure I'd win in a straight duel. Has she always been this way?'

Marco began to stroll down towards the Rialto Bridge. He planned for them to cross over the famous bridge and then head back to the *palazzo* to collect his boat for the afternoon. 'As long as I can remember.'

'But why? It's usually the other way round, isn't it? Pressure on the daughter to marry? I'm sure you're a catch and all...' The dimple was out again and he couldn't stop smiling back in response even though his mother's obsession with his future was his least favourite topic. And it wasn't easy to put into words.

'It's not about me, not really. She's obsessed with the past, the future, the *palazzo*. Venice is changing, has been for the last fifty years. More and more real estate is owned by foreigners, many of whom don't live here, which means more and more families moving onto the mainland. Both my parents came from ancient Venetian families, together they owned a lot of real estate, a lot of businesses around the city.' He allowed himself a brief smile. 'We're a city of traders, of merchants. Even I, though I wanted to set out on my own, trade goods back and forth. It's in my blood, like the sea.'

'What does that have to do with marriage?'

'It's about not letting the old bloodlines die out, with keeping a Santoro in the *palazzo*, running the family business, sons at his knees, just like the old days. Now Bianca is getting married—and to another scion of an ancient family—her attentions can be fully focussed on me. London might not be far enough. I may try Mars.'

'Would it be so bad? Marriage?' She held her hands up, laughing as he turned to look at her. 'That's not a proposal, by the way, not even a leading question. Just plain curiosity.'

'I'm the Santoro heir,' he said. 'It's a position that comes with privilege, sure, but also with expectations.

I'm the only son. And from the moment I was born I was reminded that I had a duty to the family, to the name, to Venice. That what I want doesn't matter, that to pursue my dreams is a selfishness unbefitting a Santoro.' He could hear his father shouting the words as he spoke them. 'Marriage is part of that responsibility. So to me it isn't something natural, something healthy, something good. It's a heavy expectation I'm expected to bear. And now my father is gone…' He swallowed as he said the words. It still didn't seem possible. Venice seemed emptier without him, the *palazzo* hollower. 'Now I'm not just the only son, I'm the only remaining male, it's become even more imperative to my mother that I marry and soon. But the more she pushes, the less ready I feel. And I love my city, my family, of course I do. But I won't sacrifice myself, my integrity to tradition.'

'Have you told her?' Sophie asked softly. 'Told her how you feel. That you're not ready.'

His mouth quirked into a smile; if only it were that easy. 'Many times. But she only listens when she wants to. Hears what she wants to hear.'

'It's not good to let misunderstandings grow, let resentments fester.' There was a quiet certainty in Sophie's voice.

'I think we understand Mamma too well, Bianca and I. She was orphaned young, raised alone by her grandparents in an old *palazzo*. They had a title, an illustrious ancestry but no wealth. When she married my father she wanted security and a large family. Together they built up an empire to rival that of the early Santoros, but they had to settle for a small family. After Bianca she just couldn't conceive again. So she turned her attentions to grandchildren, to building the dynasty she always dreamed of. She thinks she knows best what will make us happy. I don't hurt her on purpose, but we have such different ideas on the way I should live.'

Hurt was inevitable. Every time he said 'no'. Every time he chose his own path. But if he didn't, then what had it all been for? The hard-fought-for independence, the ten years of estrangement, the knowledge he would never make it up with his father.

The knowledge that his father might even yet have been here, still alive, if Marco had been a different kind of man. More pliable, obedient.

'So you live in a different country and seldom come home?' Sophie was shaking her head. 'I don't know, Marco, it's a solution, but it doesn't sound like a good one. Not at all.'

And the worst thing was, Marco knew she was right. But what other choice did he have?

CHAPTER SEVEN

'DID YOU AND Marco have a good day yesterday?' Bianca's eyes were sly as she looked at Sophie in the mirror. 'Mamma was disappointed you didn't come back for supper. She was so looking forward to getting to know you better.'

Sophie circled Bianca, checking every seam and every hem. The dress was gorgeous, far bigger and more ornate than she would have chosen personally but perfect for a wedding as imposing as Bianca's promised to be. But Bianca's new curves spilled out of the silk ballgown's sweetheart neckline, turning it from daring to borderline indecent, and it was a struggle to get the zip up at the low back—in fact Sophie had decided against forcing it, not wanting to snag the delicate fabric.

'Lovely, thanks. We spent the morning at the palace, and then we had lunch with your mother, so I hope she wasn't too disappointed we missed supper, and then Marco took me out onto the lagoon for the afternoon.' He'd pointed out some of the more notable islands, promising to bring her back to visit one or two before the end of their trip, and then he had taken her to dine at an island hotel. Sailing in through the private water gate to be escorted up to the glassed-in terrace with views across to Venice itself had been the most romantic thing

Sophie had ever experienced. If only she hadn't felt so tired and her appetite hadn't been so capricious. And if only she hadn't replayed Marco's words over and over in her mind. *You can see why I asked you here.*

She wasn't sure why those words had pricked her. She had been under no illusions about his sudden invitation; Marco hadn't brought her here because he'd been struck down with instalove—and she'd accepted for that very reason. But to have him spell out so baldly that she was a mere ploy to keep his mother happy was a little bruising to her pride.

But then again, after one lunch with his mother she fully accepted his reasons, sympathised with them even. Only, it would be nice to be more than convenient, to really matter to someone… She stopped still, staring down at Bianca's elaborate train. Where had that thought come from? She was happy on her own, remember? Not at all interested in a relationship.

But maybe one day. If she chose better, found someone who valued and cherished her the way her friends were loved and cherished, then maybe she could take that risk. Because if she did spend her life hiding from the possibility of love, did spend her life thinking she wasn't good enough, then Harry won after all, didn't he?

'Right.' Sophie blinked back unexpected, hot tears. What on earth was wrong with her? It was time to remember why she was here and not on a plane back to London. 'There's no way this dress is going to fit the way it is. Luckily your hips and waist have only increased by the smallest amount, so it's a reasonably easy fix, no major restructuring needed, but we do need to do something about the neckline.' She hesitated, searching for the right words. 'I could re-bone the bodice, but I still think you'll look more top-heavy than you intended. So what I'm proposing is that in addition to letting out the seams and adjusting the zip I make you a lace overdress. It's up to you if you just want it for your top or to cover the skirt as well. Look, I'll show you.' She picked up a gossamer-thin scarf and deftly twisted it around Bianca, pinning it in place.

'You need to imagine this is lace,' she warned Bianca. 'This is just to give us an idea.'

Sophie stepped back and pursed her lips as she fixed her design in her head. 'The beading on your skirt is lovely. It would be a real shame to cover it up with lace,' she decided. 'Let's go with a lace bodice. I'll find buttons to match your beads, tiny ones, and it can button up your back.' She shot Bianca a reassuring smile. 'I'll sew those on at the very last minute to make absolutely sure it fits.'

Bianca stared at herself in the mirror, hope flaring in her expressive dark eyes. 'Will it really work?'

'Absolutely.' In fact the more Sophie thought about it, the surer she was. 'I think it will be stunning. I can give you capped sleeves, little straps just off the shoulder—or we could go really regal with full-length sleeves, so decide what you'd prefer. The most important thing is making sure the lace matches the exact colour of the dress. Not all ivories are created equal. Do you have a swatch I can use?'

Bianca nodded, her eyes bright with tears. 'Thank you, Sophie. I can't begin to tell you how much I appreciate this, how much it means that you haven't just fixed my problem but made my dress even better.' She caught a tear with her finger, wiping it away, pulling a watery smile as she did so. 'If there is anything I can do to repay you...'

'No repayment necessary, I promise. I'm happy to

do it. Let's get you out of the dress before you spoil the silk with your tears and I'll take a look at the zip. It only needs a few millimetres, I think, to be comfortable. I might not even need to add an insert. Unpicking the stitches and redoing it might be enough.'

It took a few minutes to manoeuvre Bianca out of the many folds of the dress, but eventually Sophie hung the layers of net and tulle and silk back up, smoothing the silk out with careful hands as she figured out the best way to deal with it. 'I wonder if I could get my hands on a tailor's dummy,' she pondered. 'If I put a dummy on a dais, I would find it easier. There must be somewhere I could source that from. I'll draw up a list of all we need: lace, silk, thread, buttons.'

'*Sì*, none of that should be a problem. The best place for lace is Burano, one of the islands. I'll ask Marco to take you. It's very pretty. I think you'll like it.'

'Sounds perfect.' Sophie turned to look at Bianca. The Italian girl sat on her unmade bed, a robe loosely drawn around her, the magnificent mane of hair spilling around her shoulders, tears still shimmering in her eyes.

'I'm sorry, Sophie, I'm not usually such a mess. The thing is…' she took a deep breath '…I didn't eat too much over Christmas, nor am I that stressed about the wedding, not really. It's just that…I'm having a baby and I haven't told anyone yet.'

'You're what? But that's wonderful. No wonder you've gone up over two cup sizes and barely gained a centimetre around your waist! How far along are you?'

'The doctor says ten weeks. I only realised at the end of last week. I've always been irregular, so I didn't notice any changes there, but I was always crying, or suddenly really hungry and then really nauseous. I've been so tired, light-headed. And I can't even cope with the smell of coffee, let alone the taste. Honestly, for someone with so many qualifications I can be very stupid, but I just didn't realise what was wrong. It wasn't like we were trying.'

Sophie perched onto the bed next to Bianca and patted her arm a little awkwardly. 'But this is good news, surely? After all, you're about to get married.'

'*Sì*, it is, at least, it will be, when I get used to it. I just thought we'd have time to *be* married before starting a family.'

'So,' Sophie asked gently, 'why the secrecy?'

'Antonio is stressed about the wedding, it's so big, I just don't want to give him anything else to worry about. I will tell him,' she said defensively as Sophie raised her eyebrows. 'I was planning to tonight—telling you was the first time I've said it out loud. It wasn't as hard as I expected.'

'And your mother will be over the moon.'

Bianca's mouth twisted. 'Oh, *sì*, Mamma will be delighted. But I won't be telling her until after the honeymoon. She can be a little overpowering.' She giggled. 'Okay, a lot overpowering. She already tried to take over the planning of the wedding, make it into her dream wedding, not mine. I'm not ready for her to take over the baby as well, not until I know how I feel about it all.'

'That makes sense.' But Sophie's mind had wandered back to something Bianca had said earlier. Something about not noticing that she was pregnant because she was irregular. Sophie was the complete opposite. In fact she was like clockwork, every twenty-eight days. Usually…

Frantically she counted back. Almost five weeks had passed since she had spent the night with Marco.

Over five weeks without her period. Her regular-as-clockwork period...

'That's all great, Bianca, I mean congratulations again and I can't wait to get started. I just remembered, I didn't pack for a week-long stay and there's a few things I need, so I'm just going to go out and grab them...' She collected her bag and backed out of the door still babbling inanely. 'When I get back we'll talk lace, okay? I won't be long.' The last thing she saw as the door swung shut behind her was Bianca, upright and staring at her in complete surprise.

Smoothly done, Sophie.

But she couldn't wait, not another second, not while this big *what if* was thundering through her body, beating its question with every thud of her heart.

Although she found her way out of the *palazzo* easily enough, having earmarked enough landmarks to find her way to the main hallway and back up to her room, as soon as she set foot outside it was a different matter. Sophie plunged into the alleyways and back streets searching for the green cross that meant pharmacy in a dozen different languages. But each road seemed to lead her nowhere, a dead end with water rippling gently at the end, round in a gently curving circle back to the same square over and over.

And what would happen when she reached a pharmacy? She could barely order a pizza in Italian let alone a pregnancy test and she doubted her mime skills were up to scratch.

You're being ridiculous, she told herself. *You used protection, you were careful, he was careful.*

But the rest of Bianca's words came back, almost visible, floating around her in the still, cold air. Emotional? Check, look at the pity party she'd held for herself on

New Year's Eve, the tears just now. Light-headed and tired? For a couple of weeks now. Nauseous? Yes, a low level, almost constant feeling of sickness. All kinds of things set it off. She hadn't been able to stomach even the smell of wine for ages; it had been an oddly teetotal Christmas and New Year's Eve.

Sophie stopped dead in the middle of the street. Of course she was pregnant. How could she not have known—and what on earth was she going to do now?

'Sophie, Bianca mentioned you wanted to visit Burano. Would this afternoon be convenient?'

Sophie skidded to a stop outside the salon and fought an urge to hide her handbag behind her back as if Marco might see through the leather, to the paper bag within. It had been a mortifying experience, but thanks to the Internet, her phone, some overly helpful shoppers and a very patient pharmacist she had finally got what she needed.

Well, two of what she needed. She hadn't paid that much attention in Science, but she was pretty sure all experiments could go wrong.

'Marco! Hi! Yes, Burano, this afternoon, sounds wonderful, great.'

One eyebrow rose. 'Are you okay?' He sauntered over to the salon door and she had to fight the urge to step away.

'Fine, I've been out. I got a little lost, that's all.'

'The best way to learn Venice is to get lost in her,' he said, but there was a quizzical gleam in his dark eyes as he looked at her.

'In that case we'll soon be the best of friends.' Sophie knew she was acting oddly, but she needed to get out of this hallway and up into the safety of her room and find out for once and for all. 'What time do you want to leave?'

'If we leave here just after noon, we could stop for lunch along the way.'

'That sounds wonderful. I just need to talk to Bianca then, take another look at the dress and get a swatch of material. Shall I meet you back here in an hour? Great. See you then.'

She barely registered his response as she walked as fast as she could up the stairs, slowing a little as she tackled the second and then the third staircase until finally she was twisting open the door to her room, throwing her bag onto the bed, grabbing the paper bag and rushing into the bathroom, tearing open the plastic on the box as she did so…

She was pregnant. Two tests' worth of pregnant.

Sophie sank onto the bed with a strangled sob, throwing her hand across her mouth to try to keep the noise in. Idiot. Fool. Stupid, stupid girl. It was different for Bianca. She was engaged to a man she loved, she had a great career, a life ready and waiting for a baby. What did Sophie have? A fling with a commitment-shy man she barely knew, a shoebox of a flat, an un-fulfilled dream and a job scrubbing toilets and serving drinks. How was she going to fit a baby into her flat, let alone her life?

She slumped down on the bed and stared up at the ceiling, every fat cherub leg, every beaming cherub grin on the fresco an unneeded reminder. The thing was she *did* want children. Had planned to have them with Harry—although she had never got him to admit the time was right. Thank goodness. She shuddered; if she had had his baby, would she ever have got out? Ever freed herself or would she still be there now? Holding down a job, taking care of the house, looking after the kids while Harry lied and cheated and manipulated...

But Marco wasn't like Harry. He was, well, he was... 'Face it,' Sophie said aloud. 'You know nothing about him except he doesn't want to get married. He's rich. He's handsome. He's good in bed. He seems kind, when it suits him to be...' Added together it didn't seem an awful lot to know about the father of her baby.

Father. Baby. She swallowed a hysterical sob.

She had to tell him; it was the right, the fair, thing to do.

And then what? He might walk away although, she conceded, he didn't seem the type. Sophie wrapped her arms around herself, trying to hug some warmth into her suddenly chilled body. He might accuse her of entrapment. Think this was done on purpose...

He didn't want to get married, she knew that, and that was okay. After all, they didn't really know each other. But what about when his mother found out? She wanted grandchildren, heirs, and here Sophie was carrying a Santoro heir as a good little wife should.

She shivered again, nausea rolling in her stomach. She'd been free for one year and six months, independent for such a short while. No placating, no begging, no reassuring, no abasing, no making herself less so someone else could be more. No eggshells. She was pretty sure Marco wasn't another Harry, she knew his mother had all the best intentions, but if they knew she was pregnant, she would have every choice stripped away, be suffocated with kindness and concern and responsibility until every bit of that hard-won independence shrivelled away and she belonged to them. Just as she had belonged to Harry. Besides, Bianca was getting married in a week. This was her time. It wouldn't be fair to spoil her wedding with the inevitable drama Sophie's news would cause.

I won't tell him yet, she decided. *I need to know him first, know who the real Marco is. Know if I can trust him. I'll get to know him over this week and then I'll tell him. After the wedding.*

Marco manoeuvred his boat out of the Grand Canal with practised ease. It came more naturally than driving, even after a decade in London. Sometimes he thought he felt truly alive only when he was here on the water, the sun dancing on the waves around him, Venice at his back, the open lagoon his for the taking.

'Warm enough?' He'd elected not to take the traditional, bigger family boat with its polished wood and spacious covered seating area. Instead they were in his own small but speedy white runabout, which didn't have any shelter beyond the splash screen at the front. He'd reminded Sophie to wrap up warmly for the journey over, but she was so pale and silent maybe she'd underestimated the bite of the January wind out in the lagoon.

'Hmm? No, thanks, honestly I'm toasty.' He could see her visibly push away whatever was occupying her thoughts as she turned to him and smiled. 'Bianca says Burano is beautiful. I'm really looking forward to seeing it.'

'It is,' he assured her. 'Very different from Venice, but equally stunning in a quieter way.'

'Did you visit the islands a lot when you were younger? What about the rest of Italy? It's such a beautiful country. It must have been wonderful to have had it all on your doorstep,' she added quickly as he raised an eyebrow at her series of questions.

'It is beautiful and, yes, most of our childhood holidays were spent in Italy. Venice gets so hot and busy in the summer and we have a villa by Lake Como, so every summer we would spend a month there. And I don't remember a time when I didn't explore the islands. Every Venice child grows up able to handle a boat before they learn to ride a bike.'

'And swim?'

'*Sì*, and swim.'

'I still can't imagine what it was like, actually living here, crossing water to get to school. It just seems impossibly exotic.'

'Not when it's your normal. To me, your childhood in Manchester would have seemed equally exotic. What was your route to school? A bus?'

'I doubt it. Suburbia is suburbia, nothing exciting there. But a school boat? Now, that's fun.' And once again she turned his question aside effortlessly. Was there some dark secret there or did she really think her past was of so little interest? 'What else did you do when you were little? Were you a football player or addicted to video games or a bookworm?'

'None of the above. If I wasn't messing around on a boat, I was always trying to find a way to do some kind of deal.' He grinned at her surprised expression. 'I told you, we're an island of merchants, sailors, traders. Oh, it's been several hundred years since we had any influence, since we controlled the waves, but it's still there in any true Venetian's veins.'

'What did your parents say?'

'Oh, they were proud,' he assured her. 'So many families forgot their roots, watched the *palazzos* crumble around them as the money ran out. My mother is a big believer in a good day's work, no matter who you

are.' Proud right until she realised his independent en-
trepreneurial streak wasn't just a phase.

It was as if Sophie had read his mind. 'Was she disappointed when you set up for yourself? Left Venice?' She
leaned against the windscreen, half turned to face him,
eyes intent on him as if the answers really mattered.

'Yes. She's convinced one day I'll get over my little rebellion and come home, settle down and take
over the family affairs.' He paused as he navigated the
boat around a buoy. 'Of course, since my father died
she's been keener than ever and at some point I need
to make a decision about where my future lies. But
right now she's not ready to give up the reins no matter what she says—she'll spend every second of her
retirement second-guessing every decision I make. I
have a while yet. Besides…' Marco had always known
the day would come when he would have to step in, but
he wanted to see how big his own business could grow
first. He already turned over several million euros an-
nually, and there was plenty of room to expand, new
territories to trade in.

'Besides what?'

'Bianca. Maybe she could take over the Santoro hold-
ings. She's an extremely talented businesswoman, she's
got exactly the same heritage as me and I know she
wants a family, so she could hand the business on, just
as my parents wanted.'

'That makes sense. Hasn't your mother ever considered it?'

'Neither of my parents have. In many ways they were
very old-fashioned. Bianca's a woman, so in their eyes
when she marries she'll no longer be a true Santoro.
But it's just a name…' And if Bianca did take over the

business, the *palazzo* and provide the heirs, then he would be free.

Was it the perfect solution—or was he merely fulfilling his father's prophecies and eluding his responsibilities? Marco had no idea. It all seemed so clear, so simple in London, but the second he set foot back in Venice he got tangled up in all the threads of loyalty, duty and family he'd spent most of his life struggling to free himself from.

They had reached the open waters of the lagoon and Marco let out the throttle, allowing the boat to zoom ahead. 'I miss this,' he admitted. 'This freedom.'

'I can imagine. I know there's a harbour in Chelsea, but sailing up and down the Thames must be a little sedate after living here. What do you like to do in London for fun? Apart from attending parties, that is.'

Marco eased off on the throttle and let the boat slow as Burano came into view. 'Is this an interview?' He was teasing but noted the high colour that rose over her cheeks with interest. 'An interrogation? Will you lock me up in the Doge's palace if I answer wrongly?'

'Yes, right next to Casanova. No, no interrogation, I'm just interested. We're spending all this time together and I know nothing about you. I need to be prepared if you want your mother to think we're a real couple. What if she gets me alone? Imagine how suspicious she would be if I don't know your favourite football team, or how you take your coffee.'

'Black, strong, no sugar and of course I support Venezia despite our current ranking. Thank goodness our national team is a little more inspiring.' Sophie was right, he realised. If they were acting the couple, it made sense to know more about each other. Besides, she was fun company, insightful with a dry wit he appreciated. 'How about you? City or United?'

'Me?' She blinked. 'My family is City, so I am by default, but to be honest I'm not really bothered. We were a bit divided on gender lines when I was a child. My father would take my brothers to matches, but I was eight years younger and so I was always left behind with my mother, who was definitely *not* interested. I think she thought sport was invented to ruin her weekends.'

'Did that annoy you? Being left out by your brothers?'

She wrinkled her nose. 'No one likes being the baby of the family, do they? But my mother encouraged it, I think. By the time I was born my brothers' lives revolved around sport. Footie, cricket, rugby—it's all they talked about, watched, did. She always said she was delighted to have a daughter, an ally at last.' She sounded wistful, her eyes fixed on the sea.

'You weren't into sport, then?'

Sophie shrugged. 'I didn't really have the option. Like I said, Dad would take the boys to matches or whatever and Mum and I would be left behind. Besides, she was determined not to lose me to their side. She had me in classes of her choosing as soon as I could walk. Dance,' she confirmed at his enquiring look. 'I wasn't kidding when I told you at the Snowflake Ball that I'd done every kind of dancing.'

'A dancer? Professionally?' It made sense. She had the build, petite as she was, strong and lithe, and he dimly remembered her mentioning it on New Year's Eve.

'Could have been. Mum thought I'd be a ballerina. She wanted me to train properly at sixteen, dance at Covent Garden one day.'

'But you didn't want to?'

She shook her head. 'It's not just about talent, it's luck, build, you know, having the right body, discipline but most of all drive. I was good, but good enough? Probably not. I didn't want it enough. I stopped just before I turned sixteen. It broke her heart.'

She looked down at her hands and he didn't pursue it—he knew all about breaking parental hearts, was a gold medallist in it. 'What did you want to do instead?' It wasn't just about polite conversation; he was actually interested. His hands tightened on the wheel as the realisation dawned.

Sophie smiled, slow and nostalgic. 'The thing I did really like about ballet, about performing, was the costumes. Every show involves a lot of net and tulle and gluing sequins—I loved that part. I was always much happier with a needle than a pointe shoe. So I guess I'm lucky, trying to make a go of the thing I love. If I'd become a ballet dancer, I'd be over halfway through my career by now. Not that I can imagine I'd have had much of one. Like I say, I was never driven enough.' She stopped and stared as they neared the pretty harbour and the brightly coloured fishermen's cottages came into view. 'Oh, my goodness, how beautiful. Where's my camera?' She turned away, grabbing her camera and exclaiming over the colours, the boats, the sea, the sky.

As he guided the boat into the harbour, mooring it at a convenient stop, Marco's thoughts were preoccupied with Sophie, still chattering excitedly and snapping away. Why was he so intrigued by her? Sure, she was fun, they had chemistry and she was proving extremely helpful in calming Bianca's ever more volatile nerves and keeping his mother off his back. But next week she would return to London and their brief relationship would be over. There was no point in prolonging it when they both knew they weren't heading anywhere. Short, sweet and to the point just as all perfect liaisons should be.

But what would it be like not to feel as if every relationship was ticking towards an expiration date, not to worry about getting in too deep, about not raising expectations he had no intention of fulfilling? For every new woman to be an adventure, a world to be explored, not a potential trap? He'd never cared before, happy with the limits he set upon himself, upon his time, upon his heart. But, for the first time in a really long time, as he helped Sophie ashore, felt the warm clasp of her hand, watched her face alight with sheer happiness as she took in every detail on the colourful island, Marco was aware that maybe, just maybe, he was missing some colour in his perfectly organised, privileged, grey life.

CHAPTER EIGHT

IT WAS THE MOST beautiful commute in the world. How many people travelled to their office by boat? Marco took a deep breath, his lungs glad of the fresh salty air, a much-needed contrast to the polluted London air he usually breathed in on his way to work. No, he thought as he steered his boat across the lagoon towards the dock at the mainland Venetian district of Mestre, this was a much better way to spend his early mornings.

Marco hadn't intended to work from the Santoro Azienda offices, but he found it easier to concentrate away from the *palazzo*. Bianca was staying at home until her wedding and every room was full of tulle or confetti or wedding favours—it was like living in a five-year-old girl's dream doll's house. Besides, working at the *palazzo* meant working in close proximity to Sophie and that, he was discovering, was distracting. And if his mother and sister were at home, then they kept interrupting him to ask his opinion on everything from how the napkins should be folded to where Gia Ana should be seated, given that she had fallen out with every other member of the family.

And when they *weren't* at home, then it was almost impossible for him not to seek Sophie out on some barely disguised pretext—or for her to casually wander by him—knowing that within seconds their eyes would meet, hold, and, like teenagers taking advantage of an empty house, they would drag each other into the nearest bedroom… There was something particularly thrilling about the illicitness of it all, the sneaking down corridors, the stolen kisses, the hurried pulling off clothes or pulling them back on again. Not that his mother or Bianca were fooled for a moment, but that wasn't the point. It was all about appearances. His mother would only countenance an engaged couple sleeping together under her roof. Or not sleeping…

Yes, working at the *palazzo* certainly had its benefits, but he had far too much to do to allow himself to be continuously distracted, so, for the last couple of days, knowing his mother was so busy with the final details for the wedding she was unlikely to be at work, he had taken to heading off to the office early, returning home during the long lunch break to meet up with Sophie, who was spending most of her mornings working on Bianca's dress. He didn't have to come home, she'd assured him, she was happy to explore Venice on her own if he was too busy, but he was enjoying rediscovering his city, seeing it through her eyes as she absorbed the sights and smells of the city.

The Santoro Azienda offices were a short walk away from the dock. As his parents' real estate and other business interests had expanded and they had taken on more and more staff it had become increasingly clear they needed professional offices out of the *palazzo*. The decision to base the offices on the mainland hadn't been taken lightly, but for the sake of their staff, many of whom no longer lived on the islands, it had made sense and twenty years ago they had moved into the light, modern, purpose-built building. All glass and chrome, it was as different from the *palazzo* as a building could be.

Until last week Marco hadn't set foot in the offices in ten years. It was one of the many things he'd regretted since he'd shouldered his father's coffin to walk it down the aisle towards the altar—and yet he still couldn't see any other way, how he could have played things differently. It took two to compromise and he hadn't been the only one at fault.

Marco strode through the sliding glass doors and, with a nod at the security guard and the receptionists, headed straight for the lifts and the top floor, exiting into the plush corridors that marked the Santoro Azienda's Executive Floor. Left led to his parents' offices, right to the suite of rooms he was using. He hadn't turned left once since he'd returned to the building.

He stood and hesitated, then, with a muffled curse, turned left.

His parents had had adjoining offices on opposite corners of the building, sharing a PA, a bathroom and a small kitchen and seating area. He'd been in his teens when they'd relocated here, spending many days in one office or the other being put to work, being trained up to manage the huge portfolio of properties and companies they owned. No one had ever asked him if it was what he wanted. If they had noticed that he was happier rolling his sleeves up and engaging on the ground level, they ignored it. He was destined to take over and his interest in art and antiques, in dealing directly with people, was a quirk, a hobby.

'A multimillion-euro hobby, Papà,' he said softly. Not that it would have made any difference.

His father's name was still on his office door and Marco stood there for a long moment staring at the letters before twisting the handle and, with a deep breath, entering the room. It was a shock to see that nothing had changed, as if his father could walk in any moment, espresso in hand. The desk still heaped with papers, the carafe of water filled on the oak sideboard, the comfy chair by the window, where his father had liked to sit after lunch and face the city while he took his siesta. Photographs covered the walls, views of Venice, of buildings they owned, goods they made, food prepared in restaurants they owned. There were no photographs of Marco or Bianca. 'The office is for work,' his father used to say. And work he had, in early, out late, deals and successes and annoyances his favourite topic of conversation over the evening meal.

Marco picked up a piece of paper and stared at it, not taking in the typed words. Was his mother coping, doing the work of two people? She hated delegating as much as his father had, didn't like handing too much power to people not part of their family.

They were as stubborn as each other.

He barely registered her footsteps, but he knew she was there before she spoke.

'Marco.'

He closed his eyes briefly. 'Hello, Mamma.'

He turned, forced a smile. In the bright artificial office light he could see the lines on her forehead, the hollows in her cheeks. She was working too hard, still grieving for his father.

'You've been home for two weeks and yet I barely see you.' Her voice might be full of reproach, but her eyes were shrewd, assessing his every expression.

'I've been busy. As have you.'

'Sì, weddings don't organise themselves. Maybe you'll find that out one day.' She linked her arm through his and gave a small tug. 'Come, Marco, take coffee with me. Let's have a proper catch-up.'

Words guaranteed to strike a chill through any dutiful child's heart. 'No coffee for me, Mamma. I have a lot to do.'

She stepped back and looked up at him. It was many years since she had topped him yet he still had the urge to look up—she carried herself as if she were seven feet tall. 'You work too hard, Marco. A young man like you should be out, enjoying himself. Sophie must be feeling sadly neglected.'

'I doubt it. She's making herself a dress for Bianca's wedding. I'm not sure I would be of much help.'

'Clever girl. She's so creative.' Her eyes flickered over his face and Marco stayed as expressionless as possible. 'We lack that in our family. We're all good at facts, at figures, at making money, but none of us has any creativity. It would be nice…' Her voice trailed off, but he knew exactly what she meant. Nice to breed that creativity in. 'She has such lovely colouring as well, the peaches-and-cream English complexion.' As if Sophie were a brood mare, waiting to be mated with a prize stallion.

The old feelings of being imprisoned, stifled, descended like physical bars, enclosing him in, trying to strip all choice away. His mouth narrowed as he fought to keep his cool. 'Yes, she's very pretty.'

'Oh, Marco, she's beautiful. And so sweet. Bianca adores her, says she is just like a sister. We'll all miss her when she returns to London. We'll miss you as well. It's been lovely having you home.'

'Luckily for Bianca they have invented these marvellous little devices which make it possible to communicate over large distances. In fact she usually has one glued to her hand. I'm sure she can speak to Sophie as much as she would like to.'

His mother walked over to the desk and picked up the fountain pen his father had always used. 'My own mother always said one of her greatest joys was watching you and Bianca grow up.'

This was a new one. 'Nonna was a very special person. I miss her.'

'She was in her early twenties when I was born, and I, of course, was very young when I had you. She was still only in her forties when she became a grandmother. Young enough to be active, to be able to play with you. Of course, her dearest wish was to see you marry, have a family of your own.'

'She was taken from us too early.'

'I will be sixty next year, Marco. Sixty.'

He was impressed; she didn't usually admit to her age. 'And you don't look a day over forty-five. Are you sure you have the right year?'

But she wasn't in the mood for gallantry, barely raising a smile at the compliment. 'I want to see my grandchildren, Marco. I want to know them, watch them grow up, not be an old lady, too tired and ill to be able to play when they finally arrive.'

Marco sighed. 'Mamma…'

'I want you back home, back here, where you belong, heading up the Santoro family. I want you settled down and married with children of your own.'

'I know you do. It's all you've ever wanted.'

'I just want you to be happy, Marco.'

He fought to keep his voice even. 'I know. But you have to accept that happiness comes in many different forms, in many different ways. I like what I do. I like London.'

'And what of me? Of the business?'

'There are other options. Bianca, for instance. Come on, Mamma, you must have considered it. Bianca is more than fit to take over from you. She's the best of us all when it comes to figures, she's ambitious and she's a Santoro to her fingernails, no matter who she marries and what her last name is. Don't overlook her. You'll be doing all of us a disservice.'

His mother only smiled. 'You think I haven't considered her? That your father didn't? Of course we have. You're right, in many ways she's the cleverest of us all and when it comes to the finances there's no one I would rather have in charge. But she doesn't have what your father had—what you have—she doesn't have the flair, the inspired spark.'

Guilt flared as she compared him to his father and Marco's hands curled into fists involuntarily. 'I don't know what you mean.'

'Yes, you do,' she said, staring at him as if she could imprint her words into him. 'Bianca and I can manage, we can audit, we can run—but you and your father can build. Can take an idea and make it grow, see where opportunity lies and grab it with both hands. I'm not discounting Bianca because she's a woman and getting married, I'm discounting her because she won't grow the company like you will. Because you are the heir your father wanted.'

Bitterness coated his mouth. 'Papà didn't want me to be inspired. He didn't want me to be anything but an obedient clone. He sat in this room, at this desk, and told me if I went to England, continued to mess around with antiques, we were finished.'

'They were just words. You know what he was like. Words came too easily and he never meant them—it was what he did which counted. And he was proud of you, Marco. He followed your every move. People would tell him of you, people you worked with in Venice, further afield, would seek him out to talk of you and he would drink in every word.'

The ache in Marco's chest eased, just a little. 'He never said, never showed that he even knew what I was doing…'

'You didn't give him the opportunity. Besides…' she shrugged '…he was too proud to make the first move. He was proud, you are proud and here you are.'

'He sat there and disowned me and when I disobeyed him he…' But he couldn't say the words.

'He had a heart attack,' she finished calmly. 'It wasn't your fault, Marco.'

Easy for her to say. He knew better; he'd always known. 'Of course it was. If I had settled to be what he wanted…'

'Then you wouldn't be you. He knew that. But it hurt him that you barely returned. That from the moment you went to London you never again spent a night under our roof.'

Misunderstandings, pride, stubbornness. Family traits passed on from father to son. 'I couldn't. I didn't dare. I couldn't let his health blackmail me into compliance, nor could I let him work himself into one of his passions. It was better to stay away.' He stopped, bleak. 'He died anyway.'

'*Sì.* But not because of anything you said or didn't say but because he didn't listen to his doctor, didn't listen to me, didn't exercise or take his pills or cut down on red meat. Stubborn. But it's not your fault, Marco. That first heart attack would have happened anyway, you must know that. We're lucky we had him for another ten years.'

But Marco hadn't had him; he'd lost his father long before. 'And now it's too late, he's gone and he didn't even know I said goodbye.'

Her eyes were soft with understanding, with love. 'He knew. You came straight away. He was conscious enough to know you were there. Forgive yourself, Marco. Nobody else blames you for any of it, nobody ever did. But I would like you to come home, at least to be here more often. To advise me even if you won't take over. I just want to see my son more than a couple of hours once or twice a year.'

'Yes.' His mind was whirling. Why had his father never told him that he was proud of him, never said he hadn't meant a word of the bitter denunciation that had left him in the hospital and Marco in exile? But his mother was right. Marco hadn't stayed away just out of fear he would trigger another heart attack, he'd stayed away out of pride. Just as bad as his father. Maybe it was time to let some of that pride go.

'Yes,' he said again. 'I can be here more often. And I can't promise you I'll take over, but I can advise—and make sure you have the right people in place to help you. You need to delegate more, Mamma, and accept that people who aren't Santoros can still care about the company.'

'It's a deal.'

Relief flooded through him. They had compromised and, for the first time, he didn't feel that she had tried to manipulate him; she had respected his decision. He would, should spend more time in Venice. It was only right that he at least took a board role in his family company.

He bent, kissed his mother's cheek and turned to leave but stopped as she called his name softly. 'Marco?'

'Yes?'

'Ten years wasted, Marco, out of pride, out of anger…' She paused. 'Don't make that mistake again. I know you say you aren't ready to marry and I know you are angry with me, with your father, for what happened ten years ago. But don't let that pride, that anger, push Sophie away. She's a lovely girl, Marco. But I don't think there will be second chances with that one. You need to get it right.'

'Mamma, we've only just met.'

'I know, and I am staying out of it.' Despite his prickle of annoyance he couldn't help an incredulous laugh at her words. 'Just think about it. That's all I'm asking. Just take care with her.'

'Okay.' He could promise that with an easy mind. Taking care came easily to him; he knew how to tread for an easy relationship and an easier exit. 'I'll take care. Now I really have to get on.' But as he walked away her words echoed in his mind. *No more second chances.* He didn't need a second chance. He liked Sophie, he liked her a lot, enough to know that she deserved a lot better than anything a man like him could offer. He should thank her though, for all her help. He might not be able to offer her happy ever after—and she probably wouldn't take it if he did—but he could offer her one perfect day. It was the least he could do. It had to be; it was all that he had.

CHAPTER NINE

To Sophie's amazement Marco was still in the breakfast room when she came down, having overslept again. She stopped and hovered at the door, stupidly shy.

How she could feel shy when he'd left her bedroom just four short hours ago, how she could still feel shy after the things they'd done in that bedroom, eluded her and yet her stomach swooped at the sight of him and her tongue was suddenly too large for her mouth, like a teenager seeing her crush across the hallway.

They hadn't eaten breakfast together since that first morning. He was usually already out working when she came downstairs, their first communication of the day at lunch. Lunch was civilised, easy to navigate, but breakfast? Breakfast was an intimate meal. She wasn't ready for breakfast…

His presence wasn't the only thing that had changed. The atmosphere in the *palazzo* seemed lighter somehow, less fraught. Less weighted with the air of things left unsaid, when the silences were more eloquent than words. For the first time since the party she and Marco had stayed at the *palazzo* for dinner last night and Marco hadn't tensed up too much when his mother had quizzed Sophie once more about her future plans and shot him meaningful glances every time she did so. Marco's mother was very charming, but over the space of the evening she'd ramped up the inquisitional levels to almost overbearing, her hints so broad Sophie hadn't known where to look half the time. She'd aimed for obliviousness, but it was difficult to look unknowing when she was invited to try on Marco's dead grandmother's engagement ring, asked about her perfect honeymoon plans or how many children she wanted and didn't she think her eyes with Marco's colouring would look cute in a baby?

She might, possibly, have been able to laugh the whole thing off if it weren't for the pregnancy. Guilt, embarrassment and fear mingled in a toxic concoction every time Marco's mother opened her mouth. Every time Signora Santoro mentioned children guilt shot through Sophie, like a physical pain. It took everything she had to sit and pretend everything was okay, not to jump up and announce her pregnancy in a rush of tears. She still thought it was fair to wait until after the wedding, it was just a week's delay after all, but she knew in her heart she was deceiving Marco, lying to him by omission.

And part of her knew it wasn't Bianca's welfare really driving her, it was fear. She'd spent so long living her mother's dreams, only to crush them when she'd walked away, the rift still no way near repaired. Then she'd allowed Harry to set her course, making him the sole focus of her life. This family was so certain, so overbearing, so grand and overwhelming—what if they tried to take control as soon as they knew about the baby? Had the last year and a half given her enough strength to hold firm and make her own choices?

Time would tell, but she needed these days to prepare. To try to work out exactly what she, Sophie

Bradshaw, wanted, before the Santoro expectations descended onto her.

She took a deep breath and walked into the room, hooking a chair and sitting down, swiping a piece of brioche off Marco's plate as she did so. The key to fighting off both the tiredness and nausea, she'd realised, was carbs and plenty of them. The way she was eating she'd be sporting plenty of bumps long before the baby actually started to show.

'Good morning. All on your own?'

Marco folded his newspaper up and pushed it to one side. Sophie really liked the way he focussed his full attention on the people he was with, apologising if he checked his phone or took a call. He never kept his phone on the table when they were out, never scrolled through it when she was speaking. Harry had never made any secret of the fact every contact in his phone, every game, every meme, every football result came before her. 'You just missed Mamma and Bianca. They told me to remind you that you can join them at any time. Apparently the twenty times they asked you last night wasn't a pressing enough invitation. Are you sure you don't want to go with them?'

Sophie grinned. 'Your mother, Bianca's future mother-in-law, all five of her future sisters-in-law and her three best friends all alternately talking in Italian so I sit there gaping like a goldfish before switching to English to quiz me on your intentions and my potential wedding plans? There's not a spa luxurious enough to tempt me.' She realised how ungrateful that sounded and backtracked quickly. 'I like them all well enough, in fact I love Bianca and your mother individually…'

'But together they strike fear into the heart of the bravest warrior?'

'They really do. Besides, the day after tomorrow it's the wedding and I fly back to London the morning after that. I'm making final adjustments to Bianca's and the bridesmaids' dresses tomorrow, which makes this my last free day here. I want to make the most of it. Explore Venice one final time.'

'Do you want some company?'

Happiness fizzed up at the casual words. 'Of course, but don't you need to work? Don't worry about me if so…'

Giuliana, one of the maids, set a cup, a small tea-pot and a plate laden with sweet bread, slices of fruit, cheese and a couple of pastries in front of Sophie. Her preference for herbal tea first thing had caused some consternation in the caffeinated household at first, but the staff had eventually adjusted to both tea and her very un-Venetian need for a breakfast more substantial than a few bites of something quick. Sophie nodded her thanks, grateful as the familiar ginger aroma wafted up, displacing the bitter scent of coffee and settling her queasy stomach.

'A few days off seems like the perfect plan right now,' Marco said as Sophie started to tuck in. 'I need time to think about where my business is headed, how I can continue to grow and still meet my obligations to the family business.' His mouth twisted into a rueful smile. 'I realised yesterday that even if I don't want to take over I still need to be involved. Besides, when I started out I used my contacts here to source antiques, but it was important for me to be in London to build contacts for the other side of the business, the people I would sell to. I've been based there ten years, own a house in Chelsea. In many ways it's my home.'

Right there and then the chasm between them widened even further. Sophie rented a shoebox on the top floor of a building on a busy road. Buses thundered past at all hours of the day and night, streetlights lit up her room, casting an orange glow over her dreams, and the bass from the flat below provided a thudding soundtrack to everything she did. Half her pay went straight to her landlord. Owning a home of her own was a distant enough dream, her city shoebox well out of her range. A whole house? In Chelsea? Not for the likes of her.

It was all going to make telling him about the baby even harder. If only they were equals financially... She pushed the thought away, adding it to her ever-lengthening list of things to worry about in the future. 'But now?'

'I still need an office and a base in London, but those contacts are secure. I have a whole global network of dealers, buyers, designers who know and trust me. I'm having to work a little harder on the Italian side now. There's a new generation of suppliers coming along and I don't have the same links with them, the same trust. It means I'm no longer the automatic first choice and that could impact my future stock.'

'So, you need to spend more time here?' Her heart twisted. She had no idea what her future held, but she hadn't expected to have a baby with a man she wasn't committed to, a man who spent half his life out of the country.

Suck it up, she told herself fiercely. *This will be your reality. Deal with it.*

'I do. But these are thoughts for another day. I'm very much aware how much we owe you, Sophie. Bianca would have imploded if you hadn't stayed. Let me make it up to you. Anything you want. How do you want to

spend the day? A trip to the lakes? To Roma? Buy out
the whole of the lace shops on Burano?'

Guilt twisted again. She'd had her own selfish reasons for staying, for getting close to Marco's family.
But she couldn't pass up this opportunity to spend a
day with the father of her child—and she didn't want
to. She wanted to spend the day with him, to get to
know him a little better, to have one last carefree day
before she shattered his world. 'Nothing so elaborate.
Show me your Venice, Marco, the things you love most
about the city. That's what I'd like to do today. If you're
okay with that.'

'Really? That's what you want to do? You're willing to take the risk?' He looked surprised, but he was
smiling. 'In that case I'll meet you back here in half an
hour. Wear comfy shoes and wrap up warm. We may
be out for some time.'

CHAPTER TEN

SOPHIE INSTANTLY FELL in love with the Dorsoduro. Although there were plenty of tourists around, exclaiming over the views and taking selfies with the canals and bridges as backdrops, it had a more relaxed air than the streets around the Rialto Bridge and Saint Mark's square, a sense of home and belonging, especially once they reached the quieter back streets and small tree-lined squares. Amongst the grocery and souvenir shops, the cafés and restaurants, she spotted some gorgeous boutiques, specialising in stationery, in paints, in textiles as well as enticing pastry and confectionery shops that made her mouth water and she itched to explore further. 'Can I go shopping before lunch and then explore this afternoon? I'd really like to look at those textiles if I could.'

'Of course. I'm not sure how we've managed to miss this area out of our tours,' Marco said. 'We spent some time in the east of the *sestieri*, but somehow we haven't wandered here.'

'That's because we were meant to come here today. It's been waiting for me all week, an old friend I haven't met yet.'

'That's exactly what this area is, an old friend. If I ever lived back in Venice full-time, I wouldn't want to live in the *palazzo*. I'd prefer a little house tucked away in the back streets here. Something smaller than the London house, overlooking a canal.'

No one Sophie had ever met who lived in London had ever wanted something smaller. Curiosity got the better of her manners. 'How big *is* your house in London?'

Marco shrugged. 'Four bedrooms. It's just a terrace, round the back of the King's Road. Three floors and a basement, courtyard garden.'

Sophie managed to keep walking somehow. *Just* a terrace. *Just* round the back of the King's Road. She often walked those streets, picking out her favourites from the ivy-covered, white and pastel painted houses, knowing that houses like that, lifestyles like that, were as beyond her dreams as living on Mars.

She'd known that Marco's family was rich, knew he had enough money to buy handmade suits and frequent expensive bars, but somehow she hadn't realised that Marco was rich—really rich, not merely well off—in his own right.

It made everything infinitely worse.

It took two to make a baby, she reminded herself. This wasn't her fault. She wasn't trying to trap him, to enrich herself at his expense. But it was what people would think. It might be what he would think and she couldn't blame him. It would all be so much easier if he were a little more normal, if his family hadn't made the idea of fatherhood, marriage and settling down into his worst nightmare. If she thought he'd be happy with her news, not horrified…

Preoccupied, she hadn't noticed where they were walking, barely taking in that Marco had turned out of the narrow road to lead her through an arched gate and onto a rough floor made of wooden slats, leading down to the canal. Wooden, balconied buildings took up two sides of the square, the open canals the other two, and upturned gondolas lined up on the floor in neat rows.

'Marco!' A man dressed in overalls, wiping his hands on a rag, just as if this were a normal garage in a normal town, straightened and strode over, embracing Marco in a warm hug. Marco returned the embrace and the two men began to talk in loud, voluble Italian. Sophie didn't even try to follow the conversation, even when she heard her name mentioned; instead she pulled out her camera and began to take pictures of two young men bending over a gondola, faces intent as they applied varnish to the curved hull. It was the closest she'd got to a gondola in all the time she'd been here; Marco owned his own boat, of course, and had made it clear that gondola rides were only for tourists. She'd not argued but couldn't help feeling a little cheated out of the quintessential Venetian experience.

'*Sì...sì, grazie.*' Marco embraced the man again and Sophie whipped the camera round to capture the moment, his body completely relaxed, his smile open and wide in a way it never was at the *palazzo*. His family were only a small part of his world here. He had his business contacts, yes, family obligations and friends— but also this whole other life. His own friends and interests, left behind when he started a new life in London, and yet still obviously important. This was what he would be returning to when he started to spend more time here. Leaving behind the network of business friends he spent his time with in London for people who really knew him. Sophie swallowed. She could go back to Manchester tomorrow and not meet one person who would make her smile the way Marco was smiling now.

'Ready?' He stepped over an oar and re-joined Sophie.

'For what?'

'I thought you wanted to go shopping and I have a few things I need to buy. *Arrivederci*,' he called over his shoulder as they exited the yard as speedily as they had entered it.

Sophie looked back, wishing they'd had more time for her to take in every detail. 'Is that where gondolas go to die?'

His mouth curved into the rare genuine smile she loved to see, the smile she liked to draw out of him. 'No, it's where they go to get better. Tonio's family have been fixing them for generations. When we were boys he swore it wouldn't be for him, swore that he would travel the world, be his own man…'

'What happened?'

Marco shrugged. 'He travelled the world and realised that all he wanted was to come home and run the yard. Now he's the most respected gondola maker and fixer in all of Venice.'

It didn't take long to reach the shops Sophie had noted when they'd first entered the Dorsoduro and she was immediately torn between a textile shop specialising in hand-woven materials and a traditional mask maker. She hadn't had to dip too far into her carefully hoarded money so far; a few ingredients for the meal she'd cooked Marco, material from a warehouse for her dress and for Bianca's wedding gift, but she wanted to buy presents for her friends if possible.

'I have a few errands to run,' Marco said as she wavered between the two. 'See you back here in an hour? I know the perfect place for lunch.' And before she could respond he was gone. Sophie checked her watch. She had just under an hour and streets of tempting little shops to explore; there was no time to waste. With a deep breath and a feeling of impending bankruptcy she opted for the mask shop.

It was like stepping into another world, a world of velvet and lace, of secrecy and whispers, seductive and terrifying in equal measure. Sophie turned slowly, marvelling at the artistry in every detail, her eyes drawn to a half-face cat mask, one side gold, the other a green brocade, sequins highlighting the slanted eye slits and the perfect feline nose. She picked it up and held it against her face, immediately transformed into someone—something—dangerous and unknown. She replaced it with a sigh of longing. The gorgeous carnival masks, all made and painted by hand, were definitely beyond her means and having seen the real thing she didn't want to waste her money on the cheaper, mass-produced masks displayed on souvenir stalls throughout the city. Likewise she soon realised that the colourful fabrics, still produced on traditional wooden looms, would bankrupt her.

Three quarters of an hour later she was done, choosing beautiful handmade paper journals, one for each of her friends. Turning as she exited the shop, she saw Marco sauntering towards her, a secretive, pleased smile on his face. 'Done already?' he asked as he reached her side. 'I usually have to drag Bianca and Mamma out of these shops kicking and screaming.'

'I could just look at the colours and the workmanship for hours,' Sophie admitted. 'I very nearly came home with a cat mask. But options for wearing such a thing in London are sadly limited. Not that I can imagine actually wearing it. It's a work of art.'

'You should see the city at *carnivale*. It's not just the masks, the costumes are out of this world—hats, dominoes, elaborate gowns. You would go crazy for the colours and designs. My mother has five different outfits and six different masks, so each year she changes her look completely.'

'What about you? What do you wear?'

'I go for the simple black domino and a half-mask, but it's many years since I've been here during *carnivale*. The city gets a little fevered. It's easy to get carried away.'

After a light lunch at a pretty café overlooking a narrow back-street canal they explored the rest of the vibrant district, wandering down to the university, visiting churches and museums as they went. The afternoon flew by and it was a surprise when Sophie realised it was late afternoon and their wandering no longer had an aimless quality to it. Marco was walking with intent as they retraced their steps back to the gondola yard they had visited earlier. The gates were closed now, but Marco knocked loudly on the wooden door and almost immediately one large gate swung open. Sophie didn't recognise the owner at first. He'd changed out of his overalls and into the striped top and straw hat of a gondolier, although, in a nod to the season, he had put a smart black jacket over the top.

'This way,' Marco said and steered her towards the jetty. A gondola was moored there, gleaming black in the fading light. Warm velvety throws were placed over the black leather seats, several more were folded on the two stools that provided the only other seating. 'It gets cold,' Marco said briefly as he took her hand and helped her step into the gently rocking boat. 'Welcome aboard, *signorina*.'

The rug was soft and warm as Sophie wriggled into one of the two main seats, placed side by side along the middle of the long narrow boat. Marco picked up another blanket and draped it across her knees and Sophie folded her hands into the fabric, glad of the extra coverings. Her tights and wool jacket were good enough protection against the chill while she was moving and the sun was out, but, sitting still as the evening began to reach dark fingers along the sky, she was suddenly very aware it was winter. Marco set a basket on the small table in the middle of the seating area before gracefully stepping aboard and taking his seat next to hers. It was a narrow space and she could feel the hard length of his thigh next to hers, his body heat as he slipped an arm around her shoulders and shouted something unintelligible to his friend. The next moment the moorings were untied and the boat began to glide away from the dock, moving smoothly down the canal.

Marco leaned forward and, with a flourish, took two champagne glasses and a bottle out of the basket, and set them in front of her, followed by a selection of small fruit and custard tarts, beautifully presented in a lavishly decorated box.

'It's far too early for dinner,' he explained. 'But I thought you might enjoy a picnic. And don't worry, I've remembered your 'no drinking in January' rule. The bottle is actually lightly sparkling grape juice, although it really should be Prosecco.'

Sophie didn't need Prosecco, the unexpected sweetness of the surprise he had so carefully planned more intoxicating than any drink could possibly be. The grape juice wasn't too sweet, the tartness a welcome relief against the flaky pastry and sugared fruit of the delicious tarts. Replete, she snuggled back against Marco's arm and watched Venice go by. She'd spent many hours on the canals, but the city felt closer, more magical from the gondola, as if she were in a dream, part of the city's very fabric.

Marco had obviously planned the route with his friend in advance and the gondola took them into several hidden corners of the city, going through water gates into some of the *palazzos* and even slipping beneath churches into secret passages. Their route took them through the back waters and quieter canals and at times it was as if they were the only people in the city, even their gondolier fading into the background as, with a final burst of orange and pink, the sun finally began to sink into the water and the velvety dusk fell.

'I don't know why you said a gondola was a tourist trap. It is the most romantic thing that has ever happened to me,' Sophie said as the last of the day disappeared, their way now lit by the soft gold of the lamps, their reflections glowing in the murky water.

'More romantic than you knocking me over in the snow?'

She pretended to think about it. 'Almost. Even more romantic than you chasing me into a cupboard on New Year's Eve.'

'I have fond memories of that cupboard,' he said and she elbowed him.

'Nothing happened in that cupboard, unless you're mixing me up with someone else that night.'

'Oh, no, you are definitely one of a kind,' Marco said softly. 'The first girl who ever ran away from me.'

'I find that hard to believe.' But she didn't. She found it hard to believe that she ever had run away, that she had had the strength of will to walk away that first night and again on New Year's Eve. 'Is that why you asked me here, because I walked away?'

'Ran,' he corrected her. 'One sight of me and you

were tearing through that ballroom like an Olympic medallist in heels. And maybe that's why. I was intrigued for sure, wanted to spend more time with you.'

And now? She wanted to ask, but she didn't quite dare. The carefully orchestrated romance of the evening was perfect but could so easily be a farewell gesture. 'You didn't bargain for quite so much time,' she said instead. 'Thank you, Marco, I know you were blindsided by your sister, but thank you for making me feel welcome, for making me feel wanted...'

He leaned over then, pulling her close, his mouth on hers, harder than his usual sweet kisses, more demanding. He kissed her as if they were the only two people in the whole of Venice, as if the world might stop if she didn't acquiesce, fall into it, fall into him. The world fell away, the heat of his mouth, his hands holding her still, holding her close all she knew, all she wanted to know. Her own arms encircled him as she buried one hand in his hair, the other clutching at his shoulder as if she were drowning and he all that stood between her and a watery grave.

It was the first time he'd kissed her for kissing's sake, she realised in some dim part of her mind. That first night they didn't lay a hand on each other until they were in the hotel room, New Year's Eve she had walked away from his touch—but if she hadn't, she knew full well they would have ended up in that same hotel room, the kiss a precursor, a promise of things yet to come. It would have been another hotel, not his house; close as it must have been, that was too intimate for Marco, not her flat, too intimate for her.

Even here in Venice they were curiously separate... Oh, he kissed her cheek in greeting, held her arm to guide her, but there were no gestures of intimacy; no holding hands, no caresses as they passed each other, no cuddles or embraces. No kisses on bridges or boats. Kisses, caresses, embraces—they were saved for under cover of darkness, saved for passion and escape. But there could be no passion or escape here in the middle of a canal, visible to anyone and everyone walking by. This was kissing for kissing's sake. Touching for touching's sake. This was togetherness.

Her heart might burst—or it might break—but all she could do was kiss him back and let all her yearning, her need, her want pour out of her and into him. Savour each second—because if this was it, if this was a farewell gesture, she wanted to remember every single moment, remember what was good before she blew his world apart.

Sophie hadn't expected the evening to continue after the gondola ride, but after they reluctantly disembarked Marco took her to a few of his favourite *bàcaro*, small bars serving wine and *cicchetti*, little tapas-type snacks. In one *bàcaro* Sophie was enchanted by the selection of *francobollo*, teeny little sandwiches filled with a selection of meats or roasted vegetables. 'They're so tiny it's like I'm not eating anything at all,' she explained to a fascinated Marco as she consumed her tenth—or was it eleventh? 'Less than a mouthful doesn't count, everyone knows that.' In another she tried the tastiest meatballs she had ever eaten and a third offered a selection of seafood that rivalled the fanciest of restaurants. One day, she promised herself, she would return when the smell of the different house wines didn't make her wrinkle her nose in disgust and she could sample the excellent coffee without wanting to throw up.

She had no idea how long they spent in the friendly,

noisy bars as early evening turned into evening. Marco seemed to know people everywhere they went and introduced her to all of them until she had completely lost track of who was a school friend, who a college friend and who had got who into the most trouble in their teens. Everyone was very welcoming and made an effort to speak in English, but Sophie was very conscious of their curious glances, a confirmation that Marco seldom, if ever, brought girlfriends back to Venice.

'Okay,' Marco announced as Sophie was wondering if she could possibly manage just one more *francobollo*. 'Time to go.' She glanced up, surprised; she'd assumed that this was the purpose of the evening, that they didn't have anywhere else to go.

'Go?' she echoed.

He nodded, his face solemn but his eyes gleaming with suppressed mischief.

Sophie got to her feet. They couldn't possibly be going out for dinner, not after the almost constant snacking starting with the pastries in the gondola and ending with that last small sandwich, and it was too dark to head back out on the water. She was relieved that she'd dressed smartly that morning, and some bright lipstick and mascara had been enough to make her look bar ready; she just hoped it would work for whatever Marco had planned next. 'Okay, I'm ready. Lead on, MacDuff.'

It didn't take them more than five minutes to reach their mystery destination, a grand-looking *palazzo*, just off St Mark's Square. The main door was ajar, guarded by a broad, suited man, and to Sophie's surprise Marco produced two tickets and handed them over. The man examined them and then with a nod of his head opened the door and bade them enter. They were ushered through a grand hallway, beautifully furnished in the formal Venetian style, up the sweeping staircase and into a grand salon, where around sixty people were milling around, all smartly dressed. In the corner a string quartet were tuning their instruments.

One end of the room was empty, furniture carefully placed in a way that reminded Sophie of a stage set; chairs had been placed in semicircles facing the empty area. 'Is this a recital?'

'Not quite. Have you been to the opera before?'

'The opera? No, never. Is that what this is? In a house?'

'*La Traviata,*' Marco confirmed. 'Each act takes place in a different room in the *palazzo* so that the audience is both spectator and part of the scene. It's one of my favourite things to do when I'm home. I thought you might enjoy it.'

'Oh, I'm sure I will.' Sophie knew nothing about opera, had no idea if she would like the music, but it didn't matter—what mattered was the effort Marco had put into her last free evening here. The effort he had put in to show her the parts of Venice that meant something to him, show her the city he loved and missed. 'Thank you, Marco. This is the loveliest thing anyone has ever, ever done for me.'

He smiled, but before he could reply they were asked to take their seats.

The next couple of hours passed by in a blur of music, of song, of spectacle, of tears. Sophie was so engrossed she didn't notice the tears rolling down her face as Violetta sang her swansong, not until Marco pressed a handkerchief into her trembling hand. It wasn't just the music, moving as it was, it was the setting, it was the night as a whole, it was the realisation that these were the last innocent hours she and Marco would spend together, that whatever happened after this would be heavy with expectation. She wanted to freeze every second, frame them, remember it all.

'Did you enjoy that?'

She nodded, wrapping her scarf a little tighter as they exited the *palazzo* and turned into St Mark's Square. The moon was low and round, casting an enchantment on the ancient buildings, lit up and golden by the street-lights. 'I loved every bit of it,' she said. 'The whole evening, Marco. Thank you.'

He caught her hand, a boyish carefree gesture, and as he did so realisation rocketed through her, sudden and painful in its clarity. She was in love with him. Deeply, relentlessly, irrevocably in love with him. How had this happened? Maybe it was hormones, her version of mood swings, an emotion that would drain away when she hit the magic twelve-week mark. Maybe it was fear, fear of raising the baby alone in a tiny flat on a busy main road. Maybe it was simply the novelty of being treated as if she mattered, as if she was worth something by a man worth everything.

Or maybe it was real, that elusive alchemy of desire and compatibility and friendship.

She rose onto her tiptoes, pressing a soft kiss to his bristled cheek in thanks. He moved as she did so, catching her in his arms, capturing her mouth under his so that her light embrace was turned into something more powerful. She allowed him to take control, leaning into him, into his warmth and strength. Allowed him to claim her as his. Because she was, his. But that was almost irrelevant. How could she tell him when he was already burdened by his family's heavy expectations? How could she tell him she loved him when she still had to tell him about the baby? Her love would be one more load for him to bear, one more expectation for him to manage and she couldn't do it to him. She had this night, this kiss. They had to be enough.

CHAPTER ELEVEN

BIANCA QUIVERED AS the music struck up and she clutched his arm even more tightly.

'Hold on in there,' Marco said. 'Not long to go.'

'I'm not nervous, I'm excited. I love Antonio and I can't wait to marry him, to start our life together, I just…' She faltered, her dark eyes tearing up, and he squeezed her hand.

'I know, you wish Papà was here. I do too.'

'He liked Antonio. I'm glad about that. Glad he got to know him, that they respected each other. He'd have liked Sophie too.'

'Bianca, Sophie and I aren't…'

She turned and looked straight at him, beautiful, glowing with her hair caught up behind the heirloom tiara, her veil arranged in foamy folds down her back. 'Not yet, but you could be. I see the way you look at her when you think nobody's watching you.'

'And how's that?'

'You look the way I feel about Antonio, that's how.'

'I think you're seeing what you want to see. I like her, of course I do, I admire her…'

'Fancy the pants off her?' Bianca's mouth curved into a wide grin and she waggled her perfectly plucked eyebrows at him.

'The mouth on you. And a bride at that! Yes, I find her attractive too, but that's not…' He stopped, unable to find the right words.

'That's not what? What falling in love is? I never had you down as the stars and flowers type, Marco. Falling in love might be instantaneous, strike-me-down, can't-live-without-this person, all-consuming lust when you are sixteen, when you're twenty. It's meant to be like that when you're young. But when you grow up, when you're an adult, then love is something slower but stronger. You start off with like and admire and attract and over time it grows and becomes all the more powerful for that. But you have to let it grow, not run away the first chance you get.'

Marco stared down into his little sister's face. 'When did you get so wise?'

She smirked. 'I always was. Now stand up straight and get ready to support me down this aisle. These heels are ridiculous and I have no intention of tripping and prostrating myself at Antonio's feet!'

The music swelled, their cue. He bent slightly and kissed Bianca's cheek. 'Ready, *sorellina*?'

She inhaled slowly, her hand shaking as she did so. 'Ready. Let's go get me married.'

Bianca had chosen to marry in the gorgeous Church of Santa Maria dei Miracoli, partly because of the sumptuous décor and partly, Marco suspected, because she'd liked the idea of standing at the top of the marble staircase to make her vows. There weren't quite enough seats for all the guests and people were standing at the back and along the sides, all three hundred pairs of eyes staring right at Marco and Bianca. Marco barely noticed them; he was searching for the one person he wanted to see, Bianca's words hammering through his brain with every step they took.

Like, admire, attract.

Was she right? Was it that simple? If so, why did the very thought of it feel so terrifying? So insurmountable? And yet…he inhaled, his heart hammering fast, louder than the organ music filling the great church. And yet in some ways it made perfect sense.

As they neared the front of the church he caught sight of Sophie, elegant and poised, standing next to his mother. If he hadn't known that she had whipped her dress up in just two days, he would never have believed it; she looked as if she were wearing the most exclusive designer fashion. She'd opted for a silvery grey damask material, which shimmered faintly under the chandelier lights. It was a seemingly conservative design, wide straps at her neck with the neckline cut high, almost to her throat—a stark contrast to the deep vee at her back, exposing creamy skin down to the mid-point of her spine. The bodice fitted tightly right to her waist and then the material flared out into a full knee-length skirt. The look was deceptively demure—but the dress fitted the contours of her body perfectly, the material lovingly caressing every slight curve. She'd twisted her hair up into a loose chignon confined by a silver band showing off the graceful lines of her neck. She was elegant and sophisticated, easily outshining the more elaborate and colourful dresses crowding the pews of the ornate church.

She looked right at him and smiled, a soft intimate smile, and his chest tightened. Two days ago he had promised her a perfect day. It hadn't been altogether altruistic; payment for all the work she had put in on the wedding, work that had ended up going way beyond altering one dress; distraction for him as he mulled over the momentous decision to step back into the family business, to spend more time at home; seduction, he'd wanted the kind of day that would make her boneless with desire because sex with her was out of this world and they had so little time left. No, his reasons hadn't been altogether altruistic.

But she hadn't demanded fine wines and five-star restaurants, she'd asked him to show her his world. He hadn't realised it at the time, but the price of her day was far higher than the most expensive restaurant in Italy. He'd paid her in intimacy, in revealing parts of his soul he kept hidden from the whole world.

Like, admire, attract.

Surely, despite the short amount of time he'd known her they had gone way beyond those three words and he'd no idea how it had happened, how he'd let his guard down. He'd kept himself so safe, most of the women he'd met over the last decade or so had as little interest in his inner life as he had in theirs. They cared about his name, his family, his prospects, his money. They made superficiality all too easy, all too attractive.

But Sophie wasn't like that. She was visibly shocked by his wealth, unimpressed by his name. And still he hid. Because if she found him wanting, it would matter; this time it could hurt.

Marco escorted Bianca up the stairs towards the altar and her waiting groom. She'd forgotten about him, about the church full of people waiting to see her get married, all her attention on Antonio, her eyes shining and luminous. He crossed himself as they neared the altar and, as if in a dream, waited to play his small part, before descending the steps to join Sophie and his mother, leaving Bianca making her vows, readying herself for a life in the family she chose, not the one she was born to.

The church hushed, the only sound the voices of the priest, Bianca and her new husband as they repeated vows with heartbreaking sincerity and emotion. All his sister's usual theatrics had disappeared as she gazed at the man she was promising to love in sickness and in health.

'I couldn't understand a word, but that was beautiful.' Sophie gulped as the crowd burst into enthusiastic applause as Bianca and Antonio embraced for the first time as husband and wife. 'She looks so gorgeous. Like the perfect bride. And they look so happy...' Her voice wavered. Next to her one of Marco's aunts was sobbing, on his other side his mother was still applying her handkerchief. Marco looked around wildly, but he was trapped; there was no escape from wet-eyed, sniffing females.

At least no escape until he was crushed into the narrow pew as his mother elbowed her way past him. 'Oh, Sophie, *grazie, cara*. You performed miracles. Hey, Chesca, this is Sophie, Marco's *ragazza*. Did you see how she transformed Bianca's dress? *Sì, bellissima.*'

His mother kept up her chatter as they made their way down the aisle. She was obviously buzzing from the wedding and wanted everyone to know how Sophie had helped—binding the English girl ever closer to the family, he thought wryly. 'Yes, she and Marco are very close, he's quite besotted,' he heard her confide more than once. 'We expect an announcement any day now.'

Her whispered predictions didn't surprise him, his lack of anger did. But she was wrong; there would be no announcement. Things had moved too fast, so fast he'd barely noticed that they were out of the shallows and heading towards the deep water. Sophie was going home tomorrow and perhaps it was for the best. Enjoy the short time they had left, then put a stop to it before he let her down. He might not mean to, but he would. It was his hallmark after all.

Sophie had been aware of the stares before the wedding started. It was worse than the party at Epiphany. Then, she had been new to the city, unaware of the subtext. Today she knew all too well that everyone was looking at her and wondering if she would be the next Santoro bride. She had been the subject of more than a few cool, assessing once-overs from expensively clad and groomed women, the contemptuous flicker of their eyes judging her and finding her wanting.

But the stares intensified once the ceremony was over. Marco's mother was making it very clear that she considered Sophie one of the family, introducing her to what seemed like every single one of the three hundred guests. Even worse, she told everyone she could about how Sophie had 'saved' Bianca's dress. Sophie knew that if Ashleigh were here she'd be telling her to milk the situation for all she was worth, think of future commissions and suck it up, but she felt guilty taking all the credit—she'd only adapted what was already there after all.

The whole wedding party walked the short distance between the church and the *palazzo* where Bianca and Antonio were hosting their wedding reception. There had, Sophie gathered, been some heated family debate on the venue, the Santoros wanting to hold it at the family home, but Bianca preferring a neutral venue—and for she and Antonio to pick up the tab. 'Mamma wants to control every little detail as it is,' she'd explained to

Sophie. 'The only way I can guarantee having things the way I want them is to pay for it myself.'

And goodness knew what she had paid. The couple had taken over one of the most illustrious hotels in Venice for the evening, demanding sole use of the fourteenth-century *palazzo* for their guests. Sophie had been intimidated by the faded glory of the Santoro home, but this fully restored *palazzo* took her breath away, from the bright frescos adorning every wall and ceiling to the marble staircase, the huge terrace overlooking the Grand Canal, furnished with tables, chairs and throws to wrap around the hardier wedding guests venturing out in the January chill, to the ballroom in which the reception was being held. This was an immense room, decorated with elaborate, huge gold frescos, the ceiling high above adding to the feeling of grandeur and space. She had waitressed at some glitzy events over the last eighteen months, had seen some fabulous occasions, but nothing came close to the sheer grandeur of this wedding, this room, this family.

What on earth was she doing here?

'Signorina Bradshaw?' She jumped at a gentle tap on her elbow, turning to see a petite brunette with a wide smile, conservatively dressed in a smart, dark blue suit. 'Hello. I am Flavia, fashion reporter for *Marchesa* magazine.'

That was another unexpected facet to today's wedding. She had known the Santoros were rich, had known that the family was old Venetian blue blood, but it simply hadn't occurred to her that there would be outside interest in the wedding. It came as a shock when she realised several newspapers and magazines had been waiting outside the church and the high society *Marchesa* magazine had permission to cover the early part of the reception. Sophie resisted the urge to smooth down her dress and did her best to smile. 'Hi, yes, I'm Sophie Bradshaw.'

'You are here with Signor Santoro?'

'Erm…yes.' That wasn't exactly privileged information and Marco's mother had already announced it to pretty much the whole of Venice. The reporter looked at her expectantly and Sophie struggled to find something else to say. 'It was very kind of him to ask me along to such a beautiful occasion.'

There, she knew her role was to act as a buffer between Marco and his family's expectations, but at least she wasn't publicly staking her claim. The journalist didn't look convinced, raising a sceptical eyebrow before plastering on her smile. 'The big news is, of course, the wedding dress. Everyone has been raving over it and I hear you are responsible for making some big last-minute changes?'

Sophie paused. She didn't want to say that Bianca had put on weight and she certainly wasn't going to mention the pregnancy. 'I…'

'Sophie saved me.' The bride swooped down upon them, kissing Sophie exuberantly. 'My dress was beautiful, yes, but too plain for such an occasion, not entirely appropriate for a church wedding. And she took this beautiful dress and made it unique and special.' She twirled round, allowing the accompanying photographer to take pictures. 'Look at the stitching, and these beautiful buttons, and how she took it in here and here. She made the dress she's wearing too. Don't be fooled by how simple it looks. It is truly *elegante*.'

To Sophie's relief, once her photo had been taken, one with the bride and one posing self-consciously by herself by one of the three huge windows, the journalist moved away. Sophie scanned the crowds but couldn't see Marco anywhere and she couldn't face another round of being introduced as the new member of the family. It was probably a little futile checking her hair and make-up after the magazine had taken her photo, but she knew she needed a few moments to ready herself for the rest of the event.

She'd always found large social events intimidating, much preferring quiet evenings to a big crowd. Make the crowd larger, wealthier and effortlessly chic, add in a language she didn't speak and she was officially way out of her depth.

Luckily it didn't take her long to find the ladies' room. The door led into a large sitting area, filled with inviting-looking seats and sofas and several dressing tables, each piled high with cotton wool, hair spray and even straighteners for maximum primping. A door at the other end led to toilets and sinks and, as another guest came through, Sophie noted the opulence of the marble sinks and the gilt fittings. She suspected the individual toilet stalls might be bigger than her own shower room back in London—not that difficult: most cupboards were bigger than her shower room.

Sinking onto one of the sofas with a sigh of relief, Sophie told herself sternly she had five minutes to get herself together before heading back in. Things were coming to a head, that was all. She was leaving first thing tomorrow—really going this time—and she had to tell Marco about the baby before she did so. He hadn't mentioned anything about seeing each other in London, so she couldn't assume that there would be an easy opportunity to tell him once she was back.

She closed her eyes and wished, just for a moment, that things were different. That she and Marco really were as together as his mother assumed, that she would be joining this loud, overbearing, terrifyingly opinionated, loving, inclusive family. Not once had Sophie felt not good enough. Not when she hadn't known how to address the maid. Not when she couldn't follow the conversation, not when she admitted she made most of her clothes, not when Marco had realised she was worrying about money.

She'd never once felt good enough for Harry. Which was ironic because now she could see she was far, far too good for him.

If she weren't pregnant, would she act any differently? Be more honest about how she felt? It was too difficult to know; she *was* pregnant and although that made everything infinitely more complicated she couldn't be sorry. Besides, Marco's mother was right: she and Marco probably would make a beautiful baby.

Opening her eyes, Sophie jumped. Three terrifyingly elegant women had sat opposite her and were all staring at her in undisguised curiosity. She managed to raise a smile and said, 'Weddings are tiring, aren't they?'

They nodded as if one. All three were wearing their glossy, expensively cut hair down in the kind of swishy style Sophie always envied and were all dressed exquisitely in labels Sophie wasn't sure she'd ever seen outside glossy magazines.

The woman in the middle leaned forward, her eyes bright. 'May I ask you something?' she asked in heavily accented but perfect English.

'I suppose so,' Sophie said warily.

'How did you do it?'

'Do what? Bianca's dress? It was…'

'No,' the woman on the left interrupted her. 'Although that is very impressive. No, how did you tie Marco down?'

'How did I...? I haven't... I mean, we're not engaged.'

'Yet.' With a heavy emphasis. 'I dated him for three years. Mamma was planning my dress, Papà was ready to buy us our own house, and then *poof...*' the woman on the right clicked her fingers '...he was gone. He told me I had trapped him, that he didn't want to be tied down.'

Sophie's stomach lurched. Would he feel the same way when she told him she was pregnant? Trapped?

'I'm sorry to hear that.'

'I was humiliated, heartbroken, and he never told me why. Just left, went to England. Left me to pick up the pieces alone. I should hate him...' Her voice softened. 'I tell myself I hate him...'

'But you...' one of her friends chimed in.

'Everyone is talking about it...'

'Living at the *palazzo*, friends with his sister...'

'What's your secret?'

'I don't know whether to pity or admire you.'

'Or envy you.'

Sophie swallowed. Marco had been completely up front from the very beginning. He'd told her this was temporary, fun, a one-time thing, but at some point she'd allowed herself to hope for more. There was no point deceiving herself any longer. It wouldn't change anything. She was having his baby; he had to know. Those were the inescapable facts.

'I'm sorry,' she said. 'But I really have to go. If you'll excuse me?'

With a deep breath she got to her feet. It was time to find Marco—whatever happened next was entirely up to him.

CHAPTER TWELVE

MARCO SCANNED THE ROOM. One minute Sophie had been with his sister, the next she had completely disappeared. He was pretty sure she could take care of herself, but in a room that seemed to be comprised solely of his extended family and women he used to date, even the most hardened party-goer would need backup.

Hell, *he* needed backup. That was why she was here, wasn't it?

'Marco.' He jumped as she came up behind him, laying one pale hand on his sleeve.

'There you are. I was thinking you must have been cornered by my great-aunt Annunciata.'

'No, not yet. Look, could I have a word? In private?'

Her hand wasn't the only part of her that was pale. Her cheeks were almost white, her lips bloodless. Anger rose, hot and hungry. Had someone said something to hurt her? 'Is everything okay?'

'Yes, I just need to talk to you about something.'

Marco looked around. The door to the terrace was ajar and it looked as if nobody else was braving the sharp winter air. He took her hand, her fingers sliding into his as if they belonged there, and led her outside. Trees in pots lined the walls and vines twisted around the railings. He selected a table at the far end of the terrace and pulled out a chair for Sophie, tucking one of the blankets left out for the purpose around her shoulders as she sat.

'I was talking to some of the other guests just now. They all knew you.'

'Did they?' He raised his eyebrows. She sounded solemn. Solemn at weddings wasn't usually good.

'One of them was an ex-girlfriend of yours. She's a little bitter. Apparently you practically left her at the altar.'

Understanding dawned. 'You were talking to Celia, which I expect means she was flanked by Beatrice and Elena. They usually work as a team.'

'I didn't get their names.'

Something was off here and he couldn't work out what. 'It's a bit of an exaggeration to say I left her at the altar. We were never formally engaged.'

'So what happened? I deserve to know,' she added. 'If looks could kill, I'd currently be laid out on the floor of the women's bathroom and wedding guests would have to step over my corpse to get to the sinks.'

Marco rubbed his eyes wearily. Celia was so intrinsically mixed up with the events that had led to him leaving Venice, to the row with his father, that he'd done his best to not think of her at all over the last decade. He should have known he couldn't return home without the whole sorry business being dredged up again. 'It sounds like a bigger deal than it was,' he said, staring out at the Grand Canal, following a small open boat with his eyes as it cruised slowly opposite. 'Celia and I started seeing each other after I finished university. We were together for about three years.'

'She said you just disappeared.'

'It wasn't quite like that. She was pretty, a little crazy,

fun, all the things a man in his early twenties finds attractive. I guess I thought I was in love, thought she loved me, not that I had any idea what love was.' Bianca's words floated back to him. She was right; it had been infatuation, not love. He sighed. 'She was a welcome distraction from home. I was just starting out, collecting and reselling, developing a client list, building up a reputation, but my father thought I was wasting my time—and told me every chance he got.'

'That must have been difficult.'

'It was challenging,' he admitted. 'But I was young and driven and wanted my own path. I thought Celia agreed with me, but gradually I realised she wanted very different things. She didn't love the Marco Santoro who was passionate about his business and happy to start from scratch if he had to. She loved the Santoro heir with all the privileges that entailed and she kept pushing me to listen to my father. To give in.'

'But you didn't.'

'I didn't. So we'd argue, she'd cry, I'd feel guilty, we'd make up. It was an exhausting cycle mirrored by the constant battles with my father. Soon I realised she spent more time at the *palazzo* than I did, that she was shopping with Mamma and going out with Bianca, that she was already considered part of the family. Hints were dropped, more than hints, that a proposal would be nice. Her father took me aside and made noises about buying us a house as a wedding gift. Nonna presented me with her engagement ring and told me how proud I made her.'

Sophie put a cold hand on his. 'That must have been difficult.'

He'd been trapped. Each way he'd turned, an impossible choice. Give in and live a life he didn't want or stand firm and disappoint everyone who loved him. 'My life was just beginning. It should have been full of possibilities. Instead everyone I knew, everyone I loved, everyone I respected was trying to narrow it down, to cage me in. The girl I thought I was falling for had been replaced with a woman I didn't recognise, a woman who didn't want me as I was but wanted to change me, mould me.'

'But she didn't succeed. You walked away.'

Celia had succeeded in one way: she *had* changed him. All that youthful optimism and hope had been replaced with wariness; his home had become a prison.

'I decided I had to leave Venice. I couldn't carry on being scrutinised and criticised at every turn. I told Celia, gave her the option to come with me. She laughed at first, thought I was joking. When she realised I was serious…' He shook his head. 'The contempt in her eyes. I realised then that it was the package she wanted, not the man.'

'She was a fool.'

'She was ambitious. Oh, don't think I spent the next ten years weeping over my lost love. I was relieved more than heartbroken. Besides, it just confirmed what I already knew. That what I was mattered more than who I was and I was tired of it, tired of Venice, tired of all their expectations. So I went to see my father and told him I was done.'

'How did he take it?'

'Not well. He got so angry he collapsed with a suspected heart attack.'

'Oh, Marco.'

'And I went anyway. He was in the hospital and I packed my bags and left. I knew if I stayed the guilt would suck me in and I would never be free, so as soon as the doctors said he should make a full recovery I was out of Venice and starting again. I barely saw him after that, a couple of times a year of guarded pleasantries and then it was too late. For both of us.'

'I'm sure he knew you loved him. I'm sure he was proud of you.'

'Maybe.' Suddenly he was tired of it all. Of the guilt, of the uncertainty. 'All I knew was that I wasn't good enough. Not as a son, as an heir, as a partner. It's been easier—safer—not to get involved. Not to allow anyone to let me down. Allow anyone to look at me and tell me I'm not enough as I am.' Safer but ultimately unsatisfying. Short-term relationships, friendships based on business not deep-rooted companionship, family kept at arm's length. No wonder he'd worked eighteen hours a day, seven days a week. He'd had very little else.

He looked at Sophie as she stared out onto the Grand Canal, her profile sad and thoughtful, and for a moment he wondered what would happen if she told him he did matter, he mattered to her. Would he be able to believe her—or would he brush her off, turn away?

Time stood still, the air shimmering over the water while he waited an eternity for her to speak. She swallowed, a convulsive shudder, and her hand pressed on his, icy now in the winter chill.

'I don't believe you're not enough, Marco, at least I hope you are, more than enough. Not for me, I know that's not what you want, but for your child. I'm pregnant, Marco. I'm having a baby, your baby.'

CHAPTER THIRTEEN

SHE COULDN'T LOOK him straight in the eye. Instead Sophie stared at her hand, still covering his, gleaming pale white in the moonlight, and waited. Marco had stilled under her touch, turning to marble the second the words left her mouth.

'Pregnant?'

'Yes.' She waited for him to ask the obvious questions. *Are you sure? How do I know it's mine?* But they didn't come. Relief flooded over her as he nodded slowly.

Only to recede as he looked straight over at her, eyes hooded. 'Then we had better get married.'

It wasn't a question.

It was an assumption. Sophie's heart sped up.

'Married?'

'London would be best. Three weeks from now. We'll tell everyone we wanted to keep it quiet. We don't want this kind of fuss.' He shrugged in a way that encompassed all of Bianca's wedding.

No, Sophie didn't need three hundred guests, had no desire to book out an exclusive old *palazzo*, say her vows in a world-famous church. But when—if—she got married she would want her friends, her family there. She would want it to be a celebration of love, just as

Bianca was so clearly celebrating her love for Antonio today. Not a clandestine affair hidden from the world as if she were ashamed.

And if—when—she got married she wanted to be asked. She didn't need an extravagant proposal, but she would hope that any future husband wouldn't just *assume*…

'Marco, I…'

'Then we'll return here. You can live at the *palazzo*. You'll need family around you and you don't want to go back to Manchester. Besides, I need to be either here or London, so it has to be Venice. I can sell the London house, get a flat for when I'm there. I will have to travel a great deal, another reason why you'll need my family close by.'

That was how he saw her future, was it? Here in Venice, safely tucked away with his family, the family he'd spent over ten years avoiding as much as possible, while he stayed in London.

She opened her mouth, but he ploughed on. 'I don't think we should tell anyone anything yet. You can go back to London as planned tomorrow. I'll be back in a week. I'll arrange for somebody to move your things into my house this week.'

It was obviously all decided. All taken care of in less than a minute's decision-making. It didn't matter what she thought, what she wanted. She was a problem to be taken care of. A problem he had solved in record time.

It wasn't that she didn't love Venice, that she couldn't imagine living here, although she wasn't sure she would ever feel at home in the huge, ancient *palazzo*. It wasn't that she didn't adore Marco's family, overbearing as they were, because she did. But it had taken Sophie far too long to get to the point where *she* made the decisions about her life. She wasn't about to hand over control to someone else. Just go along meekly with his plans like an obedient little wife.

'Marco, stop. We don't need to decide all this now.' She couldn't help the slight emphasis on the 'we'. 'Let's take a few days to think about it and talk about it then, when you've had time to digest everything.'

He got to his feet, body half turned away, the message clear; this conversation was over. 'There's nothing to decide. Look, Sophie, you might not like it. You don't have to like it. This doesn't fit my plans either.' Hurt lanced through her at his cold tones, at each distinct word. 'But what's done is done and we need to act like adults, put our own preferences aside.' He smiled then, a wintry half-smile that left her colder than his earlier bleakness. 'We get on well enough. We have chemistry. There are worse foundations for marriage.'

'Yes, but there are better foundations too.' She looked up at him, putting every ounce of conviction she had into her voice. 'Marco, it's the twenty-first century. We can both be involved, be good parents without needing to be married. We don't need to live together, or even *be* together. We just need to respect each other and work together. I need you to listen to me, to consult me, not to make pronouncements that affect my entire life and expect me to jump to.' Sophie could hear the quiver in her voice and swallowed, holding back the threatened tears. 'I know you don't want to get married and so thank you for suggesting it. But I don't think a reluctant marriage is the best thing for me or for the baby.'

She stood up, the blanket slipping off her shoulders as she did so. 'I am heading back to the *palazzo*. Please make my apologies to Bianca. I'm going to get my plane tomorrow and I'm asking you to give me some space.

Please don't come to my room tonight or offer to drop me off in the morning—I think we both need some time to think. Think about what's best for *all* of us.'

Head held high, she touched him lightly on the cheek before turning and walking away. She'd been expecting anger or denial. Not this cold acceptance. But secretly, buried so deep down she'd hardly been aware of it, she'd been hoping for more. Maybe not love, she wasn't that much of a fool, but liking. An indication he wanted to be with her. Not cold, hard duty.

But it looked as if cold, hard duty was all he had to offer—and it wasn't enough. She deserved more—even if her heart was breaking as she turned and walked away. But better a cracked heart now than a lifetime with someone who didn't want or respect her. Better a cracked heart than allowing someone to dictate her life. Because she'd allowed that to happen twice, and she'd had to fight to be free twice. Last time she'd vowed never again and she'd meant it. She meant it now. No matter how much it hurt.

CHAPTER FOURTEEN

'I CAN'T BELIEVE there are so many photos of you. It's like Marco and his family are famous!' Ashleigh was once again searching through Italian gossip sites on Sophie's laptop.

'Not famous exactly, it's just they're a really old family. A really old rich family. A bit like minor royalty.' Sophie turned her head, not wanting to catch a glimpse of Marco, even on screen. He hadn't texted, hadn't called. A week of radio silence. She'd asked for time, asked for space, but this was beginning to feel a lot like punishment. 'Marco and Bianca are gossip-column staples. Her wedding was a big deal. Not that I knew that when I offered to fix her dress. I'd have been far too terrified.'

'So that makes you the mother-to-be of minor royalty,' Grace said.

'I can't believe you're pregnant.' Emma was staring at Sophie's stomach. 'You haven't put on an ounce.'

'I have, many ounces, but half of it is Italian food,' Sophie pointed out, but Emma's words brought her situation home. It was too easy, back in the safety of her flat, of her routine, to hide from her future. But that future was growing rapidly and she couldn't hide it for much longer. 'And I can't believe it either. There are moments when I'm thrilled—and then I start panicking again. I don't know how to be a mother. It's not like I have the best relationship with mine.'

'Sure you know how,' Ashleigh said with a soft smile. 'You know how to be an awesome friend. You're over halfway there.'

'Besides…' Emma jumped to her feet and stepped over to give her a hug. Sophie leaned gratefully on her shoulder, glad of the support. 'You have us. We're going to be the best team of aunties-stroke-fairy-godmothers any child ever had. You're not alone, Soph. Don't ever think it.'

'And I wouldn't worry about your future. I predict amazing things,' Grace said, wrestling the laptop away from Ashleigh. 'Not only is the whole of Italy wild about the alterations you made to Bianca's dress, but they love the going-away outfit you made her too. I've seen dozens of blogs and articles raving about it. Now your website is finally going live…' she shot a mock stern look at Sophie '…and people can actually *order* your clothes, success can't be far away.'

'Long-deserved success,' Ashleigh chimed in, holding up her cup of tea in a toast.

Sophie blinked back tears. Not only had her friends collected her from the airport, smothered her with affection, tea and cake, waited patiently until she had been able to find the words to tell them about the baby—and about Marco and her feelings for him—but they had also gently encouraged her to capitalise on her new-found design fame, helping her put the finishing touches to her website and testing it for her so when it went live—any second now—she could be confident it worked. Ashleigh had also helped her organise her space in the tiny flat so that finished designs could be photographed in a clutter-free space and her material was neatly stacked, giving her more room to work. Potential customers could either choose from her small collection of existing stock or order by design, choosing the material they liked best from her assortment of vintage prints or sending their own for her to make up.

One day she would like to have a larger collection of ready-to-buy stock—but for that she would need a studio and storage, possibly a couple of seamstresses. No, tiny steps were best. If she could just make enough to keep herself and the baby afloat, then she would have options; she didn't want to need Marco's money. She *would* like his emotional support though.

Which was ironic—he had money to spare but support, real support, was much harder for him. Maybe too hard.

'Right, we have to get off.' Ashleigh hauled herself to her feet. 'Are you sure you don't want to come, Sophie?' Grace's fiancé was hosting a glamorous fundraising event at his hotel and all three of her friends were attending. Funny to think that just a few months ago they would probably have all been waitressing for it.

Which reminded her, she needed to discuss hours and jobs with Clio. Heavy cleaning and too much standing around were probably out, but Sophie wanted to ensure she had some steady income while the first orders came in. Her waitressing days weren't behind her yet.

'I'm sure. I'm exhausted by nine at the moment. Besides, I want to stalk my inbox and wait for an order.'

'It won't be long,' Grace said loyally, dropping a kiss onto her cheek. 'If you need a hand, well, I can't sew. Or cut out. But I am very good at parcels—and making tea.'

'You'll be my first port of call,' Sophie promised, kissing her back and then embracing Emma and Ashleigh in turn.

The flat felt larger without her friends—a little larger—and a lot emptier. Sophie put her laptop on the kitchen counter and refreshed her email. Nothing. Maybe her friends were wrong, maybe the publicity and excitement over Bianca's wedding dress and the two-piece, sixties-inspired going-away outfit she had gifted the bride were just a storm in a teacup and wouldn't translate into sales.

But she couldn't believe that, wouldn't believe it. After all, photos of Bianca were everywhere and not just in the Italian press; a few British sites had picked up the chatter about the 'London-based designer' and had run short pieces extolling her as one to watch. Every piece used the same photo, taken at the wedding, Sophie in her grey dress smiling up at Marco, handsome in his tuxedo. Her heart turned over at the picture. They looked so happy, so together—to a casual observer as if they were head over heels in love. But she wasn't a casual observer.

Impatient to shake her bad mood, Sophie grabbed her pad and pencil. The success of Bianca's wedding dress made her wonder if there might be more bridal commissions in her future and she wanted to be prepared…

Stretching, she realised she'd lost track of time. Over two hours had passed while she'd sketched her first attempts at twenties-, fifties- and sixties-inspired bridal gowns. Not too bad, she decided, standing back and taking a fresh look. She'd like to get some samples started soon, a heavy silk for the twenties dress, lace and chiffon for the fifties dress and embroidered velvet for the sixties-inspired design.

As she moved the pad further away her hand knocked

the keyboard and her laptop screen blared into life, opening onto her brand-new inbox. Only, it wasn't empty as it had been when she last looked; no, there were four unopened emails sitting there and they didn't look like spam… With a trembling hand she clicked on one and scanned the message; would she be able to design a wedding dress and what were her fees?

Sophie took a deep breath; she'd been right to turn her attentions to bridal. The second was from a boutique here in Chelsea asking if they could discuss stocking some of her designs, the third another enquiry, this time for an evening gown. So far so good. No actual money but the possibility of work. The fourth, however, came from the automated payment system she had set up. She took a deep breath and clicked. 'Yes!' she shouted. 'Yes!' An order, a real order for two of her dresses, a shift dress in a polka-dot pink and a copy of the dress she'd worn to Bianca's wedding in a gorgeous green flowered cotton. She had done it! She was a real designer with real sales to people she didn't know.

She looked round, wanting to jump up and down, to babble her excitement into someone else's ear, to have someone else to confirm that, yes, the emails said exactly what she thought they said. But there was nobody there; her shoebox had never felt so spacious, never felt so lonely. She could text her friends, of course. They would be delighted. But, she realised, sinking back onto her stool, the euphoria draining away, she didn't want to impress them. She didn't need to witness their reactions.

She wanted Marco there, celebrating alongside her. She wanted to see him look impressed, to tell her how proud he was. But he was a long, long way away. Emotionally, physically, in every way that mattered. She'd thought she'd been lonely in the past, but it didn't compare to how she felt now. Completely and utterly alone. She couldn't let that stop her. She'd pulled herself back from the brink before, she could do it again. Besides, it wasn't all about her, not any more. She had to be strong for the baby—she simply had no other option.

Marco took another look at the address. He hadn't thought too much about where Sophie lived, but he'd assumed it would be in a flat in one of Chelsea's leafy streets, possibly sharing with a couple of friends. Not on this noisy, busy road, cars honking horns impatiently as they queued three abreast, fumes acrid in the damp air.

'Number one eight one,' he muttered, coming to a stop outside the right building. There was a takeaway on the ground floor and Marco grimaced as the scent of greasy fried chicken assailed him. The door to the flats was a dingy green, the doorstop covered in thrown-away boxes and discarded chicken bones. No way was any child of his growing up here, he vowed.

He scanned the names, almost illegible against the long list of buzzers, but before he found Sophie's name, the door opened and a young woman barged out, leaving the door ajar. Marco added security to the list of undesirables and shouldered it open. He needed Flat Ten. He looked at the door at the end of the ground floor—number one. It looked like he was going up…and up and up. Another item for his list: too many stairs. How on earth did she think she would cart a baby up here?

It was easier to list all the reasons for Sophie to move than it was to face the other list, the list that had brought him to the door. The list that started with how big, how lonely his bed felt every night, the list that included how much he missed her. The list that concluded that he didn't want to live in the Chelsea house or Venice on his own. The list that told him he had reacted badly to the news of her pregnancy, that he might be a little too convinced of his own eligibility, possibly bordering on arrogant where his marriage prospects were concerned. He patted Nonna's ring, secure in his top pocket. He would do better this time. He had to.

Finally he made his way to the top floor. Sophie's door was the same dull navy as all the other flat doors, but the handle was polished and two terracotta pots filled with lush greenery brightened the narrow landing. Marco shifted, nervous for the first time since he had boarded the plane this morning fired up with purpose. Before he could start listing why this was a bad idea he raised his hand and knocked firmly at the door.

'Mr Kowaski, have you forgotten your keys again? It's okay, I... Oh.' The door was fully open and Sophie stood there, shock mingling with something Marco couldn't define but hoped might be pleasure. 'How did you get in?'

'A neighbour.'

'They're not supposed to just let people... Not that it matters. Come on in.'

She stepped back and Marco entered her flat. There wasn't much of it, a small attic room, a large dormer window to the right the only natural light. A sofa ran along the wall to his left, opposite him a narrow counter defined the small kitchen, a high table barely big enough for two by the window. He'd been on larger boats.

The furniture was old and battered, but the room was scrupulously clean, the cream walls covered in bright prints and swathes of material, the sofa heaped with inviting throws and cushions. Along the wall adjoining the window a clothing rail lined up, dresses hanging on it in a neat row and drawings and patterns were pinned up on a huge easel.

There was no door between the living space and her bedroom, just a narrow archway. Through it he could see a single bed and two more rails bulging with brightly patterned dresses and skirts.

He walked over to the nearest rail and pulled out the first dress. Just like the outfit she'd worn to Bianca's wedding—just like everything he'd seen her in—it was deceptively simple. She obviously took her inspiration from the past, each outfit having a vintage vibe, but the detailing and cut gave it a modern twist.

'So this is what you do.' She'd said she wanted to be a designer, he'd seen her work first-hand, but he hadn't appreciated just how talented—just how motivated—she was, not until he stood in the tiny flat, more workspace than home. He'd met so many Chelsea girls over the last few years, women with family money who pottered around playing at being designers or artists or jewellers. He'd assumed Sophie belonged to their tribe, although looking back the signs were there: how careful she was with money, how little she spoke about her family. It was painfully clear how much he'd misjudged her, how little he knew about her.

'This is what I do. It's taken me a long time to get even this far. I don't make a living from it yet. In fact…' she took a deep breath '…I owe you an apology. I didn't mean to mislead you…'

'About what?'

'When we met, that first night. I was at the party but not as a guest. You didn't see me because I was invisible—I was waitressing there. I was supposed to be waitressing at the Snowflake Ball as well. Only, my friends played fairy godmother and bought me a ticket.

That's how I make ends meet, have done since I moved to London. I work for Maids in Chelsea, cleaning, shopping, bar work—whatever is needed.'

Her blue eyes were defiant, her chin tilted, hands bunched on her hips. 'You worked and produced all this? When did you find time to sleep? To eat?'

The defiance dimmed, replaced with relief. 'Sleep's overrated.'

'You didn't lie. You told me you were a designer. Looking at all this, I'd say that's exactly what you are. These are incredible.'

'Thank you.' She twisted her hands together. 'But you didn't come here to pay me compliments. I know we need to talk, but it's late and I'm really tired. Could we meet tomorrow and do this then?'

She did look exhausted, he realised with a pang of guilt. Purple shadows darkened her eyes, her hair, twisted up into a loose ponytail was duller than usual, her lips pale. She looked more vulnerable than he'd ever seen her and he ached for the right to take care of her. She was carrying his child. *His.* It was almost impossible to imagine, her body still slender, seemingly unchanged, and yet his blood thrilled at the realisation. He'd been running from this commitment for so long yet now he was confronted with the actuality he was filled with a primal joy. A determination to do better, be a better father than he had been a son, to not make the same mistakes his own father had made but to love his child no matter what their aspirations, who they wanted to be.

'We can, but I just need to say one thing. I'm sorry for how I reacted, when you told me about the pregnancy. It was such a shock, so unexpected. I needed to fix it, solve it. That's what I do.'

'I understand.'

'I made assumptions about you, about us. That was wrong. But I've missed you, Sophie. All this week I keep turning to speak to you, to see your reaction, and you're not there. That's my fault, I know, and it's up to me to make things right.' It was his turn to take a deep breath. He had never thought he would ever reach this point, but now he was here it made sense as nothing had ever made sense before. Maybe this was destined, the meeting in the snow, the baby, bringing him to this point.

Reaching into his top pocket, he pulled out the small black box. Sophie's eyes widened and she retreated back a step, but he took her hand in his, sinking to one knee like an actor playing his part. 'Sophie, it would make me very happy if you would do me the very great honour of becoming my wife.'

He smiled up at her, waiting for her agreement.

'No. I'm sorry, Marco, but I can't.'

CHAPTER FIFTEEN

SOPHIE STEPPED BACK one more step, pulling her hand free of his. A chill of loneliness shivered through her and she had to fight the urge to tell him she'd changed her mind, of course she would marry him. But he wasn't here for her, not for Sophie Bradshaw, he was here for the mother of his child. Here because it was the right thing to do. And she appreciated that, she really did. But she couldn't stake the rest of her life on it. 'I'm sorry,' she repeated.

Marco slowly straightened, regret mingled with anger and embarrassment clear on his face. 'I see.'

Ten minutes ago all Sophie had wanted was the coolness of her newly washed sheets, to burrow under her duvet and fall into the kind of heavy, dreamless, all-encompassing sleep her body demanded. She'd asked him to wait until tomorrow, told him she was tired and yet he'd still overridden her wishes. The only difference from last week's conversation was that this time Marco had couched his demand for marriage as a request.

A request he clearly expected her to acquiesce to.

No, nothing had changed. 'I appreciate that you think getting married is the right thing to do, especially knowing how you feel about marriage, but I can't.'

Eyes grim, mouth narrowed, he nodded once. 'Then

there's nothing else to say.' Marco turned, clearly heading for the door, out of her flat and potentially out of her life. Out of their child's life.

Sophie wavered, torn. She wanted him involved, but he expected so much, too much. But, dammit, she knew she owed him an explanation; after all, it wasn't his fault it wasn't enough for her. At least a dozen women at the wedding would have leapt at his first decisive statement; they'd have swooned at a ring and a bended knee—after saying yes, of course. 'Would you like a drink? I think I have a beer in the fridge.'

He stilled, stopped. 'That would be nice, but you're tired.'

'I am, but you're here now. Sit down.' She nodded at the sofa. 'I'll bring you a beer.'

Sophie busied herself for a few minutes, opening the beer, making herself a peppermint tea and pouring some crisps into a bowl and setting it on the tiny portable all-purpose table, before sinking into the sofa next to him. Next to him but not touching. She pulled her legs up before her, propping her chin on her knees, her arms hugging her legs, wanting the warmth, the support. Neither spoke, the silence neither hostile nor comfortable, more a cautious truce.

'I owe you an honest explanation, at the very least,' she said after a while. 'It's not easy for me to talk about, even to think about. I'm not very proud of my past.'

His eyes flickered at that, but he didn't say anything. Instead he took a long drink from the bottle of beer and settled back against the sofa, his gaze steady as he watched her. Sophie stared past him, her eyes fixed on the wall behind him, tracing the colours in the material hanging there, following the pattern round and round. 'For most of my life I thought my only value was in how happy I made others. My parents weren't cruel, not at all. I had everything. Private school, lovely clothes, everything I needed except for freedom, except for autonomy. My mother liked a project, you see. She's very determined, very focussed.' She smiled. 'I often wonder what will happen when she meets your mother. They'll be the definition of the unstoppable force versus the immoveable object. Scientists should study them under test conditions.'

She sipped her tea, her gaze still fixed on the material. It was hard to untangle her feelings about her mother; they were so complicated. She'd been so loved, Sophie knew that. But the burden of expectation had been crushing and Sophie wasn't sure she'd ever stop being resentful, stop wishing for a more carefree childhood. A childhood that had prepared her for adulthood instead of leaving her wide open and vulnerable.

'I think I mentioned before that I was born quite a long time after my brothers. It was like being an only child in many ways and I was quite isolated. My mum liked to pick out my friends, my clothes, my activities, and I soon learned that my role in the family was to make her happy—and she was happy when I did exactly what she wanted. It's dangerous, linking love to approval, making a child feel that it's conditional. And that was very much how I felt. I didn't dare complain, I didn't dare disagree because when I had her approval I knew I was loved. But I wasn't happy. My school was quite a long way away from my home and I was dancing most evenings from a young age, so I didn't have many friends. Ashleigh was my closest friend, but I only knew her for a short while and then her family moved back to Australia. By the time I hit my mid-teens I was a bit of a loner and really naïve.

'My mother had planned for me to apply for professional training when I was sixteen—but I think I told you in Venice that my heart wasn't in it. It was the first time I had said no, first time I'd let her down and she didn't hide her disappointment in me. But I felt free for the first time. I started to go out, to gigs to see local bands, to make my own clothes and find my own look. The more I started to work out who I wanted to be, the harder she tried to hold on. We had such terrible, horrible rows, said nasty, vicious things.'

They had both been guilty, she knew that. But Sophie had still been a child in many ways and her mother had left her in no doubt that she wasn't good enough, not any more. That Sophie's own style, her own wishes, her own hobbies were wrong and behind her bravado her fledgling self-confidence had begun to crumble.

'That was a long time ago. How are things now?'

'Fragile,' she admitted. 'Uncomfortable. That's why I rarely go back to Manchester.' She found a smile. 'See, we do have some things in common.' But their solutions to their family problems had been drastically different. Marco had taken control of his life, made a huge success out of his passions, his business. Sophie? She had run from one controlling situation to another.

She took another sip of the comforting tea and tried to order her thoughts. She hadn't spoken about Harry since the day she had finally come to her senses and walked out of the door. If she told Marco, it would be like probing a wound to see if it had really healed or still bubbled with infection.

'Like I said, I was a bit of a loner and really naïve. Ripe to be exploited. I met Harry at one of his gigs. He was the singer—all brash confidence and raw sexuality. I had never seen or spoken to anybody like him before and I was besotted before we even spoke. When he singled me out I thought I was the luckiest girl alive. It was every teen cliché come true. My parents hated him, of course. He was older than me for a start, arrogant, entitled. Looking back, he was just really rude, but I thought he was authentic and being true to himself. The more they tried to stop me seeing him, the more attractive he got.'

'How old were you?'

'Seventeen, a really young seventeen. I thought I was Juliet, of course, brimful of forbidden love.' Her mouth twisted into a wry smile. 'There is nothing more guaranteed to drive your hormonal teenaged daughter into the arms of a complete sod than to try to stop her seeing him. If they'd relaxed and made him welcome, or at least pretended to, maybe I'd have seen the truth a lot sooner.'

Maybe.

'Things were tense for a year. Home was like a battlefield, every sentence an ambush. My parents couldn't cope. Their sweet, biddable daughter had been replaced by a foul-mouthed hellion. I drank, stayed out all night, ditched school—and of course Harry encouraged me all the way. It shouldn't be an excuse, but, remember, I needed approval to feel loved and Harry's approval was intoxicating. I lived for it—and he knew it. Eventually my dad put his foot down in a "not in my house, young lady, you live in these walls you obey my rules" kind of way and I said "fine". Packed my bags and walked out the day I turned eighteen.'

He echoed her thoughts. 'We're both runaways, then. You're right, we do have something in common.'

'Only, you moved to a new city and started a successful business. I moved into a squat three miles away and became a cook, cleaner, cheerleader and paid heavily for the privilege. Harry had me exactly where he wanted me. My original plan had been to go to college and study art and textiles while living with him, but he persuaded me I'd be wasting my time. That I wasn't that talented, that original.' To her horror she could feel the tears gathering in her eyes and swiped her sleeve angrily against them. 'He said I'd be of more use getting a job so we could get a flat—obviously he was too busy being a musician to dirty his hands with real work. So instead of college I worked in a greasy spoon café. I was there for six years. I paid for our flat and our food. I cleaned our flat. I cooked our food. I soon learned not to ask Harry to do anything, not to expect anything from him. Including fidelity.'

She swiped her eyes again. 'I know what you're thinking because I'm thinking it too. Why did I put up with it? Why did I let him treat me that way? I think it every day. He made me feel like I was completely worthless, that I couldn't do anything, be anyone without him. That I was lucky to have him. And I believed him. The worst part is that every now and then he'd do something sweet, remind me why I fell in love with him in the first place. I lived for those moments, craved them, would lie there every night he didn't come home and relive every one of them.'

His hands had curled into fists and a primal part of him welcomed his anger. 'He didn't deserve you. You know that, right? You left, you got away.'

'Eventually. We were at a wedding and when he saw the head bridesmaid his tongue was practically hanging out. I'd turned a blind eye to his flings before, but when he kissed her on the dance floor—in front of his friends and family—I knew I had to get out before he destroyed me completely. I called a taxi, packed my things and went straight to the train station. I didn't trust myself not to waver if I saw him.'

'That was very brave.'

'I was running on adrenaline,' she admitted. 'If I'd thought about what I was doing, moving on my own to a city I didn't know, to a place where I knew no one, I would have just given up.'

But he was shaking his head. 'You're stronger than you think, Sophie. When I look at you I don't see a victim or weakness. I see a survivor. I see resilience. I see strength.'

Warmth flooded through her, not just because of his words but because of the respect she saw in his eyes. 'It's been a slow journey, Marco. I don't feel strong, not all the time. I've worked really hard to get to this place. My flat is tiny and horribly overpriced, but *I* pay the rent for me. It's my home, my sanctuary. I've finally put my designs out in the world. I have friends here, good friends. I'm my own person.'

'You'd still be your own person if you married me. I wouldn't stand in your way.'

She would give anything to believe him—but she didn't. 'When I told you about the baby you went into decision-making overdrive. We would do this, I would do that, this is how it would be. I know you were thinking of me and the baby, but I can't live like that, Marco, not again.'

He had paled, his eyes hard. 'You think I'm like your ex? That I would control you? Put you down?'

'No, no...' She reached a hand out to him. 'You're nothing like Harry. Your kindness was one of the first things I lo...liked about you. But you do like things your own way. That's why you moved to London in the first place. You're used to being in charge and I won't risk losing myself. I won't be the peacemaker, the compromiser again. I can't.'

She needed him to understand, desperately hoped that he did, but his mouth was grim.

'I understand, Sophie, I really do. But this isn't just about you, not any more. You might not like it, but my role now is to take care of you and our baby and I won't let you push me aside. You've come a long way, but you need to learn to let go, to trust me not to hurt you.'

She opened her mouth to tell him she did, but she couldn't say the words. He sighed. 'There's a difference between protecting you and controlling you. I have to do the first, but I can promise you I'll never do the second. I'm here, Sophie, for you and for our baby and I'm not going anywhere. The sooner you accept that, the better. Thanks for the drink. I'll see myself out.'

She sat frozen as he got to his feet. Two seconds later the door clicked behind him and he was gone. Part of her was relieved he still wanted to be involved, that she wouldn't have to bring the baby up alone, but his parting words rang in her ears. *The sooner you accept that, the better.* He was wrong; she wasn't accepting anything and no man would ever tell her what she could or could not do ever again. 'Damn you, Marco,' she whispered as she got wearily to her feet, the cold bone deep inside her. 'Why didn't you ask me what I want rather than telling me what you think I need?'

He said he respected her, now she needed him to show it. It was a poor substitute for love, but Sophie suspected it was all she was going to get. The question was, would it be enough?

CHAPTER SIXTEEN

'ARE YOU SURE you don't want me to come with you? Hold your hand?'

Sophie smiled, touched at the concern in Ashleigh's voice. 'It's a scan. I don't think it hurts.'

'That's not the point,' her friend said firmly. 'It's a huge moment, and on Valentine's Day too. You're going to need someone to hold the tissues.'

'I'm not dragging you away from Lukas on your first Valentine's Day. What kind of best friend do you think I am? Besides, it's different for you loved-up types, but I've never made a fuss about the fourteenth of February. It's just a day.'

Ashleigh's voice took on the dreamy tinge she always used when talking about Lukas. 'I think Lukas is planning dinner in Paris from all the not so subtle hints, but we can get a later train. I don't mind at all.'

'No, go to Paris, be happy and in love. I'll email you a picture of the scan, okay?'

'Only if you're sure.'

'More than sure. Now go and get ready to look surprised. *Au revoir.*'

'Email me straight away, love you.'

'I love you too.' Sophie clicked her phone off and suppressed a sigh. It would have been lovely to have her oldest and best friend with her when she met her baby for the first time, but there was no way she would butt in on Ashleigh's first Valentine's Day with Lukas.

She turned her phone over and over in her hand. She didn't *have* to go alone. After all, there was someone else who was probably just as keen to meet his baby. Their baby.

She hadn't met up with Marco at all over the last few weeks, partly because he was travelling and partly because he seemed to be respecting her request for space and time. It hadn't stopped him sending details through for potential flats and houses he 'wondered' if she might find more suitable or arranging a delivery service to supply her with home-cooked meals she just needed to heat up. She told herself that she should be mad at his officiousness, but she was so busy and tired the meals were a godsend and she couldn't help but concede he had a point about the flat. Hers was too small, too noisy and up too many flights of stairs.

The only problem was that every property he sent her was way, way out of her price range. She was pretty sure he was expecting to pay for wherever she moved to and knew that unless she suddenly sold every outfit she had made she was going to have to accept in the short-term at least. Necessity didn't make it easy though. 'For goodness' sake,' she told herself. 'At least he's not expecting you to support him. That's a huge improvement, right?' But much as it made sense it still felt like the first step on a very slippery slope.

She sighed. They did need to talk and a scan was a good, positive place to start. Before she could change her mind she called up his name and pressed Send. It was the right thing to do.

* * *

'*Buongiorno.*'

Marco scanned Sophie with a critical eye, nodding with satisfaction as he noted the shadows had disappeared from under her eyes and her cheeks had colour once more. Her hair was freshly washed and full of its usual bounce and her eyes no longer had the sad, defeated look he'd taken away with him when he'd left her a few weeks ago. 'You look beautiful.'

'Hi.' She smiled shyly at him and his heart squeezed. It had taken every single ounce of self-control he possessed not to call her or pop round over the last few weeks, but he had promised her, promised himself, that he would give her the control she needed, the time she needed. It had seemed like an eternity.

He'd thought he'd missed her when she left Italy, but that was nothing to the way he'd felt over the last few weeks. He'd thrown himself into work, but it had been almost impossible to concentrate when all he could think about was how he had blown it, how he had destroyed the best thing that had ever happened to him. Through arrogance, through ignorance.

Marco wasn't sure when he had fallen in love with Sophie, but he did know that this pain in his chest, the ache in his heart, the constant knowledge that something fundamental was missing, was love. He suspected he had fallen for her at some point in Venice. He was sure he loved her when he'd walked away from her flat, when he knew he'd let her down and had no idea how to fix it. When he'd decided that he had to respect her decisions, her choices, no matter how much it hurt him to do so.

He'd hoped that it would simplify things, but, looking at her nervous smile, he realised it complicated everything. If he told her how he felt, he suspected she would feel manipulated, think that he was saying what she wanted to hear, not what he felt, and after the last few weeks he wouldn't blame her.

He usually had all the answers, but today he had nothing. 'Thank you, for asking me here today.'

'I should have given you more notice. It's lucky you were in London.'

He hadn't left London, although he'd given her the impression he was away. He couldn't have left her if his business depended on it. What if she needed him and he was nowhere to be found? He'd let down one family member through pride. That was more than enough.

'I'd have found a way to get here. What do we do now?'

'We go in there, register, I have to drink lots of water and then we meet our baby. Ready?'

Our baby. The words hit him with full force. He, Marco Santoro, was going to be a father. Excitement mingled with pride filled him and he vowed he would do anything and everything to keep his child safe and secure. To make him or her happy. For the first time he understood why his mother fretted and planned and pressured him. Why his father had insisted he knew best no matter what Marco said or felt. They too felt this way; misguided as they might have been, they had just wanted to protect him. He just needed to remember that his version of happiness might not be the same as his child's. He took a deep breath. Yes, he was ready for fatherhood and all it entailed. '*Sì*, let's do this.'

'I can't believe this is our child.' Marco took another look at the black-and-white picture in disbelief.

'I know, it does look a little like an alien, doesn't it?

Do you think I got beamed up onto a spaceship and just didn't realise it?'

'Shh, the *bambino* will hear you. An alien indeed.' He snorted. 'With that nose? This is a Venetian baby for sure.'

'The next scan we can get in colour, you can properly see features and everything. Did you mind that they didn't tell us the sex? We could go for a private scan if you wanted to find out.'

Hope flared at her casual use of 'we'. 'I don't mind either way. Do you want to know?'

'Yes and no,' she admitted. 'It would be handy for names, but I'm not really a pink for a girl, blue for a boy type. I just want it to be healthy and happy.'

'It will be.' He knew he sounded serious, but he would lay his life down for that little alien without even blinking.

They'd reached the hospital doors and Sophie paused. 'I know you're busy, but do you have to get back? I'm really grateful you've given me some time, but there's a lot of things we need to talk about. It's all feeling very real at the moment.'

'I can clear my diary.' He already had, but she didn't need to know that. 'Where do you want to go?'

'Anywhere outside. It's so nice to have a dry day after two weeks of rain, I want to take advantage of it.'

Marco agreed. The torrential downpours of the last two weeks had added to his impatience as he'd waited for Sophie to get in touch.

'I could eat though,' she added. 'Before I kept eating to stop me feeling sick. Now I just want to eat all the time because I am ravenous. The books tell me I need to be really healthy, but my body just wants carbs, the greasier and unhealthier, the better. You can tell the baby is half Italian the amount of pasta and pizza it demands.'

'I think I know just the place.' He hesitated. 'Unless you have somewhere in mind?'

'No, go ahead. And while we're talking about food, thank you for arranging for those meals. There have been times when I was too tired to even make toast. They have been brilliant.'

Marco exhaled. Bianca had announced her pregnancy shortly after he'd last seen Sophie and had mentioned how tired she was in the evening and what an effort making dinner was. The difference was she had Mamma taking around dishes of pasta and Antonio to cook for her; he'd hated to think of Sophie exhausted and hungry all alone. 'So the meals come under protective and not controlling?'

She nodded. 'They do. They also come under thoughtful and sweet. I really appreciate it.'

It was a start. If he had his way, she'd be living with him and wouldn't need to cope on her own. But he had agreed to respect her wishes—it didn't mean he couldn't make things a little easier for her though.

Marco hailed a cab the second they left the hospital and gave directions as he opened the door for Sophie. Neither of them spoke as the taxi crawled along. It was barely three miles to their destination, but in London traffic that could mean an eternity. As they sat there Marco was assailed by homesickness for the city of his birth. Yes, Venice could be insanely crowded, but just five minutes on a boat and he could be in a deserted spot the tourists would never discover. London had been a wonderful adventure, the place where he had grown up, established himself, become a man in his own right, not just the Santoro heir, but he was ready to move on.

Except Sophie was here—and so his child would be here. Which meant London was his home too for the foreseeable future.

'I don't know this area at all.' Sophie was looking around as the taxi inched its way around Hyde Park heading north. 'I spent my first few nights in London at a cheap hotel near Euston while I looked for work and, once I had the job, rented a flat as close by the office as I could afford. Luckily I had a small savings account I'd kept from Harry—if he'd known, he'd have spent it on guitars or booze or a lads' holiday. I was saving up for a wedding or a baby. Luckily I came to my senses before either of those chained me to him, but it did mean I could afford the first six months' rent while I started to make a life for myself here. But I'm ashamed to say I haven't explored London much at all in the year and a half I've been here. I'm usually working for Clio or working for myself at home.'

She sounded so matter of fact, Marco couldn't imagine how hard it must have been starting afresh in a new city where she knew no one, had nothing. He had already had some contacts when he'd made the move over, a fledgling business and money enough to make the move easy and comfortable. Being his own man was so important to him, but, he acknowledged ruefully, it was easier to start from a position of privilege with a network of contacts than it was completely alone and from scratch. He might have the more successful business, the expensive house, the influential network, but Sophie had a grit and determination he could only hope to emulate and learn from.

He'd thought she was beautiful the first time he'd met her, shivering in the snow, enjoyed her company over the first couple of glasses of wine. He'd been intrigued by her lack of interest in pursuing a relationship with him, a refreshing attitude to his jaded soul, and been taken aback by her horrified response to his family's wealth and influence. There was a grounded realness to Sophie he hadn't come across before. Her experiences could so easily have made her bitter, but instead, although she maintained a guard over her emotions, she was willing and ready to embrace life, to try new things whether it was a small challenge like driving his boat or a huge one like motherhood. He wanted to be with her every step of the way. He just had no idea how to make her believe he meant it.

Marco was quieter than usual. Partly because, like her, he was overwhelmed by the scan bringing the baby to life before their eyes and partly, she suspected, because he was trying his best to show her that he had taken her wishes on board. How long he would manage to consult her before taking any step, from hailing a taxi to opening the door for her, she wasn't sure, but she was touched to see the effort he was making with such sincerity.

The taxi had dropped them off just north of Paddington by a canal filled, to Sophie's delight, with colourful narrowboats. 'They call this area Little Venice,' Marco explained. 'It isn't a patch on the real thing, naturally, but it has a real beauty of its own.'

'I love narrowboats,' Sophie said, staring around her with fascination. 'I've always wanted to live on one and travel from place to place, you know, with pots of herbs and flowers on the roof and maybe a dog.'

'Lovely in summer,' he said doubtfully. 'Probably less romantic in late November when it's been raining for weeks and you can't dry your clothes.'

'It's always sunny in my imagination.' They began walking along the towpath, Sophie peeking in at each boat they passed, squeaking in excitement when she spotted something novel whether it was a cat curled up in the sun or a riotous selection of flowers and vegetables covering the entirety of the boat.

He didn't say that the *palazzo* overlooked a canal on one side, that the terrace and courtyard were big enough to grow all the herbs and flowers she desired, that the heating kept it toasty warm in the colder months and the shuttered windows and thick walls provided shade and coolness in the summer. He didn't need to; she knew it as well as he did.

She knew there were plenty of empty salons just waiting to be put to use, rooms she could line with rails filled with her designs, a drawing board set up by the window, her sewing machine in one corner, a cutting-out table in the other. All that could be hers, she only had to say the word.

But space and money weren't enough. All she wanted, all she'd ever wanted was unconditional love. And for that she'd have gladly lived on a narrowboat through the fiercest of storms.

'There are several cafés on boats, one of which is an Italian deli run by a Venetian man. I can vouch for the quality of both his pasta and his bread. How hungry are you?'

Sophie considered. She could always eat, but was she actually hungry? 'You know, I think if I get a snack to sustain me I would rather walk first, eat afterwards. Is that okay?'

'Of course, it's still early. Why don't we walk up to Regent's Park and decide what to do next from there?'

After a black coffee for Marco and a bottle of sparkling water and a toasted ciabatta filled with mozzarella and tomatoes for Sophie at what was, she conceded, the best Italian café she had been to in London, they headed north towards Maida Vale and Regent's Park. The sun was warm, a gorgeous contrast to the dampness that had characterised most of February and added to the almost holiday atmosphere along the canal side. A family passed them, a baby snug in a sling against its mother's chest, a curly-haired toddler swung high on his father's shoulders. Sophie and Marco paused on the towpath to let them walk by and then stood looking after them as the couple chattered and laughed as they pointed things out to their small son.

Sophie's heart ached. Would she and Marco ever walk along with their baby in such compatible ease or would it be the polite handovers and lonely nights of a civilised joint custody?

'They look happy,' he said softly as if reading her mind.

'Yes.'

He put a hand on her shoulder and she looked up, surprised, to see a serious expression darkening his eyes. 'Sophie, I just want you to know that I am here for you, whatever you decide to do, however you decide to do it. I know how important your independence is to you. I admire…' he paused, a smile twisting his mouth '…I really admire how hard you've fought for it, fought for everything you've achieved. You should be so proud. I am. I just want you to know that.'

Sophie's heart began to speed up, her throat constricting as she listened to him.

'It's yours, whatever you need, my house in London or the *palazzo* in Venice or somewhere new. For me they are just places, but I want to help you find a home, the right home for you and the baby. If you'll let me. I don't have much else to offer, I realise that now. Strip away my name, strip away my family and there's not much there. I told myself that I didn't need them, that I was enough by myself, yet at the same time I coasted along comfortably on all they brought me. I admit, I didn't think I needed to ask whether you wanted to marry me or not. I'd spent so long running from marriage it didn't occur to me that you might turn me down, want something different for your life. I was an arrogant fool.'

His eyes, still steady on hers, were heavy with sadness and she impulsively lifted a hand to his cheek. 'No, you had good reason to feel that way. I was with you, at that wedding. I saw how people looked at you. I heard what they said. And if I was someone else, if I hadn't been so broken, then maybe I would have said yes. Maybe respect and chemistry would have been enough.'

He shook his head. 'No, you were right. Love is the only basis for marriage. It should be. It's hard enough to succeed at something so huge without starting out short. I didn't think I was the kind of man who could love, but you've taught me differently.'

Her pulse began to hammer so loudly the rest of the world was drowned out. Was he saying what she thought he was saying?

'I thought of love as selfish, as needy, as constrictive. I thought love meant giving up who you are, what you are. But now I know it means wanting the best for someone else regardless of the cost to you. Tell me what you need from me and I'll do it. Anything. All I want is to be the best father I can be to our child, to make you as proud of me as I am of you.'

All the surety had been wiped away, replaced with

a heartfelt expression and the kind of tenderness Sophie hadn't believed could exist in the world, not for her. Scarcely believing, she stared into his face and saw the truth blazing out. He loved her, not because of what she could do, nor because of how she made him feel, but because of who she was.

'Anything?' She couldn't believe her voice was so steady.

'Anything,' he confirmed.

'Then marry me.' She hadn't even known that was what she was going to say, but as soon as she said the words she knew they were right. That they were perfect. 'Marry me three weeks from now in a small ceremony here in London. Just like you wanted, only with the people we love and the people who love us celebrating with us because a wedding should be a celebration, always.'

'It should. I was a fool to think any differently. Sophie, are you sure? You don't have to do this.'

'Surer than I have ever been about anything. I love you, Marco. Saying no to you was the hardest thing I've ever done, but I couldn't be with someone who didn't love me again, not even for the baby.'

'You won't need to,' he vowed. 'Because I love you more than I ever thought possible.' He grinned. 'See how far I've come? My *machismo* is not even slightly dented by your proposal.'

'You did propose to me twice first,' she pointed out. 'Although the first time was more of a fait accompli than an actual proposal.'

Marco caught both her hands in his. 'Not only do I accept your proposal, but I'll make you a promise, here and now, as binding as any wedding vow. We're a team. I'll always remember that. I won't ever try to control you, try to stop you from fulfilling your dreams, from being the person you want to be.'

'That's all I need.' She laced her fingers through his; now she could hold on to him she didn't want to ever let go. 'That's all I ever needed. Your promise and you.'

And as he bent his head to hers to seal their bargain with a kiss Sophie knew she was home at last. London, Venice, a narrowboat cruising the country, wherever Marco was she would be too. She finally had a place of her own.

* * * * *

If you loved this story, make sure you catch the rest of the magical Christmas quartet
MAIDS UNDER THE MISTLETOE!

A COUNTESS FOR CHRISTMAS
by Christy McKellen

GREEK TYCOON'S MISTLETOE PROPOSAL
by Kandy Shepherd

CHRISTMAS IN THE BOSS'S CASTLE
by Scarlet Wilson

She knew that she didn't really owe him an explanation.

After all, he was a public servant and this had been done in the service of the public. The public had a right to know. But she had made him a promise, so she felt the need to explain why she'd gone back on it.

"I know I promised that you'd have the final say, but I've got people I answer to and they insisted that the segment go on tonight as is. It turned out pretty well, I thought." She crossed her fingers that he saw it that way, too.

"You lied to me." It wasn't an accusation but a flat statement. It carried with it not anger, but a note of genuine disappointment. And that made her feel worse than if he'd launched into a tirade.

"I didn't lie," she replied. "I had every intention of showing you the clip first." When he said nothing, she felt uncomfortable, despite the fact that this ultimately wasn't really her fault. "The station manager wanted to air it before the other stations got it. I'm sorry, but these things happen. Listen, if you want me to make it up to you—" she began, not really certain where this would ultimately go.

He cut her short with two words. "I do."

* * *

Matchmaking Mamas:
Playing Cupid. Arranging dates.
What are mothers for?

TWICE A HERO, ALWAYS HER MAN

BY
MARIE FERRARELLA

MILLS & BOON

First Published in Great Britain 2017
By Mills & Boon, an imprint of HarperCollins*Publishers*
1 London Bridge Street, London, SE1 9GF

© 2016 Marie Rydzynski-Ferrarella

ISBN: 978-0-263-92264-6

23-0117

Our policy is to use papers that are natural, renewable and recyclable products and made from wood grown in sustainable forests. The logging and manufacturing processes conform to the legal environmental regulations of the country of origin.

Printed and bound in Spain
by CPI, Barcelona

USA TODAY bestselling and RITA® Award–winning author **Marie Ferrarella** has written more than two hundred and fifty books for Mills & Boon, some under the name Marie Nicole. Her romances are beloved by fans worldwide. Visit her website, www.marieferrarella.com.

To Charlie
For stepping up
And
Taking care of me
When I couldn't.
After all these years,
You still manage to surprise me.

Prologue

"Oh, Maizie, it's just breaking my heart, seeing her like this."

Maizie Sommers quietly pushed the gaily decorated box of triple-ply tissues she kept on her desk toward her friend, waiting for the woman to collect herself. Connie Williams had called her first thing this morning, asking to see her.

Maizie knew from her friend's tone of voice that she wasn't asking to see her in her professional capacity—at least not in her professional capacity as an award-winning Realtor.

But Maizie had another vocation, an altruistic one that was near and dear to her heart, as it was to the hearts of her two dearest, lifelong friends, Theresa Manetti and Cecilia Parnell. All three were career women who did quite well in their respective chosen fields. But it was the one avocation that they had in common that brought them the most joy. The one that carried no monetary reward whatsoever, just one that made them feel good.

All three were matchmakers.

It had begun quite innocently enough. The three of them had been friends since the third grade. In the years that followed, they had gone through all the milestones of life together, great and small—not the least of which was widowhood. And all three were also blessed with children. Maizie had a daughter, as did Cecilia, while Theresa had a daughter *and* a son.

Their four children were all successful in their own rights—and they were also maddeningly single. Until Maizie decided that her daughter, an ob-gyn, needed more in her life than just delivering other people's babies. She needed a private life of her own. Joining forces with her two friends, Maizie began to closely monitor and review the wide variety of people all three of them dealt with.

Thanks to their professions—Theresa ran a catering company, while Cecilia had a thriving housecleaning service—Maizie quickly and secretly found the perfect "someone" for her daughter.

Theresa and Cecilia were quick to follow her example, and soon all three of *their* children were matched to their soul mates, as well.

Nothing bred more success than initial success and so a passion was born. Maizie, Theresa and Cecilia began helping the children of other friends, all while always managing to keep the principals involved in the dark, thinking it was fate rather than three very artful women that had intervened in their lives for the better.

So it didn't surprise Maizie at all to be sitting in her office today across from one of her friends, quietly waiting for the request she knew was coming. Connie wanted her to find someone for her daughter, a reporter with a prominent local news station.

Connie pulled out a tissue and wiped away the tears that had slid down her cheek despite her best efforts to the contrary.

"Ellie puts up a brave front and whenever I ask her, she tells me that she's fine, but she's *not* fine. A mother knows, Maizie," the older woman insisted, stifling a sob.

Maizie offered her an understanding smile. "Truer words were never spoken," she agreed. Then, gently, Maizie asked her friend, "How long has it been now?"

"Two years," Connie answered. She didn't even have to pause to think. She knew it to the exact day. Remembered how stricken her daughter had been when she'd found out that her husband, a recently discharged, highly decorated Marine sergeant had been killed while trying to save a couple who were being robbed at a convenience store.

"She goes on with her life, goes on with her career, but I know in my heart nothing's changed. If anything, she works harder these days, spends long hours both in the field on assignment and at the studio, overseeing the editing of her work, but it's like everything froze inside her since that day."

Maizie nodded. "I can imagine how awful it must have been for Ellie to find out that the news story she was being sent to cover involved her own husband."

There had been a mix-up when the story had come over the wire and the name of the hero of the piece had been accidentally switched for the name of the owner of the convenience store where the robbery had occurred. When Ellie and her cameraman had arrived on the scene, the ambulance had already come and gone. It wasn't until she was in the middle of covering the story, talking to the two grateful people her husband had saved, that her cell phone had rung. Someone from the hospital was calling her to notify Ellie that her husband had been shot and had died en route.

"Ellie went numb when the call on her cell came in. The poor thing barely kept from fainting in front of everyone. Her studio was exceedingly sympathetic, and Ellie, well, she just froze up inside that awful, awful night and she still hasn't come around, no matter what she tries to tell me to the contrary."

Connie looked at the woman she was counting on to change things for her daughter, her eyes eloquently entreating her for help.

"Maizie, she's only thirty years old. Thirty is much too young to resign from life the way she has. Ellie has so much to offer. It's just killing me to see her like this." Connie pressed her lips together. "If I say anything to her, she just smiles and tells me not to worry. How can I not worry?" she asked.

Maizie placed her hand over her friend's in a comforting gesture, one mother reaching out to another. "I'm glad you came, Connie. Leave this to me."

The woman hesitated, her gratitude warring with a host of other feelings—and one main one that she gave voice to now. "If Ellie knew I was trying to find someone for her—"

"*You're* not," Maizie pointed out. "Let me look into this and I'll get back to you," she promised. In her mind, she was already summoning her friends for an evening card game, happily telling them that they had a brand-new assignment of the heart.

Nothing was more satisfying to them—except, of course, for the successful execution of said operation.

Maizie couldn't wait.

Chapter One

It felt as if mornings came earlier and earlier these days, even though the numbers on the clock registered the same from one day to the next. Even so, it just seemed harder for Elliana King to rouse herself, to kick off her covers and find a way to greet the world that was waiting for her just outside her front door.

It wasn't always this way, she thought sadly. There was a time that she felt sleeping was a waste of precious hours. Those were the days when she would bounce up long before the alarm's shrill bell officially went off, calling an end to any restful sleep she might have been engaged in.

But everything had changed two years ago.

These days, her dreams were sadly all empty, devoid of anything. The first year after Brett had been taken from her, she'd look forward to sleep because that was when he visited her. Every night, she dreamed of Brett, of the times they'd spent together, and it was as if she'd never lost him. All she had to do was close her eyes and within a few minutes, he was there. His smile, his voice, the touch of his hand. Everything.

She'd been more alive in sleep than while awake.

And then, just like that, he wasn't. Wasn't there no matter how hard she tried to summon him back. And getting up to face the day, face a life that no longer had Brett in it, became progressively harder for her.

Ellie sat up in bed, dragging her hand through blue-black hair Brett always referred to as *silky*. She was trying to dig up the will to actually put her feet on the floor and begin her day, a day that promised to be filled from one end to the other with nothing but ongoing work. Work that was meant to keep her busy and not thinking—not feeling.

Especially not feeling.

Work was her salvation—but first she had to get there.

Still trying to summon the energy to start, Ellie glanced at the nightstand on her left. The nightstand that held her phone, the lamp that was the first piece of furnishings Brett and she had chosen together—and the framed photograph of Brett wearing his uniform.

A ghost of a smile barely curved her lips as she reached out to touch the face that was looking back at her in the photograph.

And without warning, Ellie found herself blinking back tears.

"Still miss you," she murmured to the man who had been her whole world. She sighed and shook her head. "Almost wish I didn't," she told him because she had never been anything but truthful with Brett. "Because it hurts too much, loving you," she admitted.

Closing her eyes, Ellie pushed herself up off the bed, taking the first step into her day.

The other steps would come. Not easily, but at least easier. It was always that first step that was a killer, she thought, doing her best to get in gear.

She went through the rest of her morning routine by rote, hardly aware of what she was doing or how she got from point A to point B and so on. But she did, and eventually, Ellie was dressed and ready, standing at her front door, the consummate reporter prepared to undertake a full day of stories that needed to be engagingly framed for the public.

She knew how to put on a happy face for the camera.

No one except those who were very close to her—her mother; Jerry Ross, her cameraman; and maybe Marty Stern, the program manager who gave her her assignments—knew that she was always running on half-empty, because her reason for everything was no longer there.

Several times Ellie had toyed with the idea of just bowing out. Of not getting up, not going through the motions any longer. But she knew what that would do to her mother and she just couldn't do that to her, so she kept up the pretense. Her mother, widowed shortly before Brett had been killed, would be devastated if anything happened to her, so Ellie made sure nothing "happened" to her, made sure she kept putting one foot in front of the other.

And just kept going.

"But sometimes it's so hard," she admitted out loud

to the spirit of the man she felt was always with her even if she could no longer touch him.

Ellie took a deep breath as she opened the front door. It was fall and the weather was beautiful, as usual. "Another day in paradise," she murmured to herself.

Locking the door behind her, she forced herself to focus on what she had to do today—even though a very large part of her wanted to crawl back into bed and pull the covers up over her head.

"I know that look," Cecilia Parnell said the moment she sat down at the card table in Maizie's family room and took in her friend's face. "This isn't about playing cards, is it?"

Maizie was already seated and she was dealing out the cards. She raised an eyebrow in Cilia's direction and smiled.

"Not entirely," Maizie replied vaguely.

Theresa Manetti looked from Cilia to Maizie. She picked up the cards that Maizie had dealt her, but she didn't even bother fanning them out in her hand or looking at them. Cilia, Theresa knew, was right.

"Not at *all*," Theresa countered. "You've got a new case, don't you?" She did her best to contain her excitement. It had been a while now and she missed the thrill of bringing two soul mates together.

"You mean a new listing?" Maizie asked her innocently. "Yes, I just put up three new signs. As a matter of fact, there's one in your neighborhood, Theresa," she added.

"Oh, stop," Cilia begged, rolling her eyes. "You know that's not what Theresa and I are saying." She leaned closer over the small rectangular table that had seen so many of their card games over the years as well as borne witness to so many secrets that had been shared during that time. "Spill it. Male or female?"

"Female," Maizie replied. She smiled mysteriously. "Actually, you two know her."

Cilia and Theresa exchanged puzzled glances. "Personally?" Cilia asked.

Maizie raised a shoulder as if to indicate that she wasn't sure if they'd ever actually spoken with her friend's daughter.

"From TV."

Cilia, the more impatient one of the group, frowned. "We've been friends for over fifty years, Maizie. This isn't the time to start talking in riddles."

She supposed they were right. She didn't usually draw things out this way. Momentarily placing her own cards down, she looked at her friends as she told them, "It's Elliana King."

Theresa seemed surprised. "You mean the reporter on Channel—?"

Theresa didn't get a chance to mention the station. Maizie dispensed with that necessity by immediately cutting to the chase.

"Yes," she said with enthusiasm.

"She didn't actually come to you, did she?" Cilia asked in surprise.

"A girl that pretty shouldn't have any trouble—" Theresa began.

"No, no," Maizie answered, doing away with any further need for speculation. "Her mother did. Connie Williams," she told them for good measure. Both women were casually acquainted with Connie. "You remember," Maizie continued, "Ellie was the one who tragically found out on the air that her husband had been killed saving a couple being held up at gunpoint."

Theresa closed her eyes and shivered as she recalled the details. "I remember. I read that her station's ratings went through the roof while people watched that poor girl struggling to cope."

"That's the one," Maizie confirmed. "As I said, her mother is worried about her and wants us to find someone for Ellie."

"Tall order," Cilia commented, thinking that, given the trauma the young woman had gone through, it wasn't going to be easy.

"Brave woman," Maizie responded.

"No argument there," Theresa agreed.

Both women turned toward Cilia, who had gone strangely silent.

"Cilia?" Theresa asked, wondering what was going on in their friend's head.

Maizie zeroed in on what she believed was the cause of Cilia's uncharacteristic silence. Maizie was very proud of her gut instincts.

"You have something?" she asked.

Looking up, Cilia blinked as if she was coming out of deep thought.

"Maybe," she allowed. "One of the women who work for me was just telling me about her neighbor the other day. Actually," Cilia amended, "Olga was making a confession."

"Why?" Theresa asked, puzzled.

Maizie went to the heart of the matter. "What kind of a confession?" she pressed.

"She told me she offered to clean the young man's

apartment for free because it was in such a state of chaos," she explained. "And Olga felt she was betraying me somehow with that offer."

Theresa still wasn't sure she was clear about what was going on. "Why did she offer to clean his place? Was it like a trade agreement?" she asked. "She did something for him, then he did something for her?"

"It wasn't like that," Cilia quickly corrected, guessing at what her friend was inferring was behind the offer. "She told me that she felt sorry for the guy. He's a police detective who's suddenly become the guardian of his ten-year-old niece."

Maizie was instantly interested. "How did that happen?"

"His brother and sister-in-law were in this horrific skiing accident. Specifically, there was an avalanche and they were buried in it. By the time the rescuers could get to them, they were both dead," Cilia told her friends. "Apparently there's no other family to take care of the girl except for Olga's neighbor."

Theresa looked sufficiently impressed. "Sounds like a good man," she commented.

"Sounds like a man who could use a little help," Maizie interjected thoughtfully.

Maizie took off her glasses and gazed around the table at her friends. Ideas were rapidly forming and taking shape in her very fertile brain.

"Ladies," she announced with a smile, "we have homework to do."

"But I don't need a babysitter," Heather Benteen vehemently protested.

"I told you, kid, she's not a babysitter," Colin Benteen told his highly precious niece, a girl he'd known and loved since birth. Life had been a great deal easier when the only role he occupied was that of her friend, her coconspirator. This parenting thing definitely had a downside. "If you want to call her something, call her a *young-girl-sitter*," he told Heather, choosing his words carefully.

"I don't need one of those, either," Heather shot back. "I'll be perfectly fine coming home and doing my homework even if you're not here." She glared accusingly at her uncle, her eyes narrowing. "You don't trust me."

"I trust you," Colin countered with feeling.

Heather fisted her hands and dug them into her hips. "Then what's the problem?"

"The problem is," he told his niece patiently, "that I know the temptation that's out there." He gave her a knowing look. "I was just like you once."

"You were a ten-year-old girl?" Heather challenged.

"No, I was a ten-year-old boy, wise guy," he told her, affectionately tugging on one of her two thick braids. "Now, humor me. Olga offered to be here when you come home and hang around until I get off."

She tried again. "Look, Uncle Colin, I don't want to give you a hard time—"

"Then don't," he said, cutting Heather off as he grabbed a slice of toast.

Heather was obviously not going to give up easily. "I don't like having someone spy on me."

"Here's an idea," he proposed, taking his gun out of the lockbox on the bookshelf where he always deposited his weapon when he came home at night. "You

can get your revenge by not doing anything notewor-
thy and boring her to death."

The preteen scowled at him. "So not the point,"
she insisted.

He wasn't about to get roped into a long philosophi-
cal discussion with his niece. She had to get to school
and he needed to be at work.

"Exactly the point," he replied. "Olga will be here
when I'm not, just as she has been these last few
weeks—and we're lucky to have her. End of discussion," he told her firmly.

"For there to have been a discussion, I would have
had to voice my side of it," she pointed out, all but
scowling at him in a silent challenge that said she had
yet to frame her argument.

Colin paused for a moment as he laughed and shook
his head. "Sue me. I've never raised a ten-year-old before and I want to get this right."

The impatient look faded from her face and Heather
smiled. She knew that they were both groping around
in the dark, trying to find their way. Her uncle had
always been very important to her, even before she'd
woken up to find that the parameters of her world had
suddenly changed so drastically.

She gave him a quick hug, as if she knew what
was really on his mind. Concern. "We'll be all right,
Uncle Colin."

"Yes, we will," he agreed. He pointed toward the
front door. "Now let's go."

For the sake of pretense, Heather sighed dramatically and then marched right out of his ground-floor
garden apartment.

* * *

Less than an hour later, Colin found himself halfway around the city, tackling a would-be art thief who was trying to make off with an original painting he'd stolen from someone's private collection in the more exclusive side of Bedford.

The call had gone out and he'd caught it quite by accident because his new morning route—he had to drop Heather off at school—now took him three miles out of his way and, as it so happened today, right into the path of the escaping art thief.

Waiting for the light to change, Colin saw a car streak by less than ten feet away from him. It matched the description that had come on over the precinct's two-way radio.

"Son of a gun," he muttered in disbelief. The guy had almost run him over. "Dispatch, I see the vehicle in question and I'm pursuing it now."

Turning his wheel sharply, he made a U-turn and proceeded to give chase. Despite his adrenaline pumping, he hated these chases, hated thinking of what was liable to happen if the utmost care as well as luck weren't at play here.

He held his breath even as he mentally crossed his fingers.

After a short time and some rather tricky, harrowing driving, he pursued the thief right into a storage-unit facility.

"You've got to be kidding me," he muttered under his breath. Did the guy actually believe he was going to lose him here? Talk about dumb moves...

He supposed he had to be grateful for that. Had the thief hit the open road, he might have lost him or

someone might have gotten hit—possibly fatally—
during the pursuit.

As it was, he managed to corner the man. Colin
jumped out of his car and completed the chase on foot,
congratulating himself that all those days at the gym
paid off. He caught up to the thief, who had uninten-
tionally led him not only to where he had planned on
hiding this painting that he'd purloined but to a number of others that apparently had been stolen at some
earlier date.

It took a moment to sink in. When it did, Colin
tried not to let his jaw drop. Things like this didn't
usually happen in Bedford, which, while not a sleepy
little town, wasn't exactly a hotbed of crime, either.

"Wow, you've been quite the eager beaver, haven't
you?" Colin remarked as he snapped a pair of hand-
cuffs on the thief's wrists.

"Don't know what you're talking about," the thief
declared. "Never saw these other paintings before in
my life," he swore, disavowing any previous connection.

"And yet you came here to hide the one you stole
this morning," Colin pointed out. "Small world,
wouldn't you say?"

"I never saw these before!" the slight man repeated
loudly.

Colin shook his head as he led the thief out to his
waiting car. "Didn't your mama teach you not to lie?"
he asked.

"I'm not saying another word without my lawyer," the thief announced, and dramatically closed
his mouth.

"Good move," Colin said in approval. "Not much

left to say anyway, seeing as how all these paintings speak for themselves."

Desperate, the thief made one last attempt to move Colin as he was being put into the backseat. "Look, this is just a big misunderstanding."

"Uh-huh."

Panic had entered the man's face, making Colin wonder if he was working for someone else, someone he feared. "I can make it worth your while if you just look the other way, let me go. I'll leave the paintings. You can just tell everyone you found them."

Colin smiled to himself. It never ceased to amaze him just how dumb some people could be. "Maybe you should have thought of the consequences before you started putting this private collection together for yourself." He saw the thief opening his mouth and sensed there was just more of the same coming. "Too late now," he told the man.

With that, he took out his cell phone and called in to the station for backup to come and collect all the paintings. There were going to be a lot of happy art owners today, he mused. They wouldn't be reunited with their paintings immediately, since for now, the pieces were all being kept as evidence, but at least they knew the art had been recovered and was safe.

He glanced at his watch as he waited for his call to go through.

It was just nine thirty, he realized. Nine thirty on a Monday morning. His week was off and running.

Chapter Two

Maizie put as much stock in fate as the next person. She didn't, however, sit back and just assume that fate would step in and handle all the small details that were always involved in making things happen. That was up to her.

Which was why she was on the phone that morning calling Edward Blake, an old friend of her late husband's as well as a recent client she'd brought to Theresa's attention. The latter had involved Edward's youngest daughter, Sophia. Theresa had catered her wedding reception at less than her usual going rate.

Maizie used that as her opening when she placed her call to the news station's story director.

What had prompted her call was a story she heard on her radio as she was driving into work. The opportunity seemed too good to pass up. That, she felt, had been fate's part. The rest would require her help.

"Edward," she said cheerfully the moment she heard him respond on the other end of the line, "this is Maizie Sommers."

There was a pause, and then recognition set in. "Maizie, of course. How are you?"

"I'm well, thank you," she replied as if she had all the time in the world rather than what she assumed was a clock ticking the minutes away. She knew how the news world worked. "I just called to see how the newlyweds were doing."

"Fine, fine," Blake asserted in his booming baritone voice. "They're not looking for a house yet, though," he told her, obviously assuming that was why she was checking in with him.

"No, I wouldn't think so," she answered with a laugh. "It's much too early to start thinking about dealing with things like escrow and closing costs and homeowner associations." She paused for just a beat, then forged ahead. "But I did call to ask you a favor."

Their friendship dated back to the final year in college. Edward had been a friend of her late husband's. They had pulled all-nighters, helping each other study and pass final exams. "Name it."

"That news reporter you have working for you, Elliana King," Maizie began, then paused so that the woman's name sank in.

"Ah, yes, great girl, hardest worker I've ever had," the station manager testified fondly with feeling. "What about her?"

"I just heard about what could be a good human-interest story for your station and thought you could send the King girl to cover it."

"Go on," Blake encouraged, intrigued. He genuinely liked and respected Maizie and was open to anything she had to pass on.

"According to the news blurb, a police detective in Bedford chased down this supposedly small-time art thief and wound up uncovering an entire cache of paintings in a storage unit that had been stolen in the last eighteen months. I thought you might want to send someone down to the precinct to interview this detective." And then she played what she felt was her ace card in this little venture. "So little of the news we hear is upbeat these days."

"Don't I know it," Blake said with a sigh. And then he chuckled. "So you're passing on assignments to me now, Maizie?"

"Just this one, Edward."

There was more to this and he knew it. Moreover, he knew that Maizie knew he knew, but he played his line out slowly like a fisherman intent on reeling in an elusive catch than a station manager in a newsroom that moved sometimes faster than the speed of light. "And you think I should assign King to follow up on it."

"Absolutely," Maizie enthused, adding, "She has a nice way about her."

"Oh, I agree with you. She definitely has a rapport with her audience," Blake said. When he heard nothing more illuminating on the other end, he asked, "Okay, what's really going on, Maizie? Is this some kind of a matchmaking thing?"

"I have no idea what you mean, Edward," Maizie told him in far too innocent a voice.

"Right. Belinda told me what you and your friends are up to in your spare time," Blake said, referring to his wife. And then he became serious. "If you think you've found a way to get the pain out of King's eyes, go for it. You've got my vote."

Relieved that the man was so easily on board, Maizie tactfully pointed out, "What we need is your assignment, Edward."

"That, too. Okay, give me the details one more time," he instructed, pulling over a pad and pencil, two staples of his work desk that he absolutely refused to surrender no matter how many electronic gadgets littered his desk and his office. His defense was that a pad and pencil never failed.

"Don't get too comfortable," Jerry Ross warned Ellie just as she sank down behind her desk in the overly crowded newsroom.

The six-two onetime linebacker for a third-string minor-league football team strode over to the woman he followed around with his camera a good part of each day, sometimes successfully, sometimes only to see his footage ignobly die on the cutting room floor.

"Up and at 'em, Ellie," he coaxed. "We've got ourselves an assignment."

Ellie had just begun to sit down but instantly bounced back up to her feet again. She was more than ready to go wherever the assignment took them.

Two years ago it would have been because each story represented a fresh opportunity to put her stamp on something that was unfolding. Now it was because each story necessitated her having to abandon her private thoughts and focus on whatever the news report required from her. The first casualty was her social life, which she more than willingly surrendered. She really didn't have one to speak of now that Brett was no longer in her life.

"Where to?" Ellie asked.

Jerry held up the written directive he'd just received for them. "Blake wants us to do a story about this police detective at the police station."

"Blake?" she questioned, puzzled. She fell into step beside her cameraman as he went out of the building and to the parking lot where their news van was waiting for them. "You mean Marty, don't you?" Marty Stern was the one who handed out their assignments, not the station manager.

"No," Jerry insisted, "I mean Blake." It had struck him as odd as it did her, but he'd learned not to question things that came from on high. "This assignment came down from Edward Blake himself."

She hurried down the steps into the lot without even looking at them. "Why?"

Reaching the van, Jerry shrugged as he got in on the driver's side. He glanced over his shoulder to check that his equipment was where he had put it earlier. It was a nervous habit of his since there was no place else his camera and the rest of his gear could be. The cameraman always packed it into the van first thing on arrival each morning. But checking on its position was somehow comforting to him.

Satisfied that it was there, he turned forward again. "That's above my pay grade," he told her. "I'm just relating the message and telling you what he said he wanted."

After putting the key into the ignition, Jerry turned it and the van hummed to life.

"All I know is that this detective had just swung by Los Naranjos Elementary School to drop off his kid—a niece, I think Blake said—and he almost tripped over the thief. Who cut him off as he raced by." Jerry told her with disbelief. "Anyway, when the detective followed the guy, he wound up cornering him in a storage unit. Guess what else was in the storage unit."

Ellie was watching the cluster of residential streets pass by her side window. The tranquil scene wasn't even registering. She felt more tired than usual and it was hard for her to work up any enthusiasm for what she was hearing, even the fake kind.

"It's Monday, Jerry. I don't do guessing games until Tuesday," she told the cameraman as if it was a rule written somewhere.

Undaunted, Jerry continued his riveting edge-of-her-seat story. "The detective found a bunch of other paintings stored there that, it turns out, had been stolen over the last eighteen months. It's your favorite," the cameraman pointed out. "Namely, a happy-ending story."

"Not for the thief," Ellie murmured under her breath.

Jerry heard her. "That's not the lede Blake wants us to go with," he told her. "Turns out that this isn't this detective's first brush with being in the right place at the right time."

"Oh?" Ellie did her best to sound interested, but she was really having trouble raising her spirits this morning. She'd resigned herself to the fact that some mornings were just going to be worse than others and this was one of those mornings. She needed to work on that, Ellie told herself silently. Jerry didn't deserve to be sitting next to a morose woman.

Maybe coffee would help, she reasoned.

"Yeah," Jerry was saying as he navigated the streets, heading for the precinct. "I didn't get the details to that. Figure maybe you could do a follow-up when you do the interview."

She nodded absently, still not focused on the story. Out of sheer desperation, Ellie forced herself to make a few notes. Something had to spark her. "What's the detective's name?"

Jerry shrugged. "Blake said we're supposed to ask the desk sergeant to speak to the detective who uncovered the stolen paintings."

"In other words, you don't have a name," she concluded.

The curly-headed cameraman spared her an apologetic look. "Sorry. Blake seemed in a hurry for us to get there. Said the story had already been carried on the radio station. Wanted us there before another news station beat us to it."

Well, that was par for the course, Ellie thought. She sighed. "Why is it that every story is *the* story—until it's not?"

She received a wide, slightly gap-toothed smile in response. "Beats me. All I know is that all this competition is good for my paycheck. I've got a college tuition to fund."

"Jackie is only five," she reminded him, referring to the cameraman's only child.

Jerry nodded, acting as if she had made his point

for him. "Exactly. I can't let the grass grow beneath my feet."

Jerry stepped on the gas.

The police department was housed in a modern-looking building that was barely seven years old. Prior to that, the city's core had been domiciled in an old building that dated back to the '50s and had once contained farm supplies. People still called the present location the *new precinct*. Centrally located, it was less than five miles from the news station. They got there in no time flat, even though every light had been against them.

Ellie got out first, but Jerry's legs were longer and he reached the building's front entrance several strides ahead of her.

"Ladies first," the cameraman told her, holding the door open for Ellie.

She smiled as she passed him and headed straight for the desk sergeant's desk. She made sure she took out her credentials and showed them to the dour-faced man before she identified herself.

Even so, the desk sergeant, a snow-white-haired man whose shoulders had assumed a permanent slump, presumably from the weight of the job, took his time looking up at the duo.

The moment he did, Ellie began talking. "I'm Ellie King and this is my cameraman, Jerry Ross." She told him the name of her news studio, then explained, "We're here to interview one of your detectives."

White bushy eyebrows gathered together in what seemed to be a preset scowl as the desk sergeant squinted at her credentials.

"Any particular one?" he asked in a voice that was so low it sounded as if he was filtering it over rocks.

"Detective," he said a bit more loudly when she didn't answer his question. "You want to interview any particular one?" His voice did not become any friendlier as it grew in volume.

"The one who caught that art thief," Jerry answered, speaking up.

The desk sergeant, Sergeant Nolan according to the name plate on his desk, scowled just a tad less as he nodded. "You wanna talk to Benteen," he told them.

The moment Nolan said the name, it all but echoed inside her head.

It couldn't be, Ellie thought. *Breathe, Ellie, breathe!*

"Excuse me," she said out loud, feeling like someone in the middle of a trance. "Did you say Benteen?"

"Yeah. Detective Colin Benteen," the desk sergeant confirmed, acting as if each word he uttered had come from some private collection he was loath to share with invasive civilians. Nolan turned to look at a patrolman on his right. "Mallory, tell Benteen to come down here. There're some people here who want to talk to him."

Having sent the patrolman on his errand, the sergeant turned his attention to the people from the news station. "You two wait over there," he growled, pointing to an area by the front window that was empty. "And don't get in the way," he warned.

"Friendly man," Jerry commented, moving to the space that the sergeant had indicated. When he turned around to glance at Ellie, he saw that she'd suddenly gone very pale. A measure of concern entered his eyes. "You feeling all right, Ellie?"

"Yes," she responded. Her voice sounded hollow to her ears.

It was an automatic response, but the thing was that she *wasn't* all right. She'd recognized the name of the detective, and for a moment, everything had frozen within her. She tried to tell herself it was just an odd coincidence. Maybe it was just a relative. After all, Benteen wasn't *that* uncommon a name.

It had been a patrolman with that last name who had come to the scene of the robbery that had stolen Brett from her. This was a detective they were waiting for.

Because of the circumstances that had been involved and the fact that she had removed herself from the scene, Ellie had never actually met the policeman who had arrived shortly after Brett had foiled the robbery. The patrolman, she was later told, who'd tried—and failed—to save Brett's life.

But she knew his name and at the time had promised herself that as soon as she was up to it, she would seek out this Officer Benteen and thank him for what he had tried to do—even if he had ultimately failed.

But a day had turned into a week and a week had turned into a month.

After several of those had passed, she gave up the notion of finding the policeman to thank him for his efforts.

After a while, the thought of talking to the man who had watched Brett's life ebb away only brought back the scene to her in vivid colors. A scene she was still trying, even at this point, to come to grips with. She honestly didn't think that she was up to it. So eventually she avoided pursuing the man altogether.

Jerry was watching her with concern. "You don't look fine. If I didn't know any better, I'd say that you look like you're about to break into a cold sweat."

"Jerry, I already have a mother," she told him, an annoyed edge in her voice—she didn't like being read so easily. "I said I'm fine."

He was not convinced and was about to say as much when she turned away from him and toward the man she saw walking toward them. The expression on her face had Jerry turning, as well. If anything, she appeared even paler than she had a moment ago.

"You look like you're seeing a ghost," he remarked uneasily.

The universe was sending her a message, she thought. It was time to tie up this loose end.

"Not a ghost," she answered. "Just someone I never got to thank properly."

The moment she said that, Jerry knew. The name the desk sergeant had said had been nagging at him. He knew it from somewhere…

"Oh God, you mean that's him?" Jerry cried. "The policeman who…?"

She waved the cameraman into silence, her attention fully focused on the tall, athletic-looking man in the navy jacket, gray shirt and jeans who was walking toward them.

He had a confident walk, she noted, like someone who felt he had the angels on his side. Maybe he did, she thought.

Ellie unconsciously squared her shoulders as the detective drew closer.

It was time to make up for her omission. The only thing that was left to decide was whether she would do it before they began the interview so she could get it out of the way or wait until after the interview was over so that it wouldn't make the man feel awkward or uncomfortable. Viewers were always quick to pick up on awkwardness and she didn't want to cause the detective any undue discomfort. It didn't make for a good segment, and after all, wasn't that why she was here?

Ellie made up her mind. The information as to who they were to one another could wait until after she finished talking to him, for the benefit of the home audience.

It took a great deal of effort for her, but by now she was used to playing a part.

Ellie forced a welcoming smile to her face and put out her hand to the detective as he came forward. Her entire attention was now on making the hero of the moment feel comfortable.

"Hi," she greeted him. "I'm Ellie and this is Jerry, and we'd like to ask you a few questions about those paintings you uncovered."

Chapter Three

The woman standing by the front window next to the pleasant-faced hulk with the unruly hair was cute.

Beyond cute, Colin amended. There was something appealing about her that he couldn't quite put his finger on. As best as he could analyze it, he sensed an intriguing combination of sadness mixed with an undercurrent of energy radiating from her.

And, more startling and thus far more important, he realized that for the first time in months, he found himself both attracted and interested.

There'd been a time when his older brother, Ryan, had called him a ladies' man, a "babe magnet" and a number of less flattering but equally descriptive terms. And at the time, they had all been rather accurate.

But all that had been before life had abruptly changed for him. Before his brother and sister-in-law, Jennifer, had been involved in that freak skiing accident that had resulted in their being swallowed up by an avalanche. Who could have predicted this outcome when Ryan and Jennifer had gone on a last-minute spur-of-the-moment vacation because a late-season unexpected snowfall had occurred and they were both avid skiers?

Just like that, in the blink of an eye, he suddenly found himself the only family that their only daughter, Heather, had left.

His personality, not to mention his priorities, had changed overnight. He hadn't been on so much as a date since he'd had to fly to Aspen to identify Ryan and Jennifer's bodies and to pick up his niece. Heather had been in bed asleep when it had all happened. Her parents had opted to sneak in a quick early-morning ski run before she woke up—not thinking that it would be the last thing that they would ever do.

Stunned, Colin had never thought twice about assuming this new responsibility. He turned his entire life around, then and there, vowing that Heather would always come first.

He couldn't give up what he did for a living—he'd worked too hard to get to where he was. It came with its own set of dangers, and that couldn't be helped. But he could definitely make sure that any time outside his job would go to being with Heather, to making sure that she wouldn't be permanently scarred by the loss of her parents. He'd vowed that he would always be there when Heather needed him to make the night terrors go away.

But just for a moment, this petite woman standing before him took Colin back to the man he had been before all of this had happened to change his life. It made him remember just how he'd felt when a really attractive woman crossed his path.

"Detective?" Ellie prodded when he didn't seem to have heard her, or at least wasn't attempting to respond to her greeting.

"Sorry," Colin apologized, rousing himself out of the temporary mental revelry he'd fallen into. He flashed a smile at her that one of his former girlfriends had called "naturally sexy." "I got distracted for a moment."

She was about to ask him if it was because he recalled who she was, but then she remembered that she had given him only her first name. Even if she'd told him her full name, that wouldn't necessarily mean that the detective would remember her husband and that fatal night at the convenience store.

Or even if he did recall every moment of that night, there was no reason to believe that he would make the connection between her and the man he couldn't save. King was, after all, a common enough name. Most likely, Benteen probably hadn't even gotten Brett's name after everything had gone back to normal—or as normal as it could have gone back to, she silently corrected.

No, if the detective was distracted on her account, he was probably trying to place where he'd seen her before.

As if the presence of a cameraman wasn't enough of a clue, she thought wryly.

"No problem," Ellie told the detective. In her opinion, that was a throwaway line that blanketed a lot of territory. She just wanted to do this story and move on. "Your CO told us we could take up a little of your time and ask you about the huge coup you just scored."

Colin looked at her puzzled, not quite following the sexy reporter. "Excuse me?"

"The paintings," Ellie prompted. "The stolen paintings that were in the storage unit you found."

Colin nodded in response but said nothing.

"Well?" she asked, waiting for him to start speaking. Talk about having to pull words out of someone's mouth. The detective was either exceptionally modest or exceedingly camera shy.

"That about covers it," he told her.

She could see by the look that Jerry gave her that he had the same thought as she did. This wasn't going to film well, not unless she could find a way to make this detective come around and start talking. She had a feeling that he would engage the audience once he got comfortable.

"You're being modest," she said, her voice coaxing him to elaborate.

He surprised her by saying, "Bragging rights aren't a part of this job."

Okay, she thought. He *did* need to be coaxed. A lot. She had to admit that this wasn't what she'd expected. Some people, once they got in front of a camera, wouldn't stop talking. This one seemed reluctant to even start.

"Still, I'm sure that it's not every police detective who gets to take down an art thief who's been plaguing the city."

"I really can't take any kind of credit for what happened. It's not as if this was the result of long hours of planning." He shrugged. "This was all actually just a big accident," Colin told her.

The job had made her somewhat cynical. It wasn't anything that she was particularly proud of, just a fact. But Ellie was beginning to believe that the detective was being serious. He was the genuine article. And because of this, she found herself trying to reach out to Benteen.

"There's that modesty again," she said. "I tell you what—why don't you walk me through exactly what happened and we'll go from there?"

She could see by the look on the detective's face that he was about to dismiss the whole incident. It made him a rare find in her book. Most men couldn't stop talking about themselves. But the station manager obviously was expecting a story and she wasn't about to come back empty-handed. It wasn't advisable.

"Word for word," Ellie urged again. "Paint a picture for me, so to speak."

Colin glared at the camera in Jerry's hands. It was clearly the enemy. "Are you going to film this?"

"That is the idea," Ellie said breezily. "Jerry's just going to keep on filming and when we're done, it'll be edited down to about a minute of airtime. Two, tops," she promised. She could see that the detective was wavering. All he needed was a little push that would send him over to her side. She felt she had just the thing. "You get final say on the footage."

"I do?" Colin asked, not entirely certain that she was on the level. He was aware of how badly some of his fellow detectives had been portrayed to the public. He wanted no part of that.

"Maybe this'll convince you," she said, trying again.

"Your CO signed off on this because he knew this would create a positive image of the Bedford PD. And my station manager thought this would be a feel-good piece that would really go over well, especially since those pieces are so few and far between."

"Well, I guess I'm sold, then," Colin told her. What he was sold on, he admitted, was the way her clear blue eyes seemed to sparkle as she tried to convince him. That alone was worth the price of admission.

Ellie smiled at the detective.

"Good." She glanced over her shoulder to make sure that Jerry had the camera in position. He did. "All right, just tell me what happened."

"Tell you?" he asked, thinking he was supposed to talk to the camera.

"Just me," she assured him. "Talk to *me*."

That made it easier. She had a face that invited conversation—as well as a number of other stray thoughts. "I'd just dropped off my niece, Heather, at school—"

Her ears instantly perked up. "Is that a usual thing for you?" The man was beginning to sound like a Boy Scout.

"It is ever since I became her sole guardian," Colin answered matter-of-factly.

As a human-interest story, this was just getting better and better, Ellie thought. She made a mental note to ask him more questions regarding that situation so she could annotate her commentary once the film had been edited.

"Go on," she urged.

"An APB came on over the two-way radio about a

B and E that had just gone down less than three blocks away from Heather's school," he said.

She wanted to get back to that, but first she wanted him to explain some of the terminology he'd just used. "An APB and B and E?" she asked, waiting for him to spell the words out. She knew what he was saying, but the audience might not.

"*All points bulletin* and *breaking and entering*," the detective explained. He was so used to those terms and others being tossed around that it didn't occur to him that someone might not know what he was talking about.

"Okay. Go on," she said, smiling at him.

It was a smile he caught himself thinking he could follow to the ends of the earth.

But not anymore, remember?

"The homeowner called 911 to say that he'd heard a noise and when he woke up, he saw a man running across his lawn carrying off his painting. Apparently, the thief had broken in while the guy was still asleep."

She nodded, focusing on the image of a thief dashing across a lawn with a stolen painting clutched in his hands.

"Definitely not something you see every day," Ellie agreed drolly.

Colin nodded. "That's when I saw this guy driving a van that matched the description dispatch had put out. So I followed him. Turns out it wasn't all that far away," he added. "He took the painting to a local storage unit. As I watched him, he stashed the painting he'd just stolen in an ordinary storage unit. When I came up behind him, I saw that he had what amounted to fifteen other paintings inside the unit."

Colin paused in his narrative to tell her, "There've been a rash of paintings stolen in Bedford in the last eighteen months."

She looked at him, waiting for more. When he didn't continue or make any attempt to brag, she asked, "And the paintings that you saw, were they the ones that had been stolen?"

He nodded. "One and the same."

She tried to get more details. "Was this guy part of a gang?"

"Not from anything that I could ascertain," Colin told her. "When I questioned him, he said he had taken all the paintings. I think he was telling the truth."

"And he hadn't tried to fence any of them?" she asked. It didn't seem possible.

Colin laughed softly. "Turns out that the guy just likes works of art and he didn't have the money to buy any of his own, so he came up with this plan." Colin shrugged. "Takes all kinds," was his comment.

It certainly did, Ellie silently agreed. "That almost sounds too easy," she said.

"I know," he replied. "But sometimes everything just falls into place at the right time and the right way. It doesn't happen often," Colin allowed. "But it does happen."

"Well, apparently, it did for you," Ellie observed. She all but expected to see the detective kick the dust and murmur, "Ah, shucks."

Colin turned out not to be as clueless as she momentarily thought him to be. A knowing smile curved his mouth as he guessed, "You're not convinced."

The smile came of its own volition. "It's my doubting-Thomas side," she admitted.

"We're checking the guy for priors," Colin told her. "Right now he's clean, but we're not finished. I could give you an update later," he offered.

"I would appreciate it," she said, then turned toward something that she knew would interest her viewers. "Tell me more about your niece. How long have you been her guardian?"

The question caught him off guard. They were just talking about the thief's lack of priors. "Is that important?" he asked, unclear as to why it should be, especially in this context.

If nothing else, Ellie knew her audience and how to make a story appealing to them. "The viewers love to hear details like that about selfless heroes."

"I'm not a hero and I'm not selfless," he told her, his manner saying that he wasn't just mouthing platitudes or what he felt passed for just the right amount of humility. His tone told Ellie that this detective was being straightforward with her, which she had to admit impressed her. He could have just as easily allowed her to build him up without protest.

"Why don't we leave that to the viewer to decide?" Ellie suggested. "Now, how long have you been your niece's guardian?"

"Six months," he told her.

Again, he didn't elaborate or tell her any more than the bare minimum. Was he being modest? Or was that a highly developed sense of privacy taking over?

Either way, her job was to push the boundaries a little in order to get him to open up. "What happened?" she asked.

He didn't look annoyed, but he did ask, "Is this really necessary?"

She was honest with him, sensing that the detective would appreciate it. "For the story? No. This is just me asking."

That brought up another host of questions in his mind. "Why?"

She wanted him to trust her. She needed to know the kind of man her husband had spent the last seconds of his life with. Only then would she know if he had done all that he could to try to save Brett. She was aware that he had probably said he had and filled out a report to that effect, but she wanted to be convinced.

"Shut off the camera, Jerry," she said, glancing over her shoulder at her cameraman. "We've got our story. I'll meet you at the van."

Jerry looked at her skeptically, still worried about her. She hadn't told the detective of their connection yet, but that didn't mean she wasn't going to, and when she did, she might need someone there for her.

But he couldn't say anything, because it wasn't his place. And if he did say anything, he knew that Ellie would *put* him in his place because she refused to tolerate anything remotely resembling pity, even if it came in the guise of sympathy.

All he could do was ask, "Are you sure?"

"I'm sure." The words *Now go* were implied if not said out loud.

Shaking his head, Jerry took his camera and walked out.

"See you around, Detective," he said by way of a parting comment.

Turning back to the detective, Ellie picked up the conversation where she'd left it. "You asked me why before."

Colin had just assumed that she'd forgotten and would go off on another topic. That she didn't raised his estimation of her. And he really had to say that so far, he liked what he saw. Liked it a lot. Maybe there was hope for him yet. At least, he'd like to think so.

"Yes, I did." His tone gave her an opening to continue her line of thinking.

"Because I am one of those people who has to know everything," she told him simply. "That doesn't mean I repeat everything I hear or everything I know, but I *need* to know it. And once I have all the information and can process it, then I can move on."

He looked at her and made a judgment call. "So this really isn't for your 'story'?" he asked.

"No. Not directly." And then she qualified her statement. "That doesn't mean that I won't use a piece of what you tell me—but again, we'll run it by you first. You'll get the final okay."

He had to admit that he thought it a generous way to proceed. "Is this your normal procedure?"

Ellie laughed. She had no idea that he found the sound captivating. "There is no such thing as 'normal' procedure. It is what it is at the moment."

Colin paused, considering her words and if he believed her.

Like a lot of true dyed-in-the-wool detectives, he had "gut feelings."

"Gut feelings" that saw him through a lot and, on occasion, kept him safe. His gut feeling told him that the woman with the deep crystal-blue eyes was telling him the truth.

He took a chance. "They died in an avalanche."

"That had to be terrible for you," she said. It was

certainly different from the usual car crash or drive-by shooting. She managed to control her reaction so he wasn't aware that what he said had affected her.

"It wasn't exactly a walk in the park for Heather, either," he pointed out.

"You were the one who broke the news to her?" Even as Ellie asked the question, she knew that he would have taken it upon himself to tell his niece. Benteen struck her as that sort of person. She was filled with empathy for both the detective and his niece, knowing what being told news like that felt like.

"I wasn't about to let anyone else do it," he said.

No, I wouldn't have thought so.

Without her realizing it, her estimation of the detective rose up yet another notch.

Chapter Four

Jerry appeared to be dozing in the news van, but he snapped to attention the moment the passenger-side door opened.

"So, how did he take it?" the cameraman asked her.

"Take it?" Ellie repeated absently as she climbed into the van. After closing the door, she pulled on her seat belt and snapped it into place.

Jerry watched her intently for a moment. "You didn't tell him that he was there the night your husband died, did you?"

Ellie shrugged, settling into her seat. "I didn't get an opportunity." She avoided looking at Jerry as she said, "The timing wasn't right."

Jerry turned his key, starting up the van. For an instant, the music he'd had playing on the radio stopped, then resumed. Someone was singing about surviving.

"This isn't the game-winning pitch to home plate we're talking about, Ellie. Don't you think the good detective should know that he tried to save the husband of the woman who was interviewing him?"

"I don't see how that would make any difference to this story," she countered stubbornly.

"No," Jerry allowed, "but it might make a difference to him."

There was a measure of defiance in Ellie's eyes as she turned them on Jerry.

"Why? I'm going to treat him fairly. We've got nothing but glowing words for him in this spot. His CO seemed pretty high on him and I'm sure if we interview a couple of the people whose paintings were recovered, they'll talk about him like he's their patron saint come to earth."

Jerry sighed as he barreled through a yellow light before it turned red, narrowly missing cutting off a tan SUV.

"He's a good guy, yes, I get that. But that doesn't change the fact that you should tell him about your connection," he insisted.

She didn't see what good it would do and telling Benteen would force her to relive a night she couldn't seem to permanently bury.

"Why?" she challenged.

Jerry gave her a look. "Because you shouldn't be keeping it from him."

She didn't normally get annoyed, but "normal" was no longer part of her daily life.

"How did I get to be the bad guy in this?" she asked.

"You're not," Jerry told her in a voice that was much

lower than hers, "but if you don't tell him, this is going to be something that'll just fester between you and him—until it finally comes out. Think how uncomfortable you'll feel then."

"Well, it's not like we're going to be working together or we're a couple," she pointed out impatiently. "Once the story airs, we probably won't ever even run into one another."

The funny thing was, Ellie thought, that the detective was just the kind of man her mother would have picked out for her once upon a time. There was a lot about him that reminded her of Brett.

The next moment, she shut all those thoughts down. "For now," she said, addressing the point that Jerry had raised, "let's just say that maybe I didn't want to make *him* feel uncomfortable."

"Is that it?" Jerry asked. "Or is it that you just want to hold something back and maybe, oh, I don't know, spring it on him later?"

Why in heaven's name would she want to do that? Ellie shook her head.

"I think that you've been watching too many procedurals, Jerry," she told him.

The light turned red, forcing Jerry to come to a stop and allowing him to really stare at her as he said, "No, it's just that I care about you."

"Do me a favor. Care a little less," she requested. "I can take care of myself."

Jerry frowned. The light turned green and he hit the gas again. "I'm not so sure about that."

What had gotten into him? Jerry had always been her chief supporter. "What's that supposed to mean?"

"It's just that sometimes I get the feeling that you're

just sleepwalking through life, that you've decided to check out."

He pulled into a parking spot but made no effort to get out. He'd faithfully followed her around and they made a great team, but she wasn't about to hold on to him against his will.

"Are you telling me that you want to switch news reporters?" she asked suddenly. "Because if you do, I'm not going to stand in your way."

"No, I *don't* want to switch reporters." He frowned. "You know, you never used to be this touchy."

"Things change," she said vaguely.

His eyes narrowed as they bore right into her. "Do they?"

"Okay, now you're really beginning to sound like my mother, and while I really love her, I do *not* need two of her," she informed him, one hand on the car's doorknob. "You heard me. Once the piece you got today is edited, I did promise Detective Benteen that we'd let him have the final okay. When he does okay it, *then* I'll tell him. Does that meet with your approval?" she asked.

She realized that she was being short-tempered with Jerry because she knew he was right. But at the same time, she didn't want to go there, didn't want to revisit the pain that went with all that.

"You don't need my approval, Ellie."

"No," she told him pointedly, agreeing. "I don't. I also don't need you glaring at me, either."

"I'm not glaring," he protested. "I was just looking at you. The rest is in your head."

Ellie sighed. "How does your wife put up with you, anyway?" she asked as the tension began to drain from her. She'd overreacted and she knew it. Now all she wanted to do was just forget about it and get this piece in to the editor.

Jerry laughed. "Betsy worships the ground I walk on—you know that."

"Uh-huh," she murmured, getting out of the van. "Let's go get some of our background material for this story."

Jerry got out on his side, taking his faithful camera with him. "Your wish is my command."

Ellie spared him a glance as she rolled her eyes. "If only..."

Colin sighed. It had been a long, long day.

After his morning had started out with all four burners going, what with the lucky catch of that thief and his cache and then that knockout news reporter coming to ask him questions, his afternoon had turned into a slow-moving turtle, surrounding him with a massive collection of never-ending paperwork. Paperwork that he'd neglected far too long.

The trouble with ignoring paperwork was that it didn't go away; it just seemed to sit in dark corners and multiply until it became an overwhelming stack that refused to be ignored. Unfortunately, he'd reached that point today. He supposed it was a way to keep him humble, even though he wasn't given to grappling with a large ego. Philosophically, he'd rolled up his sleeves because he knew he had to do something to at least whittle down the pile a little before it smothered him.

Rather than begin at the beginning, which might have been the orderly thing to do, Colin decided to start with the most recent file since that case had been the one that brought the reporter into his life.

Besides, there was nothing like the feeling that came from actually being able to close a case rather than having it linger on indefinitely, doggedly haunting him because he hadn't been able to solve it.

What he especially liked about this last case—other than the fact that it had introduced him to the sexy reporter—was that the thief had been taken down, so to speak, without his having to fire a single shot. Not all cases involving robbery ended so peacefully.

More often than not, someone was hurt, sometimes fatally. Colin didn't admit it out loud, but he took it hard when that happened. It wasn't that he thought of himself as some kind of superhero who should be able to prevent things like that from happening. He didn't think of himself as a hero at all, but the fact that he wasn't able to prevent a fatality really ate away at him for a long time.

Maybe that was why before Heather had become his responsibility, he had lived a faster life, determined to enjoy himself as much as possible. Partly because life was short and could end at any time and partially to erase certain images from his mind.

Images like having a would-be hero's blood pool through the fingers of his hand as he desperately tried to stem the flow, desperately tried to keep the man alive. But he'd come on the scene just minutes too late. Too late to stop the gunman from firing that lethal shot, but at least not too late to take the gunman down.

It still kept him up at night sometimes or disturbed his dreams, intruding like an uninvited, unwanted visitor determined to disrupt everything. Those were the nights when Heather came into his bedroom to wake *him* up instead of the other way around.

They were a pair, he and Heather. Both trying to act as if nothing bothered them. She was becoming more like him each day, he realized, wondering how Ryan would have reacted to that little piece of news.

He found himself wishing Ryan was around to react to *anything*.

Colin rotated his shoulders, then just got up from his desk altogether. There was only so much sitting at a computer, inputting information, that a man could be expected to do.

He needed to get some air, he decided.

"See another art thief darting by?" Marconi, another detective sitting close by, asked as he looked up to see him walking out.

Colin took the remark in stride. "Very funny. I need to stretch my legs."

"Hey, Benteen, so when do we get to see that chiseled profile on TV?" another detective, Al Sanchez, asked, speaking up.

Colin merely shrugged. That alluring reporter had said she'd get back to him, but she hadn't mentioned when. "Beats me."

"I've been here fourteen years. Never had anyone come and film me," Marconi pretended to complain.

Sanchez ventured a theory. "Maybe they didn't want to risk their cameras breaking filming that ugly mug of yours."

Colin knew they didn't mean anything by it, but he ignored them anyway. The truth was that he really wasn't comfortable about being on camera. He'd been just doing his job and saw no reason for something like that to make the six-o'clock news—or whatever time it was going to be on.

Leaving the squad room, he shoved his hands into his pockets. His right hand came in contact with the card that the news reporter had given him just before she'd left.

He felt it for a moment, his fingers passing over the embossed lettering. Taking it out, he looked at the card for a long moment.

Elliana King.

Her number was written directly under that. Probably not hers, he discounted. Most likely, it was the studio number. Even so, for a moment, he was tempted to call it. But then he thought better of it. What was he going to say? "Hi, remember me? Would you like to get some coffee somewhere?"

That wasn't going to get him anywhere. She probably had her share of guys calling her. Besides, he didn't have time for things like that. He had Heather to look out for.

Colin put the card back into his pocket and just kept on walking.

Hours later, he finally unlocked the front door of his apartment. The moment he walked in, Olga Pavlova, his next-door neighbor, gathered together her things and headed straight for the door.

"Good evening, Detective," the woman said, nodding at him as she passed. And without another word, she was gone.

Which left just him and Heather. His niece was planted on the sofa in front of the wide-screen TV.

"You're watching the news?" he questioned.

"Olga says I need to be aware of the world around me. 'Is good to know,'" Heather said, doing a decent imitation of the woman's thick Russian accent.

"So how was your day?" Colin asked as he slid down next to Heather, loosening his tie as he went down.

Heather spared him a look. "I learned stuff, forgot stuff, the usual." And then she tossed the ball back into his court. "You?"

He would have rather spent twelve hours on his feet investigating a case than sitting at his desk for six battling paperwork.

"Mostly forgot stuff," he told her. He glanced at his watch. It was after six. "Did you have dinner?"

"Yeah." Her eyes were back on the screen, devouring everything she saw. "Olga brought over a casserole. She said to tell you it's in the refrigerator. It's in the refrigerator."

He laughed as he got up again. "Thanks, kid," Colin said, kissing the top of her head. "I knew I could count on you."

Colin was halfway to the kitchen when he heard Heather suddenly scream. In hindsight, it was more of a squeal, but at the time, he wasn't differentiating. He pivoted on his heel and raced back into the living room.

"What's wrong?" Colin asked, alert and looking in all directions at once. Heather wasn't the type to scream under normal circumstances. Something had either set her off or frightened her.

"Look!" Heather cried, pointing to the TV. "It's you!"

The words were partially muffled because she had

her hands over her mouth in utter surprise even as she talked. "You're on TV." Her head appeared to almost swivel as she looked from the image on the screen to her uncle and then back again. Her eyes were huge as she took in his TV image. "You didn't tell me you were on TV!"

"I didn't know," he answered, staring at the screen. The interview he'd given Ellie King this morning was being run on the evening news. "I mean, I wasn't supposed to be until I gave my final approval."

Heather had scrambled up to her knees and was staring at the image as if she had never seen her uncle before. She hardly heard him.

"You didn't tell me you met Ellie King." It was almost an accusation, as if he had kept a vital piece of information from her. "You *know* her?" she cried in complete wonder.

"No." But that wasn't entirely true. "I mean, not until this morning."

And just like that, the piece they were watching on the air was over.

"Where's the remote?" he asked Heather.

"I don't know. It was here," she said, distracted. The remote was barely on her radar. "Can I meet her?"

He was focused on finding the elusive remote. He pushed the cushions around until he finally found what he was looking for half buried under the last cushion. He extracted it, then pointed the device at the set as he pressed the rewind button.

Images did an awkward dance, moving backward until he got to the beginning of the piece.

"Meet who?" he finally asked, still looking at the TV monitor.

"Ellie King," Heather told him impatiently. "Can I meet her?"

Bringing the woman around for introductions was the last thing on his mind right now. He was annoyed, not because his vanity had been offended but because she'd lied to him. He hated being lied to.

"We'll see."

"Please, Uncle Colin," Heather begged. "She's just everything I want to be. Pretty and smart and she gets to do all these really great stories—"

Heather abruptly fell silent as the interview began from the beginning again.

Colin winced as he watched himself. He supposed that it wasn't as bad as he'd thought it was, but it still made him feel awkward. And he was still annoyed.

He didn't wait for the end of the piece this time. He tossed the remote back on the sofa next to Heather.

Taking the card that the reporter had given him out of his pocket, he pulled his cell phone out of his other pocket and proceeded to dial the number on the card.

He was bracing himself for an ordeal. He figured that he was going to have to verbally strong-arm his way to getting someone to either put Ellie King on the line or give him her number. He wasn't about to hang up without getting either satisfaction or the number.

Having worked himself up, Colin wasn't prepared to hear her voice.

"This is Ellie King. May I help you?" When no one responded, she said, "Hello, is anyone there?"

"This is Detective Benteen," Colin said, finally finding his voice.

She hadn't expected to hear from him so soon, but she should have known. The man had struck her as being on top of things. She knew he was calling about the segment they'd just aired.

She decided to get ahead of this before he tried to run her over. "Hello, Detective. We had to air your segment tonight."

"Had to?" he questioned.

She didn't really owe him an explanation. After all, he was a public servant and this had been done in the service of the public. The public had a right to know. But she had made him a promise, so she felt the need to explain why she'd gone back on it.

"I know I promised that you'd have the final say, but I've got people I answer to and they insisted that the segment go on tonight as is. It turned out pretty well, I thought." She crossed her fingers that he saw it that way, too.

"You lied to me." It wasn't an accusation but a flat statement. It carried with it not anger but a note of genuine disappointment. And that made her feel worse than if he'd launched into a tirade.

"I didn't lie," she replied. "I had every intention of showing you the clip first." When he said nothing, she felt uncomfortable, despite the fact that this ultimately wasn't really her fault. "The station manager wanted to air it before the other stations got it. I'm sorry, but these things happen. Listen, if you want me to make it up to you—" she began, not really certain where this would ultimately go.

He cut her short with two words. "I do."

Chapter Five

I do.

The detective's words echoed in her head for a moment.

Okay, what had she just gotten herself into, Ellie wondered. She really hadn't expected the man on the other end of the line to take her up on her offer, especially since it was so vague. Now she had no idea what to say to solidify the offer—or more accurately, to rescind it, which was what she really wanted to do.

But since she had made the offer and the detective had said yes, she had no choice but to at least hear him out and find out what he had in mind. She could always say no.

Taking a breath, Ellie did her best to sound cheerful as she asked, "How?"

"Do you remember that niece I mentioned when you interviewed me?"

His voice seemed to rumble against her ear, like the sound of thunder. She could feel it reverberating within her chest.

"Yes, I remember," Ellie said uncertainly.

Colin was watching Heather out of the corner of his eye. She was on her knees on the sofa and it seemed as if his niece had frozen in midmovement, completely riveted to the conversation he was having with the reporter she so obviously idolized.

Giving Heather an encouraging smile, he told Ellie, "She'd like to meet you."

"Oh?" Was that all? Ellie felt a flood of relief. She hadn't exactly known what to expect, but life had taught her these last two years always to expect the worst. This was definitely not the worst, not even close. "Sure, that would be very nice," she told him. "Where and when?"

"Well, considering the fact that we both have busy careers and Heather has school, how about sometime this weekend? Is that doable for you?" He'd anticipated some sort of in-depth negotiation. This was turning out to be easier than he'd thought. Maybe the gorgeous reporter did have a really nice side to her after all.

Ellie paused, doing a quick review in her head. So far, she had nothing planned for the weekend. "I'm not sure I can bring you and her around the studio for a tour this weekend—"

Now that he had put it out there and saw the hopeful look on Heather's face, he wasn't about to accept a rejection. "Then how about coming over to my place?"

The moment the words were out of his mouth, he

realized that sounded like a come-on and far too intimate for an innocent meeting. She'd think it was a ploy on his part—and maybe at one time, it might have been. But this was for Heather and he wasn't about to disappoint his niece if he could help it. This was the first time he'd seen the girl excited about anything since she'd come to live with him.

"Or we could meet you at a coffee shop," Colin suggested.

"Didn't you say she was ten? Isn't that a little young for coffee?" Ellie asked, wondering if the detective was telling her the truth—or if he had something else in mind by way of her making up for the unapproved aired segment.

"Yes, she's ten, but Heather has an old soul. Besides, this coffee shop serves hot chocolate, as well." Thinking the woman probably preferred everything on her terms, he told her, "Or you choose the location if my picking one makes you uncomfortable."

Was he insinuating that she was afraid to meet him? Half a dozen half-formed thoughts crowded her head extrapolating on that.

Ellie suppressed a sigh. She really missed the days when things were simpler and more transparent.

"A coffee shop is fine," she told him. "Name the place and the time. If I'm not on a story, I'll be there."

She was giving herself an out, Colin thought. He supposed he could appreciate that. But his foremost thought was of Heather, not the dark-haired reporter with the killer legs.

"And if you are?" he asked.

"Then I'll call—and reschedule," Ellie said simply.

"Sounds reasonable," Colin replied. "How does Saturday, ten o'clock, at Josie's Café sound?" he asked.

"Reasonable," Ellie said, using the same word he just had.

He began to give her the café's address and only got partway through.

"I know where it is," Ellie told him.

"Great. Then we'll see you then—barring rescheduling," Colin added for the woman's benefit.

Sensing that the next sound she was going to hear was the call being terminated, Ellie said, "Wait."

"Something else?" Colin asked.

She was probably going to regret this, Ellie thought, but she asked the question anyway. "What did you think of it?"

"You mean the segment you aired without my okay?"

She wasn't about to apologize again. She'd already told him why she'd had to go ahead with it, so she just skipped over that and went directly to her answer. "Yes. The segment—what did you think of it?"

Colin paused, then told her, "You look good on camera."

His answer caught her off guard. For just one second, she wondered if he really thought that. The next second, she shut the thought away, telling herself that didn't matter one way or another. She wanted to get his reaction to the segment.

"That's not what I'm asking and you know it. I'm asking if you liked the segment." Not waiting for an answer, she quickly emphasized, "I didn't misrepresent you or trivialize you. Actually, I think you came off quite heroically. As a matter of fact, I'd be surprised if this piece doesn't get you a few groupies."

When she'd watched the segment as it aired, she'd caught herself thinking he came off rather compelling as well as damn good-looking. Everything that was required by a hero of the moment.

"I'm not interested in groupies," he told her, dismissing her comment.

She really found that difficult to believe, given his age and his looks. Ellie decided to push that a little. Whether she was playing devil's advocate or trying to see just how genuine this detective was, she wasn't all that sure. She knew only that she wanted to hear Colin's answer, for reasons that she wasn't making clear to herself.

"A good-looking man like you?" she scoffed. "I find that very difficult to believe."

"Maybe in another life, I might have been interested," he allowed. "But I have a niece to raise now," he reminded her.

The man sounded a bit too noble, but who knew? For now, she didn't have any more time to wonder about him. Another story had come up on her schedule and needed her attention.

"I'll see you on Saturday," she told Colin pleasantly.

"See who on Saturday?" Jerry asked just as she hung up the phone on her desk.

She hadn't heard the cameraman come up behind her. "You need to get squeaky shoes," she told him. When he gave her a look that said he wasn't about to be distracted, she answered his question. "That detective we did the story on today."

"To finally tell him how you're connected?" Jerry

asked, curious. "Good for you. Did he call to tell you that he was having trouble placing you but that your name was sticking out for some reason?"

"No, he didn't," she said, trying not to get annoyed.

"Then why did he call?"

"He wants me to meet his niece."

Jerry dropped into the chair opposite her desk. Even sitting, he towered over her. "How's that again?" he asked, confused.

She gave him an instant replay. "The detective called, not very happy that we went ahead with the story without his okay—"

"The way you promised him," Jerry interjected, nodding his head.

"Yes, the way I promised him," she said between gritted teeth. And then she willed herself to calm down. Jerry meant well. There were just times that he didn't know how to go about it. "What did I do for a conscience before you came into my life?"

Jerry never hesitated. "My guess is that you were depraved and conniving."

Her eyes narrowed as she looked at him. "At least I didn't have to worry about someone eavesdropping on my conversations."

"Consider it a trade-off." He drew his chair in closer. "So how did you wind up saying you'd meet his niece?"

She smiled. "Seems his niece is a fan. At least, that's what it sounded like."

"So you're giving her a tour of the studio?" Colin asked.

From what she'd heard, the weekend promised to be rather hectic at the studio. Besides, this could be something she could save for a later date, like a virtual ace in the hole to be played when she felt she needed it.

Why was she making long-range plans about this man anyway? she silently asked herself. This was most likely going to be just a one-time thing. Done and over with. No reason to think otherwise.

She sounded like the typical distant celebrity as she said, "I thought it might be better just to do a little one-on-one. You know, answer her questions, give her an autographed photo, that kind of thing."

Jerry nodded. Crossing his arms before him, he gave her a penetrating look. "Any reason for the special treatment? Or do you feel that guilty about lying to our local hero?"

She frowned, enumerating it for her cameraman one more time. "A, I didn't lie. The station manager overruled me. B, I don't feel guilty about anything. And C, he isn't my local hero."

"Okay, then why are you doing this?" he asked.

"Maybe I'm just a nice person," she replied.

"Look, Ellie, I'm the first one in your corner—you know that. And yes, you're a nice person, but this is an extra mile here you're going. Maybe two. I'm just curious as to why."

He knew her too well, Ellie thought. Seeing no reason to keep this from him, she told him. "The girl lost both her parents six months ago. Maybe I feel like we're kindred spirits," Ellie said. "Anyway, he made it sound as if she was excited to meet me. I didn't see why I couldn't meet her. Satisfied?" she asked.

He gave her what his wife referred to as his "electric smile." It lit up his face and the immediate area. "Always."

"Uh-huh," she said dismissively, on her feet. "Let's get going. We've got another segment to film."

"I hear and obey," he told her as he followed her out.

For the rest of the week, the rendezvous she'd made with the detective over the phone to meet his niece was never far from Ellie's thoughts. It seemed to hover over her like a distant hummingbird that just wouldn't find a place to alight no matter how long it fluttered.

At least once a day, if not more, Ellie thought about calling and "regretfully" rescheduling. As the days until Saturday steadily disappeared, the idea of rescheduling grew more tempting.

In all honesty, Ellie had no idea what she was afraid of but her nerves were definitely on edge. It was somewhat akin to being aware that an earthquake was imminent and just waiting for the tremors to begin— without having a clue as to when they would hit.

It wasn't the prospect of meeting a ten-year-old that unsettled her. She got on fairly well with children, as well as with adults. But for some reason, it was the girl's uncle who had made her nervous.

Maybe she unconsciously blamed the detective, she theorized. Maybe, deep down in her soul, she felt he could have done something more and saved Brett. Or if he'd just arrived two minutes earlier, he could have prevented the robber from shooting Brett altogether.

No, she told herself fiercely, staring at her reflection in her bedroom mirror, she had to stop doing this to herself, had to stop coming up with what-ifs. Because it didn't matter "what if." What mattered was that it hadn't happened according to any one of the dozen scenarios she'd created. It had happened just one way and that way had resulted in Brett being the hero he always was and paying for that quality with his life.

To wonder about some other possible outcome was just going to make her crazy and she had to stop. Brett wouldn't have wanted her to continue to do this to herself. He would have wanted her to be happy. To live her life, she silently insisted.

So why was she looking into the mirror and crying? Ellie upbraided herself, angrily brushing the tears away with the back of her hand.

"Damn, now I've got to put my makeup on all over again," she complained. "You can't go meet this fan looking as if you've been peeling onions all morning," she told herself.

Taking a deep, steadying breath, Ellie went into her bathroom to wash her face and put on a fresh one. If she didn't hurry, she was going to be late.

"She's late," Heather observed, frowning, clearly worried about being stood up. They were sitting at a table in the café and it was fairly crowded, the way it was every Saturday at this time of day. Heather's eyes had been glued to the front door since they had arrived. She spared half a glance in her uncle's direction before her head whiplashed back into position. "Is your phone on?" she asked him.

"My phone's on," Colin assured his niece.

She put her hand out, still watching the front door. The hot chocolate in front of her was half-consumed and growing cold. "Can I see it?"

"Certainly not a trusting little girl, are you?" Colin quipped, shifting so he could get his cell phone out of his pocket.

"Trust but verify—you taught me that," Heather reminded him.

He laughed softly. "I didn't think you were listening." Rather than hand her the phone, Colin held it up in front of her so that she could see for herself. "Satisfied?"

She saw that it was active. "And you've got the ringer on?"

"Yes," he answered her patiently, "I've got the ringer on."

Heather frowned again. The door opened, but it was just a couple coming in. Heather sighed. "She said she'd call if she wasn't going to be here, right?"

"That's what the woman said. Heather," Colin said kindly, "she's probably just held up by traffic."

Instead of agreeing with him, Heather took the phone he still held in his hand and deftly pulled up the Sigalert app on it. Looking away from the door for a moment, she scanned the various routes.

"No traffic jams," she informed her uncle, handing the phone back to him.

"Then maybe she got a late start."

Colin looked at his niece. She was both old and young at the same time. An old soul trapped in a pre-teen's body and dealing with all those strange new feelings that were colliding with one another. Most likely, he was going to be in big trouble in about another year or two—if not sooner.

He supposed he should get Heather prepared just in case this didn't play out the way she hoped. "And even if she doesn't come, Heather, it's not like it's the end of the world."

Wide green eyes turned to him, clearly distressed. "I told my friends I was meeting her," she lamented.

Something didn't sound right. "Wait, I thought when I asked you just recently how things were going, you told me that you weren't making any friends." That had caused him some concern at the time.

Heather lifted her chin defensively. "Well, I made them."

"When?" he asked suspiciously.

"When I said you were bringing me to meet Elliana King," she told him, striking an innocent air.

"Heather, those aren't really friends," he said gently.

She was way ahead of him. "I know that, Uncle Colin. But I've got to start somewhere."

An old soul, he thought again as he rolled his eyes. "Sometimes I wonder who's raising who here."

"You're older, so you're the one raising me," she said matter-of-factly. Her heart-shaped face turned up to his, a hint of sadness welling up in her eyes as she made herself face the truth. "She's not coming, is she, Uncle Colin?"

"We don't know that yet." But if she didn't, he intended to go down to the news studio and make the woman realize how much she'd hurt his niece.

"But she's not," Heather insisted.

"Tell you what," he suggested. "Why don't I order you another hot chocolate? And when you finish drinking that, if that fancy news lady isn't here yet, we'll go home."

"And write her a nasty letter?"

"You bet," he agreed. "So nasty that the paper will burn her fingers when she holds it."

He was doing his best to hide his annoyance. The

woman had set the terms for this meeting and now she was disappointing Heather. It was one thing to go back on her word with him—he was thinking of the segment that had been aired—but quite another when it came to his niece. He took that as a personal affront and he promised himself that if Elliana King thought she'd heard the last of this, she had another think coming.

At the very least, she had—

"She's here!" Heather declared excitedly, rising in her seat and pointing toward the shop's entrance. Tugging urgently on his sleeve, she all but squealed, "She's here!"

Chapter Six

At first glance, Josie's Café seemed crowded, but then, Ellie already expected that. She'd had to park her car by the auto-parts store on the opposite side of the strip mall because there were no spots to be had by either the café or the round-the-clock fitness gym that was right next to it.

Saturday was the day that everyone was out catching up on their lives, mostly at the same time, Ellie thought wryly as she looked around the café, looking for Detective Benteen and his niece.

She was late and part of her wondered if maybe they had given up and left. She was late by only fifteen minutes, but she knew some people could be impatient and intolerant, easily feeling snubbed if strict punctuality wasn't adhered to. She'd actually thought of calling Benteen from her car to tell him she was on her way, but since she'd said she'd call only if she *wasn't* able to make the appointment, she'd been afraid he wouldn't answer and just take that as a signal to leave.

So Ellie now stood near the front entrance, scanning the small café and trying not to block other people's paths as they made their way in or out of the cozy family-owned establishment. The noise level was definitely up and that made focusing somewhat more difficult.

And then she saw them.

Oddly enough, it wasn't the young girl waving her arms and standing up by their table who caught Ellie's attention. Instead, she'd zeroed in on the detective who was seated next to the waving girl, his expression appearing somewhat grim.

Obviously, Ellie surmised, she'd incurred his disfavor by her late arrival. Well, that could be easily handled.

Waving back to the girl, Ellie quickly wound her way in and out of the pockets of space between people and tables as she forged a path to the table.

The first thing she did was to greet the girl rather than the detective she already knew.

"Hi! You must be Heather," Ellie said cheerfully, putting out her hand to the preteen.

Heather was at the age where she was testing the waters of being cool about things, but that role was abandoned for the time being as she eagerly put her hand into Ellie's and shook it with no small amount of enthusiasm.

"Yes, that's me. And you're really Elliana King," she cried.

"Last time I checked," Ellie answered with her

trademark warm, sunny smile. And then she added just a touch of contriteness to her voice as she said, "I'm sorry I'm late."

"Oh, we didn't notice," Heather told her loftily. "Did we, Uncle Colin?"

Colin had no idea why Heather was saying that, but he was wise enough to play along. This meeting was, after all, strictly for Heather's benefit.

"I don't own a watch," he said by way of backing up Heather's claim.

Colin saw amusement entering Ellie's eyes. He caught himself thinking that the woman had very expressive eyes. Beautiful expressive eyes.

Not that it mattered one way or another, he told himself as an afterthought.

"Even so, I am running late and I apologize. I hope you haven't been waiting long," Ellie said to the young girl.

As was her habit, she quickly took note of Heather's physical features, drawing a few conclusions. The pre-teen was willowy and taller than the average ten-year-old. That she was thin told Ellie that Heather didn't seek solace in food, which in turn told her that the girl either had extremely strong willpower or she was well adjusted with a good sense of self. Possibly both.

Heather instantly shook her head in response to Ellie's statement. "Oh no, we just got here ourselves."

Ellie glanced at the two cups on the table. Both more than half-empty.

"I guess they served you as you came in," Ellie said. "Must be good service here."

Rather than get flustered, Heather never missed a beat. "Oh, very good service," she attested.

Ellie smiled as she nodded, giving the girl another point for poise. Both Heather and her uncle were still on their feet. The latter had gotten up as she approached the table, which told Ellie that he'd been schooled in manners, something that wasn't all that common anymore.

"Well, let's sit down so we can get better acquainted," Ellie suggested.

Heather bobbed her head in agreement as she took her seat. Colin sat only after they did.

"Can I get you coffee?" Heather offered eagerly, bouncing up again.

Colin put his hand on his niece's shoulder and gently pushed her back into her seat. "I'll get Ms. King what she wants to drink so you two can talk," he said accommodatingly. Turning to the reporter, he asked, "What would you like?"

To ask you if you did everything you could that night.

The words popped into her head out of nowhere, startling her and making Ellie painfully aware that as much as she denied it, Jerry was right. She needed to tell the detective about their connection so it didn't hang over her head like this.

Soon, she promised herself.

Ellie forced a smile to her lips as she said, "Coffee, please."

"Decaf?" Colin asked. A lot of women he knew preferred the nonstimulating form of coffee.

But Ellie laughed at the question. "Not on your life. I need as much fuel as possible."

A woman after his own heart, he thought. "Cream and sugar?"

Ellie shook her head. "Black as midnight."

Heather looked pleased by the reporter's choice, Colin thought. "She likes her coffee the same way you do, Uncle Colin."

There was affection in his voice as he smiled at his niece. "Yes, I heard. Be right back," he promised a moment before he was all but swallowed up by the crowd he stepped into.

He'd said the words to his niece, not to her, Ellie noted, as if to reassure the girl he wasn't leaving her alone. Heather didn't strike her as being particularly insecure or nervous. Maybe it was habit, she guessed. In any event, she had to admit that she liked the man's protective attitude toward the girl. For someone who was new to this position of guardian, he seemed to be doing all right.

As if to confirm her thoughts, the next moment Heather said, "He's the best."

Ellie nodded, absently acknowledging the girl's testimony.

And then Heather seemed to roll the statement over in her mind again. "Well, maybe a little more than he used to be."

"How so?" Ellie asked. Even if the woman in her had more or less retreated from the human race, the reporter in Ellie was curious about everything.

Heather seemed to choose her words carefully before answering. "He's just getting the hang of being a dad instead of an uncle."

That told her that he'd been a presence in the girl's life even before her parents had died. It spoke well of the man. Usually someone Benteen's age didn't have time for girls unless they were over the age of eighteen.

"So he's different now?" she asked Heather.

Heather nodded. "A little. He checks my homework and does a bunch of other stuff he didn't do when he was just my uncle."

"And how do you feel about that?" Ellie asked.

Heather appeared to consider her answer before giving it.

"Okay, I guess." And then a lightbulb went off over her head. "Hey, are you interviewing me?" the girl asked.

Ellie was nothing if not warm as she gave her answer. "Well, I'm getting to know you and that's the way I get to know people, so yes, I guess in a way I am interviewing you. Do you mind?" she asked.

"No, it's cool."

Ellie smiled. "And so are you," she told Heather. The girl beamed in response, obviously thrilled by the compliment. "Would you like to be a reporter someday?"

Heather paused to seriously think the question over. "I'm not sure yet. First I want to graduate the fourth grade."

Ellie bit the inside of her bottom lip to keep from laughing. She didn't want to hurt the girl's feelings. "I see you have your priorities straight."

The next moment, Colin rejoined them at the table. "Here we go," he said, "Coffee, black as midnight, just as you requested." He placed the cup in front of Ellie and then took his seat. He noticed that Heather was practically beaming. "So, what are you two talking about?"

"Graduating fourth grade," Ellie answered him. Humor entered her eyes as she looked back at his niece. "And having your priorities straight."

Colin picked up his own cup and pretended to toast them, then took a sip. "Okay, I guess I'm all caught up, then," he commented.

"Would you like to ask me any questions?" Ellie asked, looking at Heather.

Heather looked as if she was fairly bursting to ask questions. The only problem was which to ask first and which to leave for a later time. "Do you ever get nervous?"

"You mean on the air?" Ellie asked. She smiled in response. "Sure, lots of times."

"Really?" It wasn't that Heather didn't believe her; she looked as if she was thrilled to discover that her newest idol was human.

"Really," Ellie repeated.

"But you never look nervous."

Ellie leaned in confidentially toward the girl. "Want to know a little trick?"

"Sure!" Heather answered enthusiastically.

Ellie told her the truth. "That's because I pretend it's just the person and me, talking as if we were old friends."

"Like we're talking now?" Heather asked as she realized that was exactly what was happening. Ellie was talking to her as if they had always known each other.

"Like we're talking now," Ellie confirmed.

The woman was good with Heather, Colin thought, and he appreciated it. Because she was, he didn't want to abuse Ellie's time or her patience.

"If you have anything else you want to ask Ms.

King, why don't you do it now?" Colin urged his niece. "I'm sure that Ms. King is very busy and we don't want to keep her from her work."

Ellie looked at him, masking her surprise. He was actually using the excuse she had prepared to use. But now that she was here, she found that despite her reservations—and that one rather dark cloud that was hanging between them—she wanted to stay awhile. She was enjoying Heather's company. The girl was both older than her years and yet still refreshingly untarnished and innocent. That was rare these days when ten-year-olds were going on twenty in ways that would take innocence away from them.

"Actually, I cleared this morning so I could do this," she told Heather, throwing the detective a quick glance, as well. "So go for it," she encouraged. "Ask away."

Heather grinned like a child who had just been admitted to Santa's workshop in late November. All the newly built toys had yet to be wrapped up and accounted for—so she could have her pick.

"Okay."

They'd been talking for more than an hour. For the most part, it had been Heather asking questions and Ellie answering them. Occasionally, Colin would slip in a question himself. He had to admit that he was surprised that the news reporter turned out to be so accessible and human.

He hadn't known exactly what to expect when he'd initially set up this meeting. He supposed he'd expected a plastic would-be celebrity, someone playing the part of a so-called reporter/personality until she grew tired of answering questions or pretending to answer questions. But Ellie King wasn't plastic. Unlike some of her counterparts, she seemed to be *very* genuine. He appreciated the fact that she was interacting with his niece and treating her not like an underling or a child but like a person who mattered.

As for Heather, he could see that she was really enjoying this. It did his heart good to see her like this. It was the first time he'd seen the old Heather, the girl she'd been before her life had been so cruelly stripped of both her parents. Before she was made to face the fact that life had a very real dark underbelly.

He realized that he had the reporter to thank for that, at least in part. By paying attention to Heather, by treating her like a person whose feelings were important, the woman had allowed this side of Heather to resurface.

He was about to say something to Ellie to get her to understand that he was grateful for this when his cell phone began to ring, interrupting his train of thought. Colin frowned even before he checked the screen to see who was calling.

Part of him already knew.

Wound up like a top, Heather abruptly stopped talking and glanced at her uncle as he took out his phone and swiped the screen to take the call.

Ellie saw the look on the girl's face. "Something wrong?" she asked Heather.

"It's probably work," Heather said in a subdued voice, suppressing a sigh.

"I've got to take this," Colin told her. With that, he left the table.

"Does this happen a lot?" Ellie asked the girl, trying to sound sympathetic at the same time.

"It happens enough times," Heather confirmed. She shrugged philosophically, trying to make it seem as if it didn't bother her. "They need him."

"I'm sure they do," Ellie told her, putting her hand over the girl's.

Heather smiled her gratitude.

The call was short. They always were. Pocketing his phone, Colin came back to the table. He didn't sit down. By the look on Heather's face, he knew that she already knew what he was going to say. For once he really wished he didn't have to, but there was no way around it.

"Sorry, honey. We're going to have to end this. I've got to get you home and get Olga to come to stay with you."

"Olga's the Russian lady next door," Heather explained to Ellie before turning her emotive eyes up to her uncle. "Do you have to go?" she asked.

"I'm sorry, Heather, but I'm afraid so." He turned toward the reporter. "Thank you for meeting us like this. It was really very nice of you—"

Ellie cut him off before he could finish. "There's no need for it to end."

"I'm afraid there is. I've got to get Heather home," Colin began to explain again in case the woman didn't get it.

Ellie held her hand up, stopping him again. "Why don't I follow you and stay with Heather while you're gone?" She flashed a smile at Heather. "We girls can just keep on talking."

For a second, Colin was speechless, fully aware that

Heather was pleading with him with her eyes, asking him to agree. In good conscience, he knew he couldn't.

"I don't know how long I'll be gone," he told the woman.

He couldn't expect her to hang around until he came home. Olga, on the other hand, was accustomed to popping over and remaining until all hours. Besides, he paid the woman for her time. She'd initially protested, but they'd worked out equitable rates. Fortunately, her work time at the cleaning service was flexible enough for her to be able to make these arrangements.

Ellie, however, seemed determined. She must have seen how much Heather wanted to go on talking with her.

"I fully understand," she told the detective. "Tell you what. Why don't you give me this Olga's number and if I have to leave for some reason before you can get back, I'll call her to come over?"

At that point, Heather stopped pleading with her eyes and her mouth took over, as did her hands, which she used to clutch his arm, as if that would somehow give her more leverage.

"Please, Uncle Colin? Say yes."

He in turn looked at the reporter making what he considered to be a rather generous offer. "You sure about this?"

"I said I cleared my morning—and to be honest, I cleared the rest of my day, as well. I was going to go shopping," she confided. "But this is a lot more satisfying than going shopping. Apparently, I underestimated the number of questions Heather would have for me." Her eyes met Heather's and she winked at the girl. "Seems like we just started to scratch the surface."

Heather mouthed "Thank you" to her, then turned back toward her uncle.

"Please?" Heather begged again.

Colin sighed. "If I say no, I'm an ogre," he commented.

"And we really can't have that," Ellie told him even as she appeared to agree with his conclusion. "Nobody likes an ogre."

He'd always had trouble saying no to Heather, although now that he'd become both mother and father to her, there were instances when he had to. But this didn't really need to be one of them. And as long as the reporter didn't seem to mind, who was he to say no?

"All right, as long as you're all right with this, I'm not the one who's going to kill this little get-together," Colin said.

Heather was all but bouncing up and down in her seat. "Oh, thank you!" she cried excitedly.

"Okay, then, where are you parked?" he asked Ellie, getting down to logistics.

"In the north forty," she quipped, standing up. "Why don't you give me a few minutes to pull up in front of the café so that I can follow your car? Better yet, give me your address in case I lose sight of the car."

Before he could try one more time to demur, Heather was rattling off their address. Ellie quickly wrote it down on her napkin and put it into her purse.

"Got it," she announced.

You certainly do, Colin couldn't help thinking, feeling as if he'd gotten swept off his feet by a hurricane. And with that, it was a done deal.

Chapter Seven

Colin was completely and utterly exhausted as he unlocked his front door.

For a while there, it looked as if he wasn't going to be able to come home at all tonight. But then he caught a break and just like that, the case was put to rest. At least as far as he was concerned.

They'd been shorthanded at the station, so when the call went out regarding an Amber Alert, his was the next name on the backup rotation and he'd been called down. But it had ended well, which ultimately was all that really mattered.

Colin finally let himself into his apartment. Not for the first time he thought, *Thank God for Olga.* Otherwise he would have been really hard-pressed to get someone to stay with Heather at a moment's notice the way his job at times necessitated.

As he closed the door behind him, Colin heard the TV. He recognized some of the dialogue. A series marathon was running on one of the cable channels. Olga favored that program, telling him she watched it in order to try to perfect her English. He suspected the fact that the leading man was exceptionally good-looking might have had something to do with it, as well.

Walking into the living room, he was about to greet his neighbor but then stopped dead in his tracks. Instead of the pleasantly rounded grandmotherly woman who periodically brought over baked goods and "leftovers" that suspiciously didn't look as if they were leftovers at all, he was looking at Ellie King sitting on his recliner.

"You're not Olga."

Ellie'd been dozing off and on during the last hour but was now instantly awake. She sat up, her eyes meeting his.

"I don't know if that's an observation or an accusation," she responded, the corners of her mouth curving.

Glancing past the woman, Colin saw that his niece was on the sofa, curled up like a kitten and very soundly asleep.

"What happened?" Colin asked.

Ellie's brain still felt slightly foggy. She rose from the recliner, pulling herself together. "What do you mean?"

Colin rephrased his question. "Why didn't you go home?"

"We didn't finish talking. Your niece *really* likes to talk," she told him with a laugh.

"And you stayed?" he asked, surprised. Colin noticed that Heather was covered with a throw that he kept on the back of the sofa. This had to be the reporter's work.

"Well, it seemed kind of rude to walk out on Heather in midsentence. Besides, I was enjoying her company." She glanced at the girl and smiled. "And I kind of think she was enjoying mine."

In his mind, there was no doubt. "Oh, I'm sure she was. She couldn't wait for Saturday to come so she could meet you. But once she fell asleep, why didn't you call Olga to come over?" he asked. "Don't you have somewhere else you have to be?"

It was one o'clock in the morning. The only place she had to be at that time of night was in bed.

Ellie shrugged, dismissing his question. "If I did, Detective, I assure you I'd be there. No, this turned out to be one of those rare days where I was the mistress of my own fate, able to spend my day doing anything I wanted to."

"So you chose to spend it with a ten-year-old?" he asked incredulously. That didn't sound very plausible to him. Ellie was considered a celebrity of sorts. Celebrities didn't choose to hang out with ten-year-olds unless they were related to them.

"A very precocious, entertaining ten-year-old," Ellie amended. There was a fond expression on her face as she looked at the sleeping girl again. "She's really a great kid," she told him.

"I know," he responded, looking at his niece. "That's why I worry about her." He wanted to protect her, to keep Heather from getting hurt. But there was no way to Bubble Wrap her world—or even her.

"You shouldn't," Ellie told him. "In my humble

opinion, Heather's amazingly well adjusted and bright, and I have a feeling she'll go far." Her eyes shifted back to the detective. "And she speaks very highly of you, you know."

"You talked about me?" Colin asked her, clearly surprised.

"*She* talked about you," Ellie clarified, not wanting him to get the wrong idea. "I just listened. In her estimation, you're about ten feet tall and stop just short of leaping over tall buildings in a single bound," she said, amused.

Because Heather was asleep in the living room and he didn't want to wake her just yet, Colin indicated that they should move into the kitchen. He pulled out a chair at the table and sat down.

Debating her exit, Ellie decided to join him for just a minute. "There's some dinner, if you're interested," she told him. When he looked at her curiously, she pointed to a covered pan on the stove.

"Olga stopped by?" he asked. If she had, why hadn't the woman stayed?

The next moment, Ellie answered the question for him. "No, I made it."

"You cook?"

Someone else might have taken offense at his obvious stereotypical view of her, but Ellie let it go, choosing instead to just be amused.

"I can do more than hold a microphone in my hand, yes," she said, addressing a more elaborate question that she assumed was going through his mind. "Nothing fancy, just some fried chicken breasts," she told him, adding, "They're still warm, if you're hungry."

The moment she said the word, he realized that he

actually was. Very hungry. With good reason. "Other than the coffee this morning, all I've had is some stale pizza left over in the break room, so fried chicken sounds pretty good to me, warm or cold."

She was already uncovering the pan and taking out a piece of chicken to put on a plate.

"Then by all means, eat," she urged, placing the plate in front of him. Without thinking, she took a seat opposite him. "Did you get your bad guy?"

For just a moment, Colin lost himself in the taste of the chicken cutlet he'd bitten into. It wasn't just good; it was *very* good. He relished it, then realized that the woman had asked him something. The words, however, were lost to him.

So he looked up at her, puzzled. "What?"

Ellie began to explain. "I assumed that whatever called you away involved a bad guy of some sort. I was just wondering if you got him."

She flashed a smile at him, knowing that she was invading territory he might not be at liberty to talk about yet. In her experience, police personnel had this maddening habit of asking questions but not answering them when they were involved in an ongoing case. It always made her want to dig deeper.

When the detective didn't say anything in reply, she assumed that this was another one of those "no comment" instances. Ellie began to get up from the table. "You don't have to tell me," she said, resigned.

He was eating—and really enjoying—the chicken she'd made. His mouth was full of the savory flavor, which was why he couldn't answer her. In lieu of that, he made a noise and waved her back down in her seat.

"You want me to sit. Okay." She complied, sinking back down in the chair for the moment. She noted how he was doing away with the piece of chicken she'd served him. Some would call it doing it justice, she thought, rather pleased.

"Is this because you want me to stick around until you're sure I didn't poison you?" she deadpanned.

"You don't look like you'd poison anyone," Colin told her when he could finally speak.

"Ever see a picture of Lucrezia Borgia?" Ellie posed innocently.

Colin shook his head before taking another forkful of the crisp chicken meat. "You do like to keep people guessing, don't you?"

"That's what makes life exciting," Ellie replied. "Well, since you're still obviously alive," she began philosophically, getting up again, "I'll consider dinner a success and let myself out."

She was about to walk out when she heard Colin say, "We got him."

Turning around to look at the detective, Ellie asked, "Excuse me?"

"You asked if we got the bad guy," he reminded her. "We did."

She smiled, pleased that he'd answered her but now exceedingly curious about the details that went with the story.

"Congratulations," she told him, doubling back to rejoin him.

"He wasn't actually a bad guy," Colin said, amending his previous statement. "Maybe a more accurate description of him is that he wasn't a bad person—he was just very frustrated."

Reclaiming her chair, Ellie sat down for a third

time. He'd phrased it that way on purpose, she thought, to lure her back in. That in itself surprised her. She would have thought he'd be happy to see her go.

How about you? Why aren't you making good your exit? Why are you hanging around the man who couldn't save your husband?

She didn't have a good answer to that.

Instead, she heard herself telling him, "You know I'm not going to let it go at just that, don't you?" The expression on his face told her that he knew. But he was eating again and his mouth was full. "I can wait," she said, leaning back in the chair.

"It was an abduction," he revealed once his mouth was empty and he could speak again.

That got Ellie's attention and she slid to the edge of her seat. "He kidnapped somebody? Who?" This time when Colin brought the fork up to his lips again, she caught his arm, stopped him. "Who?" she repeated.

"His daughter." Colin shook his head. Both parties were to blame in this. "It was a custody battle gone really wrong. Father got tired of being stonewalled, so when it came time for him to bring his five-year-old daughter back after a scheduled visit, he didn't. The mother had a meltdown and called us."

"And you found him?" Ellie asked, clearly impressed. She made no effort to hide the fact.

He didn't want to make it sound as if he was the hero of the piece. It was luck more than anything else. "There was an Amber Alert out. Someone called in saying they'd spotted the father's car going south on the 5 Freeway. We wound up cornering the guy twenty miles outside of San Diego."

"You?" she asked specifically.

"And the other detective in the car," he added. "It was a team effort."

She knew how these things worked. What she was surprised at was that Benteen was being so modest. The man really didn't like being in the spotlight. "How's the little girl?" she asked.

"Scared." The scene played in his mind again. It had been difficult to witness and even more difficult to do "the right thing."

"She didn't want to leave her father. Seems she wanted to be with him instead of her mother."

"Little girls do love their daddies," Ellie commented. However, that wasn't always the case, which caused her to ask, "Did she say why?"

Colin recalled the little girl's words. "'Daddy's more fun.' She said her mother had too many rules she had to follow."

"Rules can be good," Ellie interjected, thinking of what Heather had said about her uncle having been more fun before she'd become his responsibility. She couldn't help wondering if the girl had ever said that to the detective. That could have been the reason he seemed so sensitive retelling the tale.

"Yeah, but a kid needs fun," Colin countered. He frowned slightly, thinking of the man they had taken into custody. "Hated having to take the guy in. All he wanted was to be with his daughter." He sighed. "I told him that he and his wife should have found a way to work it out for the little girl's sake—and that he could still try."

"In a perfect world…"

Her voice trailed off, but Colin knew what she was

saying. In a perfect world, there would be happy end-ings no matter how rocky the road to get there might be.

If only...

"But this isn't a perfect world," Colin said, more to himself that to her.

A shaft of sadness speared through her, making her heart ache. Tears came into her eyes even though she tried to block them. Sometimes all it took was a word, a familiar scent, a lyric, and she was catapulted into the past, reliving it again. Always with the same ending.

"No," she whispered, "It's not a perfect world."

For a second, Colin thought that the woman had been affected by the story he'd just told her. If that was the case, the reporter had an incredible sense of empathy, he felt, amazed.

And then, literally out of nowhere, a fragment of a thought darted through his mind, bringing with it a flash of the last case he'd had as a patrolman. He was on his knees in a convenience store, desperately try-ing to stop a man's life from oozing away.

Why the hell had he thought of that now? Colin upbraided himself. What possible connection did it have with the case he'd had tonight?

And then he realized it *wasn't* the Amber Alert case that had made him think of the other one; it was the name. The reporter's last name.

King.

He looked at the woman now, then dismissed it. It couldn't be. King was a pretty common surname. If there had been a connection between her and the man who had died on the floor of that store that night, the reporter would have said something.

Wouldn't she?

Sure she would. Talking was what she did. She would have brought it up by now.

He was just tired, Colin told himself. More than tired, he was wiped out.

"Something wrong?" she asked him, approaching the subject cautiously, like someone tasked with defusing a bomb.

"No," he said, then explained, "Just something I thought of. But it doesn't make sense." Colin shrugged, dismissing the stray thought. "It's nothing, just my overworked mind."

That was her cue to leave. More like escape, Ellie silently corrected. In either case, the man needed his sleep. So did she, although she didn't sleep all that well anymore.

"And I'm keeping you up, so I'm going to leave now," Ellie told him, getting up.

"You also fed me," he said, indicating the empty plate. "And I have to say that was really good."

She took the plate and deposited it into his sink. "Well, you don't 'have to,' but I'll take it as a compliment."

He rose to his feet because she had. "Do you do this kind of thing often?" he asked.

She turned to look at him, bemused. "What? Take compliments?"

"No." He nodded toward his sleeping niece. "Go out of your way like this to spend time with a fan."

Ellie smiled as she shrugged. "Why not? It's good for my ego."

She didn't strike him as someone with an ego. He also noticed she didn't answer the question. He let it go. "I know that you made her day. Heather really appreciated this—so do I."

She picked up her messenger bag and secured it across her shoulder. "Call it payback."

Colin wasn't following her. "For what?"

That had just slipped out and she hadn't meant it to. Her mind scrambled to do a little damage control, searching for an explanation she could give him.

"For the interview segment I did on you earlier this week," she finally said.

"Oh, that." He waved it away as he walked her the short distance to the front door. "To be honest, I really didn't think I was going to get to review the footage before you aired it."

She didn't understand. "Then why did you call to tell me I lied?"

"Probably to teach you not to make promises you couldn't deliver—and I thought it might be a way to get you to agree to meet Heather," he admitted. "I was just hoping you'd give her an autograph or something." He glanced back into the living room, where his niece was sleeping. "This is something she's going to remember for a long, long time," he told the reporter.

Ellie put his words into a more realistic setting. "Until she gets her first crush on a boy and he's nice to her."

Colin groaned. "Boys. Oh God, I hope that doesn't happen for another ten years or so."

"Good luck with that," Ellie laughed. "Your niece is very advanced for her age," she pointed out. "Try another six months—or less."

He almost seemed to go pale right in front of her eyes. "You're kidding, right?"

"Do you even remember girls at that age?" she prodded. "Think back to when you were ten or eleven."

"I was a saint," he told her. He almost managed to say the words with a straight face.

"I really doubt that." Ellie gave him a highly skeptical look.

"What makes you say that?" he asked, doing his best not to smirk precisely because he *did* recall himself at that age.

"Let's just call it keen reporter's instincts," she told him, patting his face. "Good night, Detective," Ellie said as she crossed the threshold onto his doorstep. "It's been an interesting evening in more ways than one."

"Same here," he told her.

Colin stood in his doorway, watching as the woman walked to her car in guest parking. He continued standing there as she got in behind the steering wheel.

"Good night, Ellie King," he murmured.

As he closed his door, Colin couldn't shake the feeling that he was missing something.

Chapter Eight

The deliveryman threaded his way across various cables and wires that were on the studio floor, not an easy feat, given that his vision was partially blocked by the large profusion of flowers he was carrying and charged with delivering. Whenever possible, he stopped to ask where he could find the intended recipient of the flowers.

The last person he asked pointed him to Ellie's desk. But when he set down the arrangement, there was no one sitting at the desk.

Haplessly, the deliveryman looked around for someone he could snag long enough to have them put their signature on the electronic pad he'd tucked under his arm.

"Um, I need to have someone sign for this," he said, raising his voice and hoping to get someone's attention.

Hearing what almost amounted to a plea as he entered the bull pen, Jerry quickly cut across the floor to Ellie's desk in order to put the man out of his misery.

"Here, I'll sign," Jerry volunteered. With a flourish, Jerry signed his name with the stylus that was attached to the pad. Giving the pad back to the deliveryman, he glanced at the effusive basket and commented, "Nice arrangement."

"Boss insists on the best," the deliveryman replied, glancing over the pad to make sure everything was in order. An automatic smile momentarily came over his lips as he said, "Have a good day."

"Yeah, you, too," Jerry murmured. Because he had signed for the delivery, he felt that gave him the right to peek at the card, which he did. And then he smiled. "Well, well, well."

"'Well' what?" Ellie asked, entering the room from the opposite direction. She'd just finished reviewing several upcoming segments with the program manager, including the one he wanted taped today. The clock was ticking.

Jerry stepped back, giving her a clear view of her desk. He gestured grandly toward the basket. "Well, it looks like someone made a good impression on someone else."

Seeing the flowers for the first time, Ellie stopped walking. No one sent her flowers. Her first thought was that it had to be a mistake. The flowers were meant for someone else.

She looked at Jerry. "Where did those come from?"

"My guess is it wasn't the flower fairy." He grinned, unable to contain himself. He parked himself on the edge of her desk, leaning his hip against it. "So, you talked with the detective like I suggested."

Her eyes widened. "These are from him?" she asked, quickly crossing the rest of the distance to her desk.

"See for yourself. There's the card." Jerry pointed to it. Cocking his head to underscore the innocent tone he affected, he asked, "Who's Heather?"

"Detective Benteen's niece," Ellie answered, searching through the flowers for the card. "You ask more questions than my mother." Finding the card, she pulled it out. "What are you doing reading my card, anyway?"

"Someone had to sign for the flowers," he told her. "I figured that entitled me to see who sent them." Since she hadn't acknowledged what he'd said earlier, he repeated himself. "I guess you and the good detective had that talk and came to terms, eh?"

Ellie refused to answer him. Instead, she read the card. *Thank you for Saturday. I haven't seen Heather this happy in a long, long time.*

Ellie looked up to see Jerry watching her smugly. She knew it would have been a lot easier just to let her cameraman assume that he was right, but she wasn't in the habit of lying, even about minor things, and she didn't want Jerry thinking she'd followed his advice when she hadn't yet. The man had a big enough ego as it was.

"If you must know, no," she said, annoyed. "We didn't have that talk. He asked me to meet his niece. Turns out that she's a fan, so I said sure. We met at Josie's Café. It was only supposed to be for an hour, but while we were talking, he got a call telling him to come to the scene of a crime. I volunteered to stay with his niece until he got back."

It was more complicated than that, but there was no point in going into babysitting neighbors or any of the rest of what had been involved. She was trying to keep her story streamlined.

Ellie glanced at Jerry and saw the knowing expression on her cameraman's face. It was bordering on a smirk.

"Don't give me that look," she told him.

"What look?" he asked innocently.

"You're grinning," Ellie accused.

"Who, me?" he said with far too much feeling. "No. I'm just enjoying listening to you tell your story." And then he gave up the ruse. "It's just nice to see you getting out again."

"I wasn't 'getting out,'" she insisted, knowing that the cameraman thought she'd gone out with the detective. It wasn't like that. "I was just—" Ellie gave up. There was no point in beating her head against the wall. Jerry was going to see things his way no matter what she said to the contrary. "Oh, never mind. Marty wants us to cover a story at Bedford's animal shelter. Grab your gear," she ordered.

"Animal shelter?" Jerry repeated as he hurried after her. "Are you sure?"

"Yes, why?" She spared him a look over her shoulder. To her relief, the flowers—and the reason for them—had been forgotten.

For now.

"Last time we did one of those stories, I came home with a geriatric dog and a rabbit. Betsy wasn't very happy about it," he recalled. "If I come home with anything else, she's going to put us all out on the drive-way."

Ellie laughed because she knew Jerry's distress was genuine. He might talk big, but he had a heart made out of mush.

"Just stay strong, Jerry—and remember to say no," she advised.

"I can't help it if I have a marshmallow center," he protested, hustling behind her.

"It goes well with your marshmallow build," Ellie deadpanned.

Jerry grumbled under his breath. Ellie pretended not to hear him. At least he wasn't asking any more questions about her meeting with the detective, she thought, relieved. She had a hard enough time trying to figure out why she'd done it herself, much less answering any of the questions Jerry could come up with.

The next moment, she put the whole thing out of her mind. She had a segment to tape and it deserved her full attention.

The assignment ran twice as long as she'd anticipated.

The shelter, it turned out, was also planning to have an adopt-a-pet event that following Saturday and the people in charge were using the volunteer drive she had been sent to cover to promote that.

Ellie had always had a weak spot for animals. Caught up in the story, Ellie found herself losing her heart to a mixed-breed puppy with the improbable name of Pancakes. Pancakes was all paws, licking tongue and tons of unbridled energy.

Before she realized it, Ellie had paid the very nomi-

nal fee the shelter charged for the dog's shots, a cer-
tificate of ownership and a license. And just like that,
she became Pancakes's new owner.

"I can't keep you, you know," Ellie informed the
puppy, who was riding in the back of her sedan. Not
exactly riding, she amended. Pancakes was running
back and forth on the floor like a claustrophobic prison
inmate searching for an avenue of escape. "I sprung
you in a moment of weakness because you are just
the cutest thing I've ever seen, but it wouldn't be fair
to you if I took you home. I'm hardly ever there. You
need a hands-on owner." Coming to a stop at a red
light, she glanced over her shoulder to her frantic furry
passenger. "You realize that, don't you?"

Ellie sighed. "Lord, I must be losing it—I'm having
a conversation with a dog. A one-way conversation."
At which point the dog yipped. "Okay, maybe not so
one-way," she corrected herself, putting her foot back
on the accelerator. "But you still need someone who
can walk you and play with you. I'm hardly home long
enough to put my laundry away."

Pancakes yipped again, louder this time.

"You need a keeper, you know." And then she
thought of the flowers on her desk.

Belatedly, she remembered that she hadn't had a
chance to call Benteen to thank him yet. This would
be a way to thank him and to get Pancakes a home that
was more suited to his energetic personality.

Ellie smiled. Two birds with one stone.

Perfect!

"Hang on, Pancakes—I'm going to take you to your
new home."

Ellie made a sharp right at the next corner.

* * *

Fifteen minutes later, overzealous puppy in her arms and carrying a bag of dry dog food she'd bought at the shelter, Ellie found herself standing in front of Colin Benteen's door. She knocked once and mentally crossed her fingers that he was home.

Colin had gotten home in time to watch the evening broadcast of the news with Heather. She talked through most of it until the segment with Ellie came on. Then his niece became as silent as a tomb, rabidly watching every move her idol made and listening to every word as if each one of them was a singular golden pearl of wisdom. The fact that Ellie's segment tonight was filmed in the city's animal shelter, with Ellie surrounded by a dozen yapping dogs and one duck that seemed to think it too was a dog, only endeared her all the more to Heather.

The segment and Heather's reaction to it were still very fresh in his mind as Colin went to answer the door. He hadn't heard from Ellie and was beginning to wonder if perhaps he'd overstepped his bounds by sending her flowers.

Had he offended her? Or maybe she felt that he was crowding her. Since she hadn't called, he could only assume that it was one or the other, or possibly a combination of both.

Then he opened his door and all his theories and suppositions were immediately placed on hold. It was as if she had materialized out of his thoughts and onto his doorstep. What really captivated his attention was what she appeared to be holding in her arms.

At first it just looked like a mass of moving light tan fur mixed with shafts of white. But the very next moment it barked and the mystery of what she was holding was solved.

Like an international call to attention, the bark also managed to instantly draw Heather to the door. The next moment, she was grinning from ear to ear.

"Ellie, you're here!" she exclaimed excitedly.

"Bearing fur," Colin observed wryly.

"Actually," Ellie said, doing her best to hold on to Pancakes, who was doing *her* very best *not* to be held on to, "I came to bring Heather a present."

Heather's eyes suddenly widened to the point that they looked as if they were in danger of falling out. "That's for me?" she cried, immediately assuming that her new best friend was referring to the dog that was just barely contained in her arms.

Ellie turned toward Colin, who was still holding the door open like a conscientious sentry. "May I come in?" she asked him.

"Sorry." Realizing that he was standing there rigidly, Colin stepped back and opened his front door farther. "You took me by surprise," he admitted by way of an excuse.

"This was all very spur-of-the-moment," Ellie said, indicating the puppy she'd brought over. "I was shooting a segment at the local pet shelter today and this puppy—"

Heather cut in. "We just saw it!" She pointed toward the TV monitor as if it would bear her out. "The duck was funny."

"The duck has serious issues," Ellie cracked.

Heather's eyes never left the puppy that was frantically searching for a way to jump down, twisting and turning like an escape artist in a straitjacket. Not standing on ceremony, Heather began to pet the puppy's head and was rewarded with a tongue bath on her hand. Heather giggled.

"Is this the puppy you were holding on the show?" she asked eagerly.

"The puppy I was *trying* to hold on the show," Ellie corrected.

"Did they give him to you?" Heather asked.

Ellie laughed. Out of the corner of her eye, she saw the smile that came to the detective's lips. She wasn't sure if he was laughing at her or at the situation. For now she left it unexplored.

"It's a her," she corrected. "And it was more like she just refused to let me leave once we stopped rolling."

"I guess it looks like you have a puppy, then," Colin concluded as he joined his niece in petting the hyper animal.

"What's her name?" Heather asked.

"Pancakes," Ellie told her. "Don't look at me," she told Colin. "I had nothing to do with it. That's the name she came with."

"And she's yours?" Heather asked, still stroking the puppy.

"Well, I paid her fees," Ellie said, transferring the puppy from her arms to Heather's. "But she's not exactly mine," she continued. When both Heather and her uncle looked at her for an explanation, Ellie told them, "I'm not home long enough to give this dog the proper attention." She kept her gaze on Heather, deliberately avoiding making eye contact with Colin for the time being. "I thought that maybe you'd like to have a pet."

Heather looked so happy that for a second she

looked as if she was about to burst. "You're giving Pancakes to me?" she cried, barely able to contain her joy.

Ellie glanced toward the detective. She knew this was a roundabout and underhanded way of doing this, but she was rather desperate. "If it's okay with your uncle," she qualified.

Heather instantly turned her expressive green eyes on her uncle. "Please, Uncle Colin?" the girl pleaded. "Please?"

As if to reinforce her new would-be owner's pleas, the puppy began to madly lick Colin's face.

Laughing, Colin held the dog at arm's length before telling his niece, "You're going to be the one responsible for this bundle of fur."

"Absolutely!" Heather vowed.

Colin wasn't finished. "You'll have to walk her, feed her, make sure she stays off the furniture—and doesn't chew the furniture," he emphasized, pulling the puppy away from the corner of the sofa that Pancakes had begun to attack. The puppy was clearly teething.

"Yes, yes, yes," Heather answered each question with enthusiasm. She scooped the puppy back up into her arms, giggling as she felt her neck being licked. "So I can keep her?"

"For now," Colin warned. "But if you fall down on the job, if you start forgetting to feed her, to play with her, she's going to have to go back."

"To the shelter?" Heather cried, obviously stunned that her uncle could be that strict, even though it was a known fact; one that Ellie had emphasized in her story, that the shelter had a no-kill policy no matter how crowded it became.

"No, to the news reporter who brought her," Colin told her, glancing at Ellie.

Ellie put her arm around the girl's shoulders, giving her a light squeeze. "I'm sure that she'll do an excellent job, won't you, Heather?" she asked, looking down at the preteen.

"I will, oh, I will," Heather promised keenly.

"If you're interested," Ellie told both Colin and his niece, "Pancakes has had all her shots." She opened her messenger bag and took out several sheets of paper documenting the puppy's care and the shots she'd received. "Here's her health history and her license. She's all paid up for a year."

Colin took the papers from her and placed them on the counter. "And you're not keeping her because—?"

"I don't have enough time to properly take care of her." She looked at the bundle of love on four paws. "It's a shame and I wish I did, but it just wouldn't be fair to Pancakes to keep her locked up all day when I'm away, working."

Still holding the puppy in her arms, Heather was being rewarded with a bath of what she referred to as "doggy kisses." She looked, Colin noted, as if she'd died and gone to heaven.

"You can come visit her anytime you want," she told Ellie.

She appreciated the invitation, but there was something else to consider. "I think that might be up to your uncle, honey."

Both Heather and Ellie stared in his direction.

On the spot, Colin saw no reason to put up any obstacles. When he came right down to it, he welcomed an excuse to see the sexy reporter more often. She was really beginning to intrigue him—and it was obvious that Heather idolized her. She'd managed to get to his niece the way he hadn't been able to in six months.

"Sure, why not?" he said.

"Okay," Ellie said, nodding, "I'll take you up on that sometime." About to leave, she suddenly remembered what had been behind this visit in the very first place. "Oh, by the way, I almost forgot. I loved the flowers."

"So you did get them. Good."

She felt she owed him an explanation as to why she'd been so remiss expressing her thanks. "They arrived just as I had to go do the animal-shelter story, so I didn't have an opportunity to call you. You didn't have to send them," she added.

"And you didn't have to stay as long as you did Saturday, or prepare dinner," he told her.

Ellie nodded. "I guess then we're even."

He glanced at the puppy that seemed to be all teeth and paws as she climbed up Heather's arm. The puppy was like the very personification of trouble.

"Oh, I don't know about that," Colin speculated, then laughed. "I think the balance might be just a little off in this case."

Ellie inclined her head, unaware that her smile had managed to captivate the detective. "Maybe you're right. I'll pay for any initial damages," she offered.

He nodded. "That would be a start." And then he changed the subject. "Have you had dinner yet?"

"No, I came straight here from the shoot with the dog."

"You have plans for dinner?" Colin asked.

"Chewing it," she responded. Heather giggled.

"How about if you do that chewing here?" Colin nodded at the puppy. "You might be in good company for that."

"Are you inviting me to dinner?" Ellie asked him.

His smile was slow and all the more sensual because it took its time. "Apparently."

"Then yes," she said as if she actually had a choice rather than finding herself held in place by that smile on his lips, "I'll stay."

The dog yipped even as Heather cried, "Yay!"

Colin nodded. "I guess it's unanimous, then," he told Ellie as he turned to walk into the kitchen. "Hope you're not starving," he added. "This might take a while."

Chapter Nine

"What are you making for dinner?" Ellie asked, following him into the kitchen. "Maybe I can help."

Colin removed a flyer he'd mounted on the refrigerator before turning round to face her.

"No, I've got it covered," he said, holding up the flyer. "Dialing the phone is pretty much a one-person activity."

"You're calling for takeout?" she asked him in surprise.

"Yes. Pizza," he specified. "Why? What'd you think?"

"Well, I thought you meant that you were going to cook it since you said it was going to take a while," Ellie answered.

"So does delivery after I make the call," he pointed out.

She debated just bowing out and letting him make his call. It was the simplest thing to do. But since he'd extended an invitation to her, she felt almost obligated to help out.

"Is your heart set on pizza?" she asked.

"Not particularly, but the wait time for pizza is the shortest and there's a Pizza King's less than a mile away," he pointed out, indicating the flyer in his hand.

Ellie moved past him and opened his refrigerator. She did a quick inventory of its contents—not exactly teeming, but not barren, either—then moved on to his rather limited pantry. That *was* relatively barren except for an unopened container of flavored bread crumbs and a few miscellaneous spices, origin unknown.

"Give me a few minutes," she told him. Then, looking up because she sensed he hadn't moved an inch, she said, "Go play with the puppy."

"What are you going to do?" he asked. The way he saw it, there wasn't very much to work with in either the refrigerator or the pantry. Just exactly what did she have in mind?

Ellie merely smiled and answered, "Make magic. Now go. Magic doesn't happen if you're watching for it."

Colin shook his head. The woman didn't look it at first, but she really was rather stubborn.

"Whatever you say. You change your mind and want to bail, here's the number of the pizza place," Colin told her, returning the flyer to the refrigerator and securing it with a magnet one of the real estate brokers had left on his doorstep.

"I won't be needing it," Ellie told him, pushing up her sleeves.

He had to admit he was enjoying this. "You sound very sure of yourself."

She spared him one last look before she shooed him out of the kitchen. "I am. Now go watch your niece play with the puppy."

He had no recourse but to do as she said.

"This was in my refrigerator?" Colin questioned less than half an hour later as he sat at the table with his niece and Ellie.

For the puppy's part, Pancakes had assumed an alert position between him and Heather, waiting for something to fall on the floor by either accident or design. Gifted with a strong sense of smell, as all dogs were, the puppy was already salivating.

"And your pantry," Ellie added. "In rough form," she allowed, "but it was definitely there."

"And what's this we're eating called again?" he asked.

"She said it was a frittata," Heather told him with the confidence of youth.

He got a kick out of the knowing way she'd answered him. "Oh, and you know what that is."

"Sure." She turned toward Ellie with a smile. "It's what we're eating, right, Ellie?"

"You're supposed to call her Ms. King," Colin corrected his niece.

Ellie had never been a stickler for formality and this whole evening was anything but formal. "I think we've come to the point where she can call me Ellie," the reporter told him. "And for the record, you can make a frittata as long as you have a few eggs and bread crumbs. The rest of the ingredients are really dealer's choice. You mix together a little meat, a few chopped-up vegetables, add in a little salt, a little cheese, maybe some mustard and you really *can't* mess things up. The ingredients kind of take care of each other."

"This is really good," Heather enthused. The girl looked hopefully at her new idol. "Can you teach me how to make it?"

"Anytime," Ellie told her.

Colin had eaten his first portion with gusto. A second helping gave him more time to actually examine what it was he was putting into his mouth.

"This is kind of like an omelet," Colin said after a moment.

"I'd prefer to think of it as an omelet's second cousin once removed," Ellie interjected. "It's in the family and related, but really not the same thing," she qualified.

"Where'd you learn how to make that?" Heather asked.

The answer came out before Ellie could stop the words or think to rechannel them into something less telling. Something that didn't open up a door that was supposed to remain shut.

"My husband taught me."

Colin and Heather both looked at her sharply, and Heather was the first to speak. "You're married?" she asked, appearing to soak up information about her role model like a sponge.

"I was," Ellie answered quietly, her trademark sunniness temporarily missing.

Colin continued staring at her, his attention caught by her subdued voice. Something distant stirred in his head and then the next moment, it faded into the background before he could snare it long enough to examine it.

"What happened?" Heather asked.

"Heather, that's not any of our business," Colin rebuked her.

But it was yours, Ellie thought, eyeing the detective.

Out loud she told Heather, "He died trying to defend some people."

There was an enormous amount of compassion and sympathy in the young face as Heather looked at her. "Was he a policeman like Uncle Colin?"

"No, he was a Marine," Ellie told her. "Anyone for seconds?" she asked, abruptly changing the subject and her tone of voice, going from somber to cheerful although she had to force the latter.

Heather pushed her plate forward. "Yes, please." And then she added in a lower voice, "I gave some of the frittata to Pancakes."

"I had a feeling," Ellie told her with a knowing nod. "You?" she asked, turning toward Colin.

"Sure, why not?" Colin responded gamely.

While she'd had to mix together a potpourri of ingredients for the main course, there was no lack for dessert. Olga had brought over a cherry pie last night and over half of it was still in the pie tin, waiting on their pleasure.

"Is Olga a relative?" Ellie asked, curious as to the dynamics that were involved since he'd already told her that the neighbor could be called upon to stay with Heather whenever he had to take off on a case. Apparently, the woman also seemed to be in the habit of dropping off baked goods and main courses, as well.

"No," Colin told her, getting three dessert plates.

Ellie took out three forks and one large knife. "Just a good neighbor."

"Uh-huh." She presented Colin with the knife, leaving the portion size up to him. "How old is this good neighbor?" Ellie asked.

"Why?" After cutting what was left in half, he divided that up into thirds.

Ellie shrugged. "Well, I wouldn't want the woman thinking that I'm trying to muscle in on her territory," she said.

"Oh no, Olga doesn't think like that," Heather assured her before her uncle could say anything. "Besides, Olga's really, really old."

Ellie laughed at the emphasis in Heather's voice. She could distinctly remember being that young only a little while ago. "What's old to you?" she asked, then took a guess. "Forty?"

Heather shook her head, sending the ends of her hair whipping about her face as if they'd been caught up in the wind. "No, even more than that."

"Olga's like the grandmother I never had," Colin clarified as the puppy all but ran up his side. "Although she does tend to move around rather quickly," he added. There was admiration in his voice. "I thought she was retired until she told me that she worked for a housecleaning service. She offered to clean my place for free."

"Why?" Ellie asked, gazing around. "Your place looks pretty clean to me."

"That's because Uncle Colin and I cleaned it up right after she said that," Heather volunteered.

Cherry-pie dessert consumed, the little girl was the first one down on the floor, lying flat on her back as her new pet walked along her stomach before losing her footing and falling off in a light tan heap.

Rather than remain seated at the table, Colin joined his niece. He grinned now, listening to Heather's delighted laugh as she played with Pancakes.

Picking up the conversation's thread, he said, "I figured if the woman was actually offering to clean my place for free, it had to be really bad. So Heather and I got busy and cleaned it up."

Not wanting to be left out, Ellie joined them on the floor. They looked like they were having a great deal of fun.

Colin's self-discipline in the face of his neighbor's offer impressed her. "Most men would have just taken her up on her offer instead of doing what you did," Ellie told him.

Reaching out, she scratched Pancakes behind her ears. The puppy whirled around to look at her and tripped over her own oversize paws. The next moment, she was picking herself up as if nothing had happened, her boundless energy still very much intact.

"Wouldn't seem right," Colin said truthfully, going on to say, "I don't know why I let it get out of hand like that." He shrugged. "Sometimes it just takes seeing a thing through someone else's eyes to make you realize what's wrong." As he said it, something seemed to click in his head again. And then, just like before, it was gone.

Ellie saw the pensive expression that momentarily came over his face. "You've got a strange look on your face," she observed.

"You ever have a thought that insists on playing

hide-and-seek with your brain, turning up and just as you try to catch it, it vanishes?"

"Sure. Some people claim that's evidence of a past life," she told him, wondering if something was causing him to make the connection between the past and now. Not a past life, but just the past, as in two years ago.

Not wanting to get into it tonight—they'd all had a very nice evening and she didn't want it to end on a bad note—she added flippantly, "Me, I just call it stress. There's only so much you can crowd into your brain and hope to retrieve it."

Colin wasn't up to any deep soul-searching tonight, so he shrugged. "You're probably right."

Ellie smiled, more to herself than at him. "I usually am," she replied. And then she glanced at her watch. It was late. Later than she'd anticipated.

She quickly got to her feet. "I'd better go—it's getting late."

Heather scrambled up with ease, all while clutching the puppy against her.

"Oh, do you have to?" she cried. "Can't you stay longer?" she begged.

"I stay any longer and I'll have to move in," Ellie quipped.

Heather took the remark and ran with it, turning to her uncle to ask, "Can she, Uncle Colin? Then she could be the one to bring me to school and—"

"No, honey, I was just kidding," Ellie hurried to say, setting the record straight.

The little girl sounded as if she could just keep extrapolating on the topic until she was adopting her by evening's end. Ellie wanted to save the detective from the awkward situation of explaining why he couldn't have an almost perfect stranger moving in. That "talk" was something she assumed the detective would save until such time as he had a girlfriend who wanted to move in with him.

Where the hell had that come from? Ellie silently demanded. And why in heaven's name was she even *thinking* of something like that? It wasn't any business of hers what the detective did—and with whom.

This was all just a short interlude in their lives, in *her* life, nothing more, Ellie insisted. There was no reason to make anything more of it than it already was—which was nothing. They were barely friends, much less anything more.

"Sorry," she said to Colin, apologizing that her thoughtless comment had caused what she assumed was a moment of discomfort on his part. "Now I'd *really* better be going."

Colin looked a little perplexed. "Nothing to be sorry about," he told the woman, puzzled as to why she would even say something like that. "I'm the one who probably should apologize. We've kept you much too long," he said.

Some of the tension drained from her. Ellie laughed, then held up her wrists.

"Yes, please remove the chains so that I can be on my way." The next moment she told him, "Let's just call it even. Nobody kept anybody and a very good time was had by all."

"Actually, you're right. Heather had a ball and I had a good time, too," he said, realizing that it was true. He looked down at the puppy, who looked like trouble that was about to happen. "Of course, if Pancakes winds up destroying anything really important, I'm sending you the bill."

Ellie nodded her head. "Fair enough."

They were at the door but something within Colin was reluctant to have it end just yet. He wanted a few more minutes with the woman.

He glanced over his shoulder toward his niece. Heather was back on the floor, bonding with the puppy, who was finally losing a tiny bit of her steam.

"I'm just going to walk Ellie to her car," he called out. "You two will be all right?"

"Sure," Heather piped up. "Pancakes'll take care of me."

"I'm not so sure about that," Colin confided to the woman next to him. "If anything it's the other way around."

"You're probably right," Ellie agreed. Then, because she didn't want to put him out, she said, "You don't have to walk me to my car. I'm parked just a few feet away."

"Then it'll be a short walk," he replied.

Ellie had always been one to choose her arguments. Arguing over something so minor seemed pointless, so she just went along with him.

Checking his pocket for his keys, Colin pulled the ground-floor-apartment door closed behind him. Looking around the immediate parking area, he asked, "Where's your car?"

She pointed to her light blue sedan. It was parked right in front of the rental office.

"It's not *that* close," he commented.

"But it's not in the next state, either," she countered.

"Humor me," he told her, shortening his gait until

it matched hers. "I'm a cop. Most cops are obsessed with safety."

"South Bedford doesn't strike me as being a very dangerous area."

As a local reporter, she would have heard something to the contrary if that was the case. As it was, the city was known as one of the very safest of its size in the country.

"It's not," he agreed. "But there's always a first time."

Ellie merely nodded as she said, "Uh-huh."

"Now you're humoring me."

"It's what you told me to do, remember?" she reminded him.

A minimum of steps, no matter how slowly taken, brought her to her sedan.

"Well, here we are," she announced, "at my car. Nice and safe," she added.

The rental office was closed for the night; all its lights but one were turned off. Night, with its autumn chill, had descended. She should have brought a sweater, Ellie thought. The temperature drop at night this time of year could be drastic.

"Cold?" he asked, noticing that she was trying unsuccessfully not to shiver.

"I'll be inside my car in a second," she told him.

He took that as a yes and was tempted to put his arm around her for momentary warmth.

Colin refrained and instead stepped back as she unlocked the driver-side door.

"You're still using a key," he observed.

She laughed at herself, admitting, "I'm old-fashioned. A key makes me feel like I'm in charge."

"Is that important to you?" he asked. "Being in charge?"

"Sometimes," she acknowledged. "Other times," she allowed honestly, "not so much."

"I'm sorry if the conversation got a little too personal back there," Colin apologized, referring to the questions his niece had asked. "Heather tends to ask a lot of questions."

"Yes, I know, but that's all right," she said a little too quickly. "She has an inquisitive mind. Maybe she'll make a good reporter someday," Ellie speculated.

The conversation faded, its last strains drowned out by the sound of crickets making noise, each searching for a mate to spend the long night with.

There was a full moon out and as Colin looked on, it bathed Ellie in its light. As she turned to tell him good-night, Colin felt a very strong pull in the center of his gut.

At one point in his life, he would have just gone with it rather than trying to analyze it. But those times were behind him.

Or so he'd thought.

Despite Ellie's bravado, he couldn't shake the impression she gave him of a delicate, frightened doe that had to be approached with caution. Otherwise she'd take off.

The last thing he wanted to do was scare her off.

But the first thing he wanted to do, he realized with unmistakable clarity, was kiss her.

Chapter Ten

It was as if the world had suddenly, inexplicably slowed down to a crawl and everything from that point on was happening in slow motion.

There were only a couple of feet between Ellie and him, but they were eliminated not rapidly but almost a fraction of an inch at a time.

Colin drew closer; their faces drew nearer, ever nearer. Maybe he was imagining things, but he was almost certain that some of the distance between them, small as it was, was dispensed with by Ellie.

And then, at the final moment, just before his mouth came down on hers, Colin gave up thinking altogether. He just surrendered to the ever-growing attraction that had been between them all along.

He gave her ample time to stop him or turn away if she wanted to.

She didn't.

When Ellie didn't pull away or protest, he deepened the kiss and then put his arms around her to draw her even closer to him.

Colin hadn't fully realized how much he'd wanted this until just now, until it was actually happening. And it wasn't that he missed the experience and just wanted to kiss an attractive woman. He really wanted to kiss *her*, Elliana King.

When he felt Ellie threading her arms around his neck while they were still kissing, something within him cheered and he could have sworn he saw fireworks going off in his head.

At least it seemed that way.

It had been so long, so very long, since she'd let herself feel like a woman. She'd forgotten how really wondrous it could feel. Adrenaline raced through her, heightening her reaction. Everything within her pleaded "More" as she felt Colin deepen the kiss, making her literally ache.

Making her remember.

Everything inside Ellie sped up. Her breathing, her pulse, her reaction. Colin's arms enfolded her, pulling her closer, all but making her a part of him.

Colin's arms felt strong.

He made her feel safe.

Her defenses melted away.

And then the alarms in her head went off.

She was wrong.

She wasn't safe. She'd *never* be safe—she knew that. Pain was always just a heartbeat away, waiting to dismantle her, to consume her. Her only defense was not to allow herself to feel anything, not ever again. She couldn't set herself up for another fall, another heartache. This time, when, not *if*, it happened, it would completely destroy her.

At the same time guilt flooded through her, guilt over betraying Brett's memory. Brett was gone and she was alive. After two years it still made no sense to her. She didn't understand how she could keep on drawing breath in a world where he no longer was.

Appalled at what she'd just allowed to happen, what she was *guilty* of doing, Ellie suddenly braced her hands against the muscular chest that had been only a moment ago pressed against hers and she pushed Colin away with all her might.

"No," she cried, pulling her head back. "I can't. I'm sorry. I can't."

The words tumbled out over each other. She struggled not to break down in sobs as she quickly got into her vehicle.

In her hurry to escape, Ellie didn't even buckle her seat belt when she drove away. She left a stunned Colin in her wake.

"What the hell just happened here?" Colin murmured to himself, completely confused.

He hadn't a clue.

But he damn well intended to find out. He stood there for a moment, trying to figure out what had just transpired. Trying to understand why she'd been so warm and pliable in his arms one moment and then bolting like a bat out of hell that had been set on fire the next.

Turning around, he headed back to his apartment. Someone else would have just chalked up what had occurred to flaky behavior, but Colin wasn't the type who put much stock in those kinds of one-size-fits-all labels.

And even if he were, Ellie King just wasn't that kind of person. By no stretch of the imagination could she be regarded as "flaky."

Something else was at the bottom of this.

The whole incident was still very much on his mind the next morning.

Could he have misread the signals she'd been giving off, he asked himself. He wasn't usually wrong when it came to making judgment calls about people, either on the job or off.

No, something else was going on and he needed to find out what if he was to ever have any peace of mind about this.

He needed to get to the station to do some research.

To that end, he wanted to leave early. As with everything else in his life since he'd become a guardian, it required multiple steps.

He convinced Heather to hustle, not an easy accomplishment when all his niece really wanted to do was stay home and play with her new pet, all the while talking about what a great person Elliana King was.

Even as he got his niece out the door early, it didn't end there. He had the puppy to consider. For the sake of the rest of his furniture, he put a bowl of the dog food that Ellie had brought plus a bowl of water into the bathroom and closed the door.

Pitiful whining began almost instantly.

"Pancakes is going to think we're punishing her,"

Heather lamented even as he steered his niece through the doorway and out of the apartment.

He'd already noticed teeth marks on the corner molding by the kitchen.

"No, I did that so we don't *have* to punish her when we get home tonight." He opened the car's doors. "I'll pick up a puppy crate today," he promised. "Problem solved."

Heather climbed into the car, automatically reaching for her seat belt and buckling up.

"A crate?" she cried in dismay. "You're going to lock Pancakes up in a box?" she wailed indignantly.

"Actually, I heard somewhere that dogs like being in a crate—it's like their own little cave, their own space to defend." Backing out of his parking space, Colin saw the dubious way his niece looked at him. "I'm not making this up, Heather. It's on the internet," he told her. "Look it up."

Since they both knew that she was far more proficient on the computer than he was and could easily check out what he was telling her, that seemed to placate her, at least for now.

He only wished that the problem with Ellie could be so easily resolved, Colin thought ruefully.

The root of the problem, he decided after he'd dropped Heather off at school, had to be with Ellie's husband. She'd told Heather that he'd died. Maybe the woman had unresolved feelings about his death, or even more likely, she felt disloyal being attracted to another man.

No ego failing to thrive here, Colin thought, mocking himself.

In order to begin to understand why things had suddenly gone south last night, he would have to educate himself about the woman he found himself so attracted to.

The good news, he thought as he walked into the squad room, was that everyone's life was an open book to some extent these days. While he himself had little time for that—the tools of social media just did *not* interest him—he knew that others did.

Nowadays everyone in the public eye, celebrities, politicians, actors, newscasters, all of those people, depended on having a following—obviously the more the better for the purposes of their careers. Which in turn meant that Elliana King's life had to be accessible to him.

Colin decided, at least to start with, to go the easy route, so he just did a search on her name.

There was no shortage of sources.

He highlighted the first websites in the list, forgoing various videos, reviews and the comments written in by others. He wasn't interested in what anyone else thought of her. What he wanted to find out about was Ellie's background. Not the name of the station where she got her start, or what schools she graduated from—that was information to look into on possibly another day. He was specifically interested in the fleeting comment Ellie had made to his niece when Heather had asked her if she was married.

He had a feeling that the answers he was seeking and her abrupt about-face last night could be found there. Unearthing her bio didn't take him long. He waded through paragraphs of information until he got to the crucial part.

As he was reading, the muscles in his jaw slackened. He read the pertinent paragraphs he'd found several times to make sure he hadn't misread them.

And then he went into his own back files. Specifically, the last case he'd had as a uniformed officer.

It all came back to him.

"Damn it, that's why," he muttered.

"Why what?" Sanchez asked, looking up. Coming in late, Al Sanchez had just put down his coffee container and pulled up his chair.

Their desks butted up against one another and Colin now looked across that expanse. He hadn't realized he'd said anything out loud. Glancing up, he locked eyes with the man he'd only recently been partnered with. His old partner had switched departments at the same time that Sanchez's partner had retired. Theirs was not a marriage made in heaven, but it was comfortable enough and growing more so.

"Nothing," Colin murmured.

"Sounded like a pretty loud 'nothing' to me," Sanchez contradicted. "Give." When Colin made no response, Sanchez got up from his desk and circled around behind his new partner. "We catch a cold case?" he asked, reading the information on the screen.

Rather than close the window, Colin decided to leave it open. Sanchez was the type to keep digging once his interest was aroused.

"No, it's a closed case," Colin said. "My last case as a uniformed officer. A convenience-store robbery that went wrong." He recalled it now as vividly as if it had happened yesterday.

Sanchez read a few lines and began to nod. "Yeah, I remember that one. That's the one with the Marine who'd just come home after a couple of tours of duty. He tried to stop this guy from robbing a young couple and caught a bullet for his trouble."

Colin turned his seat to look at his partner, curious. "Why would you remember this case?"

"Because of that reporter on the local news station, the woman who was covering it. She fainted on the air and that created a hell of a stir. Didn't you see it?" Sanchez asked, surprised.

Colin shook his head. "No."

Back in those days, he never even turned on the TV monitor in his apartment. He'd been too busy enjoying the company of the fairer sex to spend his time watching images on the screen.

"Why'd did she faint?" Colin asked. The tingling feeling he was experiencing told him that he might just be onto why Ellie had reacted the way she had last night.

Sanchez blew out a breath. "Well, it seems that no one told her that the guy who saved that couple at the convenience store from being shot—and got killed for his trouble—was her husband," he recalled.

Colin could only stare at his partner. "What?"

Sanchez nodded. "Yeah. He'd only been home a couple of days and was just picking up a carton of milk on his way home when he saw what was going down and put himself in harm's way to keep that young couple from getting hurt. The robber panicked and started shooting. That was *your* case?" Sanchez asked in disbelief. He shook his head in amazement. "Small world, I guess."

"Too small," was all that Colin would say.

It explained a lot.

What it didn't explain was why Ellie hadn't said anything to him. She had to have known of his involvement in the case. He was the officer on record and if she'd covered the story, she had to know that he was the policeman who'd taken down the killer—and the one who'd tried to save her husband.

Tried and failed, Colin reminded himself grimly. He could still see the Marine's blood oozing through his fingers as he vainly applied pressure to the wound to try to stop the bleeding.

Damn it, Colin thought in frustration, that was what had been nagging at him all this time, what kept trying to surface only to fade away again. This was that elusive memory that refused to take shape, the one he kept trying to catch hold of but just couldn't.

Why hadn't Ellie said anything to him? he asked himself again in exasperation. When she'd first shown up at the station to do that interview with him, she must have known then who he was. She'd said that she'd done her homework—that meant getting his background. She was far too much of a professional not to have known the connection between them.

And yet she hadn't said anything.

Why?

Colin felt confused, conflicted.

His mind peeled apart the situation in a dozen different ways with none of them yielding a satisfactory conclusion. About the only thing he knew at this point was that he needed to collect himself before he talked to Ellie about it.

Right now he felt like someone who had just walked over a land mine. He was still intact, but just barely—and very likely to say the wrong thing.

Wanting to distract himself—and calm down—Colin used his lunch hour to go to the pet store to purchase the puppy crate he'd told his niece about. While he was at it, he stocked up on several different kinds of dog treats and another bag of dry dog food, this one manufactured by a chef who prided herself on being able to prepare food equally appetizing for man and beast.

He dropped all that off, along with a couple of chew toys that he thought might come in handy, in his apartment.

Colin remained there only long enough to release Pancakes from the bathroom and place the puppy into her new home away from home, the puppy crate. He felt that the puppy needed to get accustomed to it before Heather came home.

Once he finally got back to the station, Colin called Olga, leaving a detailed message on her answering machine about both the puppy and the new crate, explaining everything.

He fervently hoped the woman liked dogs.

The remainder of the time that he spent at the station, Colin focused on work, giving it his undivided attention. Apparently, the witless art thief he'd caught the other day—the one that had brought Ellie into his life—wanted to make a deal with the assistant DA. The latter had said that his presence was needed to verify and back up several facts of the case.

While Colin always invested himself in his job 100 percent, he couldn't block out the thoughts about Ellie that were at the back of his mind, slowly eating away at him.

For that reason, Colin couldn't wait for his day to

finally be over. He just prayed that nothing would come up at the last minute, the way it was wont to do at times, necessitating his presence beyond the end of his shift.

The second his shift was officially over, Colin cleared out, his hasty exodus causing his partner to comment rather wistfully, "Hot date tonight?"

"I wouldn't describe it as that," Colin answered, not wanting to go into specifics.

Sanchez locked his drawer and shrugged into his plaid jacket.

"Hell, I'd settle for a lukewarm date at this point. All the wife and I do is stare at the TV—separately," he emphasized. "She's got hers on in the living room, I watch my shows in the family room."

He and Sanchez walked out of the squad room together. "Maybe you should give watching together a try," Colin suggested.

Sanchez merely shook his head at the idea. He pressed for the elevator. "She doesn't like any of the programs I watch."

"Try watching the ones she likes," Colin told the older man.

Sanchez made a face as they got on the elevator car. "I'm not that desperate," he told his partner as the doors closed.

Some horses just couldn't be led to water. "Think about why you proposed to her in the first place."

In response, Sanchez rolled his eyes dramatically. "*That* hasn't happened in a long time."

He was definitely getting too much information

here, Colin thought. He had only one last suggestion for his romance-challenged partner.

"Maybe if you watch TV with her, it might. You'll never know until you try," he told the man.

Reaching the ground floor, the elevator opened and they both got off.

"Yeah, well, maybe. We'll see," Sanchez muttered. "See you in the morning."

"Right, see you."

They parted company at the front door.

Colin hurried over to his sedan.

He had suppressed the urge to call Ellie more than a dozen times today, feeling that a face-to-face meeting with her would be far more effective than just talking to her on the phone.

He considered his options. He did *not* want to confront her at work and turning up at her home might make the woman feel he was stalking her. So the only thing left for him to do was sit in his car in the studio's parking lot and wait for her to leave the building where she worked. She had to come out sometime.

As it turned out, he didn't have long to wait.

Chapter Eleven

Ellie's heart almost stopped when she spotted Colin walking toward her. Acutely aware of the way they had parted last night, she would have preferred pretending that she didn't see him, but he had seen her looking right at him, so there was no way she could avoid saying something to him.

However, she didn't want to get into any sort of a serious discussion, either. Doing so would just bring up memories that hurt far too much.

Momentarily at a loss as to how to handle the situation, Ellie said the first thing that came to her mind.

"Something wrong with the puppy?"

"The puppy's fine. My apartment's a little worse for the wear, but I picked up a puppy crate at a pet store, so that should keep her from chewing up everything in sight while I'm not home."

"Good," Ellie said, not really listening. All she wanted to do was get away. Reaching her car, she began to open the driver-side door. "If there's nothing else, I've got to be—"

Colin didn't put his hand up to keep the door from closing, didn't block her access to it with his body. It was what he said that caused her to freeze in place. "Why didn't you tell me?"

The same heart that had felt as if it stopped beating at the sight of him now seemed to sink all the way down into her stomach. Obviously, she wasn't going to be able to make that quick getaway.

"You didn't come to see me about the puppy, did you?" she asked quietly.

She couldn't read his expression. "No, I didn't." His eyes pinned her in place as surely as if someone had nailed her shoes to the ground. And then the detective surprised her with a question. "We've interacted how many times?"

She braced herself for a confrontation. Jerry had warned her about this and he was right, she couldn't help thinking. She should have told Colin about the way they were connected before this.

Ellie shrugged. She wanted to look away, but she didn't and wanted to defend her position if she could.

"I don't know," she told him. "Honestly, I wasn't counting."

"Five," he answered in the same emotionless voice he'd just used. "Five times if you count when you interviewed me on camera and my phone call after that piece aired. We interacted *five* times and not once could you tell me that you knew that I was the one who found your husband at the convenience store that night. Why?" Colin demanded.

Ellie shrugged again, feeling helpless. Feeling cornered. She hated it, even if ultimately Benteen had a point. She *should* have told him. She hadn't. End of story.

"There was no right way to work it into the conversation."

"The hell with the 'right way,'" he told her, raising his voice as he dismissed what he viewed as flawed reasoning. "How about the right thing?" he asked. "As in telling me you knew I was the cop on record that night. How could you keep something like that from me?" he demanded, struggling to control his temper. "Were you planning on springing it on me after you were convinced that I was hooked on you? Did you want to make me somehow pay for not being able to save him?" Colin asked. "Because I tried, Ellie. I tried my damnedest to save him and it haunted me for a long time that I couldn't."

She stared at him, speechless.

"I rode all the way to the hospital in the ambulance with him, trying to bully him into hanging on even when I knew there was no hope," he told her.

Colin blew out a breath, his impotent anger beginning to subside. "I didn't know you found out about his death while you were on the air, doing the story about the foiled robbery. I had no idea until Sanchez informed me today," he said. "Maybe I should have been the one to notify you about his death, but my sergeant told me someone was sent to talk to the Marine's family, and frankly, I was glad because I didn't want to have to face them. I didn't want to tell them that I couldn't save him."

"There was no 'family,'" Ellie informed him in a still, subdued voice. "There was only me."

His eyes continued to hold hers. "And you knew I was the patrolman?" he asked her.

Ellie nodded her head slowly. "Yes, I knew," she admitted.

"Then why didn't you say something?" he asked. "I don't mean when you had that microphone shoved in my face, but afterward, why didn't you tell me you knew who I was?"

He wanted to know, okay, she'd tell him, Ellie decided—and hoped that she wouldn't wind up breaking down while she did it. "Because I didn't want to bring it up. Because I'm still trying to put it behind me." There were tears in her eyes as she looked at him. Tears she was desperately struggling to hold back. "Because it was all my fault."

That was a curveball he hadn't expected. For a second, she'd knocked the air out of him. And then he found his tongue.

"How was it your fault?"

She gave up trying not to cry. The tears slid down her cheeks. "If I hadn't told him to pick up that damn quart of milk on his way home, he wouldn't have stopped at the convenience store. And if he hadn't stopped, he'd still be alive."

"Was he passing the convenience store on his way home?"

"Yes," she answered, averting her face so he couldn't watch her crying.

Colin took her face in his hands and deliberately

but gently turned it toward him. "Then he would have seen the robbery taking place and, being the kind of man he was, he would have tried to stop it anyway."

Seeing Ellie crying this way undid him completely. Colin took her into his arms and held her. "It wasn't the milk, it was the man, and ultimately you had nothing to do with that."

Ellie resisted his offer of comfort for all of thirty seconds. And then she just broke down and really cried. Cried the way she hadn't allowed herself to cry in two years.

She cried for a long time.

Colin said nothing. Instead, he held her, letting her cry it out, his silence telling her that he was there for her if she needed him. That all he wanted her to do was feel better.

Finally, spent, Ellie drew her head back. "Oh God," she said, trying to wipe away the tears from her cheeks with her hands. "I must look like such a mess."

Colin smiled as he offered her his handkerchief. "A beautiful mess," he amended.

She took his handkerchief. "Right. You must have a very low threshold of *beautiful*," Ellie told him as she passed his handkerchief along first one cheek, then the other, drying them in earnest before she handed the handkerchief back to him.

"Actually, I don't." Colin absently tucked the cloth into his pocket. His attention was completely focused on her. "Do you feel like going somewhere for a drink?" he asked.

"A cop encouraging drinking and driving?" she asked wryly, doing her best to smile. It was a half-hearted effort at best.

"Doesn't have to be alcohol," he pointed out, then offered her some choices. "Coffee? Tea? Maybe a smoothie?"

Ellie eyed him rather skeptically and asked in disbelief, "You drink smoothies?"

He laughed softly, understanding her surprise. He wouldn't have touched a smoothie six months ago, but things had changed since then.

"Actually, I've tried a lot of things since I became Heather's guardian," he told her. "She loves them and I have to admit, some of them aren't half bad. How about it?"

She took another deep breath, trying to steady herself. "Speaking of Heather, shouldn't you be getting home to her?"

"It's okay," he assured her. "Olga's watching her. And now that she's got Pancakes, I don't think Heather even notices I'm not there."

"Oh, she notices," Ellie assured him, more attuned to his niece than he thought. "Trust me, with her parents gone, you're the center of her universe."

This time as she opened her car door in order to slide in behind the steering wheel, Colin did hold the door in place. She looked up at him, waiting for an explanation. She'd assumed that they were done; obviously not.

"You shouldn't be alone right now," he told her seriously. "Tell you what—why don't you follow me home?"

A refusal was on the tip of her tongue, but she knew he was right. She really didn't want to be alone tonight. After what had just happened here, if she was alone, it would give her time to think and magnify everything.

She supposed she could always call her mother. Her mother would be over before she had time to terminate her call. She knew that her mother worried about her. Her mother especially worried about her not getting on with her life and she didn't want to have that conversation tonight.

Colin was still watching her, waiting for an answer to his suggestion that she follow him home. Waiting for her to agree.

"I bet you say that to all the women," she said flippantly.

"Actually," he told her, his eyes still on hers, "I don't." The next moment, he deliberately lightened the mood by asking her another question. "Don't you want to see what that energized ball of fur is doing to my floorboards?" When she seemed confused, he elaborated on the situation. "I didn't know that dogs teethed."

"Well, she's a puppy, which means she's a baby dog, and all babies teethe, so I guess it's to be expected."

He supposed she was right. But just like he'd never been a guardian before, he'd also never had a pet before. This was all just one giant learning process for him.

"A little warning might have been nice," Colin told her.

"Think of it as a learn-as-you-go kind of situation," she suggested.

"Do I have a choice?" he asked, knowing that he didn't. Heather was so crazy about the dog there was no way the animal could be given its walking papers. Pancakes was there to stay.

Ellie laughed then. It was a small laugh, but in his estimation, it was gratifying to hear.

"No."

"Then I'll learn as I go," he said thoughtfully. "So, are we all set? You're following me home?" he asked, just to be clear that she hadn't changed her mind. "I know that Heather'll be thrilled."

Ellie nodded, relieved that she had an excuse. She wondered if Colin knew that.

"I can't disappoint my fan base, I guess," she agreed.

"Good," he pronounced, glad that *that* was settled. "Then I'll see you at the apartment."

As he turned to go, Ellie caught her lower lip between her teeth, debating. And then called after him just before he was out of earshot.

"Colin?"

He turned around thinking she was going to beg off after all, so he braced himself. In the end, the decision was up to her. He knew he couldn't very well drag her off by her hair. There was only so much persuading he could do.

"Yes?" Colin stood there, waiting.

She'd never had a problem with apologies. If she was wrong, she always willingly owned up to it. But this time around, it was hard. Hard for so many reasons. Now that it was out in the open, there was no turning back. It had to be done.

"I'm sorry I didn't tell you that I knew who you were right after the interview. Actually, after it happened— after Brett was killed—I did have every intention of finding you. I wanted to talk to you, to ask you questions. I wanted you to fill me in on Brett's last moments."

Since she hadn't tried to get in contact with him, he asked, "What happened?"

Ellie pressed her lips together. "I just couldn't make myself do it," she said honestly. "So I kept finding excuses and before I knew it, too much time had gone by and I felt awkward about opening up what had to be an old case for you."

That wasn't the whole truth and she knew it. Taking another breath, she told him, "I guess I felt that until I actually talked to you about Brett's last moments, I didn't have to deal with them myself. That way, the whole thing wasn't quite real to me." She flushed ruefully. "I guess you probably think that's stupid, don't you?"

Colin offered an understanding smile. "Actually, it happens more than you think."

She waved her hand at him, dismissing his words. "You're just saying that to make me feel better."

His face gave nothing away as he asked, "Is it working?"

It coaxed another smile from her. "I'll see you at your apartment," she told him.

"Okay," he agreed. "And if you're not there within ten minutes of my arriving home, I'm going to come looking for you."

"Duly warned," she responded, grateful that he had made this easy for her. Grateful that he hadn't just written her off as being a crazy woman with too much baggage for him to bother with.

The best way to handle this was not to think, Ellie told herself as she drove behind Colin's sedan. And she wasn't going to make too much of this. Benteen was just being a friend. She didn't want anything more than that.

Because if she *did* make it anything more than that, she would be setting herself up for another grievous fall fraught with pain. The man was a police detective, for heaven's sakes. Police detectives risked getting shot in the line of duty on a daily basis. She couldn't even allow herself to fall in love with a dentist and the only risk a dentist ran was possibly accidentally drilling his own fingers. The point was that most professions weren't being paid to face death on a regular basis.

A police detective was, so there couldn't be anything more between them than there was right at this moment.

That meant that she was just going over to spend some time with a friend, his niece and the overly energetic puppy she had gifted him with. Nothing else would happen.

Ever.

Granted, she had kissed him, but, she silently insisted, it was only to get that out of the way. Now that it was, she could go on without having to worry. Like Peter Pan, whose mantra was "I won't grow up," she lived by the mantra "I won't fall in love." And nothing would make her fall again.

Nothing.

When she arrived at the door to Colin's apartment some fifteen minutes later, she knocked once, mentally giving him to the count of ten before turning around to go back to her car. The drive over had waned her initial resolution to view this whole interaction between the sexy police detective and herself as something residing in the realm of playfully platonic. She was better off keeping her "interactions" to a minimum. "Minimum" did *not* include spending the evening with him, even with a dog and a niece between them as buffers.

Despite the pep talk to the contrary, she knew she was playing with fire.

Ellie was up to nine and ready to turn on her heel to leave when the door opened. She didn't know whether to cry or cheer.

But instead of Colin or his precocious, animated niece, Ellie found herself looking up at a rather tall, somewhat austere-looking older woman who wore her fading blond hair in what looked to be a braided crown woven about her head.

The next moment, she realized that this had to be Colin's next-door neighbor, Olga, the woman who offered to clean his house for free and who baked cherry pies to die for.

About to introduce herself—and possibly beg off— Ellie never got the chance to do either. The second the woman saw her, she caught her by the hand and enthusiastically pulled her into the apartment, declaring, "You must be the reporter lady," in an accent that was veritably thick enough to cut with a knife, preferably one that butchers used.

"I must be," Ellie heard herself replying as she all but flew over the threshold, not of her own accord. At the last moment, she steadied herself to keep from falling over.

Olga gave her a quick appraising look, apparently pleased with what she saw.

Olga smiled to herself.

"Your reporter lady is here," Olga announced, tossing the words over her shoulder and then adding, "And now I am not."

And just like that, the woman was gone.

Chapter Twelve

"I guess Olga approves of you," Colin told her.

Ellie turned around to find both the detective and his niece standing behind her. Heather was holding the puppy—or trying to. Pancakes seemed to have her own ideas about the situation and tried to use her hind legs to climb down the girl's body.

The older woman hadn't given her any indication that she liked her, Ellie thought. Had she missed something? "How do you know that?"

"Simple," Colin answered. "Because she let you in."

Ellie nodded, following Colin, Heather and their furry friend into the living room. "I guess she did look like she could physically block the doorway to keep me out if she wanted to."

Forgetting about Olga, Ellie turned toward Pancakes. The puppy was practically vibrating in her efforts to get free. Heather, however, had a tight grip on the dog, determined not to let her escape just yet.

"So, how's everything going with Pancakes?" Ellie asked. The words were no sooner out of her mouth than she noticed the chew marks along the floorboard where the two sides came together at the corner. "Wow, you weren't kidding about her teething, were you?"

Ellie bent down to get a better look at the damage. Apparently, Pancakes had gnawed away at the paint clear down to the drywall. "Some paint should take care of that," she told Colin, rising. "And then, after it dries, spray everything shin level and lower with bitter apple."

Colin would have been the first to admit that he didn't know all that much about painting walls, but he was fairly certain that bitter apples had nothing to do with it.

"Come again?"

"Pet stores carry it," Ellie told him, stroking the culprit as she continued to try to wiggle out of Heather's arms. "It's used mostly to keep dogs from chewing on themselves, but it'll probably do the same thing for the walls and your furniture if you spray them." She shrugged as she turned to look at him. "At least it won't hurt anything."

"Worth a shot," Colin agreed.

"Olga brought another one of her casseroles over, so you don't have to cook tonight," Heather announced with a grin, making it sound as if having Ellie prepare dinner was a regular occurrence rather than something that had happened just twice.

Ellie supposed that in the world of a ten-year-old, anything that had been done more than once fell under the heading of Routine.

Exchanging looks with Colin to make sure that his invitation to her was meant to include dinner—he nodded, so she assumed it did—Ellie answered, "Sounds good."

Heather planted herself directly in front of her. "I have to take Pancakes out for a walk so she can go to the bathroom. Wanna come?" she asked.

"Sounds even better," Ellie told her before Colin had the chance to tell his niece not to pester her. She could see the reprimand coming. "Really," she emphasized, looking at the detective.

Colin held his peace.

Serpentine patches of grass were woven all through the apartment-complex grounds, going around the various apartments and giving the development a rather rustic look reminiscent of the city's earlier days, before it was incorporated. Because of that, there was no shortage of places that Pancakes could stop and investigate. Investigation in this case consisted mainly of sniffing, sometimes so deeply that the dog wound up sneezing, something that in turn entertained Heather.

"I didn't know dogs could sneeze," she said.

"Pets are a constant source of education," Ellie told her.

"Did you have pets when you were my age?" Heather asked.

"My dad was allergic to anything with fur, so we couldn't have any pets in the house," she told the girl. "Other than a goldfish, of course, and that doesn't really count. You can't play with a goldfish," she added with a wink.

Heather giggled, then fell into silence for a moment before saying, "You can think of Pancakes as your dog, too, if you want."

Ellie slipped an arm around the little girl's shoulders and hugged Heather to her. "That's very generous of you." Heather beamed at her in response.

By the time she, Heather and the puppy returned to their starting point, Ellie felt a great deal more relaxed.

"I asked Ellie to come to my school for career day," Heather announced the moment they walked into the apartment.

In the kitchen warming up Olga's casserole, Colin stuck his head out and gave his niece a reproving look. "Heather, what did I tell you about that?"

Heather looked up at him innocently. "You said that Ellie was too busy to come to my classroom, but when I asked her, she said she wasn't."

Colin suppressed a frustrated sigh. It was a losing battle with Heather, so he turned to her target instead. "You don't have to do this, you know."

"I know. I already said yes," Ellie told him, taking the leash off Pancakes.

He knew how easily his niece could wrap him around her finger, but he couldn't allow her to do that to Ellie. "Heather's a hard person to say no to," he acknowledged, "but she can't expect you to just drop everything and talk to a class of ten-year-olds," he said, looking at Heather even though his words were directed at Ellie.

The crestfallen expression on Heather's face was enough to seal the fate of this dispute.

"That's okay," Ellie assured him. "They like this kind of thing at the station. They'll probably send Jerry to film it."

"Jerry?" Colin asked.

"My cameraman. You remember, big guy—" she held her hand up high "—curly hair."

Now he remembered. "Oh, right."

"I'm gonna be on TV?" Heather cried. She was already excited by the prospect of having Ellie come to speak to her class; having it all immortalized on film would send her over the top.

"We'll see how this goes," Ellie cautioned, not wanting Heather to get overly excited until the segment was approved. Turning to Colin, she told him, "She's got a lot in common with the puppy."

Colin merely sighed. "Tell me about it." And then he remembered the casserole he'd left on top of the stove. "Okay, let's eat before it all gets cold," he urged, ushering Ellie and his niece into the kitchen.

As she allowed herself to be brought into the kitchen, Ellie couldn't help thinking that it felt really nice being part of a family unit. She knew that it was just an illusion and only temporary, but she could still enjoy the moment and pretend that this was real.

Ellie wasn't exactly sure how it started, but a pattern seemed to begin forming, pulling her in almost without her being conscious of it.

Before she knew it, at least four, sometimes five, evenings a week would find her having dinner with Colin and his niece. Oh, there were various pretexts involved in this unfolding pattern—the first and foremost was that she had somehow gotten herself roped into helping Heather train the lively Pancakes. The goal, for everyone's sake, was to turn the ever-livelier puppy into if not an obedient pet, one who at least waited for her walk to relieve herself and who understood what the commands *sit* and *come* meant.

Ellie promised the little girl—and Colin—that more commands would come once Pancakes got those two down pat.

Training the dog took patience and perseverance and, most of all, a lot of man-hours, or in this case, woman-hours. Colin himself couldn't always be there, because the dictates of his job would call him away. Thieves, as he'd explained once to Heather, did not keep regular nine-to-five hours.

And there were times when Ellie was sent out to cover a late-breaking story. Calling Colin to make her apologies was particularly difficult whenever Heather answered the phone.

The preteen always sounded severely disappointed if she couldn't see her that evening. So much so that sometimes Ellie wondered if her absence even registered with Heather's uncle. That was when she reminded herself that they were just friends, nothing more, and there was no reason for him to be anywhere nearly as disappointed as Heather was.

After all, except for that one time, Colin hadn't even tried to kiss her again, so the parameters defining their relationship were clearly etched. They were friends, growing to be very good friends, but definitely nothing more than that.

She clung to the label for her own protection—even though at times it actually did really bother her.

"Tell me one thing," she said to Heather the morning before she addressed the girl's fourth-grade class on career day several weeks later. "Why am I here instead of your uncle? Aren't students supposed to bring a family member to these things?"

"Well, you're like family," Heather answered, saying it as if she believed that with every fiber of her being. "And anyway, you're a lot more famous than Uncle Colin is."

She didn't want the girl to get her priorities mixed up. Being famous wasn't everything. It should score very low on her list of aspirations.

"But your uncle's a police detective and that's very important, honey. The police keep our community safe."

"I know that," Heather said, dismissing the point the next moment. "But people see you on TV," she stressed. "Everybody in my class knows who you are. They all watch you," she said proudly.

Ellie gave it one more try. "Just remember, if you're ever in trouble, you call a policeman," she emphasized, "not a reporter."

Which was what she wound up telling her audience at the end of her presentation, hoping that the message registered with the class, although truthfully, she had her doubts. They all seemed far too interested in being on camera themselves.

She'd been right about her news station viewing this as a good opportunity to both promote some good publicity and get a feel-good human-interest story. Everyone wanted to know when the segment would air so they could tell their family and friends.

"So how did it go?" Colin asked that evening when he finally came home. His shift had run over. Consequently, he came home several hours after Ellie had arrived, relieving Olga.

"Your niece is a hit," Ellie told him.

"Everyone wants to be my friend now that I brought Ellie to school," she announced.

He looked at Heather, concerned about her feelings. "You know that's not going to last, right? They should want to be your friend because they like you, not because you know someone they see on TV."

"I know that. Ellie already explained that to me. But how are they going to know if they like me if they don't talk to me? Now they talk to me because I brought in Ellie."

"Hard to argue with logic like that," Ellie quipped. "If I were you, I'd start putting money aside for her college fund. This one's got the makings of a really good lawyer."

Colin laughed and shook his head. "Let's eat— I'm starved."

"Tonight's dinner is Hungarian goulash. Olga brought it over," Ellie told him. "She actually smiled at me today."

"Told you she liked you," Colin said, helping her set the table.

"Well, I wouldn't exactly go that far," Ellie countered. "But I think that Olga might be coming around since Heather told her that I went to her class for career day."

"See that?" Colin said. "A classroom of kids bests a dour Russian lady and you've got a classroom full of ten-year-olds idolizing you."

Ellie distributed the napkins at the three place settings. "That's just because they think being on camera is glamorous. They haven't seen the segments where I've had to stand out in the pouring rain, reporting on 'the storm of the century,' which turns out to be just three days of bad weather. Or the time the station had me reporting on the hurricane that was just off the coast," she recalled. "I looked like a wet rat."

He grinned, envisioning the scene. "A photogenic wet rat," Colin corrected.

That caught her off guard. Colin didn't usually compliment her. "You think I'm photogenic?"

He looked at her, amused. "You think you're not?" he countered.

"Actually," she confessed, "I haven't thought about it at all." She had to submit herself to the makeup woman daily, but she didn't bother looking to see what the final result was when the woman finished.

"Don't you look at yourself on TV?" Colin asked, surprised. Everyone he knew was keenly aware of how they looked. He'd always thought it was part of the human condition.

"No," Ellie answered with a dismissive shrug.

Heather was carefully putting glasses next to the place settings. She looked up at her idol in total surprise.

"Why not?" she asked. "If I was on TV, I'd watch me all the time."

"That's because you're adorable," Ellie told the pre-teen. "I feel too self-conscious. If I looked, I'd see all my flaws and all my mistakes."

"What if there aren't any?" Colin challenged.

"There are *always* mistakes," Ellie assured him, then deftly changed the subject. She was never comfortable talking about herself. "So, how was your day?"

"Frustrating," Colin said honestly. "There's been a rash of home invasions. So far, we haven't been able to catch who's behind them."

"What about descriptions?" she asked. Using a deep serving spoon, she doled out helpings on all three plates. "Home invasions mean that the people were at home at the time, right? Can't any of the people who were robbed give you an accurate description of the thieves?" Finished serving, she sat down and began to eat.

"They come in wearing masks and tie the people up, blindfolding them. We're not even getting an accurate count of how many home invaders there are. One couple said two—another said four. Nobody's agreeing with each other."

"Could be that there are several teams," Ellie suggested. "All working for one head guy—or woman," she amended. "What about surveillance tapes? Almost everyone has home security systems these days, or at least cameras."

"All of which the thieves disable before they get into the house," Colin told her.

"These thieves are tech savvy?" she asked.

He nodded, noticing that Heather seemed to be hanging on every word. "Looks that way."

"What are the names of the security companies?" Ellie asked.

He thought for a moment, recalling what was written on the reports. "Supreme Alarms."

"Just one name?" she asked. "Aren't there any other companies?"

He paused to mentally review the reports he'd read. "I don't think so."

"Maybe you should find out if the company recently fired anyone in the last few months. One of them might be looking for revenge. Disgruntled employees like to find a way to get back at their employers for firing them. This sounds like a perfect way to do it to me."

He grinned at her. "You are a very handy person to have around. We investigated the employees currently working for the company. We *didn't* look into any former employees," he admitted. "Don't know why I didn't think of this myself."

"See, Uncle Colin?" Heather spoke up. "Told you she was great."

Ellie quickly glossed over the compliment. "You would have thought of that," she assured him. "I just beat you to it because I love reading mystery thrillers," she told the detective.

Colin kept a straight face as he said, "Either that or you think like a thief."

"There's that, too," she agreed in the same dead-pan voice.

"No, you're not a thief," Heather piped up.

"Ellie's just kidding," Colin told his niece. "In any case, I'm going to head down to the Supreme Alert main office in the morning, see if I can get a list of terminated employees."

She didn't know why she suddenly felt the need to warn him, but she did. "Be careful."

"Always," he assured her. "Except when it comes to the dog," Colin said, looking down. Apparently, Pancakes had decided to work on the leg of the chair he was sitting on. Bending over, he urged the dog away, bribing her with a piece of meat. "What did you say the name of that spray was?" he asked Ellie when he straightened up.

He knew she'd told him about it, but he'd put it out of his mind at the time. He was beginning to think that maybe he shouldn't have.

"Bitter apple," she repeated.

"I'm buying a gallon of it first thing in the morning," he vowed.

"Good thinking," she agreed as Heather dutifully drew the puppy away, offering her a chew toy instead. Pancakes took the bait.

Chapter Thirteen

"What are you doing on Thanksgiving?"

The question, asked by Colin, came seemingly out of the blue after dinner one evening.

Ellie was helping him load the dishwasher and the question caught her completely by surprise. She didn't answer him immediately. Instead, she glanced at the calendar Colin had hung up on the wall next to the sink.

The holiday had just crept up on her this year. It seemed like one day Thanksgiving was over a month away, the next it was almost upon her. Four days away to be exact.

Realizing that Colin was still waiting for some kind of an answer, Ellie shrugged. "Same thing I usually do. I'm working." What she left out was that she'd asked to be working on that day.

"Can't you get out of it?" he asked, rinsing off the casserole dish before tucking it in on the top rack. "You have seniority. After all, you've been there a few years now, right?"

Handing him the dishwashing liquid, Ellie looked at him. "Have you been reading my studio bio?" she asked, doing her best to sound lighthearted rather than defensive.

If Colin detected a slight edge in her voice, he gave no indication.

"I'm a detective—comes with the territory. So, can you get out of working?" he asked, then added, "I've got the day off."

Ellie pressed her lips together. Thanksgiving had always been rather special to her. Brett had proposed to her on Thanksgiving Day. Moreover, the Thanksgivings that came after that, if they'd been apart because he was overseas on a tour of duty, they still managed to spend the holiday "together," thanks to Skype.

Because of the time differences involved, sometimes she had to get up at three in the morning, and sometimes the first chance he had to talk to her was far into the wee hours at night. The inconvenience didn't matter. It was well worth it to her.

After she'd lost Brett, the thought of facing the holiday alone—even at her mother's house, and her mother always had a houseful of friends coming over—was just too painful for her to contemplate.

But this year, things had changed without her being fully aware of the metamorphosis. This year, she'd somehow gotten pulled into this do-it-yourself family comprised of Colin and his niece—and the dog—and she had to admit that she did like it. This was what she'd envisioned her life to be if she and Brett had had a child.

"Well, I guess that I could talk to the program manager," Ellie said evasively. "I'm not making any promises, but maybe…" She deliberately let her voice trail off.

Colin closed the dishwasher and started the washing process.

"Good," he said as if it was already a done deal. "Because I know that Heather would love to have you join us." Hoping to sweeten the deal, he told her, "I was thinking of going to The Five Crowns and I have to call in a reservation, the earlier, the better."

Ellie stared at him. "A restaurant?" she said in disbelief. "Seriously?"

Why was she looking at him as if he'd just assumed the role of the village idiot? "Yes, what's wrong with that?"

Ellie started to enumerate why his thinking was so wrong. "Number one, good luck with getting a reservation at this late date."

"Late date?" he challenged. "It's still five days away."

"Four," she corrected. "And even if you could get a reservation, which is doubtful, you don't go to a restaurant for Thanksgiving." How could he even *think* that was acceptable?

Maybe she hadn't made the connection between all the takeout menus tacked up on his refrigerator and the fact that he'd never invited her to a home-cooked meal that *he* had made.

"You do if your cooking skills are limited to scrambled eggs and toast—usually burnt," he added.

"Well, mine aren't and it's important that Heather has a home-cooked Thanksgiving meal." It was happening again. She was getting pulled further in by volunteering to cook Thanksgiving dinner. Moreover, if she was being honest with herself, she hadn't made the offer against her will. "Okay," she said, "if I can clear the day with my program manager at the station, I'll make the turkey."

"I don't want to put you out." His protest was at odds with the broad smile on his face.

Her eyes met his. "Sure you do, but it's understandable, given the situation." At least her mother would be overjoyed that she was doing this, she couldn't help thinking. "I'm putting you on notice, by the way."

"About?" he asked, not quite sure what he was bracing himself for.

There wasn't a thing in his refrigerator or pantry she could work with—other than margarine. "If I get the go-ahead from the program manager, you and I and Heather are going food shopping."

"You're the boss," he told her, relieved that *this* was her condition and not something else.

"Right," she mocked.

She wasn't the boss in this situation, Ellie thought. If anything, she was just along for the ride. But somehow, she couldn't summon any resentment or indignation over the very gentle way she'd been manipulated. That in itself spoke volumes, but she chose not to explore that now.

In his sixth decade, Marty Stern was a thin, wiry man who was very good at his job. He always appeared to be moving, juggling a myriad of tasks, usually at the same time, and remarkably, keeping them all straight. His gift was that he always remained on top of everything that came under the heading of his job.

His approval wasn't easily won, but once it was, that person had it for life. He had a fondness for Ellie. In all the time she'd been with the station, she had never once questioned any assignment he had given her, any place he had sent her.

So when she'd knocked on his door the following morning and asked for a few minutes of his time, he had beckoned her in and heard her out.

When she'd finished, he had to admit to himself that she'd surprised him.

"Seriously?" he asked her, looking at her over his steepled thin fingers. "You want Thanksgiving off?" Given what he knew, he hadn't expected this.

"Yes. But if it puts you in a bind—" she began, about to rescind her request. She'd never been one who caused problems and maybe this had been a bad idea.

"No," Marty told her, cutting her off, "actually, I can get someone to cover your spot. I just thought you said you *wanted* to work on Thanksgiving."

"I did say that," she confirmed. "But something came up."

"A good something?" Marty asked, eyeing her closely.

"A different something."

Would she jinx it by saying yes? She wasn't normally superstitious but in the last couple of years, she had lost track of exactly what "normal" was. Ellie decided to take the safe route.

"Okay," he laughed drily, "I'll accept that. You've

got the day off. Lord knows you've earned it," he told her. "Now go get me something on that bear sighting down in Mission Viejo. Preferably some footage," he said, sending her off.

"You've got it." It was as good as a promise. She planned to do her very best.

Ellie had no sooner gotten into the news van with Jerry and started down the Santa Ana Freeway than she felt her phone vibrate.

Pulling it out of her pocket, she saw that it wasn't a call coming in but a text. She recognized the number. Colin was sending her a text.

Any word yet?

Smiling to herself, Ellie texted back, Got the day off.

The moment she sent it out, she received another text in response.

Great!

She was tempted to text back an inquiry as to whether he was experiencing a slow day, allowing him time to text, but she refrained. Instead, she put her phone away. When she looked up, she saw that Jerry was watching her.

"Never saw you texting before. Something I should know?" Her cameraman was grinning from ear to ear, as if he already had the answer to his question.

Ellie pointed to his front windshield. "Yes, you

should know that more accidents happen when you take your eyes off the road—so watch the road."

If anything, his grin got wider. There was no denying that he was very amused by all this.

"Anything else I should know?" he teased.

Ellie sighed as she sank back in her seat. "Just that your wife's a saint for putting up with you."

Threading his way onto the freeway, he paused until they merged into the left lane. "Speaking of wife, you know that our usual invitation to join us for Thanksgiving still stands if you decide to change your mind about working."

She realized that he didn't know yet. She didn't want to get into it, but then, she didn't want him being the last to know, either.

"Sorry, I've got plans," she told him, hoping that was the end of it.

It was obvious that her answer surprised him. "'Plan' plans?" Jerry asked keenly, making it sound like some sort of secret undertaking.

"Just drive, Jerry," she ordered.

His curiosity aroused, he knew better than to prod her. She'd tell him when she was ready. "Good for you, Ellie."

"Jerry—" There was a warning note in her voice as she said his name.

"I'm driving, I'm driving," he answered, backing off even more.

But she noted that he was still grinning. And, in a way, she supposed that she was, too.

"How about this one?" Colin asked two evenings later when they finally found the time to go shopping.

He was holding up a twenty-five-pound frozen turkey for her approval. Because of both their schedules, this was the first opportunity that they had to go to the supermarket together.

Ellie supposed that it would have probably been a lot quicker for her to just go alone, but she wanted to include Heather in the safari and she knew that the girl would want her uncle to come, as well, which was how they all came to be in the well-stocked chain supermarket at seven thirty in the evening, shopping for Thanksgiving.

Despite it being two days away from Thanksgiving, there was no shortage of turkeys to choose from.

"That depends on whether you want to be eating turkey leftovers for the next week and a half or not. There'll just be three of us," she reminded him. "A ten- to twelve-pound turkey will do."

"Okay." Colin put the turkey back in the open freezer where the store had placed most of their stock of birds and searched until he found one the size that she'd suggested. Picking it up, he eyed it skeptically. "Really? It looks puny."

"I'm not telling you *not* to get the larger one," she told him. "But just remember that there's just so much you can do with leftover turkey."

"I love turkey sandwiches," Heather spoke up. There was more than a trace of nostalgia in her voice as she said, "Mom would put them in my lunch all week."

The argument was settled in Colin's mind.

"A bigger bird it is," he announced, returning the smaller specimen and taking one that weighed in at sixteen pounds. In his mind, it was the perfect compromise. "What's next?"

"We need to make stuffing," Ellie said.

Colin thought for a minute. He didn't frequent grocery stores all that often. "I think I saw the boxes in the next aisle," he told her.

Ellie stopped him before he could turn on his heel. "We're not going to eat stuffing that came in a box."

"We're not?" Colin turned around to face her. "Are these rules written down someplace?" he asked. His personal rule of thumb was always the simpler, the better.

"Just work with me," Ellie told him, then rattled off the ingredients for the stuffing that her mother always made. She'd never met anyone who didn't like it. "Okay, we're going to need two packages of hot sausages, one package of medium-hot sausage, a pound of hard salami, several cans of chicken broth, some celery and two large loaves of white bread."

"All that for stuffing?" Colin asked doubtfully.

"Only if you want to do it right," she answered.

"Well, that puts me in my place," Colin replied obligingly.

Once they'd located all the ingredients she needed and placed them in the cart, Ellie turned toward Heather. "You get to pick the vegetables and the dessert."

Happy to contribute, Heather said, "That's easy. My mom always made mashed potatoes and corn on the cob. Oh, and gravy," she added.

"And for dessert?" Ellie coaxed.

That drew an even bigger smile from the girl.

"Pumpkin pie," Heather said as if she could all but taste it.

"See?" Ellie said to Colin, who was on the other side of the cart—Heather insisted on being the one to push it. She gestured to the contents in the cart. "Now *that's* a Thanksgiving dinner."

"It still has to be cooked," Colin pointed out. "That's where the real work comes in."

"Heather and I will handle it," Ellie said, looking at the girl. "Won't we?"

Heather looked as if she was willing to get started the second they got home. "You bet."

It did Colin's heart good to hear his niece sounding so happy. And he knew that he owed it, at least in part, to Ellie. The woman was becoming very precious to him, he thought.

Because the turkey weighed in at a little over sixteen pounds, it was going to need to be in the oven for four hours after it was cleaned and draped with cheesecloth, the latter properly doused with melted butter. In addition, the stuffing needed be made before that. Between toasting the bread and cutting each slice into tiny pieces, plus frying the sausages to get rid of any excess fat, Ellie knew that would take her another hour. By her calculations, she needed to get started by ten, which meant day off or not, she had to get up a lot earlier.

Even so, she was going to be busy for most of that morning. She was trying to time everything down to the minute so that all of her time was taken up with preparing the dinner. She deliberately didn't want to give herself any time to think. Thinking only made her dwell on the past—and remember what she didn't have anymore.

"Not the time for it now," she sternly told her reflection in the wardrobe mirror when she caught herself mentally drifting for a moment. "It's not about you. There's a little girl counting on you to make today special."

Heather's loss was fresher than her own and she wouldn't forgive herself if she didn't do everything she could to make this Thanksgiving a good one for the little girl.

In her heart, Ellie knew that her husband would have wanted her to do this. He would have wanted her to move on because he was that sort of a selfless person. He'd always told her that he wanted her to be happy and if anything ever happened to him, he wanted her to find someone to love.

Because you've got so much love in you, Ellie. You can't keep it all bottled up—you have to find someone to share it with.

He'd made these declarations when he was being deployed, thinking that he might die fighting for his country. Neither one of them had ever dreamed that he would meet his end stateside, not fighting for his country but defending an unarmed young couple.

"I'm trying, Brett," she murmured as she got dressed. "But you've got to help me. I can't do this alone."

And then she looked at her watch. It was after nine. She should have left fifteen minutes ago. She'd set a schedule for herself in her head, the way she did every day no matter what she was doing. It kept her organized.

It also kept her from thinking too much. And that was the way she liked it. Right now all she wanted to focus on was making a good Thanksgiving dinner. After that, she told herself, she'd focus on something else.

Her mother had told her shortly after Brett's death that the way to get through the oppressive pain and the horrific grief was to take one step at a time.

Just one step at a time, Elliana. You'll be surprised how those steps add up—and where they lead to.

Her mother had said that recalling her grief when her own husband had died.

Ellie had never hoped her mother was right as much as she did today.

Chapter Fourteen

It seemed that the very second Ellie knocked on the door, it swung open. Colin was in the doorway, a broad smile on his face.

"Wow, if I didn't know any better, I would have said you were standing right behind the door," Ellie said as she walked in.

"I was," he told her, closing the door behind her. When she looked at him quizzically, he said, "Heather alerted me. She'd been at the window watching for you for the last hour." He nodded toward the dog that was trying to snag her attention. "I don't know who's been jumping around more, Heather or Pancakes."

"Well, it's nice to be greeted with this much en-thusiasm," Ellie said, shifting the grocery bags she was carrying so she could give Heather a quick hug.

Not wanting to leave her out, she petted the bouncing dog. The latter tried to catch hold of her sleeve with her teeth, an act Ellie managed to deftly avoid.

His niece and the dog weren't the only ones looking forward to her arrival, but Colin deliberately refrained from saying anything because he didn't want to send her running back to the shelter of her car. He sensed that she was still skittish and he approached Ellie with caution.

Instead, he nodded at what she'd brought in. "What's in the grocery bags? I thought we got everything for today."

After setting the bags down on the kitchen counter, Ellie proceeded to unpack them. "These are just a few miscellaneous things I forgot to pick up during our shopping trip the other night."

Colin grabbed the item that was closest to him. "Parmesan cheese?" he questioned.

"That's for the mashed potatoes," she explained, then offered, "Do you want me to go over what everything else is for?"

"No, I'll learn as we go along," Colin answered, a bemused smile on his face.

Ellie returned one in kind. "See, you're learning already." Turning to Heather, she said, "Okay, assistant, let's get to work, shall we?"

"What can I do?" Colin asked.

Ellie turned around to regard him for a moment. "How are you at peeling potatoes?"

"You're giving me KP duty?" he asked with less than enthusiasm over the prospect.

"Extremely important KP duty," Ellie emphasized. She gestured toward the bag he had out on the counter. "We've got five pounds of potatoes that need peeling."

With a resigned shrug, he said, "I guess I can't ruin that."

Ellie made no effort to hide her amusement. "Not unless you cut off one of your fingers."

"Thanks for the vote of confidence," Colin pretended to grumble.

Ellie spread her hands wide, feigning innocence. "Hey, you were the one who said you didn't exactly shine in the kitchen."

He inclined his head as if to give her the round. He took out a knife from the last drawer on the right hand side. "You want all of them peeled?"

"Peeled and cut up into very small pieces." When he seemed confused, she explained, "They cook faster that way."

Nodding, he slid open the bag, allowing him to take the potatoes out. "Anything else?"

She was already slicing open the individual sausages, getting them ready to be put in the frying pan. "When you finish that, I need five celery stalks finely diced." She turned her attention to his niece, who was impatiently shifting from foot to foot. "Heather, your job is to toast the bread. We're going to need all the slices from both loaves."

"You got it," Heather told her happily, throwing herself into the task.

The rest of the morning was spent doing all the things that were involved in preparing a proper Thanksgiving meal. To a casual observer, it would look like just barely organized chaos, with Pancakes weaving in and out between all of them, continuously foraging for any bit of food that had been dropped on the floor. The only time the dog stopped foraging was when she found something. At that point, she disposed of it at lightning speed.

And then went back to foraging.

There seemed to be no downtime, not even when the turkey was finally basted, draped and in the oven, baking. At that point, Ellie turned her attention to making the pumpkin pie and the rolls she'd decided to add at the last minute.

Heather appeared to be in heaven and Colin, although not in heaven, was enjoying seeing Heather so involved and so content. He knew he had Ellie to thank for that.

"You realize that you were on your feet the entire time?" Colin asked when they finally sat down to eat dinner hours later. "From the minute you walked in to just now, when I finally got you to sit down to eat with us?" For a second there, he'd been afraid that she was bent on cleaning up, leaving Heather and him to eat while she tidied.

"It's no different than when I'm out on assignment," she answered. "Just a little hotter," she added, indicating the stove. He had a relatively small kitchen, so the heat was difficult to avoid and it was an unusually warm Thanksgiving, even for Southern California. "Except when they send me out of state to cover a story smack in the middle of a heat wave," she added as a postscript.

"I take it you don't believe in complaining," he said to her.

Ellie shrugged. "What good would it do?" She watched Colin and his niece, looking from one to the other, waiting for some sort of a reaction. They'd both started eating. "Well?" she finally asked. "How is it?"

Colin stared at her, pretending to consider her question for a moment before saying, "Oh, well, maybe it's a little undercooked."

"What?" Ellie cried, surprised as well as mystified. "But I timed it and the skin is just crisp enough—" She stopped abruptly because Colin had started laughing.

"I'm sorry—I'm just kidding. This is probably the best turkey I've ever had. Ow!" he cried when Ellie took a swipe at his arm. He gave her what he assumed might pass for a reproving look. "You realize that I could take you in for assaulting an officer of the law, right?" he told her.

Ellie raised her chin. "You'd have to catch me first."

"Don't tempt me," Colin told her, the expression in his eyes saying things that he didn't—or couldn't at the moment.

"He's just kidding, Ellie," Heather assured her, eating merrily. "And this is really, really good."

Ellie smiled at her fondly. "And you know why?"

Heather swallowed, then answered, "'Cause of all those things you put in?"

Ellie nodded. "Yes, but mainly because we all worked together to make it. Things always taste better when you make them yourself," she told the girl with feeling.

"Obviously, I'm going to have to make you breakfast someday," Colin told her with a laugh.

For just a second, their eyes met and Ellie felt a shiver go down her spine, the kind a person felt in anticipation of something that hadn't been experienced yet. He was talking about making her breakfast. Did he mean after they spent the night together, or was that an entirely innocent comment on his part?

You're doing it again. You're overthinking things. Take what he said at face value and nothing more.

Ellie glanced away. Looking into his eyes did unsettling things to her.

"Okay," she told him, smiling even when he went on to describe the ingredients that went into his perfect breakfast, items that had no business on the same plate. Even so, she was relieved that the dinner was a success. She began to relax and started to actually taste—and enjoy—what she had prepared.

After dinner and dessert had been eaten and savored, at Heather's behest, the three of them sat down and watched the tail end of the second football game on TV that day.

"This your idea?" she asked Colin as they settled on the sofa to watch.

He shook his head. "Not guilty. This is strictly Heather's idea," he said, nodding at his niece.

Heather was nestled between them, her attention riveted on the TV monitor. At first Heather thought the girl hadn't heard them, but then, still watching, she said, "My dad always liked to watch the games on Thanksgiving. Mom said we had to keep him company because he loved watching the games almost as much as he loved us." For just a second, she spared Ellie a glance. "It makes me feel closer to them watching the game now."

Moved, Ellie gave her a hug. She could totally relate to the need to bond across time and space.

"I've just got one question," she told Heather. "Who's playing?"

With a delighted air of superiority, Heather answered her question, throwing in both teams' stats as an added bonus.

"So what'd you think of it?" Ellie asked the little girl when the game was finally over almost two hours later.

When she received no answer, she was about to repeat her question, then stopped. Leaning in closer, she took another look and then smiled. Raising her head again, she turned toward Colin.

"Don't look now, but your little football fan is fast asleep."

"I know," he told her. He'd watched the rest of the game not because he particularly cared about the outcome but because he just liked sitting with them like this. There was something so right about it and he hadn't wanted to disturb the scene. "We lost her shortly after the third quarter started."

After getting up so as not to wake up Heather, he gently eased his niece off the sofa and into his arms. Asleep, she looked even younger than she was. "I'll just put her to bed."

Ellie was on her feet. "Need any help?"

"No," he whispered, "I'm just going to lay her down and cover her with a blanket. She's a light sleeper. If I do anything else, even take off her shoes, I'm liable to wake her up and then she'll be up for hours again. I've learned from experience that a forty-five-minute nap can really power her up. She's better off if I just let her sleep in her clothes. I'll be right back," he promised, turning away.

"Don't trip on the dog," Ellie warned in a stage whisper. Pancakes was sprawled out near the sofa, directly in his path. "Apparently, football puts her to sleep, too."

"Maybe we're onto something," Colin said with a laugh just before he made his way out of the room with Heather in his arms.

When he returned several minutes later, the TV was still on, but Ellie was no longer on the sofa or even in the room.

Colin looked around. He half expected her to be getting her things together to go home.

He knew that she'd spent almost an entire day with them, but even so, he didn't really want her to leave just yet. He liked her company, liked doing simple, ordinary things with this woman who regularly found her way into everyone's home for four or five minutes at a time.

This was different from that.

He wasn't really certain just what was going on, because he'd never felt quite like this before, never wanted to have a woman around to this extent.

But then, this wasn't just a woman; this was a unique, special woman. He couldn't help wondering what Ellie would say if he told her that.

Probably take off faster. He had to tread carefully if he wanted this—whatever "this" was—to progress.

Since she hadn't said anything about leaving, there was only one other place she could be. Ellie had to be in the kitchen, cleaning up. The dishes had previously been left where they were because of the football game. He'd just naturally assumed that he'd tackle them in the morning.

"You don't have to do that," he told Ellie, walking into the room.

She shrugged as if this was no big deal. "It's part of the process. First you cook, then you eat and then you clean up." She spared him a quick glance over her shoulder. "You really don't want to have to face this mess in the morning," she told him knowingly. "Besides, I'm almost done."

"But you're not loading the dishwasher," Colin observed. There were soap bubbles rising from a filled sink. He assumed the dishes were in there. "You're washing them."

"Sometimes," she said, keeping her back to Colin, "sinking your hands into a sink full of suds is therapeutic." And she did just that.

He came up behind her. "Is it working for you?" he asked kindly.

She didn't answer his question. Instead, she told him, "I enjoyed today. I think Heather did, too."

"Oh, I know she did," he declared with certainty. And then he told her, "Thank you."

She deflected his thanks. "I really didn't do anything. I just made a turkey."

Colin suppressed a sigh. "Do you *ever* just take a compliment?"

"Sure," she answered a bit too quickly. "If I deserve it."

"Well, there is no 'if' here," he said. "You did a really good thing and you made my niece very happy." She was still keeping her back to him and he found that a little strange. Something wasn't quite right here, he thought. "Will you just turn around from the sink and let me thank you?"

When she slowly turned around, Colin saw why she'd kept her face averted. Something squeezed his heart. "You're crying."

She knew she couldn't deny it, but she didn't want him questioning her about it.

"I get sentimental over soapsuds," she said, quickly wiping away the tear tracks from her cheeks with the back of her hand. That only made the situation worse because her hand was wet.

Colin took out his handkerchief, and ever so carefully, he wiped her cheeks. "Try again," he told her softly.

Ellie tried to turn away, shrugging off his concern, even though he'd all but melted her just now. "I'm fine," she insisted.

But he wasn't going to be put off. Colin took her into his arms.

"No, you're not," he told her. "Maybe if you talk about it—"

"No, no talking," she protested, shaking her head. "No—"

And then something seemed to just break apart inside her. She'd started by pulling away, and somehow, inexplicably, she wound up even closer to him than before. So close that the next moment, her resolve cracked. Ellie gave in to the overwhelming desire she felt to fill the emptiness inside her.

In a blinding flash, she was kissing him. Kissing him because the first time they'd kissed, she'd felt that old, familiar feeling she'd missed so much.

It was like a homecoming.

The kiss blossomed, catching her up in the feeling, reminding her how wondrous it could all be.

She wanted Colin to make her forget what she'd lost. She wanted him to make her forget the pain she couldn't seem to outrun no matter how fast she moved. The pain that seemed to fade only when he was kissing her.

With superhuman effort, he gently pushed her away from him. "Ellie, wait." Stunned, Colin struggled to rein in his own almost overpowering reaction, his own fierce desire to let all this progress down its natural path.

He was *not* about to take advantage of Ellie's vulnerability unless and until she could really convince him that this was what she unquestionably wanted.

She blinked, trying to focus. Her orientation was askew. "Why?"

"Don't get the wrong idea," he warned. "I'd like nothing better than to have this go where I think it's going. But I'm not going to let that happen unless I think that you really want this, too. That you're not just doing it because things have gotten out of hand."

Ellie stared at him, her mind not fully processing what was going on. "You're going to make me beg?"

"No, not beg," he said quickly. "Just convince me." It was almost a plea on his part.

The words were finally penetrating. She knew she should just back off, go home before she did something she would regret.

But going home might just be the thing that she *would* regret. "Wow, are you asking for this in writing?"

He couldn't help himself. He was framing her face

with his hands, his eyes communing with hers. "No, but I want you to be really, really sure."

Were men actually this good? Was he worried about her? She felt herself being drawn even closer to him. "I didn't realize you were a Boy Scout."

"No, not a Boy Scout," he assured Ellie. "Just a man who really doesn't want you to feel like you've made a mistake in the morning."

Damn, that clinched it. Every inch of her just wanted him to hold her. To make love to her and make her feel that everything would be all right again, the way it once was.

"Shut up, Benteen," she ordered. "Shut up and kiss me."

Not waiting for him to comply, she brought her mouth up to his again. And then over and over again, effectively blowing his resolve into the same little pieces that hers had become.

Weakening, Colin tried just one more time.

"Ellie—"

He got no further. He gave in to her. He gave in to himself. The next moment, Colin was kissing her back, kissing her the way he'd wanted to kiss her these last few weeks.

Kissing her the way he'd never kissed another woman, because he'd never felt about another woman the way he did about her.

Chapter Fifteen

"It's all right," Ellie whispered, thinking Colin still expected her to change her mind when he pulled back again.

"It's more than all right," he answered, referring to the kiss that had just spun through his system, leaving him wanting more. "But not out here."

There was a time when he would have just gone with the desire pulsating through him, making love on any surface that was available. It was the act that was important, as well as the woman of the moment, not the location.

But all that had been in a life that occurred BH—Before Heather. These days, no matter what his feelings were about anything else and no matter how urgent they seemed, his niece and her welfare always had priority. That included anything that she might encounter or see that could in turn affect her in an adverse way.

"Heather might come out and find us," he explained to Ellie. "This is *not* the way I want her to learn about the facts of life."

Ellie smiled, his thoughtfulness regarding his niece really touching her. "She's ten. I'm sure she already knows. Girls grow up a lot faster these days."

Colin groaned, anticipating what he might have to deal with down the line—sooner than later. "Oh Lord, I hope not." The next moment, he tabled that discussion by sweeping Ellie into his arms.

"What are you doing?" she laughed, steadying herself by anchoring her arms around his neck.

"Can't you tell?" he deadpanned. "I'm having my way with you." Then, before she could ask him anything else, Colin covered her lips with his own, all the while carrying her to his bedroom.

He'd left his bedroom door opened. He made his way in now, then pushed the door closed with his elbow. After setting her down on the floor, he flipped the lock to ensure that Heather couldn't just walk in on them, accidentally advancing her education further tonight in ways none of them wanted.

Once that was out of the way, he gathered Ellie to him, dissolving any resistance, any second thoughts she might still be harboring about his intent by kissing her over and over. Each kiss was more passionate, more burning, than the last until the whole room seemed to be enveloped in a circle of heat—and getting hotter by the second.

It had been more than two years since she'd known the touch of a man's hand. More than two years since she'd felt this rush of desire, of heated anticipation coursing though her veins. Suddenly, she was a prisoner of her own yearning, a yearning that was all but pleading to be satisfied.

Ellie stifled a moan as she felt his fingers working apart the buttons, one at a time, that ran down the front of her sweater. She felt her skin heating beneath his fingers. He coaxed the garment off her shoulders, then tossed it aside. Her slacks were next. He undid the button at the top, then slowly slid down the zipper with his fingertip. Ellie shivered, waiting.

She felt the material being eased down along her hips even as his lips were slowly branding her mouth, her throat, then moving down to the swell of her breasts.

Her own restraint shredded apart. Ellie began to urgently undo his pants, his shirt, desperate to get all the barriers out of her way so she could run her hands along his body, could feel his taut, naked skin against hers.

Finally, there was nothing left between them except red-hot desire. Clothing dispensed with, they merged in an embrace, melding themselves one against the other, seeking to pleasure each other, seeking to absorb the pleasures they rendered to each other so effortlessly.

Within seconds, they wound up on Colin's bed, rolling about on the king-size comforter, their limbs entwined as their anticipation rose to new, almost sizzling heights that threatened to consume them both.

His arms were strong as they enclosed around her, making her feel as if she had found a new haven, somewhere where nothing could ever harm her, where nothing could find her. She gave herself up to the feelings, to the man who created them within her, stunned that this was actually happening.

She'd given up hope of ever feeling this way again because she'd deliberately banished all feelings for fear of the pain that loomed in their wake—and yet here she was, experiencing all that and more.

She was thrilled, even as fear still hovered along the outer perimeter of her consciousness.

Her heart pounding, Ellie felt him press her back against the bed, his body just over hers. But instead of doing what she expected, instead of uniting with her body then and there, Colin slowly moved down along her body, covering every inch he came in contact with in moist, open-mouth, hot kisses.

Thorough, he left no part of her untouched, beginning with her mouth, moving down to her chin, then to her throat. He continued, making his way down along her breasts, first one, then the other, his tongue artfully teasing each tip before forging an intricate trail down along her belly, which quivered as he slid his tongue along the area.

His warm breath made her tremble in agonizing eagerness as he made his way down farther and farther until he was at her inner core, his tongue moving at a maddeningly slow pace, going back and forth— creating ripening, exploding peaks within her.

Ellie grabbed fistfuls of his comforter, arching her back off his bed, first moving with and then away from the exquisite sensation, trying to absorb as much as she could without crying out.

And then the ultimate climax seized her and she scrambled, arching even higher, wanting to go on savoring forever what she was feeling—even as she knew that it was an impossibility.

The intensity waned. Spent, Ellie fell back on the bed, her eyes widening in exhausted amazement as she looked at him.

She expected that would be all.

She expected wrong.

The next moment, Colin moved his body up over hers, ready to become one with her. He'd held back for as long as humanly possible, held back because he wanted her to be ready, wanted the foreplay to show her that he was mindful of her needs, not just his own.

But he couldn't hold back his own need for her even a microsecond longer.

Linking his hands with hers, Colin threaded their fingers together and was more than ready to complete the union.

"Open your eyes, Ellie," he whispered against her ear, then lifted his head as he told her, "Look at me."

When she did, he entered her and then the dance began, a dance as old as time, as fresh as tomorrow— as unique as they were to one another.

The tempo was slow at first, but then the music in their heads increased. They went faster, then faster still, daring one another to reach that golden pinnacle, racing to get there, to bring the other along.

They did it together.

Colin squeezed her hands as the moment found them, culminating in a burst of fireworks before slowly fading into the sky of the world they had created together.

Ellie hung on to the euphoria for as long as she could until there was nothing more to hang on to. She felt the tension leave his body, felt him roll off hers. To her surprise, he didn't get up, nor did he turn over on his side and fall asleep. Instead, he gathered her to him as if she was something precious, something he cherished that he wanted to hold on to.

Ellie moved her head onto his chest. She became aware of Colin's heart beating beneath her cheek. She couldn't explain why that comforted her, but it did. And that was enough for now.

After a while—she wasn't sure just how long— he raised his head to look at her, asking, "Are you all right?"

The question made her smile. "I'll let you know when I come back to earth."

"Fair enough," he said, inclining his head, then adding, "I just wanted to make sure I didn't hurt you."

Hurt her? She laughed softly to herself. "You didn't exactly toss me off a building."

"There are a lot of ways a person can get hurt," Colin pointed out gently.

Ellie turned her body to his, feeling a flicker of desire returning. The lights were off in his room but there was a full moon out and his window was right in its path, allowing its light to come in.

He really cared, she realized. Something tugged at her heart. Ordinarily, that would have been an urgent warning sign, a signal for her to turn tail and run. But she was far too spent to run and far too naked to get very far. She remained where she was, where she wanted to be.

Ellie touched his face, her fingers skimming along Colin's cheek. A five-o'clock shade had already begun encroaching on his face. He had a kind face, she thought, and even as glimmers of fear raised their head, she was happy.

To show him how she felt, because the words were just not coming, Ellie raised her head ever so slightly and brushed her lips against his.

And then she did it again, because once was not enough.

And before she knew it, they were doing it all over again, making love as if the first time hadn't happened. As if they each needed to get their fill of one another again. Because once was not enough.

She knew she should be leaving.

Ellie promised herself that the second he was asleep, she was going to slip out of bed, gather her clothes to her and get dressed in the bathroom so she didn't wake him, then leave.

That was her plan.

But she fell asleep before Colin did, so she never got to execute her plan the way she wanted to.

And when she did wake up, with hints of sunlight beginning to tiptoe through the bedroom, the thought of making an escape somehow just wasn't appealing. So when she finally slipped out of his bed and padded her way to the bathroom to get dressed, she did so with the intention of making breakfast.

Somehow, it only seemed right to her.

Ellie crept as soundlessly as she could through his bedroom. Coming to the door, she worked the lock slowly, moving it by fractions of an inch until she had it in the unlocked position. When she finally had it unlocked, she eased the door opened, looking carefully from one side to the other. The last thing she wanted to do was run into Heather as she was leaving her uncle's bedroom.

Yes, she thought, girls knew a few more things at ten than she had at that age, but she didn't want to put that to the test, just in case Heather was still as sweetly innocent as she looked.

Relieved when she saw that the door to Heather's room was still closed, Ellie let out the breath she'd been holding and quickly made her way into the kitchen.

Once she was there, breakfast got under way.

She moved as fast as she could without making any noise. She was so intent on being silent that she didn't hear him until he was directly behind her.

"Morning, beautiful," Colin said, threading his arms around her waist from behind and hugging her to him.

Ellie jumped, stifling what amounted to a yelp.

"Hey, easy, now—it's me. Who did you think it was?" he asked her, laughing.

Spatula in hand, she turned around to face him, her heart still hammering wildly in her chest. It felt as if it was about to break out of her rib cage at any moment.

"I thought you were still in bed," she cried. It sounded almost like an accusation.

"I was, until I saw that it was empty. I thought maybe you'd taken off," he confessed, then added with an approving smile, "This is a much nicer surprise." He meant finding her in the kitchen. Then he looked around, taking in the broader picture. "What are you doing?"

"What does it look like?" she replied. "I'm making breakfast."

"I could have made breakfast for us," he told her. It seemed only right after she'd spent half of yesterday cooking for Heather and him. It seemed even more so since she'd given him an unimaginable night that he wasn't going to ever forget.

But Ellie shook her head, vetoing the suggestion. "After the way you described it, I thought we'd be better off if I made breakfast." Mischief glinted in her eyes as she told him, "I have no desire to spend the day after Thanksgiving in the emergency room, having my stomach pumped."

"It's not that bad," he protested. And then he shrugged, conceding the possible validity of what she'd said. "But it's not all that good, either."

Ellie nodded, sliding the eggs she'd just made onto a plate and then quickly taking out two slices of toast from the toaster. She buttered them quickly before cutting the slices in half and putting them on either side of the eggs.

"I like a man who knows his shortcomings," she told him.

He grinned, fighting the urge to forget about breakfast and just take her back to his bed. "As long as that word doesn't apply to last night."

"No," she assured him with feeling, "definitely not to last night." Changing the topic before she weakened, she said, "I've got coffee." Ellie indicated the coffeemaker over on the far corner of the counter.

"I'm more interested in something else you have," he told her, the corners of his mouth curving in a wicked smile.

"This morning is PG rated," she reminded him, nodding toward the hall beyond the kitchen.

The next moment, Heather came in, looking as if she hadn't fully woken up yet.

"That smells good," she said, taking a deep breath.

"Thank you—yours is coming up in a second," Ellie promised.

Heather's eyes narrowed as she looked at her, then down at herself before slanting a glance at her uncle. "How come you've got different clothes on?" she asked her uncle. "Ellie and I are wearing the same clothes we had on yesterday."

He was relieved that instead of questioning why Ellie was wearing the same clothes she'd had on yesterday, Heather had turned the question around, wondering why he was the odd man out.

"Well, um, I spilled some gravy on my shirt and decided to put on a complete change of clothes," Colin told his niece.

Her eyebrows drew even closer together as if she assessed what he'd just told her. "I didn't see any gravy on your shirt."

"That's because it happened seconds *after* you fell asleep," he said without missing a beat.

"Oh, okay." Both Colin and Ellie thought they were out of the woods—but then Heather looked at her and asked, "Did you sleep here last night, Ellie?"

Ellie wasn't comfortable with lies. Lies always led to complications. So instead, Ellie told her, "You have a very comfortable couch," hoping the little girl would just make the leap.

"I fall asleep on that all the time," Heather confided, pleased that they had something in common.

"Heather, don't forget to feed Pancakes," Colin spoke up, reminding his niece of her responsibility.

As she went to get the dog food, he whispered to Ellie, "I noticed you didn't answer her question."

"Not directly," Ellie agreed, whispering back. "It's called a nonanswer."

He wondered if she was putting him on notice. Should he anticipate nonanswers from her, as well? The next moment, he just let the thought pass.

Heather returned and placed the filled dog's bowl down on the floor. Pancakes immediately dived in and began to eat, making short work of her breakfast.

"And here's your breakfast," Ellie told her, putting her dish down on the table in the girl's usual place.

Taking her seat, Heather appeared ready to dig in.

"Those eggs look a lot better than the ones Uncle Colin makes," she observed. And then she realized that she'd hurt his feelings with her honest assessment. Crying "Oops," Heather covered her mouth.

"That's okay, kid," he said, absolving her of any guilt on his behalf. "They *are* better. Eat up."

With an exaggerated sigh of relief, Heather did as she was told.

Chapter Sixteen

She kept telling herself to back off, to leave before she became too entrenched, too complacent.

Too happy.

The longer she remained, the more she felt it was like mocking the gods, and in every Greek mythology story she'd read as a child, mocking the gods never ended well for the one who did the mocking. The gods always got their revenge.

The only problem with all these points Ellie kept raising in her mind and her pep talks to herself was that it was already too late. Too late because she was too entrenched, too complacent and too happy for words.

And yes, she was afraid, *really* afraid that it would fall apart on her, but she just couldn't force herself to leave, to end this once and for all.

Several times she'd even rehearsed the words to tell Colin: that their relationship had run its course, that it was all a big mistake on her part and that they should just stop now and go their separate ways, remaining friends.

But she didn't want to be his friend, not when being his lover was so much more fulfilling. Life had meaning again and she no longer spent the first few minutes of every morning trying to pull herself up out of an oppressive abyss.

Instead, she woke up smiling.

Besides, she couldn't end it. There wasn't just herself to think of in this relationship, she argued. She'd become incredibly fond of Heather. They had bonded over their mutual experience of losing someone—in Heather's case, two someones. She just couldn't hurt the girl by ending it with Colin and walking out of her life, too.

If she did walk out, there was no way they could visit with one another. Doing something like that, walking away from Colin, would leave the girl reeling and in the terrible position where Heather felt she had to choose sides. Hers would of course have to be with her uncle. Anything else wasn't feasible.

Any way Ellie looked at it, terminating her relationship with Colin only led to unhappiness and hopelessness.

Especially for her.

So she continued seeing Colin and thus seeing Heather, continued as if everything was all right and that deep down in the recess of her soul, she wasn't haunted by the specter of a very real fear.

A fear that was always there, in the background,

stuffed into a corner and hardly noticeable except in the right light.

So she tried not to pay attention to it and prayed that eventually, the fear would lessen or just go away altogether.

In the meantime, Ellie lost herself in the demands of her job. In her off hours, she joined forces with Colin. Christmas was swiftly approaching and he'd asked her to help him make this a memorable celebration for Heather. His goal was to keep his niece too busy to have any time to be sad.

"It's going to be rough for her," Colin speculated one evening as they sat on the couch together talking after Heather had gone to bed. "This is her first Christmas without her parents and I know it's got to be making her unhappy, but I want to do something special for her to get her mind off the pain of missing them."

Ellie looked at him and she could almost see the wheels in his head turning as he swiftly examined and then discarded ideas. And then his eyes seemed to light up.

"Maybe I'll take some time off and we'll go to Disney World for a week," he said, turning toward Ellie and becoming more enthusiastic the more he thought about the idea.

She could see how that could be a good distraction for the ten-year-old, but there was a problem.

"It's a great idea, but I can't come with you. I can't take off for a week," she told him honestly. The holidays usually meant more work, not less. "The best I can do is get Christmas Eve and Christmas Day off."

Colin was nothing if not flexible. He was already

coming up with a plan B. "Okay, no Disney World. We'll do Disneyland, instead."

Ellie shook her head. There was a problem with that, too. "Disneyland is closed on Christmas," she pointed out.

"Closed? You're sure?" he questioned, momentarily disheartened.

"I'm afraid so."

Regrouping, Colin restructured his plan. What mattered here was some sort of fun activity and the three of them being together.

"Then we'll do Christmas Eve—it's open Christmas Eve day, right?" he asked her.

She smiled at Colin, happy to confirm at least this much for him. "Yes."

"Okay, then that's the plan," he finalized. "We'll go to Disneyland on Christmas Eve day and then figure out something different for Christmas Day." Ever positive, Colin tightened his arm around her shoulders, drawing her closer to him.

"How about celebrating it on the beach, just the three of us?" Ellie asked, the idea suddenly coming to her. "It's pretty down by Laguna Beach this time of year, and there're some trees and a few benches just a little ways in from the beach. There's even this picturesque gazebo overlooking the water," she recalled. "We could pack a lunch, eat there, then look for seashells or just walk along the sand." She shifted so she could look at him. "What do you think?"

"I think that I'm lucky to have you," Colin answered, hugging her to him. "Heather and I both are."

There it was again, that feeling that they were a

unit, a family. Ellie felt the same rosy glow she always did when she contemplated their situation.

A tiny voice in her head whispered, *It's not going to last. You know that. It's not going to last.*

Her sense of self-defense instantly kicked in, shutting down the voice and blocking it.

But even so, the little voice still insisted on echoing through her brain.

"C'mon, Jerry, get a move on. We've got two stories to cover and we're not going to cover them from here," Ellie urged.

It was several days after she and Colin had made their holidays plans and she had to admit, she was really looking forward to the day. She hadn't been to Disneyland as a visitor for *years.*

She'd already reached the doorway leading out of the newsroom bull pen and doubled back to her cameraman in the time it had taken Jerry to secure the camera case he always brought with him on assignments.

Jerry raised his eyes to look at her. "Looks like someone got a double dose of vitamins this morning," he commented. "Or are you just downing too many energy drinks?"

She laughed, dismissing his questions. "If you must know, I'm just being high on life," she informed the man.

Jerry gazed at her knowingly. "Is that what you call him these days? 'Life'?" he asked with a laugh, slinging the camera-case strap over his arm. It was heavy and required balance on his part, even given his height.

"I don't know what you're talking about," Ellie sniffed, pretending as if Jerry had no idea that her life had taken this turn for the better and why.

"Uh-huh. Sure. On to more important things," Jerry said, continuing. "Betsy and I are having our usual Christmas party this weekend. You're invited." He said it as if it was an afterthought instead of all part of the hazing that he loved putting her through. "Oh, and bring Mr. Life along," he added.

"We'll see," Ellie said, grabbing another one of Jerry's cases and automatically carrying it out for him. They were a team in her eyes and there was no hierarchy to their relationship. "You take more time getting ready than my grandmother," she said, shaking her head.

"Hey, I've met your grandmother. That's a really together lady," he told her.

Ellie just made a dismissive sound. Turning to walk out the door for a second time, she found that her way was unexpectedly blocked by the program manager.

The man didn't look happy.

"I'm glad I caught you," Marty said. Instead of his usual good-natured smile, the program manager had a rather grim expression on his face.

"What's up, Marty?" Ellie asked, silently telling herself not to start coming up with dire scenarios. She had to stop being paranoid. "You giving us a third story to cover?" She glanced at Jerry, but he had no idea why the program manager had come to them instead of the other way around, either. "We might not be able to get to it in time," she warned.

She got no further.

"Something just came down over the wire," Marty

told her. His voice had never sounded so serious, so bleak. Ellie immediately felt her stomach seizing up and then sinking.

"What is it, Marty?" she asked. "C'mon, you're scaring me. What just came in over the wire?"

"Fifteen minutes ago, a local detective foiled a robbery in progress. Two guys tried to pull off a home invasion."

"You said foiled," Ellie repeated, her voice seeming to echo in her head as she spoke. She was afraid to say anything more, waiting for Marty to fill her in. Praying he wasn't going to say something she couldn't bear to hear. But then why did he look this way?

"The two burglars were taken into custody before they could make off with anything."

He was doling out information.

Why?

Her breath suddenly backed up in her throat. She felt Jerry's hand on her shoulder, as if he was silently trying to help her brace herself. She didn't want to brace herself. She wanted this to be all right.

Ellie shrugged his hand away. Her eyes never leaving the program manager's face, she held her breath as she demanded, "And the local detective?"

"He's alive but in critical condition," Marty told her. "The ambulance took him to Bedford Presbyterian."

Her voice was shaking as she heard herself ask, "You have a name?"

Marty barely nodded before saying, "It's him, Ellie. It's Detective Benteen."

For just one turbulent moment, the immediate world shrank down to a pinprick. She thought she was going to pass out—just like the first time. It took everything she had merely to struggle back to consciousness. She wasn't going to faint! She was stronger than that.

But the next moment, Ellie just wanted to flee. To run and run until she was too exhausted to take another step. It didn't matter where, just away.

She couldn't go through this again, couldn't take the fear, the horrible pain waiting to rip her apart only a heartbeat away.

She'd been through this once; she couldn't go through this again.

She *couldn't*.

And then she heard Jerry's voice breaking through the fog about her brain.

"C'mon, I'll drive you," he told her, his hand up against her back as if he was afraid she'd sink to the floor if he took it away.

"I'm not covering this story," she all but snapped at him.

"I'm not driving you as a cameraman," he told her gently but firmly. "I'm driving you as a friend."

Stricken, Ellie realized she'd turned toward Marty and was looking at him questioningly.

The program manager waved her out. "Go—don't even think about it. I'll get someone else to cover your stories today."

Ellie didn't wait to hear anything more.

She didn't remember leaving the building, didn't remember the ride to the hospital. She was hardly aware of running through the hospital's electronic doors, which barely had time to open for her.

Jerry was the one who rattled off the information

to the woman sitting at the ER desk. Ellie just couldn't speak. Her legs and body were heavy. She felt as if she was walking through a nightmare.

A recurring nightmare.

She'd been in this hospital before, faced some woman at the ER desk before only to be told that her husband wasn't in any of the beds. Beds were for the living. He was in the morgue.

She was terrified of hearing that again. Terrified that it was happening all over again. That the person she had fallen in love with against every objection her common sense had raised had been ripped away from her by some madman firing a gun.

Just like last time.

Struggling to focus, to think, she only just realized that Jerry was talking to her.

"He's in surgery, Ellie. The nurse said Colin's in surgery."

Ellie stared up at the tall cameraman, her heart pounding so hard she could barely hear him. She blinked as if that could somehow clear her ears.

"Then he's alive?" she asked fearfully.

Jerry nodded, his curly reddish hair bobbing almost independently.

"He's alive," he confirmed, looking extremely relieved, then added, "They don't like to operate on dead people."

She tried to smile at the joke he'd made for her benefit, but she found that her mouth could hardly curve. Her face was frozen. Numb. The only thing she could do was repeat what Jerry had just told her. "He's alive."

And then, sobbing, she threw her arms around

Jerry, burying her face against the lower part of his chest because that was all she could reach.

Ellie pulled herself together long enough to call Olga to inform the woman of what had happened and to ask her to stay with Heather. She tried her very best to sound positive.

"He is going to be all right?" Olga asked, her tone demanding the information, the reassurance.

"He's going to be all right," Ellie told the woman, praying that if she said the words often enough, it would be so.

She terminated the call before her voice broke. She cried the second she stopped talking.

Ellie waited in the hall outside the operating door, leaning against the wall for support. Jerry stayed with her, refusing to leave her alone.

Someone brought out a couple of folding chairs for them. When Jerry opened the first one up, placing it beside Ellie, she dropped into it, her knees collapsing at that moment.

He opened the second one for himself.

"You don't have to stay with me," she told the cameraman as a second hour melted into a third.

"I'm not leaving you now, kid," he answered. "Besides, I'm your ride, remember?"

"I can call a cab," she told him numbly.

"Oh no," he told her. "You're not getting rid of me that easily." He shifted in the chair. It wasn't exactly comfortable for a big man like him. "You want something to drink?" he offered. "We might be here for a while. I think I saw a vending machine down the hall."

Ellie shook her head. "You go get something for yourself," she told him. "I'm okay."

She was far from okay, but he knew better than to argue with her. He merely noted, "Dehydrating yourself isn't going to do him any good." Rising, he told Ellie, "Be right back."

She was hardly aware of nodding. Her eyes remained trained on the operating room doors.

Jerry was just coming back when he saw the surgeon emerging from the operating room. The short, stocky older man didn't even need a moment to look around for her. Ellie was immediately on her feet, at his side.

As she confronted the doctor, her eyes begged him to give her something positive to hang on to.

"Are you here for Detective Benteen?" the surgeon asked.

"Yes!" And then Ellie's voice cracked a little. "Is he—"

She couldn't bring herself to continue. She was too afraid to ask the question. And even more afraid of the answer she might receive.

"He's out of surgery," the doctor told her just as Jerry reached her side. "It was touch and go for a while. Detective Benteen received one bullet to the thigh, one to the chest. The latter just barely missed a major artery. A little more to the left and he wouldn't have even made it to the hospital."

"How is he?" Jerry asked the doctor before Ellie was able to find her voice.

"He's stable now," the doctor told them in a monotone voice. It was obvious that he'd been through a great many of these life-and-death surgeries. "The next few hours will be critical. If he makes it through the night, there's every reason to believe that he'll make a full recovery." Only then did the doctor's tone begin to sound a little more optimistic. "There'll be some physical therapy involved and a lot of patience, but he should be good as new, given time."

Ellie's eyes were filled with tears and she had to blink several times just in order to see. Her throat felt completely parched and almost like leather as she cried, "Thank you, Doctor. Thank you!"

The surgeon merely nodded. "Detective Benteen's going to be in recovery for a while, and then he'll be taken to his room. I really doubt that he'll wake up before morning." He reconsidered his words. "Possibly even later than that. Why don't you go home and get some rest?" he suggested, looking from Ellie to the hulking figure beside her.

It was Jerry who told him, "Doc, she's not about to leave unless you get someone to carry her out. And he'd probably have to tie her up, as well."

"I understand," the surgeon replied. He had an alternate suggestion. "You might want to go to the cafeteria while you're waiting." With that, the doctor left.

"I'll bring you something to eat," Jerry volunteered. Tucking the can of diet soda he'd brought for her into her hands, Jerry put his own can on the folding chair and went to the cafeteria.

Chapter Seventeen

Colin's eyelids felt like lead.

He was certain that he'd opened his eyes a number of times, struggling each time, only to ultimately realize that he still hadn't even managed to pry his lids apart at all.

He needed to open his eyes, needed to see where he was and if everything was all right. There was a boy, a boy he was trying to save.

Colin kept struggling for what felt like an eternity and then, finally, *finally*, he managed to force open his eyelids.

It didn't help. He had no idea where he was.

Slowly, his brain began to make sense of the scene, processing the faint antiseptic smell mingling with the scent of vanilla and lavender.

A memory stirred, gradually taking shape.

That was her scent. Her perfume.

"Ellie?"

At the sound of his voice, Ellie jolted upright. She'd spent the better part of the last twenty hours in Colin's room, sitting in the world's most uncomfortable chair beside his bed. Somewhere along the line, she must have fallen asleep and now her body was loudly complaining about it. Complaining about the very awkward, pretzel-like position she'd wound up assuming.

She ached all over, but that sensation was a distant second to what she was experiencing right now: the most tremendous amount of relief she'd ever felt.

"Welcome back, Detective Benteen," she said, blinking back tears of joy. She dragged the chair a tiny bit closer; it was all the distance that remained between the bed and her.

"Where am I?" His ordinarily powerful voice came out in what sounded like a croak.

She allowed herself to touch his face, brushing the hair back out of his eyes. "Not in heaven," she informed him.

"You sure?" His voice faded for a moment. It took another moment before he could continue to speak. "Then why am I looking at an angel?"

Wanting to laugh and cry at the same time, Ellie took his hand in hers, grateful simply to be holding it, to feel the warmth of his flesh against hers. She touched it to her cheek.

He was alive!

"Oh, you're going to have to do better than that to make up for this," she informed him once she could find her voice again.

Details began to come back to him, choppy details

that were out of order. His brow furrowed as he tried to organize them to remember them the way they occurred. "I was shot."

Ellie nodded her head, still holding on to his hand tightly. "Good guess."

His eyes suddenly became alert as more details came rushing back, sharper now.

He remembered.

"What about the boy?" he asked her urgently. "Is the boy all right?"

Before he had finally and reluctantly left her, Jerry had called the station and gotten the full story that had come across the wire. There'd been a burglary in progress. Apparently, he'd told her, no one was supposed to be home. Nothing ever went according to plan. It turned out a twelve-year-old boy had been home from school, sick. It was the boy, hiding in his bedroom closet, who'd called 911 about the two thugs who were breaking in.

Because of his proximity when the call came in, Colin was the first on the scene. The burglars, two hardened criminals with two strikes against each of them, were armed. A gun battle ensued.

"The boy's fine. The studio's probably doing a story on his 911 call right now." She suppressed the urge to beat on Colin for rushing in alone like that. "Why didn't you wait for backup?" she asked.

Colin sank against his pillow, suddenly feeling very drained again. His eyelids were trying to close. "You know about that?"

"I know everything," she told him, her voice close to cracking again. "I'm a reporter, remember?"

His eyes were already drifting shut again. "Wanted

to get them…out of there…before…they found…the…
boy. Seemed…like a…good…idea at the…time."

He was asleep again.

Ellie sighed and settled back in the chair where
she'd been since he had been wheeled into the room
from recovery.

"I'll be here when you wake up," she quietly promised the detective.

The next time Colin woke up, he realized that Ellie
wasn't the only one in the room.

Seeing him open his eyes, his niece shrieked with
joy and threw her arms around his neck. Ellie didn't
have the heart to pull her away.

"You're alive!" Heather cried happily. "I was so
scared, so scared, Uncle Colin," she confessed, trying not to cry. "Ellie said not to worry, but I kinda
did, I did worry."

When he looked at Ellie over his niece's head, she
gave him the explanation she figured he was looking for. "Heather wanted to see for herself that you
were alive."

From the recess of the hospital room a third voice
joined in. "She would not believe me when I told her
you were going to be all right. She is stubborn, like
her uncle. So I brought her here because Ellie said
it would be all right," Olga informed him matter-of-
factly. "And now we will be going back," she said
in her no-nonsense tone, addressing Heather. "Your
uncle, he is needing to rest."

"Do as she says, kid," Colin told his niece fondly.
Smiling weakly, he stroked her hair. "I'll be home before you know it."

"You promise?" It wasn't a question; it was a plea for his solemn vow.

"I promise," he told her. "But Disneyland might have to wait for a while."

"I don't care about Disneyland," Heather told him with feeling, angry tears welling up in her eyes. "I just care about you."

Colin felt himself getting choked up. Trying to clear his throat, he looked at the woman who'd brought his niece in. "Thanks for bringing her, Olga."

"No need to be thanking me," she replied in her crisp manner. "Just remember to be ducking next time."

Putting her hands on the girl's shoulder, Olga began to herd Heather out of the room.

Belatedly, Ellie called after the girl, "I'll be by later."

Colin waited until Olga and his niece left before asking, "What's that about?"

"I'm just dropping off some of my things at your apartment later tonight," she told him.

Ellie had raised more questions for him than she'd answered. "Something going on I don't know about?" Colin asked.

"Lots of things going on that you don't know about," she told him mysteriously. And then, taking pity on the man, even if he was a damn fool who'd almost gotten himself killed, she said, "I'm moving in to take care of Heather while you're lying around here taking it easy. I don't want her life being disrupted any more than it already has."

"What about Olga?" he asked. For the last eight months, the woman had been his go-to babysitter.

"This is more than just watching her occasionally. Besides, Olga has a job. She can't afford to just take off for several weeks straight."

He supposed that made sense, but something else didn't.

"And you can?" he asked, remembering what she'd said about not being able to take a week off to go to Disney World.

"I put in for a leave of absence," she explained. Marty had told her to take as much time as she needed, assuring her that her job would be waiting for her when she got back. She smiled, grateful for the program manager's support. "Under the circumstances, I have a very understanding boss. So," she informed him, "like it or not, Detective Benteen, I am in this for the long haul."

It took effort because he was so tired, but Colin smiled. "Oh, I like it," he told her. "I like it very much."

Ellie made no response. She didn't want him thinking that she was trying to play what had happened— and his temporary disability—to her advantage. All she wanted was for him to get well.

She cleared her throat, then said, "Now, if you're through playing twenty questions, you have a menu to fill out. You're going to be here for at least a few days, so you might as well have them bring you something you like to eat."

Colin waved his hand dismissively—or tried to. He just didn't have the energy for it.

"Pick anything," he told her, a wave of exhaustion washing over him. "I'm easy."

Stunned, Ellie raised her eyes to look at him. "Not

hardly." And then she looked closer. "And...he's asleep again," she murmured to herself.

Resigned, she sat down with the hospital's menus and began to fill out the selections for only the next three days, fervently hoping that she wasn't being overly optimistic.

"You're not ready to go back to work," Ellie protested loudly as she watched Colin getting dressed in his bedroom.

For the last six weeks, for Heather's sake, she'd spent her nights on his living room couch. She'd cooked their meals and overseen every one of his physical therapy exercises. All along she'd watched Colin get progressively better with what seemed like a vengeance.

Very gently, he put his hands on her shoulders and moved Ellie out of his way. He took his shirt from the closet and began to put it on.

"The doctor just gave me a clean bill of health and cleared me for duty," he informed her.

Like she cared what the doctor said. Ellie made a dismissive noise, telling him what she thought of the doctor and his clearance.

"Well, I'm not ready to clear you for duty," she stated.

"Ellie, I can't go on just hiding in my apartment," he pointed out. Finished buttoning his shirt, he tucked it into his pants.

"Why not?" she asked. "At least it's safe here. Nobody's going to shoot you in your apartment," Ellie pointed out.

Colin stated the obvious, thinking of the incident

that had taken him out of commission these last six weeks. "Unless they break in."

"Pancakes would never let them—as long as you don't lock her up in that puppy crate," she specified. "Maybe you haven't noticed, but she's been your shadow the entire time you've been home." There had been a change in the dog since Colin had come home from the hospital. "It's like she can sense you've been hurt and she wants to protect you."

"If she does, it's because she's taking her cues from you." Done getting dressed, Colin took her into his arms. "Not that it hasn't been great being with you, having you bully me around," he deadpanned, referring to the physical therapy session he'd endured in order to be able to walk without a limp, "but you need to get back to work and so do I."

"What if you get shot again?" she challenged. She managed to keep the fear out of her voice, but there was no way she could keep it out of her heart.

He wasn't about to tell her he was bulletproof. "I can't tell you that I won't—"

"Terrific," Ellie bit off.

He had to go in, but he didn't want to leave her like this. He wanted her to understand. "Life doesn't come with guarantees, Ellie—you know that. You could get killed covering your next story," he pointed out.

She frowned, shaking her head. "I do mainly fluff pieces."

"Mainly, but not always. For that matter," he stressed, "a gas main could blow up just as you're going to your next location."

Okay, now he was really reaching, she thought. "That's not exactly a regular occurrence."

"Neither is my getting shot." He took her hands in his. "Honey, the important thing is that we make the very most of every minute we have."

"I just want to have more minutes," she told him, even as she knew that she couldn't stand in his way. It made her feel completely helpless.

Colin grinned. "I'm glad you said that."

"You are?"

"Yes—" he released one of her hands and put his into his jacket pocket, reaching in for something "—because then you make this easier for me to ask."

Ellie thought she knew where this was going. "You're talking about Disney World again, aren't you?" she asked. "Because I don't think—"

"No," Colin said, cutting her off. "I'm talking about this."

"This" turned out to be the black velvet box that he was holding in the palm of his hand. He held it up to her, expecting her to take it.

Ellie stared at the box and then at him, but she made no move to take it from him.

"What is it?" she whispered.

Since she wasn't taking the box from him or even opening it, he opened it for her.

Inside the box was a gleaming marquise-shaped diamond engagement ring.

When had he had time to buy this? She looked at him with confusion. "I've been with you the entire time you've been home from the hospital. How did you—?"

"I bought this before I got shot. I was going to ask you to marry me at Christmas," he explained.

"Then why didn't you?" Ellie asked. It didn't make sense to her.

"Because I got shot," he repeated, "and I didn't want to propose to you while you were here taking care of Heather and me. I didn't want you saying yes to my proposal because you felt sorry for me."

"So you're asking me while I'm angry at you?"

This was getting too involved. He wanted to keep it simple. "I was hoping that this would make you less angry." He slipped it on her finger while he made his argument. "I love you, Ellie. I can promise to love you for as long as I live—and then do my damnedest to live for a very long time."

She still wasn't saying anything.

Colin took a deep breath and made his final offer, "If you want me to stop being a cop—"

"Yes, yes, I do," she cried. "With all my heart, I do. But you are a cop—it's what you do, who you are, and I have no right to ask you to change, because I don't want you to change. I wouldn't want you to want me to change, so I have no right to dictate any conditions," she explained. Ellie slipped her arms around his neck. "I fell in love with a cop, heaven help me, and I guess I'm going to stay in love with a cop."

He encircled her waist, holding her close to him. "So, is that a yes?"

She smiled up into his eyes. "You're a clever cop. You figure it out," she challenged.

Colin drew her closer still. For the last six weeks, he had remained celibate. He'd been too weak in the beginning and then it seemed as if either Heather or Olga or both were always around, not to mention that there'd been an endless stream of visitors and well-wishers who kept dropping by. It was never just the two of them.

It was now. Olga had taken Heather to school a little while ago.

"You know," Colin told her, "I can be late on my first day getting back."

She could feel him wanting her. "What is it that you have in mind?"

He pressed a kiss to the side of her neck before answering. "Making love with my fiancée."

She could feel herself melting already. "So you're assuming that I'm saying yes?"

"Not assuming," Colin corrected. "Praying."

Ellie smiled then, a warm smile that began in her eyes and radiated all through her, pulling him in.

"Well, lucky for you, sometimes prayers *are* answered." And then, in case there was any lingering doubt, she said, "Just to make it official, yes, Detective Benteen, I will marry you. Since you stole my heart, you might as well have the rest of me."

Colin had nothing to say about that. He couldn't. He was far too busy kissing her and making good on what he'd just promised to do.

Epilogue

Cecilia had been watching for her.

The moment she spotted Olga entering the church, she half stood up in the pew and waved the woman over.

"Olga, come sit by us," Cilia called to her in what amounted to a stage whisper.

Olga approached the pew hesitantly, recognizing her employer as well as the woman's friends Theresa Manetti and Maizie Sommers, women she'd had the occasion to meet several times in passing.

"It is all right?" Olga asked, not wanting to intrude.

"More than all right," Maizie assured the woman with a welcoming laugh. She scooted over, as did Theresa and Cilia, as well as a woman Olga didn't know, creating room for the newcomer. "If it weren't for you, this might not be taking place."

Once Olga was seated, the fourth woman rose to her feet.

"I'd better take my place up front," Ellie's mother told the others. "I don't know how to thank you," Connie Williams said, repeating the sentiment she'd voiced earlier as her eyes swept over the four women. "I've never seen Ellie looking happier. Anything you want," she told them, "*anything*, I'm in your debt."

"Our pleasure," Maizie told her friend. "It's what we all really enjoy doing, isn't it, ladies?" She addressed her question to her friends.

But it was Olga who spoke up as soon as Ellie's mother had eased herself out of the pew and made her way up to the front of the church.

"This is what they call matchmaking, yes?" the woman asked, looking from Cilia to the other two.

Cilia's smile answered her, but just in case Olga needed more verification, Theresa told her, "Yes."

Olga nodded, a satisfied, somewhat thoughtful expression on her face.

"I think I like this matchmaking. Can we be doing this again?" She looked from one woman to the other, waiting for an answer.

"You bet your buttons we will," Maizie said with a laugh, her eyes glinting with amusement as well as pleasure.

"We will be needing buttons?" Olga asked, confused as she slanted a glance in Cilia's direction.

Cilia placed a hand on the other woman's wrist. "No, dear, no buttons."

Olga's brow furrowed. Not for the first time she thought that English was a very confusing language to learn. "But—"

"You'll get used to Maizie," Cilia promised.

"Shh, it's starting," Theresa said as the strains of the wedding march began to slowly swell and fill the packed church.

Everyone rose in anticipation.

Wordlessly, her eyes fixed to the rear doors, waiting for them to part, Maizie automatically passed out three tissues she'd brought with her in her clutch purse, one for each of the women in the pew. She kept a fourth one for herself. Weddings never failed to make them tear up. She saw no reason to think that this wedding would be different.

Especially not when she saw Heather entering first, positively glowing as she took measured steps into the church, a flower basket in her hand.

Grabbing small fistfuls of rose petals in her hand, Heather happily paved the path before her with a mixture of pink and white.

And then Ellie entered, resplendent in a floor-length wedding dress, a wreath of flowers in her hair and clutching a cascading arrangement of pink and white roses in her hands.

"They just keep getting more lovely, don't they?" Theresa whispered to her friends.

"She's breathtaking," Cilia agreed.

"Colin certainly seems to think so," Maizie observed, directing their attention toward the groom.

"And that, in the end, is all that matters," Olga said in finality, adding her voice to theirs.

All three old friends exchanged looks and smiled just as Ellie reached the front of the altar, ready to join her life with the man who stood there waiting for her.

Attuned to one another's thoughts, they had no need to voice what they were all thinking: another undertaking well done.

* * * * *

*Don't miss Marie Ferrarella's next
Mills & Boon Cherish,
FORTUNE'S SECOND CHANCE COWBOY
the third book in
THE FORTUNES OF TEXAS:
THE SECRET FORTUNES
continuity, available March 2017!*

MILLS & BOON®

EXCLUSIVE EXTRACT

Sheikh Ibrahim al-Ansari must find a bride,
and quickly… Thankfully he has the perfect
convenient princess in mind—his new assistant,
Ruby Dance!

Read on for a sneak preview of
THE SHEIKH'S CONVENIENT PRINCESS
by Liz Fielding

'Can I ask if you are in any kind of relationship?' he
persisted.

'Relationship?'

'You are on your own—you have no ties?'

He was beginning to spook her and must have realised
it because he said, 'I have a proposition for you, Ruby,
but if you have personal commitments…' He shook his
head as if he wasn't sure what he was doing.

'If you're going to offer me a package too good to
refuse after a couple of hours I should warn you that it
took Jude Radcliffe the best part of a year to get to that
point and I still turned him down.'

'I don't have the luxury of time,' he said, 'and the
position I'm offering is made for a temp.'

'I'm listening.'

'Since you have done your research, you know that
I was disinherited five years ago.'

She nodded. She thought it rather harsh for a one-off

incident but the media loved the fall of a hero and had gone into a bit of a feeding frenzy.

'This morning I received a summons from my father to present myself at his birthday majlis.'

'You can go home?'

'If only it were that simple. A situation exists which means that I can only return to Umm al Basr if I'm accompanied by a wife.'

She ignored the slight sinking feeling in her stomach. Obviously a multimillionaire who looked like the statue of a Greek god—albeit one who'd suffered a bit of wear and tear—would have someone ready and willing to step up to the plate.

'That's rather short notice. Obviously, I'll do whatever I can to arrange things, but I don't know a lot about the law in—'

'The marriage can take place tomorrow. My question is, under the terms of your open-ended brief encompassing "whatever is necessary", are you prepared to take on the role?'

Don't miss
THE SHEIKH'S CONVENIENT PRINCESS
By Liz Fielding

Available February 2017
www.millsandboon.co.uk